Come Fly with Me

Come Fly with Me

Judith Whitmore

COME FLY WITH ME
Copyright © 2013 by Judith Whitmore.
All rights reserved.

Publishing Consultant, Flying Pig Media
Cover & Interior Design by VMC Art & Design, LLC

Published by Smith Terrace Publishing

ISBN: 978-0-9892157-0-1

For Wes

She opened his gift—a gold bracelet carved into the shape of a flying horse, its wings tipped with diamonds. She slipped it over her wrist.

"Pegasus. It's beautiful."

He drew her into his arms. "It's a reminder that no matter where you are, if you need me I can fly to you on a moment's notice."

Chapter 1

It nearly tore Kate Randolph's heart out seeing the grin on the girl's face. Too close to home, she told herself. But it was why she'd started Safe Haven.

The ten-year-old girl stood with her mother at the front doorway of their modest duplex. A springtime sunset disappeared over the roof line behind them.

Kate leaned down toward the girl. "No more coming home to an empty house. After school tomorrow, the Safe Haven bus will pick you up."

The girl's lopsided smile grew even wider.

"God bless you," the mother said.

"And you," said Kate.

Streetlights flickered on. With the girl's enrollment forms tucked into her handbag, Kate hurried down the concrete walkway to her Porsche. Rush hour on the 405 Freeway would be a mess. Her stomach roiled at the thought of keeping Sam waiting. Her husband had not been thrilled when she started Safe Haven, and she didn't want her pet project to be the reason she was late for supper with him. She slid into the driver's seat and eyed the clock on the dashboard. If Coast Highway wasn't too backed up, she could get to Mastro's Ocean Club before him.

Kate sat alone at a window table at Mastro's. A good-looking guy at the bar in jeans and a blazer gave her a smile and a nod. God, she hated sitting here by herself. She checked her watch again. Where was Sam? If she had known he was going to be late, she wouldn't have rushed off so fast from the girl and her mother.

Waiters bustled about the restaurant, delivering trays of sizzling steaks and fresh-caught seafood to patrons from nearby Newport Beach and Laguna. An elderly couple sat across a narrow aisle.

The woman glanced at Kate and smiled. "I saw the article about you in Orange Coast Magazine. You don't look thirty-four, and you're even prettier in person."

"Thank you," Kate said.

The woman returned to her Caesar salad.

Kate sipped her Chardonnay. When she caught sight of her hand, she reached for her purse. She groped inside and withdrew a five-carat diamond ring from a satin pouch. She replaced the little gold and ruby band on her fourth finger with the ring Sam had given her. Since he liked to see her wear it, she tried to remember to take it with her whenever they met for dinner. Under no circumstances would she ever wear it to a house visit on behalf of Safe Haven. She could never be that insensitive. She moved the ruby band to her right hand. Kate loved the ring, not just because it had been her mother's, but because she adored rubies. They symbolized romance and passion, things she wanted. She had suggested to Sam that he buy her a ruby instead of a diamond, but she had ended up with "The Rock," which spent most of its time in her purse.

She gazed across Coast Highway where the moon reflected like a silver strand of tinsel on the ocean. She thought about the girl she'd just met. Each new enrollee to Safe Haven was a victory for Kate. She wanted to share the news with Sam. She tapped her cell phone on the white tablecloth, and then she dialed his office.

"He's still in a meeting," his secretary said.

"He's forty minutes late."

"I'm sorry. I can't disturb him."

Kate waited a full hour, then dropped two twenty-dollar bills on the table and left. Furious and hurt, she retrieved her car from the valet and headed to Janet's place.

Janet, red hair in wet ringlets after a shower, answered the door dressed in sweats. "You got this dressed up just to see me?"

"Sam stood me up for dinner."

"Again?" Janet said.

They headed for the kitchen.

Janet pointed to a video case on the Formica counter. "I was gonna watch Roman Holiday. I'll make popcorn."

Kate sat on a bar stool at the counter, comfortable in the familiar surroundings. There were new gingham curtains on the window above the sink, but otherwise things hadn't changed much since she'd moved out six years ago to marry Sam.

Janet pushed a plate of brownies toward Kate. "He's a workaholic, and you're too patient. He's never going to change."

"I keep thinking he will." Kate nibbled a brownie.

"Maybe you're right," Janet said. "And maybe tomorrow I'll wake up ten pounds thinner, and I'll be speaking Chinese."

"I'm trying to make this work."

"Stop settling for safe," Janet said. "You're like those people who dream about going to Paris but never get there because they're afraid to step on the plane."

"You know I adore flying."

"And you know what I mean." Janet pulled a jar of Orville Redenbacher's from the cupboard. "Before Sam, you had a job, a car, your own room here. You're settling for safe when you could be soaring."

"I do feel safe with Sam," Kate said, but that wasn't entirely true.

Kate's cell phone rang. They both stared at the LED readout. Sam.

Janet waved the Roman Holiday CD. "We haven't had a girls' movie night in a long time."

"I'm too tired to drive home anyway." Kate picked up the cell phone. "I'll let Sam know I'm staying here tonight."

"When I was dating Derrick Randolph," Janet said, "and we needed a fourth for tennis, I wouldn't have brought you along if I thought you were going to marry the guy's father."

The following morning, dressed in a pair of Janet's white jeans and a white Gap tank top, Kate headed to the Corona Del Mar health food store that served as headquarters for Safe Haven. At eleven o'clock, Sam showed up. With his thick silvery hair and impeccable dark suit, white shirt, and matching silk tie and pocket square, he looked as though he'd wandered out of a GQ magazine.

"I'd like to speak to the president of this organization," he said.

Kate glanced at her two office assistants who sat nearby checking Sam out. She didn't want the girls to witness the confrontation that was about to occur.

She turned to them. "This is my husband, Sam."

Both girls waved.

"Hello," Sam said, flashing his "successful tycoon" smile.

Apparently mesmerized by him, neither girl turned away.

"Patty and Molly are Orange Coast College interns," Kate said. "They scour the internet for deals on sports equipment and art supplies. Running an after-school program like this is expensive. We save money where we can."

Sam strolled past the two girls, who continued to gaze at him. "So, this is H-Q for your abandoned girls project."

"The girls aren't abandoned," Kate said. "They're left alone at home because their mothers work." She wiped a bead of perspiration from her upper lip. "It's not usually this hot. The air conditioner's broken."

Sam surveyed the room, crammed with three desks, a pair of card tables, and a row of filing cabinets. "And you don't pay any rent?"

"The landlord likes what we do, but at some point he'll want this space back. We're raising money for a permanent facility." She batted her eyelashes. "Did you come to make a donation?"

Sam unbuttoned his suit jacket and pushed a stack of manila folders out of the way to sit on the corner of Kate's desk. He leaned close and whispered, "Can we talk? Please."

He touched her shoulder. The remorse in his eyes caused an ache in the pit of her stomach.

Kate reached for her handbag and turned to the girls. "How about a pizza?"

"Sure," they chorused.

Before she could get to her wallet, Sam pulled a money clip from his pocket. He peeled off several bills. "Pizza's on me."

As soon as the girls left, Sam stood. "I told you last night, I got to Mastro's right after you left. I was worried sick when I didn't see you there."

Kate squared her shoulders. "I don't like what's going on, Sam. It doesn't feel like you and I are a couple anymore. You're away on business eight to ten nights a month. You leave me hanging in restaurants...."

"Kate...."

"It's not the first time, but it was the worst." She hesitated. "Do you even love me?"

"Of course I do. I said I'm sorry."

Kate shook her head. "I made concessions to marry you because I loved you, and I appreciate that you've made it possible for me to devote my time to Safe Haven. But...."

"I made a mistake." He leaned over and kissed her cheek. "Please. It won't happen again. I promise."

She'd fallen for Sam because he'd been kind and attentive, and he embodied qualities she admired—confidence, strength, and stability. Her gaze swept over his face. He appeared genuinely contrite.

Kate sighed. "You're a difficult man to live with." She gave him a half-smile. "I'm forgiving you because, despite your flaws, I love you." She tried to ignore the other reason she would forgive Sam—she'd become totally financially dependent on him. And that scared her.

Sam picked up her purse and handed it to her.

"Come on," he said.

"I can't leave. I'm finishing a grant application."

"Too bad," Sam said, heading toward the door. He

glanced back at her and smiled. "My new plane was just delivered."

Kate hesitated a nanosecond, then grabbed her purse and straw hat and dashed out the door to catch up with him.

Turbulence buffeted the private luxury jet. Captain Rick Sanders kept cool. Hell, he'd flown thirty-six sorties over the Persian Gulf; a little light chop was nothing. His immediate concern was the rock star who'd chartered the plane. Back in the cabin, she was drunk and harassing her band members.

Rick nudged Grady Burke, the lanky young copilot to his right. "I wish we had locked cockpits like the airlines," he said.

The voice of an air traffic controller from SoCal Approach Center filled the cockpit.

"Gulfstream Echo Alpha, descend and maintain eight-thousand feet, heading two-six-zero."

Rick banked toward the newly assigned heading. A bottle of Evian tucked behind his seat rolled across the floor. Behind him, Melina, the latest one-name idol to light up the charts, rustled into the cockpit, reeking of Jack Daniels. He swiveled toward her.

"Hi, handsome," the singer said, her hair in disarray. She lifted her shirt, baring an impressive pair of fake boobs.

Rick flashed a friendly grin. He appreciated the female form as much as any man, but this was not the time or place. Pilot-in-command meant he had passengers to think about.

"It's not safe having you up here...."

Before Rick could finish, a jolt of turbulence sent the woman stumbling over a stack of flight charts.

"Watch out." Grady tried to stop her, but she careened into his lap, ending up splayed across the control wheel. She grabbed it to steady herself. The plane nose-dived. Dishes in the galley crashed, and someone in the main cabin screamed.

"She killed the autopilot," Grady cried out, struggling for control of the wheel.

"I've got the plane." Rick cut the airspeed and deployed the spoilers. White-hot adrenaline shot through him. The G-force of an abrupt maneuver could snap off a wing. He had to stop their freefall.

"Let go." Grady struggled with Melina, wresting her grip from the yoke.

With a gentle hand, Rick guided the plane back into a controlled descent.

Grady blew out a breath.

"When they cleared us down to eight-thousand," Rick said to Melina, "they didn't mean all at once."

"You know you want me." She focused her glazed eyes on Rick.

Rick elbowed Grady. "You've got the airplane." Flipping the flight attendant call switch, he climbed out of his seat.

"Come on." Rick pulled Melina to her feet. He returned the woman's shirt to its proper position. "I'm flattered, but my company forbids socializing with clients." He nudged her forward. "Now be good and go back to your seat." He used the calm, deep voice reserved for edgy travelers. No matter how irritating or obnoxious a passenger, Rick Sanders never lost his temper, and he always treated a woman with respect.

Allison, the cute flight attendant from Dallas, rushed through the open cockpit door.

Rick nudged Melina toward her and winked. "Please remind the passengers the cockpit only has two seats."

Allison mouthed the word, "Sorry." She draped her arm over the singer's shoulder. "Let's go on back to the main cabin. It's time to buckle y'all up."

Rick slipped back into his seat. Eleven hours and half as many cups of coffee had passed since the massive Rolls Royce engines on the Gulfstream, the king of corporate jets, had thrust them into the air at Le Bourget Field outside Paris.

 Grady brushed a strand of sandy hair away from his eyes. "You're a babe magnet. When I grow up, I want to be just like you." He squinted. "What's your secret?"

Rick grinned. "My uniform."

"I have the same one."

Rick shrugged. He stretched, extending his legs beyond the rudder pedals until his shoes hit the bulkhead. The captain's seat was a tight fit for his six-foot-two-inch frame, but there was nowhere else on earth he'd rather be. As if flying the sexiest planes and the biggest stars in show business weren't enough, now and again when he was starting to miss the rush of an F-18 at mach 1, his old buddy, Decatur Crane, would call with the lure of fast cash and the opportunity to live life on the edge for a few days. How much better could it get? Rick came home long enough to do his laundry, pay the mortgage on his Laguna Beach condo, and spend a few hours in the arms of his current girlfriend. Since his divorce, he never lingered.

The voice from SoCal Approach spoke again. "Gulfstream Echo Alpha, contact John Wayne tower 126.8. Have a good day."

Grady checked in with the tower. "Wind's out of the west at eight knots, and you can see all the way to Catalina."

Rick nodded. "Flaps fifteen degrees."

Grady pushed a lever. The mechanical whine and change in pitch indicated the flaps had lowered into place.

"Slowing to one hundred fifty knots," Rick said. "Landing speed?"

"One hundred twenty-eight."

"You want to take her in?" Rick asked.

"You bet," Grady said. "All the fun's in the take-offs and landings." He switched off the auto-pilot and adjusted the trim.

"When I was a kid," Rick said, gazing down on the few remaining orange groves that gave Orange County its name, "my friends and I used to ride our bicycles in those orchards. The developers won't be happy until condos replace every last tree." He blew out a breath and turned to Grady. "When we get on the ground, do a head count. Make sure everyone gets off the plane."

"Even Melina?"

"Especially her. If I have anything to say about it, this is going to be her last charter with me."

"That woman and her whole entourage are all bat-shit crazy," Grady said.

"The only body part of that woman I want to see is her ass getting into a car that's leaving."

With his copilot in charge of the landing, Rick pulled out his cell phone. *How long would it take the airlines to lift the ban on using them in flight?* He wanted a beer, a big New York steak, and then Maggie's soft and willing body. He dialed her number and waited. Her throaty voice announced no one was home.

"Hey, Maggie. It's Rick. I'll be landing in twenty minutes and on the beach by noon. How 'bout spending some time together after you get off work tonight? Let me know, honey." He tapped the screen to disconnect, slipped the phone into his worn leather chart case, and surveyed the readout on the instrument landing system.

"We're on glideslope," Rick said. "Lookin' good." At a thousand feet above the ground, he called out, "Gear down."

With a reassuring thump, the landing gear locked into place. Moments later, they touched down. The sound of the thrust reversers roared through the cabin, their force pinning Rick against his shoulder harness.

After exiting the runway, they taxied toward the Executive Terminal. A brand new Learjet caught Rick's eye, gleaming white with bold stripes of dark blue, maroon, and orange running the length of the fuselage and ending in a flower pattern on the tail. New planes, especially custom beauties like that one, held an indescribable allure for him. Like a woman, each one had a feel, a scent, and its own personality.

The new Lear was parked just outside Executive Air's passenger waiting room. Rick's boss Bob Hansen, the owner of Executive Air, stood at the bottom of the jet's stairway. A stunning blonde stepped from the plane's interior. She wore white jeans and a tight-fitting white tank top that accentuated her golden tan. Hair the color of corn silk tumbled around her shoulders, and she carried a large straw hat. The sight of her standing beside the massive jet, both bathed in glittering sunshine, made Rick's heart beat a little faster. Either one could turn a man's world upside down.

Without warning, the blonde dropped her hat and sprinted down the stairs. Waving her arms, she ran toward a catering truck backing away from a Falcon parked nearby.

"What the hell...?" Rick stared through the cockpit window.

The truck stopped. The woman skidded to her knees beside the rear wheels.

"What the heck is she doing?" Grady wondered aloud.

She stood, grease stains on the knees of her pants and

an orange tabby kitten cradled in her arms. She returned to the Lear, snuggling the ball of fluff.

Grady whistled. "That's what I call hot."

Rick shot a warning look at his co-pilot, but he thought, *Me too*.

"I'm talking about the airplane," Grady said.

"Sure."

Grady raised his hands in surrender. "Okay, I was just looking."

"You know the company rules." Rick grinned. "You don't want to go back to flying peas and carrots for Birdseye, do you?"

Rick scrutinized the new plane. "Must be Sam Randolph's Lear."

"Sam Randolph?" Grady tapped the control wheel. "I've heard that name."

"I'm sure you have. He owns radio stations and an oil field in Texas."

"Right. I saw a newspaper story about his place in Emerald Bay. It's gi-normous."

"Before we left for Europe with the band from hell, Bob mentioned the Randolph plane was coming into service with us." Rick's gaze seesawed between the woman and the Lear. "That's one sexy baby. Flies faster and higher than anything you've been in before. I can't wait to get my hands on her."

His gaze met Grady's. Both men laughed. It felt good to be a pilot.

And a bachelor.

Chapter 2

While Grady and the ground crew poured Melina, her band, and twenty-six pieces of luggage into four waiting limos, Rick grabbed his jacket from a hanger in the crew closet. He slipped it on, proud of the four gold stripes on the sleeves and shoulder boards. He smoothed his shirt into his slacks, then reached to the top shelf for his hat with the gold braid.

Looking sharp was only the outward expression of the professionalism etched into Rick's genes. Whether it was getting his hands on the last thousand pounds of fuel at a backwater airport in Mexico—just enough to make it back over the border—or flawlessly bribing a Maltese customs official intent on confiscating his passenger's cache of *Hustler* magazines, Rick's sense of duty prevailed.

He picked up his chart case, along with a lavender

Ladureé shopping bag, and headed through the cabin and down the stairway.

California sunshine warmed his skin, a welcome relief from the icy European spring. Gazing toward the new Lear, Rick recognized Sam Randolph, his face familiar from newspaper photos. The guy looked pretty fit for fifty-eight, and he still had all his hair, even if it was gray. Randolph stood on the tarmac, talking to the woman with the kitten and Bob Hanson.

A love of flight had bonded Rick and Bob, and they'd become fast friends. But lately Rick thought Bob seemed preoccupied, and whatever it was, Bob was keeping it to himself.

Bob spotted him and motioned him over. He clasped Rick's shoulder.

"Welcome home, buddy."

"Glad to be back."

Bob turned to the couple. "Sam, this is Rick Sanders, our chief pilot. This guy's the best in the business."

Rick laughed. "I pay him to say that."

"Rick hires and trains every pilot who works here. No matter how much experience a new guy has, no one flies a passenger till he says they're ready. Rick, meet Sam Randolph."

Rick reached out to Sam. "How do you do, sir?" The two men shook hands.

Bob patted the fuselage of the Lear. "Sam owns this beauty. It was just delivered. I've been showing him around the cabin."

"Hands-down, the Lear is my favorite plane," Rick

said. "The Ferrari of the skies. Nothing's faster or more responsive, unless you're flying an F-15."

Bob motioned toward Sam's companion. "Rick, this is Kate Randolph, Sam's wife.

"Nice to meet you." Kate extended her hand.

Rick took it. There was something in her touch. Her handshake felt gentle and firm at the same time. Her skin was soft and smooth. If she weren't married, he could have lingered. He pulled away. "Nice to meet you, too."

To Rick's practiced eye, she appeared to be around thirty. And man, did he know her type—wealthy and spoiled—although she did score a point for that grease stain on her white jeans.

Kate pushed a lock of blond hair out of her way, revealing thick, dark lashes that shaded sparkling turquoise eyes. She shifted the kitten. Her full lips parted in a grin. "I hope this little guy isn't part of your Terminex pest control plan."

Rick ruffled the kitten's neck. "Every once in a while a stray wanders in." Eager to unpack and unwind, he hoped he could slip away soon.

"Kate wants to be your next student," Bob said.

Rick squinted, certain he had misunderstood his boss. "What?"

Bob grinned. "Yup. She wants to learn to fly this baby."

Holy shit. Rick nearly choked at the idea. She probably had a student pilot's license.

"I'd be happy to demonstrate the features of your husband's new plane to you," Rick said.

Kate's friendly smile revealed straight white teeth.

"I don't want a demonstration," she said. "I want to learn to fly it."

Yeah, right, Rick thought. *A wannabe.* He resisted the urge to repeat the old fighter pilot joke that estrogen in the cockpit messes up the instruments. Instead, he smiled. "You know, Mrs. Randolph, this is a pretty sophisticated piece of machinery. The original Lear design came from a Swedish military fighter jet."

Sam Randolph scowled at his wife. "I don't know where you got this idea. Just because you can fly a single-engine plane around the ranch doesn't mean you can fly a twenty-million-dollar jet."

A flicker of hurt ruffled Kate's brow. It was clear her husband's lack of confidence stung. She looked directly at Rick. "I earned my private pilot's license five years ago in Aspen. I've done a lot of mountain flying."

Okay, she was gutsy. Mountain flying took nerve. Rick tried his best to be polite. "You're aware you need an instrument rating before you can fly this plane?" He hoped that hurdle would put an end to this nonsense.

Kate knitted her brows and looked puzzled. "Hmm... instrument rating?"

"It's one of the most difficult ratings to get. It takes a long time and a lot of hard training to learn to fly by instrument flight rules."

A look of disappointment crossed Kate's face. Rick felt sorry for her until she looked up with a gleam in her eye. "I got my instrument rating two years ago."

Whoa. He hadn't expected that.

"I'm sure you need more than that," her husband said.

Rick nodded. "You also need a commercial pilot's license. You can't step into a plane like this and get a type-rating with just a private pilot's license." He wracked his brain for any excuse.

Kate's eyes flashed. She straightened her shoulders. In her high-heeled shoes, she was nearly as tall as Rick. She stared at him. "Well then, I'll get right to work on that."

Sam Randolph pointed a finger at his wife. "If you're going to use the plane, just make sure it's here when I need it."

Kate patted his arm. "I will, dear."

God, these two are priceless, Rick thought.

Bob Hansen snapped his fingers and turned to Kate. "We're having safety training tomorrow. Why don't you come?"

"What would I do there?" she asked.

"Try not to fall asleep," Rick mumbled under his breath.

"It's lectures and films," Bob said, shooting a sideways glance at Rick. "We do it twice a year. FAA requirement. But it's fun, too. Between ground school and flight training, you'll be spending a lot of time here. It'll give you a chance to meet everyone." Bob met Rick's gaze. "It'll be a good introduction to the Lear. I think she'd get a lot out of it, don't you?"

"Sure," Rick replied, eyeing his watch.

"Thanks," Kate said. "I'll be there."

"Come on up to my office." Bob motioned all of them toward the modern two-story glass and stucco building that housed Executive Air. "I have an extra flight manual, Kate. You can get a head start."

Setting off across the tarmac, Bob walked beside Kate while Rick kept stride with Sam Randolph a few paces behind them. In the distance, a stand of eucalyptus trees swayed in an offshore breeze. Gazing around, Rick couldn't help feeling content. He loved it here. Not just California, but his home airport. After a long charter, he appreciated the familiar surroundings.

A white fuel truck, the Executive Air logo painted on the door, drove by. The driver slowed, stretching his arm through the open window. "Welcome back, Rick."

"Hey, Charlie." Rick waved. Yes. It was good to be home.

As they neared the building, Sam Randolph said, "Take good care of my girl."

Rick nodded, plotting his escape from his new assignment. All the captains at Executive Air were qualified flight instructors. Could he pass the job to one of them? Kate probably wanted to start immediately. Rick's hope for a few low-key weeks at home began to evaporate, but a quick turn-around and another month on the road seemed preferable to being cooped up in the cockpit with Sam Randolph's trophy wife. He was a jet jockey, not a babysitter.

When they reached the double glass doors leading into Executive Air's elegantly furnished waiting room, Rick swiped his security ID card through an access port. A buzzer sounded. He pulled open the door, allowing Kate to enter first. She smiled when she passed him, the kitten cradled in her arms. The scent of her perfume trailed behind her. Rick continued to hold the door for Sam and Bob, but his gaze remained fixed on Kate as she walked into the waiting room. He imagined her long legs would be as tan as her shoulders and arms. Recalling Grady's words, he agreed with the young pilot.

Definitely hot...and off limits.

Lila Stern sat behind the receptionist's desk, impeccably dressed in a beige suit, a strand of pearls around her neck, and her dark hair pulled into a knot. The five-foot-two, fifty-six-year-old managing director of Executive Air ran the place like a four-star general. She also watched over Bob Hansen like a mother hen. She had a soft spot in her heart for the guy that went way back.

As soon as she saw Rick, a smile spread across her rosy-cheeked face. She clapped her hands and jumped up from the chair.

She hurried around her desk, past several waiting passengers, until she reached Rick. He leaned down so she could get her arms around his shoulders. Standing on her tiptoes, she planted a kiss on his cheek.

"Welcome home, stranger. How's my favorite flyboy?"

"Lila," he said, wrapping his arms around her in a bear hug and holding her for an extra long time. "I missed you."

Rick enjoyed the special fondness Lila felt for him. Their mutual needs had paved the way to an exceptional friendship. During the darkest hour of his life, she had offered a motherly shoulder to cry on, and she had been there for him ever since. He squeezed her once more and released her.

"How is it you get better looking every day?" he asked.

She laughed. "You mean for an old broad?"

"What are you talking about?"

"I'm nearly old enough to be your mother."

"You said that, not me."

Lila stepped backwards to get a better look at him. "How was Paris? And when are you going to fly me there?"

Rick laughed. "If only you'd been my passenger. Dodging missiles over the Persian Gulf was a breeze compared to criss-crossing Europe with Melina and the band from hell. A bottle of vodka usually lasts a week on a charter. Her bass guitarist managed to go through one a day."

Lila linked arms with Rick and headed to her desk. They watched Bob and the Randolphs disappear down the hallway leading to Bob's office.

Inclining her head toward Sam, Lila lowered her voice. "When he was married to his first wife, Sam Randolph had a raging affair with that senator from Florida—you know—Ellen Gordon."

"How do you know this stuff?"

Lila smiled. "I read *People*."

"I wouldn't worry about this Mrs. Randolph," Rick

said. "She probably gets lots of retail therapy to help her."

"Not quite," Lila said. "Safe Haven keeps her busy."

Rick's brow creased. "What's that?"

"The charity she started." Lila put her hands on her hips. "An after-school enrichment program for latch-key girls. You know, sports, arts and crafts, music and tutors for homework too. Kate Randolph started the whole thing."

So she was a do-gooder. He still wasn't going to teach her to fly. Rick placed the *Ladureé* bag on Lila's desk. He grinned. "Chocolate truffles from Paris."

"You know my vices. Thank you." Lila removed a small wrapped box from the bag and inhaled its fragrance. "Mm-mm. I'm going to save them for tonight. After I take a bath, I'm going to get into bed and watch a movie. Then, I'm just going to slap these on my thighs."

Rick laughed. "If you eat them when nobody's looking, the calories don't count."

"Honey, thirty years ago I would have worried, but not any more." She pulled a pink message slip from a drawer and handed it to him. Her expression darkened. "Your *friend* called the day before yesterday."

The way she said the word *friend* meant it could be only one person. "Decatur?"

Lila whispered, "That adrenalin junkie is going to get you in a lot of trouble someday."

"Decatur's a good guy."

She touched his arm. "I worry, hon. That's all."

"What did he want?"

Lila blew out a puff of air. "You know what he wanted. Next week. A two-day job, he said."

Rick lowered his voice. "It's not like he's flying drugs."

"Yeah, yeah. Every flight is a humanitarian mission. But why does he have to involve you?"

"Because I'm his friend."

"Any pilot in his right mind would walk away from gigs like this."

Rick squeezed Lila's hand. "The pay is too good, and it all goes into a separate account."

"I know." He heard the frustration in her voice. "For your own charter company someday."

She sighed and picked up a slip of paper on her desk. "In the meantime, I just booked you on a month-long charter."

Rick smiled with relief. "Wow. You're amazing. Exactly what I needed to get out of taking on my newest student, Mrs. Randolph. Where am I going?"

"Just before you walked in, I received a call from Melina's manager. She wants to go to Tahiti, Bora Bora, Fiji. Can't remember where else. He said she needs to recuperate from her European tour. Wants to leave next week and insists you fly her."

Rick curled his right hand into a fist and pounded it into his left hand. "No way. I can't take another month of that freak show and her entourage. If anyone needs to recuperate from the European trip, it's me."

Lila shrugged. "What do you want me to do?"

"Damn it." Rick looked down the hallway to Bob's office. The rock or the hard place? It took him a moment to decide. He blew out a long breath. "Tell Melina's manager I'm training a new pilot and I'll be tied up for the next few months."

Chapter 3

The next day, morning light streamed through tall French doors that led from Kate's luxurious bathroom to a private balcony overlooking Emerald Bay and the Pacific. Her damp towel lay draped over the rim of the marble bathtub. On the velvet chaise lounge in the center of the room lay the open flight manual Bob Hansen had given her the day before. Speakers hidden in the walls filled the air with silky strains of Ella Fitzgerald.

Kate sat in a white lace bra and panties on a brocade bench at her dressing table, excitement spiraling through her.

"Sorry," she said into the phone. "This afternoon won't work." She tapped the Tailwind Flight School's business card on the counter top. "My husband and I have plans for an early dinner before the theater. But I've got to get this commercial pilot's license hurdle out of the way. Anything tomorrow?"

"How 'bout three o'clock?" the Tailwind scheduler replied.

"Perfect." Kate thanked him and hung up.

There was just no getting around it, she loved everything about being a pilot—the view from thousands of feet above the earth, the physical sensation of flight. "Even the smell of jet fuel," she often joked. She felt as at home in the air as she did in her living room. So when Rick Sanders said she needed a commercial pilot's license to acquire her type-rating in the Lear, it not only didn't faze her, she embraced the challenge.

She dropped the business card into the top drawer of her dressing table, next to two tiny pieces of aged paper she had found stuck together inside of a fortune cookie during her teens. The first read, *You will visit the moon.* Obviously the fates had her confused with Neil Armstrong. The second fortune read, *Among the lucky, you are the chosen.* The second prediction had come true. Thirty-year-old Kate Randolph felt like a lucky woman.

She loved the home she shared with Sam. Not only its grand scale and elegance, but the qualities it possessed and implied—stability and permanence. It was a world away from her childhood home, a bungalow on the grounds of a large estate where her widowed mother had worked. Separated from the neighborhood children by the invisible barrier wealth creates, Kate had returned to an empty house after school each day, filling her time with solitary activities—homework, reading, and playing their old upright piano. All the while, her yearning for her lost father burrowed into her young-girl heart, becoming an ill-defined ache she'd learned to endure.

Growing up at the edge of a gilded world challenged Kate, but she prevailed in the shadows of the mansions. Although previously left at the door to that private club of wealth and privilege, now, thanks to Sam, she owned a key, a key she used to guide and help a new generation of latchkey girls.

Kate pressed the intercom button on her phone.

"Yes, Mrs. Randolph?" a polite voice replied.

"Good morning, Patrick. How's your son's soccer team doing?"

"Still in first place. I think there'll be a trophy this year."

"Congratulations," Kate said. "How's the kitty?"

"The kids love her. They call her Wing-Ding, since you found her at the airport."

"I'm glad she's got a good home."

Sam repeatedly admonished her not to get friendly with the staff, but Kate felt awkward not connecting on a human level with those around her.

"Would you please bring my car up to the front in about ten minutes?"

"Of course, Mrs. Randolph."

After applying mascara and lipstick, Kate stood and smiled at her reflection in the mirror. Theoretically, she kept in shape for herself, but in truth, she knew Sam would settle for nothing less, and she worried about pleasing him.

She glanced at the Cartier clock on the low table nearby. *Eight-fifteen.* She needed to hurry if she intended to reach the airport on time. She'd taken up flying as a way to fill her time while Sam was away on business trips. What began as a lark became a passion and, to her chagrin, she noticed that lately she spent a lot more time with her pilot friends and the line guys at the airport than with her husband.

She heard noises from Sam's dressing room. These days, his business obligations kept him so occupied, he seemed to have less and less time for her. When they'd first met, he had dazzled her with vacations in Cap d'Antibes and St. Tropez, long weekends snuggling before the fire at his ranch in Aspen, and quick jaunts to San Francisco for a romantic dinner at a new restaurant that some celebrity chef had just opened.

But that whirlwind had rumbled to a stop.

Several months earlier a bout of melancholy had crept into her life, sunk deep roots, and blossomed into a full-blown case of loneliness. And the rumors she kept hearing about Sam didn't help. Really. How could her husband have time for another woman? He was obsessed with his radio stations. Besides, she had married him for better or for worse, and she intended to honor that vow—but did he?

Taking a last sip of coffee, she set the cup on her dressing table and ran a brush through her freshly washed hair. She pulled the crystal stopper from an antique perfume bottle, using its slim glass wand to dab some Arpége on either side of her neck. It might be an old-fashioned fragrance long out of favor, but Kate loved it. She returned the wand to the bottle, then walked through the arched doorway that led to her closet.

Brandy, her golden retriever, lay curled on the floor, her eyes fixed on Kate.

Kate bent to ruffle the fur on the dog's head. Brandy's eyes closed. "You're lucky Sam didn't want any more children. Otherwise I'd have a baby, and you'd have to share me." The idea of never being a mother shot a pang of regret through her. She rationalized her sadness away with the thought that The Haven's girls were her children.

She dressed in a pair of beige cotton slacks, a white button-down shirt and a white cashmere sweater in case the conference room at Executive Air was overly air-conditioned, then slipped her polished toes into a pair of red, Christian Louboutin high-heeled sandals.

Sam strode through the double doors that led from their bedroom. In his gray pinstripe Valentino suit and a starched white shirt with gold Tiffany cufflinks peeking out of his monogrammed sleeve, he looked every inch the business tycoon.

"You look very handsome." Kate took several steps toward him and planted a kiss on his mouth.

Adjusting the knot on his red silk tie, Sam smiled at her. "You know my motto. Clothing is the index to our contents."

Kate arched her eyebrows. "You can't possibly believe that." She laughed. "I think you should change your motto to 'I dress this way because I like to, even if I'm not meeting anybody.'"

Sam's manicured finger tapped her nose. "You know me so well." He crossed the pale pink Aubusson carpet to Brandy, and bent to scratch the dog between the ears. "I'll be late tonight," he said. "I have a meeting with the accountants about a new station in Florida."

Kate pursed her lips. "I guess I could meet you at the theater. Don't forget, we have tickets for Taylor Swift tonight."

"I can't make it. I'm going to be really late."

"But you said you would go. We have third row seats. Sam, you knew about this."

He shrugged. "Things happen. I have to take this meeting."

"No, you don't." Kate frowned. "You can cancel it. After you ditched me at Mastros it's the least you could do."

"Come on, honey, I can't help it. Invite a friend. I'm sure Janet would love to see Taylor Swift." He leaned down to kiss her cheek.

She averted her head. "You're standing me up again?"

"What do you want from me?" He pulled out his iPhone to check for new emails.

She fought back tears. "I want you to show you care about me."

He motioned around the room, eyes narrowing. "I think I take pretty damn good care of you."

She leaned against the wall. He just didn't get it. "That's not the way I need to be taken care of. I'd like to *feel* cherished."

"I'm sorry." He took several steps toward the door.

Shaking her head, Kate said, "I've hardly seen you during the past two weeks. I was excited about tonight."

Sam glanced back at her. "I'll make it up to you in Santomar. I promise."

She sighed. "You disappoint me, Sam. Why am I not surprised?"

"I can't do anything about it."

"Why did you marry me?" she asked in a whisper, scared of his answer.

Turning, he walked out of the room.

Kate's throat tightened as tears welled into her eyes. *All the more reason to get up in the air and fly away.*

A tattered pillow sat on the velvet chaise. A present from her mother after Kate's father's death, it was embroidered with a bunch of colorful balloons. On the ribbon tied around the balloons, Kate's mother had added the words, "Up, Up, and Away." Kate slumped onto the chaise and hugged the lumpy pillow to her chest. Staring at the empty doorway, she swallowed hard. *Who are you really, Sam?*

Brandy lumbered over and laid her head in Kate's lap.

Stroking the dog's silky fur, Kate checked the clock. Late. Damn it. She hastened to the mirror and wiped her eyes. Sucking in a deep breath and casting aside her disappointment, she leaned forward and said to her reflection, "I'm going to be a jet pilot." Then, she picked up her purse and the flight manual and headed for her car.

Bob Hansen sat in his wood-paneled office going over the figures prepared by his accountant. For twenty years, he had worked as much for the fun as for the money. Business was booming, but a few bad investments threatened to undermine his empire. At the top of the list was the company's sixty-four-foot Benetti motor yacht. Apparently people weren't as apt to charter a boat as they were a jet. The bank held a fifteen million dollar note on the yacht, and they were becoming impatient. If they foreclosed, and then the IRS came for their share, he'd regret not having the yacht so that he could take a header off of it. The business needed an infusion of cash. He'd have to sell off a piece of it.

He glanced past the photo on his desk of himself in his Air Force uniform to the community service awards that lined the wall across the room. With fifteen pilots and two mechanics on his payroll, not to mention an office staff of five people consumed with the task of churning out an endless stream of FAA-required paperwork, he secretly looked forward to having a partner.

Lila called on the intercom. "Marty from Flight Safety is here. He's setting up in the conference room."

"I'll be right there."

The phone rang. Bob darted to answer it, accidentally knocking over his coffee cup. He muttered an expletive, grabbed a napkin and attempted to halt the spill, but the liquid drizzled into the top drawer and oozed down the front of his desk to the floor. By the time he said hello, the caller had hung up. It was only nine o'clock in the morning. It promised to be another frantic day.

Lila poked her head in the doorway. Noticing the spilled coffee, she hurried to the bookcase and grabbed the box of tissues from the bottom shelf. She knelt beside Bob and blotted the carpet.

"I don't know what I'd do without you," he said.

She looked up, giving him a grin that hinted at their lost romance. "You've managed just fine," she murmured.

Given the hours he'd spent building his business, he had never regretted not marrying Lila. It wouldn't have been fair to her. And yet….

He pulled a handful of tissues from the box and mopped up the inside of his drawer. "I sure hope everyone stays awake today."

Lila stood. "I'll make sure the coffee pot's always full."

"None of that unleaded crap. Last year, Ted Swanson fell asleep and nearly cost us our safety certification."

Tossing the wet tissues into the trash, Lila looked out the window behind Bob's desk to the parking lot. "Ooh. She has a pretty car."

Bob turned around and watched Kate get out of her silver Porsche convertible. Grabbing a pen, he sat back and tapped it on the palm of his other hand. An idea struck him. Sam Randolph might be a good candidate to buy into Executive Air. He possessed business acumen and his wife loved to fly. Definitely a possibility.

Optimistic, Bob rose from his chair and headed toward the door. "Come on," he said, smoothing his tie. "Let's say good morning to Mrs. Randolph."

When Bob guided Kate to a seat at the cherry table in the conference room, heads turned, not just because she was beautiful, but because there had never been a woman at safety training before. Even Ted Swanson appeared to be wide awake and paying attention.

Bob rapped his knuckles on the table.

"I want to introduce you all to Kate Randolph. I'm sure you've noticed the new Lear with the great paint job. It belongs to Kate and her husband. I've invited her here today because she's going to be training with Rick for her type-rating."

All the men turned to look at Rick. Coffee cup in hand, he leaned against the wall, one leg casually crossed in front of the other. He wore khaki cargo pants and a denim shirt. His leather flight jacket hung on the back of a chair opposite Kate. Smiling, he nodded once, tacitly granting everyone the right to tease him about his new pupil.

Bob introduced the pilots of Executive Air. "Kate,

this is Pete Smalley, Ted Swanson, Grady Burke, Steve Burton." As he continued around the table, introducing the rest of the men, Kate met each man's gaze, seeming to make a mental note of their names. She smiled and said hello to each of them.

"And, of course, you know Rick." Bob gestured toward his chief pilot. "Looks like everyone's here," he said, "and there's plenty of coffee." He then motioned toward the short balding man who stood at the side of the room. "This is Marty Harris from Flight Safety. He's got a full day planned for you. So let's get started."

Bob took several steps towards the door, then paused and turned around.

"Before you guys get too cocky, I want to tell you a little something about our guest today. Before I sold that Lear to her husband, I took them both on a test flight up to their ranch in Aspen. Kate keeps a little biplane there, a Pitts."

Everyone in the room recognized the name of the fastest, most agile aerobatic plane manufactured.

"She took me on an E-ticket ride." He smiled at Kate. "We did spins, loops, and barrel rolls till I was dizzy."

A flush rose to Kate's cheeks. Bob saw her glance across the table at Rick, whose eyes seemed to widen at the news of her aviation skill.

"As if that weren't enough to knock my socks off," Bob said, "on the way back to the airport the carburetor picked up ice, and she had to land that little bird in a pasture. I'm happy to report no one got hurt. Not even the sheep. Believe me, this lady's one hell of a pilot."

He focused his gaze on Rick, praying he would charm Kate the way he did all women—paving the way for a partnership with her husband.

Recurrent safety training was mandatory for airline transport pilots, the license held by all the men seated at the table. Kate easily followed along as Marty Harris dove into a review of FAA flight regulations. But then the pilot sitting beside Kate smirked, "Getting all this?" The remark stung. To Kate, airport life was about camaraderie. It didn't matter if you were old or young, male or female, rich or not so rich. Being a pilot meant you were a member of the same fraternity. She was determined to be accepted here as one of the guys.

"Perfectly." She smiled. "If you're having trouble, let me know."

The pilot turned back to the lecturer.

The morning proceeded with talks on emergency procedures for engine and cabin fires, as well as engine failures. Just before lunch, the trainer showed them an animated video about electrical and hydraulic failures. Kate's attention was as rapt as if she were watching the latest Hollywood action film.

At noon, two young men entered the room, ferrying large silver catering trays. They placed them at the far end of the room on a long low cabinet covered with a white tablecloth and set with heavy china plates, silverware and napkins. When the group broke for lunch, a queue formed near the buffet.

Kate stood in line between Pete, the pilot who'd teased her, and another man.

"So how'd you get into flying, Kate?" Pete asked her in his thick New Orleans drawl. He seemed genuinely interested. Perhaps he was sorry for the disparaging remark he'd made earlier.

"About five years ago I was spending the summer in Aspen," Kate said. "Every time I drove past the airport, I'd see this amazing-looking biplane, midnight blue with shooting stars and comets and rainbows all over it."

"I know that plane," Steve Burton said. "I've seen it there for years."

"A real beauty." Kate grinned. "I kept thinking it would be so much fun to go flying in that plane. One day, I was driving past the airport on my way to the grocery store, and next thing I knew, my car practically turned itself into the airport, and I was standing in the flight school office making an appointment for a lesson."

By this time, Kate noticed several other pilots had gathered to listen to her. Not Rick Sanders. He stood at the far corner of the room, watching them as he made a call on his cell phone. She couldn't help noticing his rugged good looks. *A man's man, used to getting what he wants.* She heard him chuckle softly as he spoke. Wondering who he was talking to, she continued her story.

"The next morning I showed up for my first lesson. My flight instructor was this nineteen-year-old kid named Bucky. I couldn't believe I was going flying with someone who wasn't even old enough to order a beer. I got scared when he took me out to this little four-seat Cessna, unlocked the door, and said, 'Time to preflight.' I was so nervous I thought he said, 'Time to pray for flight' so I closed my eyes, leaned my head against the plane and started praying."

Everyone laughed. Kate's reminiscence led the other pilots to recount their own stories of first flights. As they ate their way through the trays of chicken sandwiches, Caesar salad and platters filled with strawberries and chocolate chip cookies, old friendships were renewed and new ones born.

They spent the rest of the afternoon in a review of every potential emergency that could occur in an airplane, including how to fix a toilet that refused to flush. At five o'clock, the class ended. On the heels of the long day, everyone jostled to collect the photocopied handouts the instructor had left at the back of the room.

Kate gathered up her flight manual and waited her turn to get near the table. After she reached it, she selected one sheet from each neat stack of paper. She swung around to leave and found herself face to face with one of the pilots. Nearly toe-to-toe, his features blurred. All she could see were a pair of crystal blue eyes, the color of the ocean in the Bahamas. The faint scent of his aftershave intoxicated her. Caught off-guard, she stared up at him. After a slight hesitation, the man took a step backwards. The straight nose and chiseled features of Rick Sanders came into focus. Kate steadied herself, fighting off unexpected desire. *God, what's the matter with me?*

"I see you're on my schedule tomorrow," Rick said. "We'll do some ground school in the cockpit."

"That'll be fine," Kate managed.

"Good. I'll meet you here at eight." He turned and walked away.

She felt as though he'd taken all the oxygen in the room with him. Kate's pulse raced. She needed air. Dashing out the door, she hurried toward the parking lot and the refuge of her car.

Chapter 4

At a quarter to eight the next morning, Rick sat hunkered down in a comfortable armchair in Executive Air's waiting room, reading the *Wall Street Journal*. He enjoyed the morning flurry of airport activity. Pilots scrambled to and from the flight planning room, plotting routes and checking weather. Catering carts arrived, and passengers made last-minute calls on their cell phones before heading to their planes. Ted Swanson, stretched out on the sofa, was taking a power nap.

Lila, looking efficient in a black suit and a white silk blouse with a bow at the neck, straightened the magazines on the glass-top coffee table. She picked up Rick's empty coffee cup. "Finished with this?"

"Yep. Thanks."

After carrying his cup to the kitchen, she returned to the reception desk.

Rick studied her, then folded the newspaper and tossed it onto the table. "When was the last time you had a date?" he asked.

"This past New Year's Eve. I took my neighbor's twelve-year-old to the movies."

"I'm serious. I worry about you being alone."

She laughed. "Honey, after two husbands, my labradoodle, Corky, is the only male I want in my house."

Sprawling back in the chair, Rick linked his fingers behind his head and watched her fill a cut-glass jar with jelly beans. When, after much effort, she couldn't squeeze the last handful into the jar, she popped them into her mouth, grinning sheepishly at him.

He recalled, with a slight sting from the memory, the day on which his friendship with Lila began. Twelve years earlier, after his discharge from the Marines, Bob Hansen had hired him to pilot the company's new Falcon 900. Flying the three-engine long-range jet was a dream job. Rick and his wife, Sandra, newly settled into a cottage overlooking Dana Point, welcomed the lifestyle change after the rigors of military life.

When his charter passengers became ill and curtailed their trip, Rick returned home two days early. As he skimmed down Pacific Coast Highway, he looked forward to surprising Sandra. On the seat beside him, a fresh-baked baguette peeked out of a white shopping bag, filling the car with a yeasty scent. Along with the bread from Dean & DeLuca in Napa, Rick had purchased a bottle of good Sonoma pinot noir and a ripe Camembert. He had even bought a bouquet of yellow roses for Sandra, although such luxuries were not in their budget.

Arriving home, he parked his Jeep in the driveway and unlocked the front door. The house was dark except for a small lamp in the living room. It cast a glow over the new chintz-covered couch Sandra had insisted they buy. Through the window that looked out on the backyard, fluttering shadows caught his eye. Rick walked into the kitchen, placed the shopping bag onto the tiled counter, and opened the sliding door. He heard music playing— vintage James Taylor, Sandra's favorite. Stepping outside, he strode across the patio and around the corner to the hot tub.

Sandra sat in the steamy water between the legs of their neighbor, moving against him. Each held a half-empty wine glass. Flickering candles cast restless shadows across naked bodies.

Rick stood silent, the roses dangling by his side. His heart hammered. He gazed at Sandra and her lover as though watching actors in a bad play.

Sandra froze. "Oh, God!" Water splashed every-where as she leaped to grab a towel.

"You're favorite color, yellow." Rick threw the roses into the hot tub, spun around, and left the house, slamming the door.

At the edge of rage, he revved up his car and screeched out of the driveway. He raced north on Coast Highway. Anger and despair fought a battle for his soul. Catching sight of Sandra's sunglasses on the seat beside him, he flung them out the window.

Gas pedal jammed to the floor, he careened through the curves of South Laguna, passing every car on the road. His world was spinning crazily. Unsure about his ultimate destination, he nonetheless intended to get there fast. He sped past the Surf and Sand Hotel, not bothering to stop at the red light.

As he rounded the bend at Forest Avenue, a woman pushing a baby stroller stepped off the curb, directly into his path. A white-hot jolt of adrenalin shot through him. Without the razor-sharp reflexes of a jet pilot, Rick would have hit the mother and child. Instead, he leaned on the horn and stood on the brakes. The tires squealed, and the car fish-tailed before it skidded to a stop mere inches from the stroller. The woman stood frozen in the light from the street lamp, fear reflected in her eyes. Rick mopped the sweat from his throbbing temples. The wild ride was over.

He drove around aimlessly, until at last he found himself in the Executive Air parking lot. He killed the Jeep's engine and rested his head against the steering wheel. Emptiness paralyzed him. *How could she betray him? Why? Now what?*

He sat there long enough for his pain to morph into hatred. Then, raising his head from the steering wheel, he straightened. *Screw her.* He would never take her back, even if she begged. He would get on with his life, but from now on, women would be for pleasure, nothing more.

He would retrieve his things from the house the next morning. For now, he needed a place to crash. The pilots' lounge. He trudged through the parking lot and pushed open the heavy glass doors to the waiting room. He glanced at the wall clock. Seven-forty-five. Everyone would be gone except for the night janitor. He strode down the hallway toward the lounge. The table lamps glowed softly, and the television was tuned to The Food Channel.

Rick dropped onto the soft, green corduroy couch and stared numbly at the screen. Looking up when he heard a noise, he saw Lila as she made her regular check of the offices before she left for the day.

Rick met her curious gaze. "I...I thought I was alone."

"Oh, honey, I'm here 'til all hours of the night." She frowned. "What's wrong? I thought you went home."

On board at Executive Air for only a few months, Rick didn't know Lila that well. He struggled for a witty reply but instead sat silent, the pain that ravaged his heart overwhelming him.

Lila crossed the room to the couch and sat beside him.

Rick looked away, a muscle ticking in his jaw as he fought for control.

She placed her hand on his arm. "What's the matter, Rick?"

The Marines had toughened Rick, and the Iraq War had finished the job by instilling in him an ability to hide even his raw emotions. Lila's compassion caught him by surprise. When he turned back to her, he gritted his teeth. "Sandra—with the neighbor." The words caught in his throat.

"*Who* was with her?"

Rick shrugged. What did it matter who? The question was why. He had loved Sandra, trusted her, and she had betrayed him.

Lila patted his shoulder. "When you need an ear to listen, I'm here." She got to her feet. "Don't move. I'll be right back."

She left the room, returning moments later with two ice-filled glasses and a bottle of twenty-five-year-old Chivas Regal.

"It's for emergencies." She poured a shot for each of them.

Rick took a long swallow. In the time it took for the amber liquid to reach his stomach, his heart closed like a tomb. "No woman ever gets to do this to me again. Not ever."

Lila took his hand and gave it a squeeze. "Give it time."

"When my father used to say, 'You can't trust a woman,' I just thought he was bitter because he had to raise me alone after my mom ran out on us." Rick managed a weak laugh. "You want to know the definition of difficult? Try being raised on a military base by a single dad. But I think the old man was right about women."

"Well, he's not right about this one." Lila stood and parked her hands on her hips. "You're coming home with me."

Too exhausted to protest, Rick left his car at the airport and climbed into her Volvo. Fifteen minutes later, she escorted him to the guest room of her immaculate little house in Irvine.

"The bed's really comfortable. Sleep as late as you want. There are towels under the sink in the guest bath. The fridge is stocked, so help yourself if you get hungry during the night."

Her no-nonsense tone and demeanor were just what he needed. "I don't know what to say, Lila. Thank you."

"You don't have to say anything." Lila smiled and kissed his cheek. "See you in the morning."

Rick spent two weeks at Lila's before he moved into his own apartment. During those two weeks, Lila made him pancakes, sewed a button on his shirt, and waited up for him on the nights she knew he'd be returning from a late charter. Rick pruned the lemon tree in her yard, praised her cooking, fixed her car, and brought her chocolates from See's. A remarkable relationship developed. The childless woman gained a son, and the motherless boy found the parent for whom he'd always yearned.

Rick watched Lila put the top back on the candy jar. Then he stood, donned his leather flight jacket, and sauntered over to her desk.

"Can you hand me the key to the Lear?" he said.

Lila opened the door to a small wooden cabinet attached to the wall behind her desk. Inside hung rows of keys, each dangling from a hook beneath a small brass plaque engraved with the tail number of the aircraft it opened. She picked up the key under the plaque that read 88SR, the SR standing for Sam Randolph. "Here you go. Eight, eight, Sierra Romeo," she said, using the phonetic alphabet familiar to aviators.

Rick tucked the key into his jacket pocket. "You can send my *student* out when she arrives," he said with a streak of sarcasm.

Lila arched an eyebrow.

"What?" he asked.

"Have a little patience, my dear," she said. "There are worse things than teaching that nice woman to fly her husband's plane."

"How do you know she's a nice woman?" Rick asked.

When Lila shut the key cabinet, the sound echoed throughout the room. She peered at Rick. "You know, you exasperate me. I'm a pretty good judge of people. Kate Randolph is way more friendly than the rest of the women who fly out of here. She's down-to-earth. And I like her." Lila shook her head. "Sometimes you're such a jerk."

Rick leaned over the counter and gave her a kiss on the cheek. "Sorry, Mom. Don't worry, I won't bite her head off. But I'm not going to treat her with kid gloves, either."

"Honestly, I don't know what's wrong with you."

"There's nothing wrong with me. It's just that she's got her work cut out for her." He smiled broadly, signaling the end of their squabble.

The smell of freshly brewed coffee caught Rick's

attention. He took two strides to the snack bar next to Lila's desk and pulled a paper cup with the Executive Air logo from the top of the stack. He poured a cup of steaming coffee, and then took a careful sip.

"When the lady arrives," he said, "send her out to the hangar." He reached into his pocket to retrieve the key. It wasn't there. He walked back to Lila's desk, setting down his cup. "I'd swear you just gave me that key."

"I did," she said.

Rick stuffed his hands into his pockets. "I know I put it here." He ran his fingertips along the inside seams, finally locating a split in the leather at the top of the right pocket. He patted the silk lining of the jacket, finding the key. He threaded it out through the hole and held it up.

"If you can ever part with that jacket for an hour, I'll fix that pocket," Lila said.

"Thanks." He tossed the key up and caught it in mid-air. Picking up his coffee, he walked out through the security doors and squinted into the sunlight. He pulled his Maui Jim's from his shirt pocket, put them on, and headed for the hangar that housed the Randolph's Lear.

Rick slouched on the leather couch inside the posh private jet. Fuming, he couldn't concentrate on reading, so he mindlessly flipped the pages of the latest *Time*

magazine. If he'd known she would be thirty minutes late, he could've stopped to pick up his laundry or done another errand. Where the hell was she?

Moments later, Kate bolted up the stairs, ducking her head to enter the cabin.

"Sorry I'm late," she gasped, dropping her shoulder bag onto the floor. Pushing up the long sleeves of her blue and white striped t-shirt, she heaved several deep breaths. She plopped into a large armchair across from Rick, her white pleated skirt flaring out over the seat.

Rick tossed the magazine onto the table next to his coffee cup. He looked at his watch, then at Kate. "If we have a lesson at eight o'clock, I expect you here at eight, not eight-thirty."

Kate straightened. "There was a lot of traffic."

He wasn't going to let her off that easy. "Either you want to learn to fly or you don't."

Her eyes flashed. "I already know how to fly. I just want to learn to fly this plane."

Rick stood. "Maybe you should set your alarm an hour earlier."

"I don't need a lecture."

Bingo. He'd hit a nerve. Feeling vindicated, he squeezed by her in the narrow aisle and walked toward the cockpit. "Let's get started."

Kate followed him. "Does your mother know how rude you are to strangers?"

"My mother doesn't know squat about me," he said. "She ran off when I was five. Haven't seen her since."

"I'm sorry," Kate said. She sounded sincere.

He climbed into the right seat and pointed to the left one. "Captain's seat."

"Is that for me?"

He looked around. "I don't see anybody else here."

She slipped into the tight space, her short skirt hiking up to the top of her thighs. The sight of her suntanned legs sent his blood surging downward.

Tugging at her skirt, Kate laughed self-consciously. "I guess from now on I'll wear slacks."

Rick leaned over, pointing under her seat. "There's a lever under there," he said in a businesslike manner. "Push it in and slide your seat until you can comfortably reach the rudder pedals."

She felt for the lever while she scrutinized the cockpit.

"Some of these instruments probably look familiar." He pointed to each as he spoke. "Attitude and airspeed indicator, altimeter and vertical speed indicator. These are just more sophisticated versions of the instruments on any single engine plane."

But that's where the similarity ended. The instrument panel, crammed with a fantastic assortment of circuit breakers, levers, buttons, gauges and indicator lights, extended far onto the side walls of the cockpit.

"My God, this looks like the Starship Enterprise. I hope I can remember what all these buttons do."

"You will if you pay attention," Rick said. He pointed across her lap. "There's another lever on the side to adjust your seat back."

As Kate felt for the second lever, Rick reached behind her to where an oxygen mask hung at the ready. He slipped it off its hook and handed it to her. "These are quick-donning types," he said, pulling his own mask from the wall behind him. He showed her how to put it on and start the oxygen flow. He felt like Darth Vader, ensconced in the thick black rubber and plastic.

"Put yours on, so you can get a feel for it," he said.

Kate slipped the oxygen mask over her face.

"Whenever your copilot leaves the cockpit, put on the mask," Rick said. "If you're flying at thirty-six thousand feet and your pressurization goes, you've got thirty seconds before you lose consciousness. There's a speaker so you can talk to air traffic control with it on." He took her hand, moved it to the base of the mask, and positioned her finger over a prominent red button. "Push this little button when you want to talk."

"That's pretty clever," Kate said.

Rick removed his mask and waited for Kate to remove hers. He replaced them both within easy reach.

Kate wrinkled her nose. "I hope I never have to use that. I don't even want to think about what happens to your ears at high altitude if the pressurization goes."

"Flying this plane is serious business. You shouldn't do it if you don't want to deal with emergencies."

"I didn't say that. I just said I hope it doesn't happen."

"Well, shit happens, and you need to be prepared. With all these technologies, many more things have the potential to go wrong. This plane isn't a toy like your other one."

She glared at him. "My Pitts isn't a toy."

"Let's just say that most people don't go from flying single engines to jets. How many hours do you have?"

"Twelve hundred."

"Twelve hundred?" He smirked. "Well, aren't you lucky? Most people don't get to sit left seat in a Lear until they've racked up a couple thousand hours."

"You're right," she replied. "I am lucky, but I refuse to do penance for it, and I don't need this crap from you. When I told Bob I wanted the best flight instructor at Executive Air, he said two words—Rick Sanders. You're stuck with me, so why don't we just get on with the lesson?" She drummed her fingers on the control wheel.

There it was, her trump card. Her plane. He worked for her. Clenching his teeth, he opened a cabinet on the back of the center console and pulled out a thick three-ring leather binder labeled, *Approach and Departure Charts*.

"The Jep charts for the entire United States are in here," he said. "If you're flying anywhere else—Europe, Mexico, wherever—get the charts from Lila." He glanced around the cockpit. "Have you noticed the location of any of the safety equipment?"

"I haven't looked yet."

He motioned toward the fire extinguisher, attached to the wall near the cockpit door, and a cabinet marked with a red cross that contained a first aid kit. Then he pointed to the ax attached to the bulkhead behind their seats.

"In an emergency landing," he said, "the exits could get stuck. You can use this to hack open a door or a window. If that happens, get yourself and your passengers away from the plane A.S.A.P."

"Why?" She arched her eyebrows. "Because after all that commotion, we'll probably need a drink?" She smiled.

"No." He didn't appreciate her joke. "Because jet fuel will be leaking all over the place, and a spark can cause the whole thing to explode."

She grimaced.

"After that, you'll definitely need a drink," he said.

"Touché."

Rick explained the rest of the cockpit layout. He couldn't ignore the fact she appeared eager to absorb his every word. He decided to lighten up a bit. Climbing out of his seat, he motioned to her.

"Come on back here," he said. "I want to show you the most important thing in the plane."

She followed him out of the cockpit, down the aisle, and halfway to the rear of the cabin.

Stopping in front of a burl wood cabinet next to the leather sofa, he commanded, "Now, pay attention."

She stood next to him, eyes fixed as he opened the cabinet door. Inside he pointed to a stainless steel panel with a spigot.

"See this?"

She nodded.

He unlatched two clips on the underside of the panel and the whole thing slid forward. The panel was actually the front wall of a half-gallon, stainless steel reservoir. Rick pointed inside.

"Anytime this plane takes off"—he tapped his finger on the panel for emphasis—"make sure this is filled." He held a stern expression as long as he could, then broke into a smile. "This is where the coffee goes."

Kate's laughter filled the cabin. *God, she's pretty*, Rick thought, suddenly wishing she weren't married to Sam Randolph. In a flash, he regained his senses. "Come on," he said. "We've got a lot of work to do. Let's take a look outside."

It took them over an hour to make a full circle of the exterior of the plane. Kate made notes in her flight manual. Rick pointed out all the items that needed to be checked in every preflight inspection, and then he quizzed her on each of them—static ports, antennae, control surfaces, and connecting hinges. He couldn't help being impressed that she remembered everything he'd said. She might be the wife of a wealthy client, but he had to admit she was the kind of student he liked. She asked the right questions, displaying her excitement so naturally, Rick started to relax.

When they had finished going over every single surface of the fuselage, Rick got on his hands and knees. He crawled under the plane, then sprawled out beside the landing gear. Motioning to Kate, he said, "Come on down here."

Kate slipped off her shoes. She pointed to the white painted floor, mopped shiny and spotless. "This hangar's so clean," she said as she crawled towards Rick, "it looks like a place that stores medical supplies, not airplanes."

"These babies are expensive," he replied. "We take good care of 'em."

Propped on one elbow, Rick pointed into the wheel

well. "When you're doing your pre-flight, you've got to get down here and check the struts. Look for cracks." He moved a bit so Kate could take a look. She eased over to see where he was pointing. When she tilted her head back to look up, Rick stiffened at the feel of the feathery softness of her long hair brushing over his bare forearm. He took a shallow breath, and then another.

Off limits, he reminded himself. *She is Mrs. Sam Randolph.*

She pointed to two small rubber tubes. "Are those for the brake fluid?"

"That's right." When she finished checking out the wheel well, she raised her head. Her hair trailed back across his arm. He let out a breath.

She gazed up at him. She was waiting for him to say something else about the Lear.

He pointed to the tires. "They're easy to blow."

He couldn't take his eyes off her. *God, she was gorgeous.*

She furrowed her brow. "Huh?"

Damn. Had he said *she's gorgeous* out loud? The last time he felt like this he was in high school. "I said, you gotta make sure the tires are inflated properly. It's easy to blow one if they're not."

He checked his watch. "It's ten-thirty. I've gotta change into my uniform. I'm flying your husband to San Francisco at eleven. I think we've done enough for today."

Rick slid out from under the plane. He offered his hand to help Kate up. When she climbed into the cabin to retrieve her purse, he called to the mechanic working on the Citation parked across the hangar.

"Hey, Ken," Rick said, pointing to the Lear. "Have this one towed up front."

Ken wiped his hands on his white overalls. "Right away."

After Kate rejoined him, Rick pushed a button on the Lear and the stairway automatically folded up. He closed the door.

Walking side by side across the tarmac back to Executive Air, Kate opened her arms wide and took a deep breath. "I could do this all day," she said.

Rick smiled. "Me, too."

They passed a variety of corporate jets parked in neat rows. Most were locked, but some had open doors with red carpets unfurled in front of their stairs. Kate peeked into all the open doors, asking how fast and far each plane could go. Rick liked the way her eyes lit up when she talked about flying. He hardly finished the answer to one question before she posed another. Her whole being seemed electrified as she caressed the fuselage of one of the planes. He smiled, understanding as only another pilot could. Perhaps he had misjudged her at the start. She was nothing like the spoiled women he'd flown before. She had an easy way about her. Maybe teaching her to fly the Lear wouldn't be so bad after all.

When they reached the office, Kate stopped. She looked up at him. "Thank you. That was fun."

"Wait 'till you get it off the ground," Rick said.

They gazed at each other a moment, not speaking, then Kate opened her handbag, fished inside, and brought out her car keys. "Same time tomorrow?"

"Fine with me. I'll see you at eight." Rick paused, then added good-naturedly, "Not eight-thirty."

Kate smiled. "You're on."

As Rick opened the door to the office for her, he pointed to her high-heels. "Leave the party shoes at home tomorrow." He winked. "We're goin' flying."

Chapter 5

Kate battled a nasty crosswind, finally sighing a gush of relief as she landed the single-engine Cessna at John Wayne Airport. She used the rudder pedals to steer the blue and white four-seater down the runway, turning the control wheel all the way to the left and raising the downwind aileron. The last thing she wanted was a gust of wind to flip them over.

"That's a wild wind," Joe, the instructor from the local flight school said. "Nice job. Make an appointment to take the commercial written exam. I'll sign you off for your check-ride today."

Full of confidence, Kate taxied to the tie-down area. A line guy signaled her to a parking space.

The cockpit radio crackled. "Eight, eight, Sierra Romeo's at the outer marker."

Kate set the brake and turned to survey the approach

path. Sam's plane was on final. She could hardly wait to tell him about her day's adventures. First, the Lear session, now this. She killed the engine and waited for the propeller to stop spinning before she opened the door.

"Thanks, Joe. Want me to lock it?"

"Naw. I've got another student coming."

She handed him the key and headed across the tarmac.

While Sam's plane made its way to the other side of the airport, Kate fished her phone from her purse. She pressed number one on her speed-dial.

Sam answered on the first ring. "Hey, baby."

"How was San Francisco?"

"Great."

"I'm here at the airport. I watched you land."

"What's up?" he asked.

"Just finished an hour's worth of chandelles and figure eights," Kate said.

"You mean like on ice skates?"

"No," Kate said. "Compulsory maneuvers on the commercial pilot's flight test. I've got a few hoops to jump through before I can get that Learjet type-rating. Anyway, I was thinking it would be fun to stop by The Balboa Bay Club. Sit on the patio, sip some wine, watch the boats."

"I think I'd rather have a quiet drink with you at home."

"No problem. It was just a thought. I'll see you later."

Kate said goodbye and crossed the parking lot to

her car. The Porsche's convertible top was down, and she tossed her purse behind the driver's seat. Exiting the airport, she headed south on MacArthur Boulevard. The wind tousled her hair, and she reached for the white Las Ventanas baseball cap on the seat beside her. After a left turn on PCH, she maneuvered through the village of Corona del Mar, stopping at See's to purchase a quarter pound of dark chocolate nougats—Sam's favorite.

Several blocks past See's, the shops and bungalows of Corona del Mar gave way to Pelican Point and the white sands of Crystal Cove. Ahead on the right, on a bluff overlooking the Pacific, stood a white clapboard cottage. The old shack, the only structure along this piece of pristine coastline, had been there for as long as anyone could remember. Its roof supported an old white sign painted with red letters that read *Date Shakes*.

Kate checked the clock on her dash. Five o'clock. Sam wouldn't want dinner until eight. She hesitated only a moment before turning the Porsche into the small parking lot. Usually brimming with customers, it was near closing time and the lot was empty. Kate set the brake, grabbed her purse from the back seat, and walked up to the window.

"One date shake."

She handed the teenage cashier three dollars, and he handed her twelve ounces of heaven.

After taking a sip, she walked to one of the tables overlooking the water and sat down to enjoy the sunset.

She heard a car pull into the lot. *At least I'm not the only one spoiling my dinner*, she thought.

The sun balanced like a golden ball at the edge of the horizon, tinting the sky brilliant shades of orange, turquoise, and pink. *God's paint palette,* her mother had often said.

"What are the chances...?" The male voice, deep and smooth, was very familiar. She was sure she could recognize it, even blindfolded.

She looked up beyond the sun-tanned hand holding the paper cup, beyond the dark sleeve with the gold stripes, and into the impossibly blue eyes of Rick Sanders.

"Be my guest." She motioned toward the empty seats at her table, willing her pulse to slow down.

Rick took the seat across from her, gesturing toward the kaleidoscope of colors. "Quite a sunset." He had taken off his tie, and the collar of his white shirt rustled in the gentle wind that rose off the ocean. The faint scent of his cologne traveled on the breeze. Kate recognized the fragrance. *Eau Sauvage.*

In the parking lot, someone exited an SUV and walked to the order window.

Rick took a slug of his shake. "Come here often?"

Kate laughed at the obvious line. "Only when I'm totally out of willpower. How about you?"

"It's on my way home," he said.

Stirring the froth with her straw, Kate looked up to see the new customer approach, balancing a Coke and an order of fries. Damn. It was the tennis pro from the clubhouse. The woman sat at another table.

Gossip spread through Laguna Beach faster than the

seasonal wildfires, and Kate didn't want her accidental meeting with Rick blown out of proportion. She hoped the woman hadn't seen her.

"My mother used to bring me here when I was a kid," Kate said. "She was a cook for a wealthy family in San Juan Capistrano."

Rick looked surprised. "You mean you weren't born with a silver spoon in your mouth?"

"Hardly." Kate laughed. "We lived in a tiny bungalow on her employer's estate."

Rick pointed toward the northeast. "When I was a kid," he said, "my dad was stationed at El Toro. First time he brought me here, I was six."

A faint longing rippled through Kate. "My dad was in the service too. He was an aviator."

"You ever take him up with you?

"He died when I was eight." She took another sip.

"Tough break when you're a kid."

Kate looked up.

With his elbows on the table, Rick had leaned in toward her. The warmth in his eyes invited her to go on.

"We used to play this game," she said. "He'd ask, 'How much do you love me?' and I'd say 'More than broccoli.' The game never ended until I said I loved him more than a date shake."

She took a steadying breath and set her cup on the table. "After he died, every trace of him vanished. My mother gave everything away. I have one photo of him."

Rick's gaze held hers, his clear eyes flashing an

intensity she hadn't seen before. It felt like staring at the sun—dangerous. She wanted to look away, but she felt helpless, like being adrift in a boat with no oars. Should she surrender? Let the current sweep her away? A voice inside said, _No_. And although she felt tempted to linger, Kate finally looked away.

Straightening, she cleared her throat. "My friends think that's why I married Sam. You know, father figure, all that Freudian stuff."

The softness left Rick's expression. "Whatever works."

Kate shook her head. "No, it's not like that. I have a wonderful husband." _Why am I telling Rick this? I hardly know him._ "I love Sam."

He seemed to look through her. His gaze made her stop. Was it sadness she saw in his eyes? No, not sadness. And then she understood. He was lonely.

Feeling uncomfortable, she blotted her lips with the paper napkin. "I need to get home. If Sam left the airport the same time you did, he'll already be there waiting for me."

"You've got time," Rick said, taking a swig of his shake. "When I drove away, your husband and Bob were having a glass of wine in Bob's office."

"Really?"

Annoyed that Sam found time for a drink with Bob after turning down her invitation to the Balboa Bay Club, Kate stood.

"Gotta go." She slung her purse strap over her shoulder. "Can't wait for my first lesson tomorrow. See you at eight." She tossed her half-finished drink into the trash and walked to her car.

Kate headed down PCH, wondering what her life would have been like if she had married a man her own age, a man like Rick. Surely she wouldn't be living in a house the neighbors referred to as "The Parthenon." And she might have had a child. *Don't go there*, she thought. She shook off the melancholy moment and switched on satellite radio. She'd already come to terms with the reality that life's joys and sorrows existed in a delicate balance.

Soon she was singing along to an old Frank Sinatra tune. *"Come fly with me, let's fly, let's fly away,"* the song went. *"If you can use some exotic views, there's a bar in far Bombay."* She couldn't help smiling. The lyrics seemed like a ticket to the realm of possibilities. High in the sky, all bets were off. The world belonged to her. It was just a matter of setting a course...east, west, freedom, escape. *"Come fly with me, let's float down to Peru...."*

She continued to sing, even as she waved and swept past the guard at the entrance to Emerald Bay. When she reached the driveway at Two Emerald Point, she pressed a button in the car and the massive bronze gates swung open. Winding her way up the long drive-way, she passed the main house, a white limestone Palladian villa with arched loggias draped in pink, red, and purple bougainvillea. She bypassed the motor court and pulled into the six-car garage. Why anyone would need more than one car was beyond her.

After turning off the engine, Kate relaxed against the gray leather headrest. She took a deep breath and smiled. What a day. She had loved her first taste of the Lear, and tomorrow she would actually fly it. Things couldn't possibly be better.

At the sound of a car engine, Kate turned. Sam pulled his big black Bentley into the space next to hers. She reminded herself of her good fortune—a handsome husband, a beautiful home, and now, a private jet. She just wished she didn't feel so restless.

She swung open her door and stepped out. Walking to the Bentley, she waited for Sam to turn off the engine. Tonight would be their first dinner together in more than two weeks. She refused to sulk about his busy schedule. When he got out of his car and closed the door, she reached up and nuzzled the side of his neck.

"Mm-m-m," she said, lingering to inhale the sweet spiciness of his cologne.

Sam smiled and put his arm around her, then kissed her on the cheek. Hardly the passionate greeting she desired.

"I hope you took a break for lunch today?" she said, linking arms with him. They walked toward the house.

"Had lunch at Fleur de Lys," he said. "Foie gras in a cherry port-wine sauce. How was flight school?"

"It was fantastic." While they strolled to the front steps, she bubbled over with details about the morning in the Lear and the afternoon in the two-seater.

Sam pushed open the carved oak door. Brandy, tail wagging, rushed to greet them.

"Hi, Brandy." Kate bent to kiss the golden retriever's head and ruffle her fur.

"Hey, girl," Sam said.

They passed through the arched stone entry, past the butler's pantry. The scent of rosemary and garlic perfumed the air.

Kate poked her head into the kitchen. "We're home," she called to Cora.

Entering the library, Kate turned on a Michael Bublé CD while Sam headed to the bar. Brandy curled up under the coffee table.

Balancing two crystal glasses filled with Dubonnet, Sam sank onto the green tapestry couch. Kate took the glass he offered her, then slid onto the sofa beside him.

He tapped his glass against hers. "To Captain Kate." He took a sip. "Just be careful when you're up there."

Kate curled up next to him, enjoying the music and the warmth of the aperitif. "This is just what I've been craving. Time alone with you." She touched his sideburn. "You know, we haven't made love in weeks."

He kissed her hand. "All I want is a quiet evening with you."

The sound of the phone on the table behind the sofa startled them both. Kate reached to pick it up without moving off the couch.

"Hello." She knitted her brow and covered the mouthpiece. "Don't we ever get a moment to ourselves?" she whispered. She held out the phone. "It's Bill Casey."

"Bill, what's up?" Sam listened while his attorney talked. By the time Bill Casey finished, Sam's face glowed red.

"What the hell's the matter with those idiots? Don't

they read contracts?" He listened again for a moment before springing to his feet. "Get over here now," he said. "We can review what you've got. I'll go to Dallas in the morning. I'll deal with them myself." Sam slammed down the phone and began pacing in front of the fireplace.

Kate uncurled from the couch. "I thought we were going to have a quiet dinner."

"So did I. But I'm buying a talk-show station in Dallas. The goddamn V.P. is moving to another station and walking off with the advertisers. I've got to meet with Bill tonight."

"Dallas in the morning?" Kate sighed. "I guess that means I won't be able to have my lesson tomorrow."

"Sorry, honey." He shook his head slowly. "Do me a favor and call Executive Air for me?"

Kate called Lila at the company's after-hours number to report the change of plans. Then she ate her dinner in the den, watching an old Bette Davis movie that was interrupted from time to time by the loud voices of Sam and Bill in the next room.

Later that evening, after she heard Bill leave, she went into the kitchen, took a carton of milk from the stainless steel refrigerator, and poured herself a glass. Sam came in, looking exhausted. Finding a plate of Cora's homemade chocolate chip cookies, he picked one up and took a bite.

"I know you're disappointed," he said. "About dinner and missing your lesson tomorrow."

Kate made no reply. She had known her husband

was a workaholic before they married. She thought that, as they made a life together, he would change. *Wrong*.

"I'm disappointed, too," Sam said. He moved toward her. "I would have much rather spent the evening with you." He took a sip from her glass of milk. "Why not come to Dallas with me? I'll just be there a few hours. You can go to Neiman Marcus. Have some fun."

That was Sam's answer to everything. Buy something nice and you'll feel better.

Kate shrugged. "Maybe I will come along. I don't have any other plans for tomorrow, and since I can't have my lesson, at least I'll be in the air."

They turned out the kitchen lights. As they walked toward the entry hall, Kate longed for Sam to touch her. Once upon a time, he would have slipped his arm around her, and they would have stopped to kiss at the foot of the stairs. Now, he walked up the wide staircase in front of her. Kate started to reach for him, but instead she wondered why he'd lost interest in her. What was she doing wrong?

Things'll be better at Santomar, she reassured herself. After all, that was one of the reasons Sam had bought the plane. Besides the luxury of being able to fly on a moment's notice to his oil field in Texas, or any of the hundreds of radio stations he owned, Sam wanted a quicker and easier way to get to their vacation house on the small Caribbean island near Virgin Gorda. *Yes,* she thought, *in a few weeks, we'll be in Santomar, away from distractions, and alone for a change.*

Chapter 6

The following morning, Rick arrived at the airport thirty minutes ahead of his passengers. The front door to Executive Air was unlocked, and he beelined toward the scent of fresh brewed coffee in the waiting area. He had stayed up past midnight getting to know the young woman who had just moved in next door. She had a drop-dead body and a pretty face. But that voice. He hoped a jolt of caffeine would be enough to erase the grating high-pitched whine from his memory. Any neighborly relations with her would have to be limited to waving hello from a distance.

Footsteps coming from the hallway to the pilot's lounge made him look up. Steve Burton, Rick's copilot for the trip to Dallas, ambled into view, his spit-shined shoes, starched white shirt, and carefully pressed uniform topped off by a Dallas Cowboys baseball cap.

"Morning," Steve said, grinning.

Rick stared at his hat. "How many of those you got?"

"I lost count last year."

Rick shook his head. "Be sure you stow that before the Randolphs arrive."

Steve peeled off the hat and started toward the door. "I'm gonna preflight the plane. See you outside."

Rick took a sip of steaming coffee and strode down the hallway to his office. The walls displayed colorful maps from every part of the world, and photos of airplanes he had flown. In one corner, a large globe sat suspended in a walnut stand. He set his cup on his desk near a stack of travel books and tossed his jacket onto the brown leather couch under the window. It landed next to a pillow painted with a map of Arizona. Large crimson letters proclaimed, *Home of the Grand Canyon*.

Rick slid into his chair and reached for the phone. He dialed the number to file his flight plan, and while he waited for someone to answer, he leafed through a stack of messages. The top one was from Decatur Crane, advising he had a new cell phone number. Rick tucked the message into his shirt pocket.

A woman's voice came on the line. "Flight Service."

"Going I-F-R," he said, "Santa Ana direct Dallas." He looked at his watch. "Half an hour from now."

He received a weather briefing for the route and filed his flight plan. No thunderheads were predicted anywhere along their way, just smooth, blue sky—the kind of day a pilot savored.

He retrieved his jacket from the sofa, slung it over his arm, and returned to the passenger lounge. He gazed through the floor-to-ceiling windows, noting the linemen had towed the Lear from the hangar to the tarmac and parked it just outside the glass doors. A red carpet lay unfurled in front of the open stairway.

Steve circled the plane's exterior, doing a thorough preflight. A ground crew in white overalls loaded catering trays into the galley, along with a half-gallon of hot coffee. They would also stock the plane's bar with an assortment of liquor, soft drinks and fruit juices, as well as an array of packaged snacks. Brand new cellophane-wrapped decks of playing cards bearing a picture of Sam's plane and its call sign would be placed throughout the cabin. When the Randolphs boarded the Lear, they would also find a bottle of Dom Perignon with a note from Bob Hansen that simply said, "Enjoy!"

From the corner of his eye, Rick spotted Sam and Kate in the parking lot. He slipped on his jacket and adjusted the knot of his tie, then brushed a piece of lint from the gold braid on his sleeve while he walked to the glass front door to greet his passengers.

"Looks like a great day for a trip to Dallas," Rick said, holding the door for them.

Randolph, dressed in a dark business suit, shook Rick's hand. "My meeting's at twelve-thirty. I don't want any delays."

"I'm ready to go when you are," Rick replied. He found it hard to take his eyes off Kate. Her blond hair cascaded over a body-hugging black top printed with small pink roses. She wore matching tight capri pants. The sight of her, along with the scent of her perfume, sent his pulse galloping. She smiled when she greeted him. *It's just business,* he reminded himself.

Rick motioned toward the plane. "We're ready to board." He stepped ahead of the couple to open the door to the tarmac. Kate passed by, and his gaze fell on the smooth curve of her back, revealed by her low-cut top. He tried not to stare.

Once they were outside, Sam paused to make a last minute call on his cell phone. Rick and Kate strolled toward the Lear.

"The weather's clear over the entire route," Rick said, "and we're going to have one hell of a tailwind. A hundred and ten knots."

As they approached the plane, Kate pointed to her black crocodile loafers. "See. No party shoes. Too bad Sam has to go to Dallas. I was really looking forward to my lesson today."

Rick held out his hand to help Kate up the stairway. "Have your lesson in Dallas." He smiled at her. "The air's the same there as it is here."

"Of course it is." She grinned back at him. "Why didn't I think of that? Let's do it."

A bell chimed, the seatbelt light illuminated, and moments later the engines roared as the Lear accelerated down the runway. Pinned to her seat beside Sam on the sofa at the back of the cabin, Kate gazed through the open cockpit door, beyond the front window to the runway. She couldn't think of anywhere she'd rather be.

She reached for Sam's hand. "Up, up, and away."

Sam squeezed her arm. "I feel like a kid with a new bicycle."

"We have so much, Sam." She planted a kiss on his cheek. "We're so lucky."

"It wasn't luck." Sam frowned. "It was my hard work."

Of course, he was right, but his remark seemed to suck the joy out of the moment.

When they reached cruising altitude and Rick turned off the seatbelt sign, Sam wandered over to the magazine rack. Kate headed to the galley to see about breakfast. She returned to the sofa with two plates of sliced papaya and strawberries. Sam read a *Forbes Magazine* while he ate. Kate nibbled a few berries and gazed out the window. Thirty-nine thousand feet below, the convoluted shoreline of Lake Powell stretched like tentacles into the Arizona dessert.

Over Alamogordo, Kate returned to the galley to heat two servings of bacon and onion quiche in the microwave.

She handed a warm plate to Sam.

"Thanks," he said. "You're a good kid."

Kate rolled her eyes.

"Sorry, honey. Just a habit." He took a bite of the quiche but stiffened when the plane shuddered.

Kate touched his arm. "Just clear air turbulence.

Nothing to worry about. I've seen pictures of these planes being tested in wind tunnels. The wings on the Lear can flap like a bird."

Sam set down his fork, picked up the intercom phone, and dialed the cockpit. "Everything okay up there?" Apparently content with the answer, he hung up the phone and continued to eat his breakfast.

"I can't believe a little turbulence would make you so nervous," Kate said. "What's going on?"

"Nothing." He shrugged. "I just wanted to try the intercom."

Sometimes Kate couldn't discern if he was telling the truth or lying. Sam baffled her now as much as he had when she'd first met him, eight years earlier, when she'd gone to Sam's Emerald Bay estate for the first time.

Janet had been seeing Sam's son, Derek; he'd arrived at the apartment on a Friday evening to take Janet to dinner.

Kate answered the door in her sweats.

"It's date night," Derek said. "Don't you have plans?"

"I did, but he got the flu. It's okay. I have papers to grade."

Derek stood by the front door while Janet gathered her purse and keys.

"We're going down to Laguna Beach tomorrow to play tennis with my dad," Derek said to Janet.

"Great," Janet said. "Why doesn't Kate join us?"

"We could use a fourth for doubles," Derek said.

Kate had always found Derek a bit cold, but a game of tennis sounded good.

"I'd love to," she said.

Later that night, when Janet returned home, she sat at the edge of Kate's bed. "It'll be fun tomorrow. The house in Emerald Bay sounds fabulous. Anyway," Janet warned, "watch out for Mr. Randolph. He's a widower. Derek claims the old man can't keep it zipped."

In spite of what Derek had told Janet about his father, from the moment Kate met Sam, she liked him. He was handsome, smart, and friendly.

After that first day of tennis, Janet teased her, "Sam likes you."

"Oh, please," Kate replied. "He's old enough to be my father."

Nevertheless, Kate began to play tennis with Sam on a regular basis. After a set or two, they would have drinks in the cabana by the pool or watch a movie in his den.

Soon after, Janet broke up with Derek.

"The guy's scary," Janet had said. "Wild temper. Too hot-headed for me."

Kate continued to see Sam. He often asked her to join him when he entertained business associates and their wives. She accompanied him to baseball games at Dodger Stadium, and to the Hollywood Bowl, where they would have dinner in his box before the concert. One warm August evening, ten months after they'd met, they sat in the box, sipping champagne and waiting for Sam's guests to arrive. He surprised her by reaching for her hand and holding it between his own.

He hesitated a moment, then said, "I'm too old to beat around the bush. I want you to marry me."

Kate gently withdrew her hand. "I thought we were good friends."

"We are," he replied. "That's why a marriage would benefit both of us. I like having a woman around. And a wife is good for business. Our age difference is irrelevant. You get along well with my friends. And if we were married, you'd have someone to take care of you."

Kate smiled at him. "What about love, Sam?"

He grinned back at her. "I love you. It's just that I'm older and think about it in different terms than you do."

"I adore my job, Sam, and my apartment with Janet. I'm not ready to get married." She leaned over and kissed his cheek. "Thank you for asking."

But then, ten days later, a drunk driver ran a red light on Crown Valley Parkway, slamming into the side of her mother's car and killing her instantly. With no siblings, no father, and now no mother, Kate turned to Sam for comfort. Her loss became the catalyst that brought them together as a couple. They became lovers not long afterward.

It was clear their age difference provided a challenge, but soon Sam convinced Kate to quit her teaching job and move in with him. A year later they were married on the lawn of Sam's Emerald Bay estate. Janet served as maid of honor, and Derek, barely a year older than Kate, and barely sober, stood beside his father.

The night before the ceremony, Sam's oldest friend, Jack Arnold, along with his wife Bebe, gave a small dinner party for the couple in a private dining room at the Montage Hotel in Laguna. The hotel was known for its collection of early California *plein-air* paintings, and Kate and Janet had wandered down a quiet hallway to admire them. When they stopped to gaze at a canyon scene with a field of poppies in the foreground, Janet turned to her.

"I hope you're not just looking for a father figure," she said.

Kate smiled. "I know what people are saying, but they're wrong. I love Sam, his command over any situation, his power to get things done. He's protective of me."

"As long as you're happy." Janet kissed Kate's cheek. "I'm going to powder my nose. Be right back."

Kate moved on to the next painting. Tilting her head to get a better view of the signature, she jumped when Derek edged up beside her. She felt his hot breath in her ear.

"You don't fool me," he whispered.

Kate spun around to face him. "Excuse me?"

He reeked of whiskey. "I got your number, bitch." The words were slurred.

Derek poked his finger repeatedly into her chest, backing her up until she was pinned against the painting. "You're not gonna get your hands on one penny of my father's money."

Since that night, Kate had become accustomed to Derek's jealousy of her relationship with Sam. What she found more difficult to abide in her marriage was the state of affairs in her and Sam's bedroom. Early on, he had been an attentive lover. Now, when he managed to find time to make love, it was fast and mechanical, as if he were in a hurry to get on to the next item on his agenda. She didn't think it was her fault. But what had changed?

The seat belt lights flashed, interrupting Kate's thoughts. She shot a speculative look at Sam, wondering if she should have paid more attention to Janet's warning all those years ago.

Rick's voice came over the speakers. "We're starting our approach into Dallas. It's eighty-nine degrees and clear. We'll be on the ground in twenty minutes. Buckle up. There'll be some light chop on the descent."

Kate stretched her arms and legs and then tightened her seatbelt.

Finishing the last drop of coffee in his cup, Sam said, "I want some new linen shirts for Santomar. When you're in town today, would you pick up three or four for me at Neimans?"

"Actually," Kate said, "Rick told me I could have my lesson in Dallas. I was planning to stay at the airport."

"We're leaving in three weeks, and I need a few things." Sam patted her thigh. "I just don't have the time to do it."

Her stomach knotted. She recognized the familiar anxiety. "Sometimes I think the only reason you married me is because your life is easier with a wife."

"That's bullshit," Sam said. "Come on. I want some new swim trunks, too. That little shop next to Armani carries the ones I like. You can have your lesson tomorrow at home."

She wanted to please Sam. She really did. But she couldn't help feeling disappointed when she asked, "What color shirts do you want?"

It surprised Rick that, after all these years, he still felt a sense of pleasurable expectation at a new student's initiation in a Lear. He couldn't wait to see Kate's expression when she blasted off the runway for the first time.

Navigating the maze of the Dallas-Ft. Worth taxiways, Rick turned to his copilot. "Call the FBO. Make sure Mr. Randolph's limo is here."

Steve reached for the microphone, then stopped. "There it is." He pointed to a gate at the side of the private air terminal that was sliding open. A black stretch limousine drove onto the tarmac and pulled into position beside the lineman guiding the Lear to its parking place.

When the engines were shut down and it was safe to exit, Rick opened the door and helped Kate and Sam out. Darting down the stairs, he hurried around the tail to the right side of the plane to meet the fuel truck he had requested. The driver of the truck, wearing white overalls and a red *Pennzoil* baseball cap, connected the grounding wire with his tough oil-stained hands, and then unrolled the thick refueling hose. "How much?" he asked, opening the fuel tank.

"Give me five hundred pounds," Rick said. "Two-fifty each side."

"You're not gonna get very far on that," the driver said.

"I'm giving one of the passengers a lesson. We're going to stay in the pattern."

The pump on the truck hummed as jet fuel flowed into the wing tanks.

"This baby's a rocket when the tanks are low and she's light," Rick said. "You can be at five thousand feet by the end of the runway."

The lineman shook his head. "No shit."

"It's awesome," Rick said, eager for Kate to experience it.

The limousine had pulled up to the left side of the plane. The driver stood at attention beside the open back door.

"Around three o'clock, you can top off both sides for our trip home," Rick said.

He walked over to talk to Sam as Kate climbed back up the stairs. "I left something inside," she said, disappearing into the cabin.

"What time do you want to leave?" Rick asked Sam.

Sam checked his watch. "It's noon now." He paused a moment to think. "I should be back here by four o'clock."

"I'll file to takeoff at four fifteen," Rick said.

Emerging from the plane, Kate held up her large straw hat. "I forgot this," she said, descending the stairs. She turned to Rick. "I've got to go into town and do some shopping," she said with a smile. "We can start the lessons tomorrow." Kate slid into the limo. Sam followed her. The driver closed the door.

Rick stared after them as they drove away, his initial

puzzlement at her change of plans soon replaced by a feeling of disappointment.

When the limousine returned at four o'clock that afternoon, Rick and Steve stood at the foot of the Lear's open stairway. They were fueled and ready to go. Rick opened the back door of the long black Lincoln when it pulled up to the plane. Only Kate got out.

"Where's your husband?" Rick asked.

"Still in his meeting," Kate said. "His colleagues are flying back to California at eight tonight in a private 737. He's going to catch a ride with them. He said for us to go on home."

The chauffeur had opened the trunk and was busy unpacking rows of shopping bags from Gucci, Armani, and Neiman Marcus.

"I wish I could have had my lesson," Kate said, heading up the stairs.

Rick shrugged. "If you weren't so busy shopping...."

Kate stopped halfway up the stairs. "You don't know what I was doing."

"Really?" Rick motioned toward the shopping bags.

"I'm ready to leave whenever you are," Kate said. She disappeared into the cabin.

Spoiled brat, Rick thought. He headed for the cockpit to obtain their clearance. Turning his head, he watched Kate settle onto the sofa and buckle her seatbelt.

After Steve loaded the shopping bags onto the plane, he closed the door and took the co-pilot's seat next to Rick. In less than ten minutes, the Lear accelerated through fifteen thousand feet, arcing toward the setting sun.

Twenty-five minutes later, when they had leveled off at thirty-eight thousand feet, Rick switched on the auto-pilot. He turned around, peering down the aisle to the rear of the plane. He could see Kate lying on the sofa, covered with the camel-colored cashmere blanket she'd purchased especially for the plane. Her head rested on a pillow.

Rick tapped Steve's shoulder. "Tell Mrs. Randolph I want to see her up here."

Steve turned around and looked down the aisle. "I think she's resting."

"That's okay. She wanted to sit up here for the flight home."

Steve unbuckled his seat belt and crawled out of his seat. Rick raised an eyebrow, smiled to himself, and turned so he could watch as Steve approached Kate's reclining form. Steve stared at Kate for a few moments before he turned around and came back to report to Rick.

"She's sound asleep."

"Then wake her up," Rick said.

In less than a minute, Kate stormed through the cockpit door. "Are you insane?"

"You said you wanted a lesson today," Rick replied in his most innocent voice.

"I walked all over town for hours in ninety-eight degree heat, and I'm tired."

"Sit down."

Kate crossed her arms and tapped her foot.

"I said, sit down."

Stepping over the center console, she flopped onto the copilot's seat and slouched down into the soft leather. "What do you want from me?"

"If you schedule a lesson with me, I expect you to be sitting in this cockpit whether we're in California, Texas, or Timbuktu. If you're going to be *my* student, you'd better take this seriously."

Her turquoise eyes lasered into him. "I am serious. You know I want to learn to fly this plane."

"This isn't something you do half-heartedly, whenever the mood strikes you. You want to get your type-rating? You'd better have your butt in this seat five days a week."

Kate stared into her lap.

"When you take your check-ride with the FAA," Rick said calmly, "you'll have an hour-long oral before they'll even get into the plane with you. They'll give you pen and paper; you'll have to sketch the electrical system, the hydraulic system, the blueprint of the fuel lines, and who knows what else. It won't be enough to show them you know how to fly. You need to know this plane inside out. And to do that, you've got to be in it, practicing. If this is what you really want, it has to be your sole priority... before shopping, or lunches, or whatever else you do."

The only sound in the cockpit was the synchronized whine of the engines.

Kate lifted her head and met his gaze. "You're right."

Her good manners triggered a hint of remorse in him for chewing her out.

"I have to fly your husband to Phoenix early tomorrow morning," he said. "We'll be back by two. Meet me at Executive Air at three o'clock. I promise you, your first take-off in command of this plane will be something you'll never forget."

Chapter 7

The next morning, Kate sipped coffee and read the *Los Angeles Times* beneath the purple canopy of the old jacaranda in the Emerald Bay garden. A white cloth embroidered with pink roses covered a table set for two. She frowned at the unused place setting across from her and pushed aside her plate of scrambled eggs and bacon.

A ladybug crawled across her napkin. She gently plucked it off and placed it on a patch of grass growing near the roots of the jacaranda's gnarled trunk. At the sound of approaching footsteps, Kate turned to see Sam coming down the path.

He sat down opposite her, pulling a flaky croissant from the breadbasket. "You were asleep by the time I got home from Dallas last night." He tore a corner off the croissant and spread it with butter.

"Pretty soon I'll have to put your picture on the pillow," Kate said. "That way, I'll remember what you look like."

He laughed. "Don't worry. We'll have plenty of time for each other in Santomar. You'll be sick of me."

"That's three weeks away. I hate to nag, but I hardly ever see you anymore. Sam, we need time alone without your accountants and lawyers or the rest of your entourage."

Sam reached for her hand. "We will." He stood.

"Where are you going?" Kate asked. "Aren't you having breakfast?"

"I've got a ten o'clock meeting in Phoenix. Lila said she'd make sure there were bagels and cream cheese on the plane."

"Croissants with butter and bagels with cream cheese are not a proper breakfast."

"Thank you for watching out for me." He kissed her cheek before he headed off.

Not long after he left, a shadow loomed over the breakfast table. Cora had come down from the house and stood between Kate and the morning sun. The woman, who wore her long dark hair in a neat French braid, folded her arms and clucked her tongue. "You haven't eaten a thing."

"I'm not really hungry."

"How about some French toast?"

"I'm just going to drink my coffee," Kate said.

Cora picked up the uneaten meal.

"Just a minute," Kate said, reaching for the plate. She

broke off a piece of bacon, bent over the side of her chair, and fed it to Brandy, who lay at her feet on a carpet of green grass.

Cora cleared her throat. "Will you and Mr. Randolph be dining at home tonight?"

Kate wiped her hands on her napkin. She suspected the cook already knew the answer to that question. "No," Kate replied. "Mr. Randolph has a dinner meeting."

When Cora turned to leave, a wave of melancholy swept over Kate. She hated how alone she felt.

"Wait, Cora." Kate tried some small talk. "Did you know my mother was a cook?"

"Yes. You told me."

The two women, despite having nothing and everything in common, stared at each other.

Cora shifted her weight from one foot to the other. "Is there something else I can get for you, Mrs. Randolph?"

Slipping her hand into her pocket, Kate pulled out an envelope. She handed it to Cora.

"What's this?" asked the cook.

"Take the evening off. I can make something for myself. Bloomingdale's is open late tonight. I want you to buy Lisbeth a really pretty prom dress."

Cora clutched the envelope to her chest before she reached out and briefly touched Kate's arm. "I don't know what to say. Thank you."

"Just have a good time with her." Kate smiled.

"You and Mr. Randolph are so good to me," said Cora.

The woman didn't need to know that Sam would

be upset if he knew Kate periodically gave extra money to members of his household staff.

"Let's not tell Mr. Randolph," Kate said. "It'll be our secret." She winked.

"Thank you very much." The happy cook disappeared through the wisteria arbor that led back to the house.

Kate gazed at the beds of yellow day lilies and lavender Johnny-jump-ups with their miniature pansy faces. This was her favorite spot on the property. Sheltered on one side by a hill covered in pink wild roses, the endless lawn stretched beyond the stately jacaranda, past a pond of water lilies, fading like a negative-edge pool into the Pacific Ocean. In fair weather, Kate preferred to dine in the garden rather than the formal breakfast room. She made sure Cora always set a place for Sam here, too, even though he rarely used it.

Pushing her chair away from the table, Kate bent to pet Brandy. The dog raised her head, laid it in Kate's lap, and closed her eyes while Kate stroked her silky fur.

"At least you love me," Kate whispered. The golden perked up her ears and licked Kate's hand.

A warm Santa Ana rustled the jacaranda's branches, showering Kate and Brandy with purple blossoms. Waves roared on the sandy beach below, reminding Kate of Santomar. She never felt lonely there. It was her sanctuary. *Soon*, she reminded herself. She sighed, tucking away her sadness.

Ruffling the fur on Brandy's head, she gazed toward the sea, drawn to the point where sunlight and water collided, shattering like shards of sparkling glass. Her thoughts turned to her upcoming lesson that afternoon. Remembering how she'd caught Rick off guard, studying her at safety training, she smiled to herself.

"Things aren't all bad," she said to Brandy. "I'm spending the afternoon with a handsome flight instructor."

From the air-conditioned interior of Sky Harbor's executive terminal in Phoenix, Rick had a perfect view through the automatic glass doors of the limos and taxis that arrived to drop off or pick up passengers. He glanced at the clock over the entrance. Sam Randolph was fifteen minutes overdue. Rick hoped the guy would arrive soon. He wanted to get back to Orange County in time to grab a sandwich and change his clothes before Kate's lesson at three.

A Lincoln Town Car pulled up. Its door opened, and this time Sam Randolph stepped out. In the car's darkened interior Rick caught the silhouette of a woman. Randolph bent to kiss her, then straightened and turned to glance toward the automatic doors, which made a swishing sound as they opened. Randolph's gaze shot past the mother and child exiting the building and landed on Rick.

With focused concentration, conveying the expectation that anything Rick saw would remain confidential, Sam Randolph stared at Rick until the doors closed.

When they deplaned an hour later in Orange County, the man clasped Rick's shoulder in a show of male solidarity and flashed his million-dollar smile. "You understand the necessity for discretion regarding business matters."

"Of course," Rick replied, wondering why Sam Randolph needed another woman when he had Kate. He also wondered if Kate knew about the other woman in her husband's life.

The clock on the wall in Bob Hansen's office at Executive Air read five minutes to three. Kate's stomach churned with the anticipation of her first take-off in the Lear. Feeling as sunny as the yellow coveralls she wore over a tight-fitting white t-shirt, she plucked a business card from a Lucite holder on Bob's desk and read it aloud.

"Worldwide aircraft charters, sales, management and acquisitions." She put the card back. "It looks like you keep pretty busy around here."

"That's the idea." Bob pushed his chair away from his desk. "But it hasn't always been suits and ties for me," he said.

He crossed the room to the bookcase and removed a picture frame from the top shelf. He handed it to Kate. "After I returned from the Gulf War, I flew cargo planes specially outfitted to transport cattle for the ranching industry. The pay was pretty good, but I got tired of that smell real fast."

Kate gazed at the faded photograph of a very young Bob, dressed in blue jeans and a white t-shirt, standing in front of a World War II era, twin-engine Convair. One of his arms cradled a leather bomber jacket, and the other was draped around the shoulder of a large black Angus. Under his pilot's cap with the oak leaf embroidery on the visor that everyone called "scrambled eggs," Bob sported an ear-to-ear grin.

Kate laughed. "The steer doesn't look quite as happy as you." She handed back the photo. "You've come a long way."

Bob nodded. "When I started Executive Air, I did most of the flying myself. Now, I've got fifteen pilots."

He set the picture back on the shelf, and then returned to his desk. Sitting back in his leather chair, he tapped his fingertips together.

He looked like he wanted to say something.

Bob picked up a pen and tapped it on the palm of the other hand. He looked directly at her.

"You know, with your love of flying, this is the kind of business you and your husband should be in."

"Wouldn't that be fun," Kate said, grinning. "The only problem is that if I worked here, I'd be too busy surfing the clouds to get any work done."

"This place practically runs itself," Bob said. "We've got a great staff."

As if on cue, Lila poked her head through the doorway. "Yeah. Great staff." She laughed. "I'm it." Her eyes seemed to sparkle when she looked at Bob. "Rick says to come on out to the plane. He's waiting for you."

The warmth in Lila's voice and her bright smile reminded Kate of her own mother. "Thanks," she said as she stood and gathered up her purse and jacket. She turned toward Bob and cocked her head. "I don't think Sam's in the market to buy another company. Besides, if my husband owned one more business, I'd *never* see him."

The Lear sat parked on the apron at the end of a row of aircraft farthest from Executive Air, aimed like a dart toward the taxiway. Kate climbed the stairs and turned left toward the cockpit. Rick already sat in the right-hand seat. In place of his captain's uniform, he wore jeans and a button-down blue shirt rolled up at the sleeves, the color accentuating his clear blue eyes.

"Hi," Kate said. The back of her neck tingled with excitement.

"Hi." Rick pointed toward the door. "Remember how to lock it?"

"Sure." Kate dropped her purse onto the floor behind the bulkhead. She knelt to secure the door bolts like Rick had taught her during ground school. After she gave the handle an extra tug to make sure it had clicked into place, she stood up. She didn't know why, but she felt shy, like a child in an adult's world. She eyed the left seat. "I guess that's where I sit."

Rick cocked his head. "Sounds like a good idea."

Stepping over the center console, Kate slid into the captain's seat. When she brushed her hand over the control wheel, she broke into a monumental grin. She tried to stop, but she couldn't. Feeling self-conscious, she turned her head so Rick couldn't see her.

"I'm going to move my seat a little closer," she said, fiddling with the adjustments. But even after she'd settled into position and turned to meet his gaze, her uncontrollable smile remained in place.

"Is there something you'd like to tell me?" he asked.

Laughing out loud, she shook her head. "I'm sorry. I'm just so excited. I can't believe I'm really doing this."

He smiled back. "You haven't done anything yet. Wanna get started?"

"You bet." Her grin disappeared, and the atmosphere in the cockpit grew serious.

Rick leaned across her to touch the green button on the instrument panel to the left of her control wheel. "That's the start button. It turns the generator and brings in the fuel." He slid his hand over the throttles. "When you move these"—he showed her how to grip them— "do it smoothly. It looks like one piece, but it's split down the middle. You can move the whole thing at once or move each side separately...left side, left engine, right side, right engine."

"Where does the key go?" Kate asked, scanning the control panel after dragging her gaze away from his strong, tanned hands.

Rick shook his head. "You don't need one."

"Really?"

"The only thing the key's good for is to lock the door when you leave."

He pointed to the right side of the throttle, tapping it as he spoke. "Always start the right engine first." He wore a sober expression. "That way, when you step out of the plane to get something you forgot in your car, you won't be sucked into the left engine."

Kate winced.

"Now, here's what I want you to do," Rick said. "But don't actually do anything yet, just listen. First, press the start button. Give it a few seconds. When you hear the generator turning, move the right side of the throttle to the idle position." He pointed out the hash marks at the base of the throttle. "The start sequence continues automatically. That's all you have to do. You ready?"

"Yes."

"Let's do it."

Kate drew in a deep breath, momentarily closing her eyes. She opened them, rubbed her hands together, then pressed the start button with her left thumb. When she heard the whine of the generator turning, she paused as Rick had instructed, then brought the right side of the throttle to the idle position. The muffled roar of the right engine spooling up spread through the cabin. She looked at Rick.

"You're doin' fine," he said. "Let's check the gauges. Oil pressure's coming up on the right engine. Fuel pressure looks good. Okay, let's fire up the left side."

Kate repeated the process and the second engine came to life, doubling the roar in the cockpit.

Rick pulled a spiral-bound booklet from a side pocket.

"Always use the checklist," he said, opening it to the first page. "The guys who think they've got this memorized are the ones you see on the news getting peeled off the sides of mountains."

Kate watched and listened while Rick went down the list, checking instruments, gauges, and control surfaces, verifying that all settings were correct. When he was satisfied that the plane was ready to taxi, he lowered the checklist to his lap.

"Okay," he said. "Here's the tricky part. All the other planes you've flown have a direct link between the rudder pedals and the nosewheel for taxiing. Press the left pedal, and the nosewheel turns to the left. Press the right one, and it turns to the right."

Kate nodded in agreement.

"It's the same here," Rick said, "except there's an electric motor that controls the nosewheel, so there's a delay from the pilot's input until the wheel actually turns."

"What difference does that make?" Kate asked.

"When we start to move, you'll see. In case you're wondering why I parked the plane all the way out here, it's because I don't want you taking off someone's wingtips your first time out."

"That would be embarrassing."

"And expensive." Rick reached for the microphone. "But you'll be fine. There's no one in your way."

He called the tower. "Eight Eight Sierra Romeo, request taxi to active."

"Sierra Romeo," came the reply. "Taxi runway one nine."

Rick met Kate's gaze. "Ready?"

Kate nodded. Shivers of excitement crawled up her back. "I can't believe I'm going to fly a Learjet."

Rick laughed. "Let's see if you can get it to the runway first. Okay. Hold down the foot brakes and disengage the emergency brake."

She pushed down hard on the top part of the rudder pedals, anchoring the plane in place. It took a moment before she remembered the location of the emergency brake. She gave it a twist, releasing it.

"You're practically on the taxiway," Rick said. "When you get on the center line, just keep it between your legs and you'll be in the right place. We're ready to roll, so ease up on the brakes."

Before Kate finished getting her hand around the throttle, Rick unexpectedly placed his hand over hers. His fingers curled hers around the cold steel, his large hand holding her small one in place.

"I want to show you how little pressure it takes to get this thing going," he said.

The sensation of his skin on hers caught her by surprise. Feeling flushed, she released the pressure on the foot brakes. Rick pushed her hand slightly forward, the throttle barely moving. Kate's pulse raced. The unexpected touch of this man, this near stranger, disrupted her ability to concentrate. Her dream of piloting this massive aircraft, the thrill she'd anticipated, now felt intensified by the sudden awareness that she sat so close to Rick, their shoulders practically touching.

The airplane groaned, advancing toward the taxiway. Rick's touch felt strong and made her feel safe. *Please don't take your hand away yet.* He was talking, probably saying something important, but she couldn't focus. The only thing she was aware of was the feel of his skin on hers. *God! What's going on? I'm a married woman, and he's just a flight instructor doing his damn job.* The seven-and-a-half ton airplane was moving. Rick took his hand away, and Kate was on her own.

She tried to keep the plane in the middle of the taxiway, but it zig-zagged farther and farther across the centerline.

"You're overcorrecting," Rick said. "Easy moves."

The plane continued to wobble toward the runway. "I can't control this," Kate said.

"Yes, you can." Rick pulled back the throttle, and she felt the brakes slide all the way forward. The plane came to an abrupt stop. "Let's start again," he said.

Kate focused intently on the nosewheel, but the plane refused to follow the straight, yellow line. Beads of sweat rose on her upper lip. Every time she moved a rudder pedal in one direction, she felt Rick move the opposite pedal to compensate.

A friendly voice filled the cockpit. "Hey, Rick. It's Pete. I'm flying with Vince today. We're right behind you in the Falcon. You look like a drunken sailor. You're makin' us dizzy, man."

"I'm making myself dizzy," Rick replied.

Kate smiled, realizing he was covering for her. The soles of her shoes tapped the rudder pedals like a Radio City Rockette's, but she only succeeded in veering further from the centerline.

"Rick." It was Pete again. This time he was laughing. "Need a map to the runway?"

Kate threw her hands in the air. "I give up."

Rick took control of the rudder pedals. "Let's try it again." He steered the plane back to the centerline. "It's all yours," he said.

Kate resumed her tap dance. "I hope this plane doesn't act like this when it's in the air," she said.

"I hope it doesn't, either."

During their stagger across the field, Rick completed the remaining items on the preflight checklist. When they reached the edge of the runway, Kate pressed hard on the brakes and the Lear thumped to a stop.

Stuffing the checklist back into the side pocket, Rick turned to her. "After liftoff, head straight out," he said. "Under ten thousand feet, you can't go more than two hundred fifty knots."

Kate listened, nodding her head.

"At the shoreline," Rick said, "turn left to one seventy and level off at eight thousand. We'll go out over the ocean and do some maneuvers." He tightened his seatbelt.

"And remember," he said. "We always do as many landings as take-offs."

Kate liked his sense of humor. She grinned. "Roger that."

Rick's blue eyes twinkled. "Ready for your magic carpet ride?"

Kate felt like a caterpillar about to burst into a butterfly. She took a deep breath. "Good to go."

Rick called the tower. "Eight Eight Sierra Romeo's ready for take-off."

A voice from the tower responded, "Eight Eight Sierra Romeo, position and hold."

Kate nudged the throttles up, a quiet roar filling the cockpit. The Lear inched forward. With help from Rick, Kate stopped on the centerline of the runway.

"Flaps ten degrees," Rick said.

She set the indicator to the appropriate mark and the flaps whined into place.

"Eight Eight Sierra Romeo, cleared for take-off."

Kate curled her fingers around the steel handles of the throttle. Once again, she felt Rick slip his left hand tightly over hers. She looked up at him.

"We're gonna' do this real smoothly," he said.

Kate's heart pounded again. She looked into his eyes, hesitating there a moment too long. His gaze immobilized her. The sound of the jet engines and the deep blue of his eyes became etched as a single memory. She would never be able to go flying again without remembering this moment and the color of his eyes.

Chapter 8

"We gotta get outta here," Rick said. "There's a plane behind us on final."

With her left hand gripping the control wheel, Kate firmly pushed the throttle all the way forward with her right hand. The Lear sprang forward as if it had been launched out of a sling shot, engines thundering, pinning Kate and Rick to the backs of their seats. For the first few hundred feet, Rick helped her keep the Lear on the centerline, but as the plane gained speed, Kate found it easier to control its path down the runway.

Kate kept her eyes focused outside the plane. Rick watched the instruments. When the needle on the airspeed indicator reached ninety-six knots, Rick called out, "V One."

Kate understood the signal to move her hand off the throttle to the control wheel. The point of no return.

Before *V One*, if she lost an engine, there would be enough room left on the runway to cut the throttle and slam on the brakes, safely bringing the aircraft to a stop. If she lost an engine after *V One*, the Lear would be going too fast to stop on the ground, and she would be committed to take-off. But at that speed, she could safely climb out with only one engine.

Within seconds Kate heard Rick's voice. "Rotate." It was the signal for lift-off. "Start pulling back now."

She pulled too hard and the plane angled steeply. She felt the wheel move forward as Rick made the correction from his side.

He shook his head. "This is a high-performance piece of machinery. Don't jerk the wheel so far. Small corrections. That's all you need."

"Okay."

"Gear up," he said.

She hesitated.

He pointed to the center of the control panel. "It's over here."

She raised the gear in time to hear, "Flaps up."

She flipped the yellow lever all the way up and heard the retracting howl of the flaps. Without the extra lift, the plane climbed more slowly. Even so, compared to the single-engine planes she normally flew, the Lear felt like a rocket.

Pulling back the throttle, Rick said, "We don't need full power anymore." The cockpit became quieter.

Kate felt like a firecracker about to explode into a million sparks. The energy from the jet engines seemed to course through the plane, up through the control wheel and into her body. She remembered a few lines from the poem "High Flight"--"*Oh! I have slipped the surly bonds of earth...and touched the face of God.*" She knew what the author meant. She felt free.

They cruised at two-hundred-forty knots, slicing through a crystal blue sky about five miles off the coast of Laguna Beach. Catalina Island was off to her right, so clear she could almost reach down and pluck a boat out of Avalon Harbor. To the left down the California coastline, she saw Dana Point, San Clemente, and Oceanside. And all around her, a magical blue sky, with not even a whisper of a cloud.

The enforced closeness of the cockpit and the accompanying sexual tension came as a shock. She reveled, lost in her own Icarian rapture, speeding toward heaven in a Learjet with Rick beside her.

Rick was speaking. What was he saying? His voice possessed a seductive quality. It sounded deep and melodious, soft and strong, all at the same time. She thought she detected a hint of an accent, then realized there was none. He simply had the voice of a man who was confident and in control. In unspoken words, his tone said, "Trust me. I won't let anything happen to you. You can take this rocket ride with me, and I'll bring you safely back to earth."

He spoke again. "Maintain eight-thousand feet."

"Okay."

"Make sure you've got the trim set right."

"Okay."

She had lost the ability to utter anything save that two-syllable word. *God, don't let me kill myself.* She glanced at Rick. *Or him.* She couldn't have chosen a worse time to realize and acknowledge her attraction to Rick.

"Relax," he said. "You don't have to hold the wheel that tight. You're doing fine. And don't forget to breathe."

For the next hour, Kate viewed herself as the marionette and Rick as the puppet master. She followed his instructions with no hesitation, executing turns, climbs, and descents.

The first several times he assigned a new heading, she over-shot it by ten degrees or more. He stayed calm and never raised his voice, only saying in his laid-back way, "Let's try that again."

After half a dozen turns to the left, Rick said, "Let's change directions. You're doin' good. Just try to maintain your altitude."

Kate hardly spoke, only occasionally swiping her hand across her brow to wipe away the moisture that had accumulated there. She took a deep breath. "This is a workout."

"You'll get used to it. You're doin' great. Let's go on up to nine thousand feet."

She pulled the wheel towards her and pushed the throttle all the way forward. The engines roared. Within seconds, they shot through twelve thousand feet, squashed into their seats by the G forces. Rick shoved the nose down and pulled the throttle back.

"Don't change the power if you want to go up or down a thousand feet. Just have your hand on the wheel and *think* about which direction you want to go; it'll practically move on its own. I told you. High performance. Easy corrections."

"Okay. I get it," she responded.

They tried again. She missed her mark by a thousand feet.

"That's better," Rick said. "Try it one more time. Remember...a light touch." On this try, she was right on the money, correct altitude and heading.

"Great. Let's end on that. I think you've had enough for today."

Kate felt like she had run a marathon. Beads of sweat trickled down her back, but she felt exhilarated.

Rick called approach control. "Eight, Eight, Sierra Romeo, requesting IFR approach to Santa Ana."

"Roger," came the reply. "Fly heading one seven zero."

When Kate heard the instruction, she turned the plane to the left to intercept the assigned heading. Rick directed her every inch of the way.

Her heart pounded with the knowledge that it was critical not to make a mistake during the landing. With fierce concentration and frequent throttle adjustments, she kept the crosshairs pegged all the way down the glideslope.

As the plane hovered above the runway, Rick said, "Throttle back. Flare now."

She pulled back the wheel, bringing the nose of the

airplane up to a steep angle. Then, she waited. The Lear slowly settled onto the concrete with only a slight bump. She exhaled. Her heart raced, driven by the excitement of her achievement. She pushed down hard on the brakes. The plane was light and slowed quickly. With Rick's help, she exited at the first taxiway and brought the plane to a complete stop. Silence engulfed the cockpit.

"I actually landed this plane." Kate grinned from ear to ear.

"Yes, you did."

She turned to him. "Can you believe it?" Beaming and exhilarated, she could barely get the words out. "It was so...so smooth...I hardly felt it touch the ground."

Rick smiled and nodded. "Great landing, Kate."

"I hope it wasn't an accident," she said. "I hope I can do it again."

"I know pilots with ten thousand hours who can't land like that," he said.

She felt sure he was just being kind to her. Nevertheless, she basked in the glow of his compliment. It made her want to continue to please him.

"For your first time out, you did great." His eyes sparkled when he smiled. He obviously recalled his first time, so he understood her emotions.

There was something special about this moment, as though she and Rick had shared an intimate experience, a memory only the two of them could ever recall. She could hardly wait for her next lesson.

"Sierra Romeo, this is ground control. Cleared to taxi to parking."

Kate nudged the throttle. In the air, the Lear had obeyed her. On the ground it zig-zagged with a mind of its own. She still had a lot to learn.

The sun was low in the sky, and the Lear cast a long shadow as they taxied to the hangar at the far side of the field. The wide sliding doors were open, but the hangar was empty.

"I've got the plane," said Rick.

When he had maneuvered the Lear into the proper position to be towed inside, he shut down the engines.

"Where are all the planes," Kate asked.

"Flying." Rick slid out of his seat. "Looks like no-body's around. Stay here 'til I chock the wheels."

He opened the door, letting in the cool evening air, and headed to the pile of chocks on the tarmac. When he had secured the plane, he gave Kate a "thumbs up."

He was waiting at the bottom of the stairs for her.

"Great job," he said, helping her down the narrow stairway.

And there it was again, the touch of his hand, the feel of his skin on hers, shattering her ability to think of anything else. The purse she carried in her other hand fell to the ground.

"Oh," she said, startled. She kneeled to retrieve it.

So did Rick.

Each holding a piece of the purse, they rose. But Rick didn't let go. He stood gazing at her, and in that moment Kate knew he had understood her reaction to him in the plane.

"I wish it could be different, Kate," he said.

"I know," was all she could manage.

He let go of the purse, then leaned toward her and brought his lips to hers in a kiss as sweet and gentle as a summer breeze.

God help me, Kate thought.

Chapter 9

K ate met Rick every morning for the next three weeks, except on those occasions when Sam used the Lear. They always spent the first hour in the Executive Air conference room, studying the airplane's operating systems and dissecting diagrams and graphs. Under Rick's tutelage, Kate gained a thorough understanding of the Lear. The kiss was never mentioned, although the memory of it haunted her.

After the morning ground school they would fly. Untethered from the earth, Kate soared and banked, so free the wings could have been attached to her instead of the sleek jet that carried them through the sky.

During their first week, they never ventured farther than the practice area over the ocean. Rick trained Kate to observe the nuances of the plane, until she could peg the indicator needles at any altitude or heading. They simulated stalls and rehearsed emergency procedures until her responses became as automatic as breathing. Soon, Rick added trips to nearby airports to practice instrument landings.

They chatted between maneuvers, discovering similarities in their backgrounds while sharing stories about their lives. Rick told tales about growing up on a succession of military bases with his father, and Kate related the loneliness she'd experienced as a latchkey child. They kept their growing attraction to each other in check. Rick knew that any relationship with Kate, other than professional, would cost him his job, and Kate intended to honor her vows to Sam. Whatever fantasies each harbored remained unspoken. Kate enjoyed her Lear training, and she knew Rick enjoyed their time together, too.

The day before Kate and Sam were scheduled to leave for Santomar, Kate taxied away from Executive Air toward the runway. She gave Rick an expectant look.

He said, "Let's head down to Palomar. It's a small uncontrolled field, and we can do touch-and-goes there without getting in anyone's way."

Once airborne, Kate turned south. At cruising altitude, she adjusted the trim and faced Rick. "I like flying with you. It's a lot of fun."

"You learn fast," said Rick.

Kate sighed. "Sometimes I wish my life were different. I'd love to just pick up and leave for London or Paris like you do."

"It would be fun to have you for a copilot," Rick said, adjusting the brightness on the radar screen.

"You're so lucky, free to fly off on a moment's notice."

"There are some drawbacks," Rick said. "You never know if you're going to be home for Christmas or your birthday. But all in all, it's a good life."

"Sounds like heaven."

"One year I had to cancel a New Year's Eve date at the last minute," he said. "I felt terrible, but I didn't have a choice. The girl never spoke to me again. So now the only woman I ever make plans with for New Year's is Lila."

"Speaking of Lila," Kate said. "The way she talks about Bob, I get the feeling that something's going on between them."

"Bob's never mentioned anything to me," Rick said.

Kate laughed. "You men certainly don't share details about your lives the way women do."

"Yes." Rick's expression was deadpan. "Men are very different from women." He grinned. "And we like the differences." He scanned the horizon. "Do you have the airport?"

She shook her head. "Not yet."

He leaned close to her, pointing straight at the runway. "Got it now?"

The airstrip sat atop a small rise, cutting a swath through the green hills north of San Diego.

"Got it." Kate pulled back the throttles, maneuvering the plane into the flight pattern.

Rick set the radio to the local unicom frequency and keyed the mike. "Palomar traffic, Lear, Eight, Eight,

Sierra Romeo is downwind." He turned to Kate. "Just land the plane, then taxi back. The runway's less than a mile. We'll do a short-field take-off."

Kate landed the Lear, using up most of the runway before coming to a stop. "You're right," she said. "This is a small field."

She swung the plane around and taxied back until they were perched at the other end of the runway, ready to take off into the wind. She knew every inch of concrete counted on such a short runway.

"Okay," Rick said. "This is just like a short-field take-off in your little plane. Hold the brakes down tight, full throttle, wait, then feet off the brakes and let her rip."

Kate knew the procedure. She firmly held down the brakes with both feet. She pushed the throttles all the way forward, allowing enough time for the engines to reach peak thrust. She still loved the now familiar feel of Rick's hand atop hers during the take-off roll, but his touch no longer distracted her.

"Feet off the brakes," Rick said.

The Lear shot forward like a bullet, covering a thousand feet of runway in seconds. Suddenly, something seemed very wrong. At the moment when Rick usually called out, "V One," he pulled back half of the throttle. The plane veered sharply left.

"You lost your left engine!"

Kate's first impulse was to jam the right rudder all the way to the floor to keep the plane from swerving off the concrete. But she failed to brake, and the plane continued to eat up the runway.

Rick jerked the remaining half of the throttle all the way back and slammed on the brakes. The plane shrieked to a stop just before it reached the end of the pavement.

Kate's heart hammered from the jolt of adrenalin.

Rick shouted, "You lost an engine before V One. You get your goddamn feet on those brakes and push them all the way to the floor and pull the throttle back if that happens."

Too ashamed to look up, Kate trembled and stared into her lap.

"What's the matter with you?" Rick's anger scared her as much as her mistake. "You know you can't take off if you lose an engine before V One. Where the hell did you think you were going?"

She turned to look at him, tears welling in her eyes.

Rick's voice thundered through the cockpit. "If you lose an engine, don't you dare hesitate. If you do, you'll kill yourself and everyone on board."

A tear spilled onto Kate's cheek, but she didn't move.

"Aw, Christ," Rick said, sinking back in his seat. He stopped shouting. "You've got to get this, Kate. It's vital."

Kate opened her mouth to speak, but fear and humiliation paralyzed her.

"I'm sorry, Kate." Rick sighed, his voice gentle. "I just don't want you to hurt yourself or anyone else." He reached out and drew his thumb across her cheek to wipe away a tear, the touch of his hand like a feather on her skin. Had Sam ever touched her with such tenderness? She gazed at him in silence, wanting to look away. But the warmth in his eyes held her there. She swallowed and took his hand.

The radio crackled. The moment dissolved.

Kate pulled her hand away, and Rick grabbed a tissue from the box behind his seat. He handed it to her.

"Okay." He cleared his throat. "You made a mistake. Just learn from it. Let's try it again."

They practiced the simulated engine-out procedure for over an hour, first one side and then the other, until it was hard-wired into Kate's brain.

On their way back to John Wayne Airport, she turned to Rick. "Nearly careening off the end of the runway really frightened me."

"That's good," he said. "It's a lesson you won't forget."

She nodded her agreement. Keeping her eye on an approaching United Airlines jet a couple of miles to her left and a thousand feet below, she said, "By the way, I was wondering about our trip to Santomar tomorrow. Who's going to be flying with you?"

"Grady Burke. He beat out every copilot at Executive Air for the booking. There was practically a stampede in the office to see who'd get to go."

"And how did Mr. Burke get so lucky?" Kate asked.

"Not luck. Smart," Rick replied. "He knows Lila does the scheduling, and he also knows she's a chocoholic. I bet the guy racked up quite a bill at See's."

Kate laughed. "Lila's my kind of gal. I don't trust anyone who doesn't like chocolate." She fine-tuned the power setting on the right engine. "There aren't any decent tourist hotels on the island. Where are you staying?"

"A little place on Tortola. We'll fly over and wait there until you and your husband are ready to leave."

"What's the flight time?" Kate asked.

"It's usually about seven hours to Tortola," Rick said. "So add on another fifteen minutes to get to Santomar. We'll have to make one stop for fuel. Do you have any preference where?"

Kate rolled her eyes. "Anywhere Sam doesn't own the radio waves. I don't want to hear him say, 'We're already here, what's the difference if I run to town and make a surprise check at the station.'"

"How 'bout New Orleans?" Rick said.

"Do you think Lila could call ahead for a catering tray of *café au laits* and *beignets* from Café Du Monde?"

Rick laughed. "Done. What time do you want to leave?"

"How about now?" Kate grinned at him. "I can't wait to get there. Flying with you in the morning and the commercial instructor in the afternoon is a lot of fun, but combined with the hours I spend raising money for Safe Haven, I'm ready to relax and sip some island punch."

Rick nodded. "A good remedy for stress."

"Wait 'til you see Santomar," Kate said. "It casts a spell on you." She sighed. "And I'm ready for some magic."

On her way home from the airport, Kate stopped at

Safe Haven's office. Satisfied that instructors and class schedules were in place for the three community centers in which Safe Haven's programs operated, she grabbed her purse and turned out the light. Opening the door, she gasped when she bumped into the owner of the health food store.

"Mr. Thompson, you startled me," she said with a laugh. "I was just making sure everything's going to run smoothly while I'm out of town."

"Those girls are lucky to have you watching over them."

"I enjoy doing it. I wish there had been something like this available when I was young and my mother was working."

Mr. Thompson shifted from one foot to the other. "I've held off as long as I could, Kate, but I'm finally going through with the remodel on the store. I need the space back."

Kate's heart sank. The program operated on a tight budget, and she hated the thought of having to cut back on classes to rent an office. She put her hand on Mr. Thompson's arm. "You've been kind to let us stay here the last three years. If we'd had to pay for office space, we'd never have gotten this project off the ground so quickly."

"I wish I had room for you to stay."

She gave the man a hug. "Thank you for all you've done. When do you need us to leave?"

"The approval from the city should take a couple of months."

"I'm leaving town tomorrow," Kate said. "I'll look for new office space as soon as I return." She was more determined than ever to find a permanent home for Safe Haven.

Later that evening at a corner table at The Sonora Grill, the hole-in-the-wall that Sam swore he wouldn't be caught dead at, Kate raised her half-empty bottle of Corona. Amid serapes, sombreros, and assorted Mexican kitsch, she toasted Janet.

"B-F-F," Kate said, clicking her bottle against Janet's.

"Best friends forever," Janet responded.

They sipped the cool amber liquid.

Kate leaned across the table and whispered, "Sam hates it when I drink beer." She took another sip. "He'd have a fit if he saw me drinking it out of a bottle."

The two women burst out laughing. Despite numerous obligations, they both still found time for a regularly scheduled girl's night out.

Janet sat back in her chair, flipping a lock of long red hair off her shoulder. She surveyed the remains of their meal of taquitos, tortas, and chilaquiles. "I'm stuffed."

"Me too." Kate glanced at her watch. "I've got to go. We're leaving early tomorrow." She motioned to their waiter for the bill. "Come on," she said to Janet. "Keep me company while I pack."

Janet followed Kate up the curved staircase in the grand foyer of the Emerald Bay house. "I love this place," her friend said. "It's like being at the Four Seasons."

"I have to admit, I love it, too," Kate said.

The women passed through the double doors to the master bedroom suite, crossed the marble floor, and turned into Kate's dressing room. Kate flipped a wall switch, and the light from eight wall sconces glowed through miniature silk lampshades.

They walked into Kate's closet. To the right was a wall of evening gowns and furs, all behind massive glass doors. Sitting beneath each gown was a pair of evening shoes designed specifically for that dress. Janet walked over and opened one of the doors. She ran her hand over a strapless, dark green Chanel gown.

"I love this dress." Janet took the matching chiffon scarf and touched it to her cheek. "It's so soft." She closed the glass door.

"Sam bought it for me on our honeymoon." Kate pulled some tank tops from a drawer. "It's six years old and I don't care how many times my friends have seen it, I'm wearing it to the Gala at the Performing Arts Center next month."

The women returned to the dressing room. Kate placed the tank tops in a small suitcase, and Janet strolled to the chaise lounge. She picked up Kate's old pillow.

"Are you ever going to get rid of this?" she said, flopping down on the chaise. She held up the lumpy pillow. "Look. It's got a hole in the seam."

"Leave that alone," Kate said, playfully snatching it away. "You know my mother made that." She set the pillow on the rim of the bathtub.

The women chatted while Kate finished packing.

"How can you go away for a week with a piece of luggage the size of a toaster?" Janet asked.

"I keep most of what I need in Santomar. These are just a few extra things."

"Quite a life you have." Janet sighed. "Sometimes I wish I had stayed with Derek."

Kate turned. "Why?"

"I know. The guy's insane." Janet shrugged. "It just looks like you and Sam are having so much fun."

"Well, looks are deceiving." Kate sat down beside her friend. "You know you can come here whenever you want. For God sakes, we have four guest rooms. And I won't smack you around like Derek did."

Janet hugged her. "Thanks." She pulled away. "Holy cow, look at the time. I've got to get up early too."

The women walked to the motor court, stopping beside Janet's blue Toyota.

"I'll call you when I get back," Kate said, opening the car door.

Janet slid behind the wheel. She pulled the door closed and started the engine.

Kate watched the car disappear down the driveway. A gust of cold wind blowing off the ocean sent her hurrying back to the house.

Kate zipped her suitcase closed, and then made her way to Sam's walnut-paneled dressing room.

An open valise sat atop the tufted leather bench in the middle of the room. Sam was packing a cotton sweater. "How was dinner?" He reached for the swim trunks Kate had purchased in Dallas and placed them in the suitcase.

"The chef outdid himself. We enjoyed the perfect pairing of guacamole and chips followed by a sumptuous feast." Kate walked to Sam and threw her arms around his neck. "You ready for tomorrow?"

When Sam returned her hug, she felt a hint of tension in his arms. "Just about," he said. He wriggled out of her grasp to pull a sport coat from one of the open closet doors. He laid it on the bench beside the valise before he shuffled through a rack of silk ties.

Kate leaned against a bank of glass-fronted drawers. "I've been ready for weeks. I can't wait to get you alone."

"I swear, you'll have my undivided attention."

Kate gazed at Sam's sport coat and the ties. "I don't think you're going to need those."

"Who knows?" he said. "We could stop in New Orleans on the way home and have dinner at Emeril's."

Kate shrugged. "Okay. I'll pack my mystery dress."

"Oh," Sam said. "I almost forgot."

He tugged open a walnut wardrobe door and pulled out a shopping bag. Inside was a large white gift box tied with a red satin bow. He handed it to Kate.

"I saw this at the Phoenix airport," he said.

"What is it?" she asked, delighted with the surprise.

"Open it and find out."

She pried off the ribbon and lifted the top off the box. Inside sat a red ceramic cookie jar in the shape of a single-engine biplane. She pulled it out.

"It looks like my Pitts. I love it. Thank you." She kissed him. "I'll make sure it stays filled with those chocolate chip cookies you like."

"That was my plan."

"I should have known you had an ulterior motive," she said. "But I won't hold it against you."

Tucking the cookie jar back into the box, she ran her finger across one of the gold-plated drawer pulls. She felt nervous asking him, but she needed to do it now. "While you're in the gifting mood, I need to ask you something. Have you given any thought to the donation I asked you about for Safe Haven? That ten acres won't last long, and it's in the perfect location—less than two miles from five different schools."

"I told you," Sam said. "It's not up to me. The board decides what charities to fund."

"But you tell the board what to do."

"Not exactly."

Kate took a deep breath. "I've never asked you for a penny for Safe Haven. I've raised all the money."

"I said I'd do what I can, but I won't promise anything."

"I swear, Sam, if your board doesn't donate to Safe Haven, I'll find a job and earn the money."

Sam stopped folding a tie and stared at her. "How would it look if Sam Randolph's wife worked?"

"I don't care how it looks. I'm committed to Safe Haven. Not just its daily operation, but finding a permanent home for the program. The community needs it. Your foundation gives away twenty million dollars a year, and I would like some of it for my girls."

Sam picked up the latest copy of *Forbes Magazine* and tossed it into his suitcase. "We'll talk about it when we get back from the island."

"Promise?" Kate asked.

"I said we'll talk about it." Sam exhaled. "All this flying and fund-raising...when I married you, I didn't plan on you doing anything except being here when I got home."

"Trouble is, Sam, you don't get home. I get lonely."

"Look around you, Kate. How many people do you think live like this?"

Kate's temple throbbed. "That's not the point, and you know it. I want my life to mean something. Those girls need me."

Sam turned away. "You need to relax, and I need to finish packing."

Kate watched him for several moments before she left the room. She returned to her bathroom and set the cookie jar on her dressing table. She felt numb and sad. Men like Sam were used to getting their own way. Despite his generosity, his needs would always dominate their relationship. She imagined decades of loneliness ahead, and a wave of panic gripped her.

She shook her head to expel her vision of despair. *I'm being ridiculous,* she thought. *We just need some time together. Everything'll be fine once we get to Santomar.*

Chapter 10

The whine of the flaps lowering awakened Kate. After a sleepless night at home, she had arrived at the airport exhausted. She'd fallen asleep right after take-off. Sitting up, she yawned and looked around the cabin of the Lear.

"You've been out cold since we left Orange County," Sam said.

Kate pushed aside the blanket. She glanced at her watch, then raised the window shade and looked down. She expected to see New Orleans and the Mississippi River. Instead, she saw rows of palm trees and the inter-coastal waterway. They were on final approach into Miami International.

She straightened. "What are we doing in Florida? I thought we were stopping in New Orleans for fuel and beignets at Café Du Monde."

"Slight change of plan," Sam said matter-of-factly. "I made a few calls while you were asleep. I'm getting off in Miami for a breakfast meeting tomorrow at the Four Seasons. But I've arranged everything. The pilots are taking you to Santomar, and then they'll fly right back here. In the morning, as soon as my meeting is over, we'll take off. I'll be there by midday."

Kate shook her head. "Oh, *Sam.*"

"I have obligations, Kate. It's only twenty-four hours."

Kate's jaw tightened. She surprised even herself when she blurted out, "I've had it with you. I want to go back to California. Now!"

"Don't be ridiculous."

"I refuse to go to Santomar alone."

"It's only one night."

"It's *always* only one night." She willed herself not to look away. "But they add up."

"I spoke to Marta," Sam said. "She's expecting you, and she's preparing a nice dinner. You can have a head start unwinding, and tomorrow we'll have lunch on the beach."

Suddenly, her life with Sam felt like a string of capitulations, like pearls on a little girl's necklace that had grown too tight and now choked the woman who wore it.

"This isn't a marriage, Sam. I don't know what this is." Kate felt dizzy. "I can't do this any more." She turned to the air conditioning vent, sucking in a deep breath of cool air. "I get it, Sam. I really do. You like me. I amuse you. But you're not in love with me. You never were."

"What's gotten into you?" He squinted at her. "Take it easy. You know you'll feel better once you settle in at Santomar. You love it there."

She couldn't believe her life was unraveling like this, in the skies over southern Florida. *Calm down, calm down.* She said the words to herself, repeating them like a mantra. Sam didn't grasp the depth of her loneliness, although he was right about one thing. She loved Santomar, and it would be good to have some time alone to sort things out.

Stuffing the fuel receipt into his pocket, Rick watched Sam disappear into a limo with an overnight bag. He'd seen Kate pull away when her husband had tried to kiss her goodbye. He was right. She wasn't happy in that marriage, and he wished he could slap some sense into Sam Randolph for cheating on her. Men with that much money—he'd never understand them.

Rick watched Kate pace the tarmac. A fleeting fantasy of her lying on a white sand beach made the corners of his mouth curl into a smile. During their flight lessons, he had sensed there was something else on fire in the plane besides the igniters in the engines. Their eyes had lingered on each other more than once. But he was determined to avoid the temptation Kate posed. Compromising his career was not an option.

He approached her as she came around the tail of

the Lear. "We're fueled and our flight plan's been filed. Anytime you're ready, we can leave."

"I'm ready now." Kate walked toward the stairs.

After locking the door, Rick buckled himself into the captain's seat, picked up the microphone, and faced the back of the plane. Kate sat on the sofa, her eyes closed and her head resting against the window. It knotted his insides; she looked miserable. He wished he could do something to fix whatever was bothering her. He wondered if she'd found out about the other woman in her husband's life.

Rick keyed the mike. "Flight time to Santomar is two hours. We'll be landing about six fifteen."

Kate nodded, but she didn't open her eyes.

Rick noted the angle of the sun. "Gettin' late," he said.

Grady lowered the landing gear.

"It'll be a quick turnaround," Rick said. "We need to take off before dark."

Santomar was part of the British Virgin Islands, a dot on the map between Virgin Gorda and Tortola. Nearly twelve hundred people lived on the southeastern corner of the island in Albert Town. The village was home to fishermen, shopkeepers and artists, all living life to the beat of calypso. The narrow streets, a carnival of colors, bubbled with restaurants, bars, a few ramshackle hotels, and a half dozen fortunetellers. Three days a week, the main dock bustled when supply boats arrived, unloading goods onto rickety push-carts or ancient trucks rusted from a decade or two spent in the salt air.

For thirty years, a small airstrip at the edge of the verdant hills behind the town had served the island. Several small inter-island flights arrived and departed each day, but all activity ceased at dusk courtesy of the absence of runway lights.

Rick banked the Lear forty-five degrees to the left, flying a slalom course through the remnants of a tropical shower. Passing over the top of the airstrip, a slash of gray amid the luxuriant landscape, he checked the windsock, and then opted to land toward the south. He headed out over the aquamarine sea, banking the Lear on his final approach to the tiny airfield. On one side of the runway, he noticed a construction project that appeared to be in full swing.

"Looks like they're building a control tower," Rick said. "You know what's next...a passenger terminal."

"Say goodbye to paradise," Grady said.

A group of people watched a steel beam dangle from a tall blue crane that swayed in the breeze. On the other side of the runway, a large man wearing a Panama hat stood beside a white Land Rover.

The Lear used up most of the runway before it came to a stop. Rick swung the plane around and taxied back to the small parking area across the field from the construction project, joining a row of single-engine planes and two private jets. A nearby wooden shack, weathered and showing signs of once having been painted green, served as the welcome area.

Rick shut down the engines and set the brake. He turned to Grady. "Get Mrs. Randolph's bags. I'll handle the passports."

After climbing out of his seat, Rick opened the door. Warm air swept into the air-conditioned plane, bringing with it the fragrances of gardenia and ginger. Rick loved the earthy smell of tropical humidity, even though it made his shirt stick to his chest. He smiled, inhaling a breath of paradise. He could hardly wait to get Sam Randolph back here tomorrow. Since there were no tourist hotels on Santomar, Lila had made arrangements for Rick and Grady to park the plane on Tortola and wait there at a beachfront hotel until the Randolphs were ready to leave.

Rick bolted down the stairs two at a time and then turned around and looked up. Kate stood in the doorway. He could hardly take his eyes off her. Her white blazer was draped over one arm, and the turquoise tank top she wore matched her eyes. Her breeze-tousled blond hair completed the picture. She looked like an ad in a fashion magazine.

"Let me help you." Rick offered his hand the way he would to any female passenger. But unlike any other passenger, when she placed her hand in his, the touch of her soft skin made his heart speed up.

As Kate descended the stairs, she waved to someone. "There's John, our houseman," she said, stepping onto the tarmac.

Rick released her reluctantly. He turned and saw a husky man beside a white Land Rover approach the plane. He also saw the sun slipping toward the horizon. He turned to Kate. "I need your passport," he said. "Grady and I have to hustle if we're gonna take off before the airport closes."

Kate fished inside her handbag. "Oh, no," she said, pulling out a cell phone along with her passport. "Sam is probably wondering where this is." She slipped his phone back into her purse. "They know us," Kate said, handing Rick her passport. "You'll be out of here in no time."

Rick walked the short distance to the peeling green shack where two customs and immigration officials, dressed in wrinkled khaki uniforms, emerged from an open doorway. On the desk inside lay evidence of an interrupted game of gin rummy.

The larger of the two men tossed his cigarette onto the pavement, stomping on the glowing ash, and then puffed out his chest. "Papers, please." He extended his hand. His lofty British accent sounded out of place, as if he had made a wrong turn outside Buckingham Palace and gotten lost.

Rick pulled the plane's registration from his back pocket, handing it and Kate's passport to the official. "She's staying." He pulled his own passport, along with Grady's, from his front pocket. "We're just dropping her off and heading right out."

The man casually flipped through the documents. Rick gazed at the approaching twilight and bit back a curse of annoyance. He didn't want to say anything that would prolong the man's show of protocol. A trickle of sweat dripped down the back of his neck.

At last, the sleepy-eyed official returned the passports and registration to Rick. "Welcome to Santomar," he said. He turned, and followed by his partner, headed back into the shack to his card game.

Rick returned to the plane to find that Grady had already unloaded the baggage. Kate was speaking to John, a large round man whose smooth brown skin was darkened further from years spent baking in the sun. A picture of tropical decorum, John wore neatly pressed white cotton pants and a matching short-sleeved white shirt, his Panama hat cradled in his hands. Kate introduced John to both pilots.

After a quick greeting, Rick looked at his watch. "Half an hour 'til sunset." He turned to Grady. "File a flight plan to San Juan. We'll pick up some fuel there, then head to Miami."

Rick started for the plane, but then stopped short when he heard an alarming screech. It was the crane. The blue metal frame buckled and twisted sideways, the off-balance load of steel swinging wildly from the end of the cable. The nearby crowd of onlookers scattered. The towering monster snapped, and then crumbled in slow motion, piece by piece, metal bending and grinding and scraping. In disbelief, Rick watched it crash to the ground. Although the tangled wreckage missed the row of parked planes, it totally blocked the runway.

Rick, Grady, Kate, and John, as well as the two customs officials, ran toward the fallen heap. The crowd returned and gathered around the operator, who had jumped from the crane moments before it collapsed. Except for scrapes and bruises, he appeared to be unhurt. A great debate ensued about whether the crane had been large enough, or if the breeze had been too strong. One thing everyone agreed—no aircraft could land or take off until the rubble was removed.

The sky turned from pink to Parrish blue. Shades of twilight unfolded across the horizon.

Rick turned to John. "Let's get Mrs. Randolph's bag into the car." Then he looked at Grady. "We're not going anywhere today. We'll get a ride into town and see about a hotel."

They all walked back across the runway.

John drove the Land Rover over the taxiway and parked near the Lear.

Kate stood quietly, appearing pensive while the men loaded her things into the back of the car. Finally, she approached Rick. "You and Grady can't stay in town. The hotels are rat traps."

Rick turned away, not wanting to be tempted by her. He busied himself by securing the plane. "Don't worry about us," he said. "We'll find a place."

She followed, standing next to him while he put the cover on the left engine. "You don't have to," she persisted. "We have a beautiful guesthouse, and it's empty. You and Grady can stay there."

Rick met her gaze. "Really," he said. "It's no problem. We've been in worse situations than this."

"I insist." She added almost plaintively, "Besides, that way I won't have to have dinner alone."

"Sounds a whole lot nicer at her house," Grady said.

As Rick stood in the violet dusk that had settled over the island, he weighed the risk of socializing with a client, especially Kate Randolph, against the prospect of a night in a dive. He sensed danger in his decision, but he capitulated.

"You win. Let's get our bags," he told Grady.

Chapter 11

Kate leaned forward from the back seat. "John, let's take the upper road. This time of day, it has the best view."

"Yes, ma'am." The houseman swerved onto an unpaved road that switch-backed away from the airport.

Settling into her seat, Kate glanced at Grady, who sat up front with John, and then she took a sideways peek at Rick. Seated beside her, he appeared in silhouette. With the sun's rays behind him, he looked almost angelic. A guilty feeling gnawed at her. Had she invited the pilots to stay at the villa for their benefit, or for hers? Sam would be furious, but she was so angry at him she didn't care. If her husband couldn't be bothered to accompany her to Santomar, she refused to be a solo act with Rick and Grady available as dinner companions and houseguests.

After bouncing along the dirt road for a quarter of a

mile, John came around a curve and stopped. Everyone leaned forward in their seats to take in the glory of Santomar.

A Peter Max sky crowned a panoramic view of Albert Town, the harbor, and the coastline. Remnants of the tropical storm had fractured the sky into a geometric palette of pink, magenta, and crimson. Powder blue swirls wrapped their arms around a golden sun, gently seducing it with the promise of a night's slumber.

"What a sunset," Rick said.

Kate agreed. "I told you it was magical."

"Best sunset I ever saw was in the Arizona desert," Grady said. "But this one's got it beat."

Feeling content, Kate sat back. "Let's head home, John."

Continuing along the dirt road, they soon rejoined the paved two-lane highway that wound through Santomar's low hills. Silvery twilight bathed the small farms that dotted the route. Sugar cane fields, once tropical jungle, shimmered in the trade winds.

John entered a hairpin curve, sending Kate sliding across the back seat. When she wound up thigh to thigh with Rick, a spark of desire shot through her. She hurriedly raised her arm to push herself away, catching him under the chin.

His hand flew to his jaw. "I might apply for hazard pay."

She wanted to put her hand on his cheek, but she stopped herself when she saw the laughter in his eyes. Why did she always feel so flustered around him?

"I'm so sorry." She slid back to her side of the seat.

"Too bad I left my catcher's mask at home."

"I try not to abuse my house guests, but sometimes I just can't help it." She smoothed her slacks. "We're almost...." Before she could finish, John slammed on the brakes. Everyone lurched forward as the car skidded to a stop.

"Watch out," said Grady.

"Shit!" said John.

Kate's heart raced. She snapped her gaze to the road.

"Wild ride," said Rick.

In the Land Rover's path, a pair of eyes glowed in the light from the car's headlamps.

John swore under his breath. Throwing the car into park, the houseman pushed open his door and jumped out.

Kate laughed. "It's not the people you have to watch out for on Santomar," she said. "It's the livestock."

The three of them watched as John approached a heifer that had wandered onto the roadway. After much pushing and prodding, the battle between man and beast ended with the houseman chasing the young cow out of their way.

Brushing off his white shirt, John returned to the car. "Sorry for the delay." He slid behind the wheel, slammed the door, and put the car into gear. "We'll be at the house shortly."

At seven-thirty the Land Rover turned off the asphalt highway onto a stone-paved road bordered by tropical plants. Passing through the main gates of the compound,

John wended the lantern-lit driveway, passing a small road to a service area and another leading to the tennis court. He brought the car to a stop beside a three-tiered fountain in the center of a wide circular courtyard. Water trickled over the fountain's upper basins into an illuminated pond lush with pink water lilies. A wide loggia surrounded the courtyard where beds of banana trees and birds of paradise shared space with ferns and red and purple fuchsia. Palm trees sprouted from oversized terra cotta pots and tuberoses scented the air.

John turned off the motor.

"Welcome to my home," Kate said to Rick and Grady.

Chirping crickets and croaking frogs, along with the distant roar of waves breaking on the shore, greeted them as they climbed out of the Land Rover.

Marta, John's wife of thirty-two years, emerged from the house wearing a short-sleeved dress and starched white apron. She rushed down the flagstone steps lined with potted red geraniums and lacy blue lobelia. She paused beside a waterfall dripping with white orchids.

"We've missed you," Marta said, throwing her arms around Kate.

Kate returned Marta's hug. "I'm so glad to be here."

"John called from the airport. I heard about the accident." Marta stepped back. "Thank God you weren't hurt." While John was formal and reserved, his wife was genial and outgoing. She eyed Kate. "But you could use a good meal."

"I'm sure you've got that covered." Kate motioned to her guests. "These are my friends, Rick Sanders and Grady Burke."

The men were fishing the bags from the car but straightened to greet the cook.

"We call the guesthouses by their colors," Marta said. "Blue, peach, and pink. I've prepared the blue house for you."

"Wait," Kate said. "What about the roof? Didn't we lose a section of tiles in the last storm?"

"It's been fixed," Marta said. "I thought you'd want them in the blue house since it has the best view and it's the closest to the main house."

Rick closed the car door. He met Kate's gaze. "Really. Any color house is fine with us."

Kate felt her cheeks flush as a prickling sensation crawled up her back. She hated what his piercing stare could do to her. She looked away. "I've got to call Sam to let him know what's happened. Come up to the main house around eight-thirty, and we'll all have dinner."

She turned and walked up the front steps with Marta. "Did the new sheets and towels from Bloomingdale's arrive?"

"Last week."

"And what about the freezer?"

"The repair man came over from St. Thomas two days ago. It works fine." Marta paused in the foyer. "Now, stop worrying about the house. It's time for you to unwind."

Kate nodded, drawing in a deep breath. "Thank

you, Marta. I'm going to take a relaxing bath. I'll see you a little later." She headed for her bedroom.

Kate's thoughts turned to Sam. Hurt and disappointed by his indifference to her needs, she believed that, by allowing him to neglect her too long, she bore part of the responsibility for his behavior. But, tired as she was of the constant heartache and loneliness, she also knew that she owed Sam a debt. His stopover in Miami for business had delivered the man she longed for right to her doorstep. She didn't know if she should feel guilty or grateful.

A twinge of concern shot through Rick as he followed John down a jasmine-scented path bordered by blooming hibiscus. Being stranded on Santomar with Kate, he had to admit, was a fantasy come true. But he counseled himself to proceed with care. A misstep by either one of them could result in dire consequences for them both.

Grady poked his shoulder. "Can you believe this place?"

"Pretty nice," Rick replied.

Towering king palms stood guard over the path. Green jasmine tendrils curled up their smooth trunks, thousands of tiny white blossoms dispatching their fragrance in every direction. The garden resembled a high-end resort with up-lights illuminating the tree canopies and glowing candles in glass hurricane shades dotting the pathways and flowerbeds. Beyond the rolling lawns, a walkway hugged a low stone wall, following the curve of a crescent of white sand. A nearly full moon reflected a silver ribbon on the aquamarine sea. The sound of waves lapping against the shoreline harmonized with the drone of restless crickets.

John stopped in front of a pale-blue cottage. A lantern surrounded by a yellow trumpet vine flickered over the entry. The houseman opened the door, motioning Rick and Grady inside.

"There aren't any keys," John said, following them. "You can lock the door when you're inside if you like."

In the living room, the lamps beside the sofa glowed, and fresh roses filled a vase on the coffee table. In the two bedrooms that flanked the living room, soft lighting fell on the king-size beds that had already been turned down. In each room, a ceiling fan stirred the air.

John demonstrated how to operate the television and video equipment, and then opened what looked like a cupboard to reveal a well-stocked bar.

"If there's anything else you need," he said, "just let me know. Dinner will be in one hour, gentlemen."

As soon as John left, Grady flopped onto the white canvas sofa. "Can you believe this place? I hope they never clear that runway."

Rick threw open a set of French doors that led out to a patio, and then leaned against the doorway, arms folded as he gazed at the ocean. A quarter mile in the distance, lights on a wooden dock reflected on the waves that rolled toward the island.

"This is the life," said Grady from the living room.

"I'd love to have a place in the Caribbean some-day," Rick said. He walked to the bar and lifted the top off a silver ice bucket, dropped an ice cube into a tall glass and filled it with Evian. "If I had a place like this, I'd never leave." He emptied the glass. Still thirsty, he opened the refrigerator. Finding no Dos Equis, he twisted the top off a Heineken and took a swig from the bottle. "I've gotta call Lila and give her a heads-up. Then I'm gonna take a shower." *A cold one.*

Not long after the first stars appeared in the sky, Rick and Grady approached the main house. Rick valued punctuality. He didn't like to be kept waiting so he did his best not to make others wait for him. At eight-thirty sharp, they crossed the flagstone patio, strode past the swimming pool, and stopped a few feet short of a glass wall, opened to expose the great room of the main house. The floors inside the home, paved in the same flagstone as the patio, created the illusion of no bound-ary between indoors and outdoors.

"Hello," Rick called, Grady right behind him. Spotting Kate as she entered the great room, the two men stepped inside to meet her.

Rick tried not to stare, but he found it impossible not to. Kate seemed effortlessly beautiful, dressed in a black tank top over white capri pants, her hair tied into a casual ponytail. He was struck by the multi-faceted qualities of her personality, and he remained astonished that Sam didn't appreciate her. She seemed as content surrounded by elegance as she was on the floor of the airplane hangar. He'd never known a woman like her. And being here with her like this, in real life and not in the cockpit, unnerved him.

"I hope you're settled in," she said. "If there's anything you need...."

He grinned at her. "Where do I sign up for your frequent flyer program?"

"Everything's perfect," Grady said, wandering toward a wall of books behind a sofa. He pulled a volume off the shelf and leafed through it.

"This property is amazing," Rick said. "How big is it?"

"The main house, staff quarters, and guest cottages sit on five landscaped acres," Kate said. "Another twenty-five acres have been left wild."

"It's paradise."

"It just shows you what a team of engineers, architects, and designers can do."

They smiled at each other, locked in a prolonged gaze that neither wanted to break. It was as if no one else existed but the two of them. Reminding himself she was married, the perfect moment ended when Rick looked away.

Kate crossed the room to the coffee table where a frosty pitcher sat on a white linen place mat.

"How 'bout a mojito?" she asked.

"Great." Grady returned the book to the shelf.

Kate poured the drinks into three glasses. She offered one to each of her guests, and then she took a sip of her own. "Nobody makes them like Marta," she said.

Cradling his drink in his hand, Rick wandered about the great room. In the glow of the lamplight, it shouted elegance, but the place felt like a ghost house. No family photos. It reminded him of the lobby of a Ritz-Carlton more than the home of a happy couple. He caught a glimpse of Kate as she showed Grady her seashell collection. Something about her tonight made him want to gather her close and protect her. She seemed so alone. As soon as he had the thought, he dismissed it. Kate's situation wasn't his problem. She was another man's wife.

"Okay if I take a look around?" Grady asked.

"Sure," Kate said. "The house is designed in the shape of a horseshoe. One wing holds our bedroom, guest rooms occupy the other, and this room is right in the middle."

Rick made a mental calculation and figured his place in Laguna would fit into the great room. Overstuffed couches, armchairs, and an enormous dining table, with a stack of board games nearby, gave the place a relaxed ambiance. Even the ebony grand piano tucked into a corner shunned formality, its bench upholstered in a casual banana-leaf pattern.

Kate strolled outside toward the pool, which appeared to be surrounded by enough chaise lounges to accommodate a baseball team. Rick and Grady followed her, and the three of them wandered about, sipping their mojitos in the moonlight. They stopped near an outdoor entertainment area fitted with an over-the-top barbeque and a fridge.

"All the rooms except the kitchen open to the garden," she said. "We're forty feet above sea level, so the view...." She didn't finish her sentence, just turned and contemplated the dark ocean below. Rick took in the view, too. Three hundred feet ahead, shimmering waves broke against a white sand beach. The sound, carried aloft by a warm breeze, mixed with the crickets and melted into Tony Bennett's croonings about a girl named Joanna from the pool speakers.

"Look." Rick pointed up to the sky, his arm brushing Kate's. "You can see Mars."

A million stars flickered overhead. In that moment, the world felt reduced to a sensual symphony of stars, ocean, warm breezes, and Kate. Nothing else mattered, only being near her. Rick couldn't help himself. He wanted to feel her next to him. He longed to ease her onto her back in the sand and make love to her till she moaned his name. A tap on his shoulder brought him back to reality. He spun around.

"Come on," Grady said.

Marta stood nearby, her hands folded across her apron. "Dinner is ready."

Kate ducked under one of the market umbrellas that sprouted everywhere. "I hope you're hungry," she said, heading for the house. "Marta's made her specialty."

An inlaid wooden table easily accommodating ten or twelve had been set for three. Rick pulled out the chair at the head of the table, holding it for Kate, then sat down to her left. The grand scale of the villa and its rich decor made Rick aware of just how far he was from his condo in Laguna. He decided to allow himself to enjoy the momentary pleasures of this place, and this woman, but he would also remember to maintain his emotional guard.

"Thank goodness you two were hungry." Kate shifted her gaze between Rick and Grady. "Marta would have been disappointed if her efforts in the kitchen had gone to waste."

Scattered grains of rice and stray herbs, all that was left of Marta's fragrant paella, clung to the sides of the clay pot in the middle of the table. Discarded mussel, clam, and oyster shells spilled over the edge of a china catch bowl.

The meal had been punctuated by stories, laughter, and two bottles of Kistler chardonnay, but Kate had managed to force down only a few bites of fish and rice. Anguish over the state of her marriage had killed her appetite. She was still picking over fresh salad greens that only hours before had been growing in the vegetable garden behind the tennis court when Marta emerged from the kitchen carrying an empty tray.

Grady rubbed his stomach as the cook cleared his dishes. "That was great." He chuckled. "When I woke up today, I was a paella virgin. You made me a pro."

Marta smiled, then gazed down at Kate's plate. "Is that all you're having?"

"It was delicious," Kate said, patting the woman's hand, "but I couldn't eat another bite."

"How 'bout running away with me, Marta?" Rick asked. "We could go to California and open a restaurant together."

"Run away with a handsome pilot? I'm nobody's fool," she said, smiling. "I'll pack my bags after I do the pots." She laughed, carrying the tray of dishes back to the kitchen. She returned a few minutes later with three bowls of plump strawberries. She set a bowl in front of Rick. "My husband says he has to come along."

"No can do," Rick said, shaking his head. "It was just supposed to be you and me." He winked at her.

Kate sipped her wine. This easy-going side of Rick helped her relax; her anxiety at last left her. In the cockpit, he had been friendly, but she'd also felt the invisible wall between them. Here at the dinner table, they were just a man and a woman, friends having dinner. But with her inhibitions dulled by the wine, she couldn't avoid some obvious thoughts. If he was just a friend, why did he stir up such intense feelings in her? How could she enjoy his stories and his company so much in the midst of her inner turmoil over her failing marriage?

She knew she'd fallen under Rick's spell. Kate sat back in her chair, looking long and hard at him. Was it her imagination, or had they shared numerous lingering glances during dinner? As she studied him, he regaled them with a story from his first job as a pilot, the year before he'd entered the military.

"I was hauling cargo every night in this big old King Air," he said. "We'd be flying over Kansas, around midnight, following Interstate 40. It goes all the way across the state without making a turn, and it's deserted late at night. Nothing but wheat fields. Anyway, we'd spot a set of headlights or taillights on the highway, and we'd turn off all the lights in the plane. Then we'd drop down to two hundred feet."

The top three buttons of Rick's island-print shirt were undone. Kate's gaze rested first on his suntanned chest, then returned to his face. *He's so sexy.*

"You don't have to worry about hitting anything," Grady said, "'cause west of Kansas City the highest thing around is a Dairy Queen sign."

Rick grinned. "Whose story is this anyway?"

"Yours," said Grady. "But you're leaving it to me in your will."

A mischievous twinkle appeared in Rick's eye. There was something about the way his white teeth flashed through his casual grin—sexy man and little boy all at once. He appeared totally at ease, obviously enjoying himself, the way pilots did when they exchanged tales. A sad ache rose in Kate's chest. If only they could all remain on Santomar forever. She hoped the runway never reopened.

Rick lifted his wine glass. "So we'd pull back the throttle and fly real slow, and just as we got to the car...." He paused for emphasis. "...we'd flip on the landing lights and jam the throttle forward."

The three of them burst out laughing.

"I'm sure we scared the hell out of those poor people. Of course, the next day there'd be all these reports about UFO sightings west of Russell."

They all howled with laughter, Grady slapping his hand on the table.

"How often did you do that?" Kate asked.

Rick cocked his head and looked abashed. "Only a few times."

She noted his thirst for danger. "I've heard about you adrenalin junkies."

He finished off his wine. "I was just a foolish kid."

Grady glanced at his watch and pushed back his chair. "Been a long day," he said. I'm gonna hit the hay." He glanced at Rick. "There are boogie boards in the closet. Wanna catch some early waves?"

"Knock on my door in the morning," Rick said. "If I'm up, I'll join you." Rising, he turned to Kate. "Thanks for dinner. I'll call the airport in the morning and get an update on the situation."

"I've already spoken to Sam," she said. "He's staying put at The Four Seasons until you can pick him up."

Hurricane candles flickered in the tropical night breeze. An awkward silence ensued before Rick said, "All right then."

Grady said, "Great meal. Thanks."

Kate stood to say good night, then watched the men disappear down the path that led to the guest house.

The glass wall separating the patio from the great room had been open throughout dinner. Kate longed to step through the opening, to be like Alice and tumble down a rabbit hole and follow Rick into a world of wild and exciting adventure.

In the swimming pool, a moth attracted by the light fluttered on the water's surface, casting restless shadows against the house. Kate strolled to the pool's edge and bent down. Leaning forward, she cupped her hands around the struggling insect, setting it on the warm flagstone deck. The moth flitted about the puddle for a moment, then, doomed by temptation, flew right back into the pool. Kate sympathized. She understood temptation.

Kate felt too keyed up to sleep. Instead of settling into her room, she filled a crystal cordial glass with homemade orange blossom liqueur and wandered down to the beach, then sat on the low stone wall to watch the ocean. Each cresting wave reflected moonbeams like Fourth of July sparklers. She sipped the sweet spirits and made designs in the soft sand with her bare feet. This was her special spot, where she came to be alone with her thoughts. The sound of the surf calmed her restless heart.

She set aside her glass. Putting her hands, palms down, on the cool wall to support herself, she leaned backward to look up at the moon. It was high in the sky, casting a silvery glow over the beach.

"I need some help," she whispered.

She stared at the star-studded sky and waited, as though she expected the moon to answer her.

I feel so alone. She swallowed hard. *I wish I knew everything's going to be okay.*

At that moment, a meteor shot across the sky. Where it disappeared on the horizon, the figure of a man appeared strolling the beach at the edge of the surf.

Kate instantly recognized Rick. What was he doing here? She thought he had gone back to the guest cottage. Her pulse jumped, and she sucked in a great gulp of air. A voice in her head said, *Run back to the house before he sees you.* But it was already too late. He waved and came across the sand to sit beside her on the wall. The butterflies in her stomach did barrel rolls.

"I thought you were going to sleep," she said.

"I don't like to go to bed right after I've eaten. That was a great dinner. Too bad your husband couldn't be here."

"If he was, he'd probably be on the phone doing some deal, and I'd still be here on the beach alone. Sorry. I don't mean to complain." She picked up her glass, offering it to Rick. "Would you like to try this? It's my specialty. I make it with orange blossoms, sugar, and two hundred proof alcohol."

He took the glass from her, sending shivers up her spine when his fingers brushed against hers.

"Thanks." Rick took a sip of the golden liqueur.

A flush of delight shot through Kate like an electric current. She had "the glitters." In high school, she and Janet used the term to describe excitement bordering on delirium. *Get a grip,* she thought.

Rick handed the glass back to her. "That stuff is sweet."

Kate smiled. "Once, Sam drank half a bottle. Then he drove into town, wearing nothing but his boxer shorts. I think that's why he likes it here. It's so laid-back. Nobody judges you."

For a while neither of them spoke. They just watched the rolling waves sparkle in the moonlight.

"I've always loved the ocean," Rick said. "My condo in Laguna is right on the beach. When I get back from a long flight, I turn off my phone, sit on the terrace, and listen to the waves."

Kate nodded. "When I was a little girl," she told him, "I remember my mother taking me to Santa Monica beach. She made egg salad sandwiches and put potato chips inside the bread. We played this card game called *Spite and Malice* for hours. It was the best time I ever had with her." Kate abruptly stood up. "I didn't mean to interrupt your walk."

Rick got to his feet, too. "I was planning to go up to the end of the cove," he said. "Walk with me?"

Kate smiled. *I'd go anywhere with you.* "Okay."

They strolled down to the water's edge, heading for the rocks that marked the end of the private beach.

"When do you think I'll be ready to take my check ride in the Lear?" Kate asked.

"As far as the flying goes, I think you could pass it now. What we need to focus on is getting you ready for the oral exam. You never know what they're gonna ask. You really need to be prepared."

"After I get my type-rating, my fantasy would be to have a job like yours so I could fly every day." Kate laughed. "I think I'll ask Bob Hansen for a position at Executive Air."

"I'm sure your husband would like that."

"He doesn't even like me working at Safe Haven."

They had reached the end of the cove. "There's a path over here," Kate said. She took the lead and headed toward a brick walkway that connected to the sand. They meandered up the gentle incline until, after a short distance, the path split in two. She pointed right. "Follow this walkway and you'll end up at the guest house."

Kate gazed at him, longing to touch him, to tell him how lonely she felt, and that she ached for him to wrap her in his arms and never let her go. She took a step toward the opposite path. "Well...goodnight," she said.

Rick smiled at her. "Goodnight." He turned and walked away.

Kate paused, watching him until he disappeared around a cluster of palms. *The Gods have played a trick.* She still loved Sam despite his faults, but she sensed that the Fates now offered her an unexpected choice. Was Rick the man intended for her? Was he her true soul mate?

Chapter 12

When the last of the sand swirled down the shower drain, Rick turned off the faucet and stepped onto the tile floor. Grabbing a towel, he dried himself, wrapped it around his waist, and tucked in the loose edge. He gave the canister of shaving foam a few shakes and lathered his face. He needed to stop thinking about Kate. Last night, she'd haunted his dreams. He drew the razor over his jaw, carving paths through the white froth. He wanted her out of his mind. The only way to do that, he concluded, was to leave Santomar. Sooner, rather than later.

He buried his face in a hot washcloth, wiping away the remaining foam. He heard Grady talking in another part of the guesthouse. Rick wandered across the tile floor, through the carpeted bedroom, and out into the living room. Grady sat on the sofa, the phone glued to his ear. Rick leaned against the wall, listening to the sea birds through the open French doors.

"What's the verdict?" Rick asked, after Grady hung up.

"They're bringing in a crane by boat from Tortola to move the one that fell. Should be here this afternoon. They may be able to clear the runway today; if not, by tomorrow for sure."

"Then we'll take off for Miami tomorrow."

"I don't think so." Grady grinned. "After they move the debris, they have to patch a hole in the runway."

"Jesus. How long is that gonna take?"

"It looks like we'll be here for two more nights." Grady punched the air. "Yes!" He'd been out boogie-boarding, and his board and fins lay in a heap on the patio.

Rick shook his head and strode back into his bedroom. He put on khaki shorts and a white t-shirt, then he headed up to the main house to deliver the news to Kate. He found her seated under an umbrella at a table next to the pool, eating her breakfast and reading the latest *Vanity Fair*. She wore white shorts and a red and white striped tank top that hugged her curves. On her feet were a pair of worn-in boat shoes.

Noticing the table was set for three, Rick sat down across from her.

"Mornin'," he said.

Kate glanced up. "Hi." She set aside the magazine. "I was just reading an article about private jet charters. People are taking their vacations with friends so they can share the cost. It's getting to be a very popular way to travel."

Rick unfurled his napkin, dropping it onto his lap. "I guess that means my job's secure."

The kitchen door swung open, and Marta appeared. She smiled at Rick and poured him a glass of fresh-squeezed orange juice. "What can I get you for breakfast?"

Rick looked at Kate's plate of scrambled eggs and bacon. "I'll take what she's having," he said.

Marta filled Rick's coffee cup and returned to the kitchen.

After removing his sunglasses and hooking them over the neck of his t-shirt, he took a sip of the steaming black liquid, feeling sure he could give up beer before he could give up coffee. Another sip, and he explained the situation at the airport.

"I spoke to Sam an hour ago," Kate said. "He's anxious to get down here."

"As soon as we can take off, we'll pick him up."

Kate frowned. "Of course, it's his own fault. I hope he's learned a lesson."

Grady's sandals flip-flopped on the flagstone. Rick and Kate looked up.

"Good morning," Kate said. She stood, shading her eyes with her hand, and gazed toward the ocean. "I'm going for a sail. Either of you interested in exploring the coastline?"

"Sure," Grady said. He looked at Rick. "How about it?"

As long as Grady went along, Rick saw no harm. "Sounds great."

"I'll meet you at the dock in an hour," Kate said,

rolling the *Vanity Fair* into a cylinder and tucking it under her arm.

Rick watched her walk into the house. She's a client, he reminded himself. Trouble was, after spending so much time with her, the boundary between client and friend felt more than a little blurred.

Kate hopped aboard the *Fancy That*, the twenty-four-foot sloop Sam had bought her as a wedding gift. She would address their troubled marriage as soon as Sam got down here, she decided. For now, she hoped a sail up the coast would clear her thinking and bring her some peace of mind.

The sailboat, tethered to the end of the private pier, bobbed in ten feet of crystal-clear water. Planting her feet on the deck, Kate tugged hard on the halyard. She pulled hand over hand, keeping her eye on the mainsail as it climbed the mast. The white canvas luffed in a gentle breeze. She hoisted the jib and cleated it.

When she heard Grady's faint, "Ahoy," she turned and waved. Both men were moving toward her.

Grady reached the boat first. He handed Kate a large basket lined with a blue and white-checkered tablecloth. "Marta said to give you this." The twenty-four-footer rocked when he stepped aboard, and again when Rick followed.

Kate handed the basket back to Grady. "Would you

mind stowing this below where it'll be out of the sun? Watch your head when you come back up."

It was only seconds before she and Rick heard the loud impact of Grady's head hitting the hatchway, the crashing sound of the rebound, and a loud wail. They rushed below. Grady lay sprawled on the floor, blood trickling from a cut above his eye. Kate grabbed a dishtowel from the galley, sank to her knees beside him, and pressed the cotton cloth firmly against his head.

Rick knelt, sliding his arm around Grady's shoulder. "Hey, Buddy," he said, helping his friend sit up. "You okay?"

Grady raised his hand to his forehead. "I didn't see that coming."

"Let's go back to the house and get you an ice pack," Rick said.

Grady staggered to his feet. Rick and Kate followed him up the stairs to the main deck, everyone careful to duck in the hatchway.

Holding the dishtowel to his head, Grady said, "You two go for a sail. I'm fine. I just need an ice pack."

Rick followed Grady onto the dock. "I'll go with you."

"That's ridiculous. Go sailing with Kate. No need to wreck her plans."

"You may need some help," Rick protested.

"I don't need help. I just need ice."

"I'll come along, anyway," Rick said.

Kate put her hands on her hips. "You two sound like Laurel and Hardy," she said. "I'll wait here for both of you."

Grady raised his free hand up in the air. "Stop, I'm fine. I'm gonna get some ice for my head and then watch some TV." His voice was firm. "You two go for a sail." He turned and walked up the pier.

Kate looked at Rick for a moment, wondering about his reluctance to sail alone with her. "Come on," she said. "He'll be fine." She felt sorry that Grady had hurt himself, but she experienced the rising excitement of having Rick all to herself. She knew she shouldn't feel that way, but quickly rationalized her feelings away. *Okay, okay. I'm married. That doesn't mean I can't have fantasies.*

Rick stepped back aboard the sloop.

Lifting a hatch, Kate pointed to the colorful contents. "Life vests are in here. Have you ever sailed before?"

Rick grinned. "Don't all pilots sail?"

Kate smiled back. "I guess they do. How about if you take the mainsail and the jib, and I'll man the tiller."

"No problem."

"Then we're ready to cast off." Kate untied the boat from its mooring, neatly winding the line around her hand before stowing it. The *Fancy That* drifted away from the dock, and when Rick tightened the mainsheet, a gentle trade wind filled the sails. Kate pulled the tiller towards her, navigating around the rocks that marked the end of the cove.

The boat segued to the open sea, heeling to starboard, its two occupants adjusting their positions to counterbalance the force of the wind. Long wisps of Kate's hair fluttered around her face. She opened a drawer and pulled out a red baseball cap, tucking her mane beneath it while watching sea birds plunge into the ocean for fish. Kate felt free, the same way she felt in her little biplane.

"Three miles up the coast, there's a secret cove," she told Rick. "It's only reachable by boat. We can have lunch there."

He nodded, as if answers were not imperative when the scenery was this breathtaking. The shoreline exploded in a riot of colors—dark green banana trees, pale green ferns, and flowers and vines that seemed to be stolen from Gauguin's palette. Wild parrots squawked from the tropical jungle, and towering over it all, pencil-thin palm trees swayed in the breeze like sentinels on alert for intruders.

They followed the coast without speaking. Then Kate spotted the entrance to the cove and pushed on the tiller, pointing the sailboat toward the narrow opening. Once inside the small turquoise inlet, the water was as still as a lake.

When they were thirty feet from shore, Kate said, "Let's stop here."

Rick lowered the sails, and Kate dropped a small anchor overboard. She watched it sink through six feet of clear water, until it found the sandy bottom beside a starfish.

"I've never seen anything like this." Rick surveyed the lush tropical forest that surrounded the inlet. "It looks like a postcard here."

Except for the narrow opening that led back to the ocean, they were completely surrounded by a white sand beach so pristine it looked as though no human had ever set foot there.

The sun, high in the sky, warmed Kate's shoulders. Tossing her baseball cap on a cushion, she pulled her tank top over her head and stepped out of her shorts. Underneath she wore a white bikini. Attached to the side of the boat was a portable ladder. Kate cast the lower rungs into the water, then kicked off her shoes and dove in.

She came to the surface and floated on her back, enjoying the rivalry between the cool water and the hot sun. Rick stood on the deck, watching her.

"What are you waiting for?" she called to him.

He peeled off his shirt, revealing a well-toned muscular torso, and followed her into the lagoon.

Kate swam to shore. Where the water was only a few inches deep, she stretched out her legs and propped herself up on her elbows, looking back toward the *Fancy That*. Rick caught up to her. Soon, he lay sprawled beside her in the shallows.

"Isn't it magical?" She trailed one hand through the water. She felt like Eve in the Garden of Eden.

Gazing around the cove, Rick nodded. "It's like a movie set." He reached across Kate's legs and pulled something off the sandy bottom. He held out his hand to show her. In the middle of his palm sat a smooth blue rock, as dark and as clear as a sapphire.

"Know what this is?" he asked.

She sat up. "A piece of beach glass," she said, ·
squinting in the bright sunlight.

"Are you sure?" His white teeth flashed a confident grin. "An old sailor would call this a mermaid's tear." He handed it to Kate. "It could have been tossed around the ocean for centuries."

She closed her hand around the piece of glass and smiled at him. She wondered if there was a woman in his life. There had to be. In an instant, she felt sad and jealous, but just as quickly chided herself. *I have a husband, for God's sake.*

"So how did you get into flying?" he asked.

"My dad had been a pilot, so I guess it was a way for me to get to know him. I have one photo of him. He's wearing a flight jacket, sort of like the one you wear."

"Mine is courtesy of the Marines."

"So was his."

Tilting her head back, Kate dipped her hair in the cool lagoon. She raised up from the water, her hair spread like a curtain across her shoulders.

"There's a legend," she said, "about a tribal chief who lived a long time ago. He was supposed to meet his young bride here in this lagoon. They had never seen each other before, and when the beautiful girl arrived ahead of the chief, she found a handsome sailor sitting on the sand. She thought he was the chief, and she went off with him. The islanders believe this is the place you come to find your true love. It's called Lover's Lagoon."

The instant she spoke the words, she regretted them. Why had she told him *that* story?

Rick flashed a smile. "If I'd known this is where

my true gal would be, I'd have come here sooner. But I don't think I'm going to find her here." He scanned the lagoon before fixing his crystal blue gaze on her. "And you can't be the one, since you're married."

Kate wanted to look away but gazed at him like an animal caught in a car's headlights.

"Are you hungry?" he finally asked.

Kate stood up. "Starved. Come on. I'll race you back to the boat."

They dined on curried chicken salad, couscous, and fresh slices of papaya. A small refrigerator supplied cold Coke and Evian. Lounging on the deck as they ate, they swapped sailing stories.

After lunch, as they gathered their picnic supplies into the basket, Rick said, "I think we should head back. We've gotten a lot of sun."

Kate stood by the tiller, enjoying a last look around. Rick placed the basket under a bench and hoisted the mainsail. He fastened the halyard but didn't realize the boom was unsecured. A burst of wind set the sail in motion. Kate saw it coming, but there was no time to warn him. The heavy wooden beam hit Rick first, throwing him into Kate, knocking them both to the deck.

Kate, lying on her back, looked up at Rick.

Sprawled atop her, Rick pushed himself up on one elbow and stared at her. "My God, are you alright?" he asked.

"I'm okay, just a little startled."

With one hand Rick grabbed for the boom, but his

other hand slipped on the wet deck and he fell on top of her again. "I'm really sorry," he said. "Did someone just wax the deck?"

"It's okay." Kate laughed. "I think I'm starting to enjoy myself."

Rick pushed himself up again. This time his foot slipped on the slick surface, sending him careening into Kate and pinning her down again. He grinned. "This is how I get girls to go out with me."

They both began to laugh.

"The next time, can you land a little to the left?" Kate tried to get up, but their laughter made it impossible for either of them to move.

Suddenly, they both stopped laughing. Face to face, they gazed at each other. Rick moved closer, his lips a mere breath away from Kate's. She swallowed hard, his gaze holding her captive. The feel of his strong body pressing down on her quickened her heart. For a moment, desire and morality played tug-of-war. Desire won. Rick's warm lips met hers in a mixture of tenderness and passion. She closed her eyes, surrendering to the intoxicating pleasure of his mouth. If she hadn't already been lying down, she would have sunk to the floor. This was wrong, wrong. Yet she responded, parting her lips and sliding her arms around his neck even as she reeled with guilt.

Rick's tongue slid past her teeth, exploring her mouth with an urgent sensuality that made her dizzy. She tumbled in a swirl of sensations...his muscular legs against hers...the sweetness of his mouth...his skin,

warm from the sun. The fantasy she had done everything to keep in check was now really happening. And
now what...?

As if reading her mind, he froze and rolled off of
her. "I'm sorry." He sat back. "I don't know what...."
His voice trailed off.

Kate pushed herself up on one elbow. "No...really...
my fault."

Rick carefully got to his feet, fastened the mainsheet, and then helped Kate up. She staggered and
leaned against the rail.

"I was out of line," Rick said. "I'm really sorry,
Kate." His eyes pleaded for forgiveness.

She reached out and touched his shoulder. "It's all
right. Don't worry. I'm not angry." She felt her cheeks
redden with shame as she thought about Sam, how
hurt he would be if he ever learned what had just
happened.

Rick shook his head. "Sure you're okay?"

Kate brushed herself off. "I'm fine. Really." She saw
his embarrassment, and she wanted to put him at ease.
"Let's just blame it on the lagoon," she said, momentarily wondering if there was any truth to the legend
there was magic in the cove.

He smiled at her. The look in his eyes said he appreciated her understanding.

She smiled back, but couldn't help thinking—*How
am I going to get through the rest of my life without feeling
so alive again?*

The clock next to the bed said seven o'clock. Kate had been lying there for three hours. Soon Grady and Rick would arrive to dine with her.

After returning from her sail, Kate had lingered in the shower, hoping to rinse away her guilt, along with her desire for Rick. Each time she thought she had herself under control, the memory of his kiss would seize her and she'd be back where she started. *Hungry for him.*

Enveloped in the soft sheets, Kate moaned, rolled onto her side, and drew her knees up to her chest. She thought about Sam alone in Miami, then winced and brought the covers over her head. But there was no hiding from the shame she felt about what had happened aboard the *Fancy That*. Thinking the sound of Sam's voice might make her feel better, she picked up the phone and dialed his cell phone. After a short pause, she heard it ringing in her purse. She'd forgotten it was there. She hung up and dialed his hotel.

"Four Seasons, Key Biscayne. How may I direct your call?"

Kate asked for Sam's room. The phone rang twice. A female voice answered, "Hello?"

"I'm calling for...is this Sam Randolph's room?"

Kate heard the caller take a breath and then the phone went dead. Her heart sped up as she dialed the number again.

"May I have Sam Randolph's room?" Kate repeated to the hotel operator.

"One moment, please."

Kate tapped her pen on the pad of paper next to the phone.

Sam answered after the first ring. "Hello?"

"I just called your room, and a woman answered." Kate's throat felt tight.

"The phone never rang here," Sam said. "They must have connected you to the wrong room. You know how inept those operators are. I'm so glad you called. I miss you, darling."

She wanted to believe him. Her marriage had flaws, just like everyone else's. She would talk to Sam about seeing a counselor when they returned home.

"I miss you, too," Kate said, trying hard to push aside her doubts. "I'm sorry we argued on the plane."

"Don't worry about it. I think you were just tired. What did you do today?"

The memory of Rick's kiss flashed through her mind. Kate flushed. "Not much. I went for a sail. How about you?"

"Keeping myself busy until the plane comes back for me," Sam said.

"What are you doing tonight?" she asked.

"I'm having a boring dinner with Howard Williams. He's the manager at WRUM, our station here in Miami. I hate to rush, but he's waiting downstairs in a taxi."

"I've invited the pilots to have dinner with me."

"That's good. You won't be alone."

Suddenly overcome by a wave of fear and doubt, she added more for herself than for Sam, "I love you."

"I love you, too," he said. "I'll see you soon."

"Goodbye, darl..." Before Kate finished her first word, the phone went dead. She always felt strange when that happened. Sam never said goodbye on the phone. He just hung up when he finished speaking. She wondered if he did that with his clients.

Cradling the receiver, Kate stared out the French doors past the patio to the ocean beyond. The sun hovered on the horizon like a glowing Chinese lantern. She wished she hadn't invited Rick and Grady to dinner. She felt like staying in bed. She tried browsing though the magazines scattered around her but tossed them aside in frustration. She'd read them all, and there wouldn't be any new ones here on Santomar for weeks. She wished she'd brought along her idea file for Safe Haven.

She had a thought. She sat up and dialed the Four Seasons again.

"Sam Randolph, please."

Sam could stop at a drug store and pick up the latest issues for her.

After numerous rings, the operator said, "There's no answer, ma'am. Would you like to leave a message?"

"No. Connect me to the front desk, please."

Sam stayed at The Four Seasons regularly, and everyone knew him there.

"Good evening, front desk."

"Hello. This is Mrs. Sam Randolph. I just got off the phone with my husband. He was about to leave the room for a dinner appointment. He's heading for a taxi out front, and I'm wondering if you could catch him on his way through the lobby. I have a message for him."

"He just passed through here. Let me connect you to the valet out front."

The valet station answered after two rings. Kate identified herself and asked for Sam.

"You missed him by thirty seconds, Mrs. Randolph," the valet said. "He and Senator Gordon just left in a hotel limousine. The driver has a phone. Do you want me to see if I can locate the number?"

"Senator Ellen Gordon?" Kate said.

"Yes."

"No, thank you." Kate hung up, rage blossoming within her. Ellen Gordon, the senior senator from Florida and chairman of the Senate Finance Committee.

"Don't worry, darling," Sam had said when she'd asked him about the rumors. "I assure you that Ellen and I are history."

"So that's why he had to stop in Miami," she whispered to herself.

She clutched the pen she held so tightly her fingernails dug painful grooves into her palm. When she opened her hand, the pen clattered to the floor. He'd deceived her. He had never stopped seeing Ellen. Their whole marriage was a sham. She had spent the entire afternoon drowning in guilt while Sam romped in Miami with his long-time lover.

Burying her head between two pillows, she hoped

the soft goose down soaked up the sound of her anger and shock.

But then she bolted from the bed, racing into Sam's closet. She yanked his white linen sport coat off its hanger and dragged it across the floor to her dressing table. She opened the bottom drawer, frantically rummaging through hair clips, bottles of suntan lotion, and extra packages of toothbrushes in search of her scissors.

"Where are they?" she said out loud.

Tears streaked her cheeks. Her hands shook as she opened another drawer, then another. Frustrated, she crumpled Sam's jacket into a ball, threw it down on her dressing table, buried her face in it, and sobbed.

Her tears finally exhausted, Kate looked up. Cutting up Sam's coat had been a ridiculous idea. He would just buy another one. She stared at her mirrored reflection. She'd worked hard at being a good wife to Sam. Obviously, her efforts no longer mattered. Would they matter to a man like Rick? She sat up straight and wiped her swollen eyes, then went into her closet to find something feminine and alluring to wear to dinner.

Chapter 13

There was no doubt in Kate's mind that her marriage was over. She had been a devoted wife. Now, she felt bewildered that Sam had even made the time for an affair. But all the signs had been there. She chastised herself for being so naive.

While she washed her face and applied her make-up, she traveled a bullet train between blinding rage, fear, and utter sadness. The title of an old Broadway musical popped into her head. *Stop the World, I Want to Get Off.* She knew there would be no easy exit from this ride.

Her husband's betrayal resurrected a carnival of youthful insecurities. *What's the matter with me? What made me think I could live in Sam Randolph's world?* Anxieties she thought she'd purged long ago reached out to grab her. *You're nobody. Why would he want you? If he hadn't married you, you'd still be alone and unloved — the two things you fear most in this world.*

She observed her reflection in the mirror as she fashioned her long hair into a French twist. Her eyes showed only a trace of redness, but they still appeared joyless. After securing her hair with one last bobby pin, she reached for a tube of lipstick and applied a soft pink gloss to her full lips.

Having abandoned any vindictive impulses to use Rick to hurt Sam as childish and out of character for her, Kate nevertheless felt desperate for reassurance that she was still desirable. She pulled her "mystery dress" off its hanger and slipped it over her head. It was the sexiest thing she owned, and her psyche needed comfort. The white silk dress tied at the back of her neck, exposing her shoulders, tan from the day spent in the lagoon, then plunged to a deep v-neck below her breasts, and down to her waist in back. Sam had named it the first time he had seen it. He had laughed, saying, "It's a mystery how so little fabric can cost so much." His moniker for the minuscule piece of clothing had stuck.

She clipped on a delicate pair of pink and white seashell earrings that dangled the length of her neck. Tiny Austrian crystal beads, sewn in among the shells, sparkled when she tossed her head. Lifting the top off a bottle of *Arpége*, she dabbed a little behind each ear and some between her breasts. She sighed. She knew she looked good. She wished she felt good.

The aroma of Marta's rosemary chicken wafted from the kitchen, reminding Kate that her dinner guests would arrive soon. Resisting the temptation to crawl back into bed, Kate took a steadying breath, crossed the bedroom, and opened the door to the red-tiled hallway. The anticipation of a showdown with Sam knotted her stomach. She hoped she could eat.

Kate strolled into the living room and sat down at the ebony Steinway. She used the piano the way other people used alcohol or tranquilizers. Making music calmed her. She lost herself in *Claire de Lune*. She loved the melodic, romantic piece.

She jumped at the sound of applause when she finished. She turned to see Rick and Grady sitting on the sofa. Both men stood. Grady wore casual khaki slacks and an island-print shirt, while Rick looked wonderful in white jeans and a pale blue linen shirt. He'd left the top three buttons undone again, forcing Kate to pry her gaze from his tan muscular chest. She pushed back the piano bench and stood.

"That was fantastic," Grady said.

Kate walked over to join them. "Thank you," she said to Grady. "Do you like Debussy?"

Grady looked puzzled. "I've never heard of him, but he sure makes nice clothes."

Rick laughed. He smiled at Kate, rubbing his chin as though scrutinizing a piece of modern art for its hidden meaning. "I didn't know you played the piano. I'm impressed." His gaze reflected the candles that flickered around the room and seemed to beckon to her.

"My mother made me practice every day. She always said, 'Someday you'll thank me.'" Kate nodded toward the piano. "She was right. I thank her every time I sit down and begin to play."

She turned back to Grady and touched his forehead. "How are you doing?"

Grady patted the purple bruise above his eye. "Not as bad I look. I feel fine."

"Whew," Kate said, grinning. "Then you're not planning to sue me for assault by sailboat?"

Rick winked at her. "We'll only consider legal action if we don't eat soon."

"We're starving," Grady added.

"Come on," Kate said, leading the way to the table. "Marta's making chocolate soufflés for dessert."

"I love that woman," Grady said. He hurried ahead to pull out Kate's chair.

An open bottle of Harlan Estate stood in front of her place setting. The red wine was too good for anything but a celebration, and Kate was sorry she had told Marta to open it. But as long as she had, they might as well enjoy it. She poured a glass for herself and her two guests.

"Sam bought six bottles of this at the Napa Valley wine auction. It's very hard to come by." She raised her glass to inhale the fragrance of the dark purple vintage, then took a sip. "Mm-mm," she said. "Liquid velvet." She took another sip.

"I hope he won't be upset we're drinking it," Grady said. "You know, without him."

"Sam Randolph gets whatever he wants," Kate said. Aware of the edge in her voice, she calmed herself. "I'm sure he'll simply order more." She quickly downed the wine, then poured herself a second glass. She drank this one more slowly, allowing the warm anesthesia to seep through her body. She wanted to forget today, forget Rick's kiss, forget Sam's lies.

But neither Marta's rosemary chicken nor the steamy chocolate souffle soothed the deep wound in Kate's heart. Despite the ongoing problems that had plagued her marriage, she'd always felt that she and Sam would find a way to work things out. She didn't believe that any longer.

She attempted to engage in the dinner conversation, but mostly she just smiled or laughed politely at Rick and Grady's aviation stories.

Rick reminisced about the time he'd flown a plane-load of boxed explosives for a mining operation. "When I landed," he said, "I asked the guy who was hitching a ride with me if he knew how the little black circles got on the top of one of the boxes. They weren't there when we left.

"'Sure,' the guy said. 'I lit some Sterno to heat up my soup.' Do you believe it? That idiot was cooking his dinner over two thousand pounds of TNT." Rick laughed, sat back in his chair, and downed the last of his wine.

Kate studied him, admiring his ability to adapt to his surroundings. He was just as comfortable in a cargo plane loaded with explosives as he was in a private villa in the Caribbean. Unlike Sam, who could only be content with his wealthy friends in their upscale hangouts, Rick possessed an easy-going attitude and self-confidence that allowed him to have fun wherever he went. With no effort at all, he charmed his companions...and seduced her.

Getting caught up in Sam's world had been easy for Kate. Getting out would be more difficult. Sam was the type of man who wanted his cake...and his cupcake, too.

She pushed her chair back from the table and stood. "I'm feeling a little tired."

Both men got up.

Grady said, "Thanks for dinner," and walked toward the open doorway.

Rick's eyes locked onto Kate's. For a moment, the only sound in the room was the ceiling fan making lazy circles above them. "I didn't get a chance to tell you before," he said. "You look fantastic tonight."

"Thank you," she said, a feeling of sadness creeping over her. Why couldn't she just get into the Lear with Rick, fly off somewhere, and forget her problems?

Rick cocked his head. "You seemed a little quiet during dinner. You alright?"

She managed a weak smile. "Everything's fine."

For a moment, it looked as if he wanted to hug her. Then he said, "Well...it was a great dinner. Thanks." He headed toward the open doorway where Grady waited.

She followed him, suddenly desperate not to be left alone. "Come up to the main house for breakfast anytime you like. Marta's in the kitchen by seven. After that, we could go into Albert Town, have lunch there."

Rick smiled. "Sounds like fun."

"Great," Grady chimed in.

"Well, goodnight," she said.

She twisted her wedding ring, watching them disappear across the patio and down the brick path. Sliding the glass door closed, she turned and meandered down the long hallway toward her bedroom. The sultry night, combined with the wine, kindled melancholy emotions. Would this be her last visit to her beloved Santomar? Shutting the bedroom door behind her, she pulled off her shell earrings and tossed them onto the bed, then unzipped her dress. When it fell in a heap on the floor, she retrieved it, hanging it neatly over its padded hanger. She pushed a button on the CD player, and Diana Krall crooned, *Do It Again*.

Changing into a pair of pink shorts and a pink tank top, Kate walked through the open French doors that led onto the patio, where she sank into a wicker armchair so she could watch the shoreline. She would wait until Rick had taken his evening stroll and then go down to the beach by herself. She craved a walk on the sand, but the last thing she needed was to complicate her life even more by running into Rick again tonight.

Kate hugged her knees close to her chest. In spite of the warm evening, she felt a chill ripple through her.

As she watched the beach, finally a figure appeared, walking along the shoreline. Rick. On his way back to the guesthouse, Kate assumed. She waited until the coast was clear, then kicked off her sandals and strolled barefoot down the brick pathway, past the palms and hibiscus and rolling lawns. Arriving at the short stone wall that separated the gardens from the beach, she stepped over it and sank to the ground, using the wall as a backrest. The sand felt soft and warm, the sound of the surf soothing.

She rested her chin on her knees and gazed over the ocean in the direction of Tortola. If she didn't stare straight at them, Kate could just make out the distant lights of Road Town, the capital of the British Virgin Islands. She and Sam had once toasted to their happiness there in an authentic English pub, drinking a glass of the local concoction the bartender had called the "Painkiller."

Kate's throat tightened. Tears formed in her eyes. She would miss this place. Sam would most likely give her a small amount of money to restart her life, but she'd have to look for a real job when she got home. She hoped she wouldn't end up sitting at a receptionist's desk at a law firm, endlessly repeating a string of partner's names followed by "one moment, please." Perhaps, she thought, Bob Hansen would hire her when she got her type-rating. Kate absentmindedly raked her fingers through the sand. Perhaps she would get a flight instructor license and teach aerobatics in her Pitts biplane. Would it be a living? Maybe.

Kate's fingers brushed against something in the sand and she plucked it up, inspecting the tiny sphere sitting in the palm of her hand, turning it over. The light of the full moon revealed a perfect little hummingbird's nest. She slid her index finger into the tiny hollowed-out space, feeling where the eggs, with their promise of new life, had once rested. Wincing at the heartbreaking emptiness of the miniature dwelling, she bolted to her feet, dropping the nest. Panicked, she gulped in a breath of air. Her impulse was to run. But where? And to whom? She had no parents, no children, and soon she'd have no husband. She felt totally alone, no better off than the bird whose nest lay on the ground. Her knees buckled. Dropping to the sand, she buried her face in her hands and wept. She cried for the empty nest, for all the empty spaces in her world. Most of all, she cried for the empty place in her heart.

Her sobs reached through the quiet night, drowning out the sound of approaching footsteps.

"Kate?"

She jumped when she heard the voice.

"It's just me," Rick said. "Sorry I startled you."

She stopped crying momentarily, but when she looked up and recognized him, she sat back in the sand and began to sob all over again.

He sat down beside her, circling her shoulders with his arm. "What's the matter?" he asked softly.

"I'm never coming back here again," she said through tears.

"Of course you're coming back here," he said, hugging her. "The runway's going to be fixed the day after tomorrow. You can visit Santomar any time you want."

Apparently he had said the wrong thing, for now she cried even harder. He wanted to comfort her, but he didn't know what to say. He waited. When he thought she might be through crying, he extended the bottle of Heineken he held. "Do you want some?"

"Just a minute," she said, sniffling. Taking a Kleenex from her pocket, she blew her nose. Then she grasped the neck of the bottle, took a sip, and handed it back to Rick.

"Thanks," she said.

"When Grady and I left after dinner, you seemed... worried or something. What's going on?"

Kate tilted her head to look up at him. In the moonlight, her face appeared luminous. Her tears had only served to make the color of her eyes more brilliant. *She should be photographed this very instant*, Rick thought.

"I've decided to leave Sam."

Rick couldn't believe what he was hearing. "But he's waiting in Miami for us to pick him up."

Kate took a deep breath, then slowly exhaled. "He's in Miami with his lover."

She knows, Rick thought. *How could any man want more when he already had Kate? What a jerk Sam Randolph is.*

"I had heard rumors," Kate said, "but didn't want to believe them. I think on some level I've always known. I'm sure you've heard of her...Ellen Gordon."

"The senator?"

"Bingo." Kate leaned back against the wall, staring out toward the ocean.

"Whew. It's going to be one long ride back to California," Rick said.

Kate sighed. "I'm not flying back with you. You can drop me in Miami when you pick up Sam, and I'll catch a commercial flight home."

Rick's mind spun. He was truly sorry she'd been hurt, but he also couldn't deny that this turn of events gave him hope. Kate would be free. He held out the bottle to her.

She took a sip of beer. "Sam's traveled so much, I'm used to being alone." She handed the bottle back to him. "I don't think being divorced is going to feel much different than being married."

A memory, dulled by time, not to mention Rick's attempt to bury it forever, crept back to him. "I know what you're going through," he said, staring straight ahead. "I never told this to anyone except Lila, but twelve years ago I came home early from a charter and found my wife in the hot tub with our neighbor."

Out of the corner of his eye, he saw Kate turn to him. "I'm sorry," she said, brushing his arm with her hand. "That must have been awful."

Her touch stirred up a caldron of chemistry from the back of his neck to his groin.

"It wasn't pretty," he said.

"So, we've both been given the boot." Kate attempted a weak chuckle.

"It's good to keep a sense of humor about it," he said. What he wanted to do was take her in his arms and hold her close. He wanted to tell her not to worry, everything would be alright. Instead, he got to his feet and held out his hand.

"How about a walk?" he asked.

She reached out, and he pulled her up. Her delicate hand felt small in his, and he was struck by the sudden urge to protect her. He let go and nudged the small of her back, leading her to the water's edge. They headed toward the end of the cove where the ocean was nearly as still as a lake. She wasn't smiling, but at least she had stopped crying.

Chapter 14

Kate and Rick strolled at the edge of the surf toward the large rock formation that marked the boundary of Sam's private beach. Kate was grateful Rick had found her. She talked and he listened, their hands and hips occasionally brushing as they adjusted their balance in the shifting sand.

When they reached the end of the cove, Kate sat down on a boulder and buried her toes in the sand.

"Life's so unpredictable," she said, leaning back to gaze at the stars. "When I married Sam, I thought our marriage would last forever, that we'd live happily ever after."

Rick took a seat beside her. "How did you end up with someone so much older than you?"

"I don't know," Kate said, shaking her head. "My friends said I missed my father. Maybe they were right." She sat up straight. "In any event, I'm no longer willing to pay the price for someone to take care of me." Shrugging her shoulders, she smiled. "So I guess that means I'll be looking for a job."

"If you find something you really like to do, it's not work."

"I'm not afraid of working. I loved being a teacher. I'm just sorry I'm not going to get the grant I requested from Sam's foundation for Safe Haven."

"Your girls' project?"

"You know about it?"

"Lila told me."

"I've got a lot of decisions to make. I don't even know where to start."

"I'm sure you'll figure out what's best." He reached out and pressed her hand. He pulled away almost immediately, but it was too late. The touch of his skin sent a shiver up Kate's arm, confirming the only benefit to the day's turmoil. The discovery of Sam's betrayal had freed her from the continual struggle to suppress her desire for Rick.

"I'm sorry you had to get stuck here," she said.

His gaze held her like a magnet. "I'm not."

The sudden awareness of her unexpected freedom made her feel bold. Besides, she knew enough about Rick to realize she'd have to make the first move. What did she have to lose? She smiled, raked one hand through her long hair. "Have you ever been swimming in the ocean at night?" she asked.

Rick shook his head, the light of the moon sparkling in his eyes. "No. Have you?"

"No. But I've always wanted to."

He didn't take his eyes off her. He didn't budge.

"Would you like to go for a swim now?"

Under other circumstances, his question would have been a casual inquiry. But at the edge of the Caribbean, under a full moon, it carried a promise of delicious danger.

Kate knew her reply would set them on a trajectory that would be impossible to control, but she didn't care. The sides of her mouth curved into a smile. "I'd love to go for a swim."

Rick stood, brushing sand off his shorts. He turned to face her. "Do you want to get a bathing suit?"

Rising from the boulder, Kate gazed up at him. She knew he already had his answer, but she said it anyway. "No. Do you?"

Without speaking a word, he slowly shook his head. His gaze locked on hers. Taking two steps forward, he slid one arm around her waist and pulled her toward him. He caressed her cheek.

Kate's heart hammered. Was this really happening?

He wound his fingers through her hair and gently tilted her head back. His mouth moved close to hers. "I can't keep my hands off you any longer," he whispered. His sweet breath felt warm on her skin.

And then, without haste, but with exquisite precision, his lips covered hers in a kiss that ignited every nerve in Kate's body. She felt swept away by the contradiction that this jet-jockey—this rugged warrior—could be so gentle.

Dizzy, Kate reached out and touched his arm, partly

to catch her balance, but also to convince herself that he was really here with her, that she wasn't dreaming.

The beach was totally secluded, hidden from the rest of the property by a grove of banana trees. They undressed slowly, leaving their clothes on the rocks. He took her hand in his, and she let him lead her to the water's edge. There they stopped and turned to look at each other. Rick cradled Kate's face in his hands, and when he gently kissed her, she closed her eyes. Her lips parted, welcoming the sweet taste of his tongue. He tucked a wisp of hair behind her ear, then brought his lips close and whispered her name.

"Kate." He said her name again, then he took her hand and they walked slowly into the sea.

The water was warm, and they flirted playfully for a while, swimming and constantly talking, only coming close enough to just be out of reach of each other. An occasional accidental touch sent shivers through Kate.

Eventually they arrived at a place where it was shallow enough to stand. They stood waist deep in the calm water, bodies glistening in the moonlight. Rick stepped in front of her, his eyes moving from her face to her body and back to her face. The anticipation of his touch made Kate feel as if she might faint.

He reached out and touched her breast, first running his thumb over her nipple, then moving his whole hand over it, caressing it in a way Sam never had. His hands traveled to her shoulders, pulling her closer. She came willingly. Their kisses were tentative at first, gentle and polite. Kate's lips swept from his neck to his eyelids, and then to his mouth, where his sweetness replaced the taste of the sea. He kissed the back of her neck, moving his hands and lips down her shoulder to her arm, and further still, until, when he could go no further, he kissed the palm of her upturned hand.

If Kate could have branded this moment into her flesh, she would have. Instead, she took both of his hands in hers, and raised them, holding them firmly against her cheek with her eyes closed. She would etch this moment into her soul, remembering the magic forever, returning to it time and again. When she was an old woman, she knew her last thoughts on earth would be of this place, this time, and this man.

Rick slid his arms around Kate's waist, drawing her closer. Her arms circled his neck. His lips sought hers again. But this time gentleness bowed to passion, their kisses setting off a firestorm of desire.

Breathless, Kate murmured, "I want to make love."

"I want to make love to you, too," he whispered back.

"But not here," she said. "Let's go up to the house."

They dressed to the sound of the surf, then Rick entwined his fingers in Kate's and they strolled the brick path back to the villa. His fantasy was becoming a reality. He replayed the scene in the water over and over in his mind. He'd never be able to forget the sight of Kate's naked body in the moonlight—the curve of her waist and her narrow hips, the way her hair fell around her shoulders and over her round breasts and perfect nipples...and those eyes. That moment on the beach was his Waterloo. He had no choice but to willingly surrender his soul to her. But in the surrender there would be victory. He would claim her for himself. She would be his.

After they passed the tennis court, Rick headed for the pool and the main part of the house, but Kate pulled him toward a smaller path.

"This way," she said, leading him to a private terrace outside a row of closed French doors. She pushed open the middle set, and he gazed into her bedroom.

A candle flame flickered inside a glass hurricane shade on the table beside the king-size bed, which had been turned down. Four pillows stood at attention against the headboard, and the crisp white sheets seemed to glow under an overhead spotlight turned to its dimmest setting. The anticipation of lying there with her intensified the urgent ache in Rick's groin.

Kate hesitated at the doorway, pivoting toward the view.

He stood behind her, placing his hands on her hips. For a moment, cloaked by the fragrance of the tropical night, they watched the moonlit waves caress the shore. Wrapping his arms around her, Rick nuzzled her neck, her scent reminding him of pink jasmine. He held her closer and bent his head to kiss her shoulder.

Turning toward him, she smiled and took his hand. "Let's take a shower and wash off the sand."

She led him past the bed through a stone archway.

To the right was a bathtub, surrounded by a stone ledge where votive candles burned, throwing flickering shadows against the walls. Next to the bathtub stood an oversized shower. More votive candles burned inside niches in its stone-clad walls.

Undressing, they tossed their clothes on the floor. Rick followed Kate into the steamy shower, where bottles of coconut shampoo and French soap sat on a shelf. They stood together under the cascade of hot water, staring into each other's eyes, hands caressing slippery bodies.

Kate sighed. "I'm glad you're here with me, like this."

By the glow of the candlelight, Rick saw desire in Kate's eyes that matched his own. "Me, too."

He wrapped his arms around her, drawing her close, and when he kissed her gently, she responded. Even under the running water, she was exquisite. But there was something aside from her beauty that captured him. She had a quality that the other women he had known hadn't possessed. She was strong and determined, and he liked that. But it was her vulnerability that made Kate irresistible.

Caressing the curve of her lower back, Rick murmured into her ear, "I want you." He turned off the faucet and stepped out of the shower, handing her a soft towel from a stack on a nearby shelf. They dried themselves.

"You can use this," Kate said, offering Rick a white terry-cloth robe that matched the one she now wore. She finished towel-drying her long blond hair, then stood in front of the mirror combing it, sheets of dark blond satin falling over her robe.

Setting her comb down, she leaned against the granite counter and turned toward him, her eyes looking downward. She played with the ends of her terry cloth belt. "The day after tomorrow, you're going to be flying my husband again. I don't want you to be embarrassed or uncomfortable. Are you going to be okay?"

You have no idea how okay I'll be, he thought. He wrapped his arms around her, pulling her close. He buried his face in the curve of her neck, where he could inhale the sweet fragrance left behind from the coconut shampoo.

"I'll be fine," he whispered. "We'll both be fine." Then he took her hand and led her to the bed.

Kate stood still while Rick untied her belt. He slid her robe off her shoulders until it tumbled to the floor. She tilted her head up to look into his eyes.

"I've only been with two men in my life," she said softly. "One was a boy in college, a long time ago."

He held her around the waist with one arm, and caressed her cheek with the other. "Don't worry," he murmured, kissing her eyes, her nose, then her mouth. "Third time's the charm." Then he stepped back and let his own robe fall to the ground, revealing his hard, muscular body.

Rick slid his hands down the sides of her neck, then over her shoulders and down her arms. Even though the night was warm, his touch brought shivers. His gaze locked on hers while his hands explored her body. His thumb traced the curve of her breast. She had never wanted a man the way she wanted him. His touch, soft yet demanding, sent a rising fever of desire through her, and she let out a soft moan. He stroked her hips and her belly, and finally the triangle of blond hair between her thighs. Kate closed her eyes, reeling from pleasure.

Rick sat down on the bed, drawing her next to him, guiding her back against the soft pillows.

"I'm so nervous," Kate said.

Propped on one elbow, Rick stretched his long, lean body out next to hers. "Just relax," he said, kissing her shoulder. "There's nothing to worry about. You're with me."

His crystal blue gaze seemed to pierce right through her, tempting her to forget about everything except her soaring desire for him.

Leaning toward her, he ran his hand over her hip to the inside of her thigh, pressing gently to part her legs. His confident voice soothed her while his skilled hands explored her body. He touched her in ways she had never even imagined, every caress, every flick of his tongue designed to bring the utmost pleasure. It was as if he knew her body better than she did—knew the secret that opened the floodgates to a torrent of exquisite pleasure. She yielded to his expertise, her nervousness obliterated by the elixir of his warm, insistent mouth.

His touch was sure and precise, and when he stroked the tender flesh between her legs, she moaned, feeling as though she might dissolve into stardust. Like a dandelion bursting upon the wind on a summer's day, she floated on a wave of rising sensations. Her whole body strove for deliverance, until at last she surrendered, a shudder of unbearable rapture rippling from her head to her toes. Gasping, she opened her mouth to speak, but the only sound that escaped her was a deep moan of satisfaction.

She felt his tongue part her lips to explore her mouth in a long, luxurious kiss. He lifted his head, and she watched a smile spread over his face.

She smiled back at him. "Don't stop."

"Not a chance." He stretched out above her, supporting himself on his elbows, and gazed down at her. Then he kissed her again, this time with unmistakable urgency. He grasped her hands, entwining his fingers with hers. She felt the whole length of his body above her, moving, slowly at first, then insistent and inexorable. And when he finally entered her, he prolonged his own pleasure, his body following the rhythm of hers, waiting for her, until at last, he erupted, groaning, filling her with joy she had never known before.

Chapter 15

The buzzing alarm awakened Rick. Heart pounding, he reached to turn it off as he looked around the room. His disorientation disappeared in an instant, years of perpetual travel inuring him to the momentary discomfort of not knowing his location.

Focusing on the burned-out candle beside the bed, he remembered the previous night. His mouth curved into a smile. Through the tangle of soft sheets, he felt the warmth of Kate's body. She slept deeply, covers tossed aside, one arm over her head, and her hair draped over the pillow and one breast. Too beautiful for words, she reminded him of a painting he'd seen at the Louvre. He wanted to draw her into his arms and make love to her again. Instead, he forced himself to quell his desire for her, and slid out of bed.

Kate stirred. "Where are you going?"

"It's five-thirty. I have to get to the guesthouse before Grady realizes I didn't spend the night there. Go back to sleep." He bent to kiss her.

She sighed and nestled into the sheets.

The sound of sea birds squawking for breakfast drifted through the open French doors, along with an early morning chill. Rick untangled the white blanket and draped it over Kate, gently tucking it around her shoulders.

He dressed in his khaki shorts. Carrying his shirt and sandals, he left through the patio doors, closing them behind him.

Hesitating a moment to gaze at the morning sky flushed with pink, Rick scanned the shoreline. He spotted Grady, who had just caught a wave, clinging to the boogie board, heading pell-mell toward the shore. After making certain no member of the staff would observe his departure, Rick hurried down the brick path.

Back at the guesthouse, he showered, shaved, and dressed quickly in white shorts and a blue Polo shirt. As he sat on his bed and studied a map of Santomar, he heard the front door open.

"Hey," Rick called out. "How were the waves this morning?"

Grady crossed the living room and paused before the doorway of Rick's bedroom. He tilted his head to one side, shaking the seawater out of his ear. "Man, they were awesome. I wish we didn't have to pick up old man Randolph tomorrow."

"Me, too," Rick said.

"I knocked on your door at five to see if you wanted to go with me. I guess you didn't hear me."

"I was really tired," Rick replied, folding the map.

"Are we supposed to make our beds here?" Grady asked, his gaze resting on the smooth bedspread under Rick.

Rick ran one hand over the bed he had not slept in. "Just a habit," he said, standing and tucking the map into his back pocket. "I'm going to walk up to the main house and get a cup of coffee. You want me to bring one back for you?"

"Sure," Grady said. "I'm gonna shower." He took two steps before turning around. "Hey. That Kate is something else, isn't she?"

Rick hesitated, and then said, "She certainly is." He wondered how much Grady knew.

After Rick departed, Kate cuddled into the lingering warmth of the sheets. She inhaled the faint but unmistakable fragrance of their combined essences. She smiled, the sensual scent intoxicating her.

Like a movie in her mind, she replayed every detail of their night together. She revisited one particular mental image over and over again. Rick's hands. She couldn't stop thinking about his hands and the glorious pleasure she'd felt as he'd caressed her skin. That the same capable hands that had fought wars and flown jets could also unleash overwhelming desire and deep satisfaction thrilled her.

Glancing at the clock on the bedside table, she swung her legs over the edge of the bed. She stretched, then padded naked into the bathroom.

She showered and put on white linen shorts, then made a halter top out of a pastel Gucci scarf. After coffee and a bran muffin from a tray Marta had brought to the room, she grabbed her purse. Determined not to think about Sam or any other problem that day, Kate turned off her cell phone, then drove the little yellow Jeep down to the guest cottage to pick up Rick and Grady.

The two men stood outside waiting for her. At the sight of Rick, she broke into a broad smile. His wink acknowledged their secret. The men piled into the Jeep, and they headed to town.

The Jeep, with its open canopy top, bounced and swayed past fields of corn, tomatoes, and peppers as Kate navigated the two-lane road to Albert Town.

She brushed a wisp of hair from her eyes, then pointed to a mountain peak. "That's Lookout Mountain," she said above the road noise. "It's the highest point on Santomar. From the top, you can see Tortola, Virgin Gorda, and Anegada. It's like heaven up there." She pointed to three billowing columns of smoke rising high in the sky. "The workers are burning the field to prepare for the next crop."

From the back seat, Grady shouted over the racket of the flapping canvas top and the wind. "Smells like burnt corn."

"Or incinerated corn bread," Rick said with a grin.

Kate laughed. "How about a scorched corn soufflé?"

They continued in this vein until they exhausted the list of corn products. Kate had traveled this road many times before, but never with the array of emotions careening around inside her today—sadness about Sam, concern about her financial future, and unspeakable joy whenever she glanced toward her passenger.

Rick sat beside her, one arm casually draped over the back of her seat. When she turned her head to catch a glimpse of him, he smiled at her and sent a ripple of excitement through her. She noticed the way the collar on his polo shirt tormented the side of his neck in the breeze. His eyes were hidden behind mirrored sunglasses, but she knew they watched her, too. His skin would be warm from the sun, and she ached to touch him, any part of him, just to convince herself she hadn't dreamed him and their night together. But she couldn't, not with Grady in the back seat, clinging to the roll bar.

Rounding a hairpin curve, Kate gasped. "Hold on." A truck had veered into their lane and was headed straight for them. She cut the wheel sharply, swerving onto the shoulder, narrowly avoiding the rickety old Ford filled with goats. The Jeep bumped and thumped over weeds and small boulders, kicking up a dust trail as it wobbled back to the pavement.

Rick laughed and adjusted his sunglasses. "Don't tell me flying's not the safest way to travel."

Kate grinned, feeling utterly buoyant.

The highway curved to the right and sloped down-hill, giving Kate and the men a bird's-eye view of Albert Town and its tiny harbor. As they approached the village, farms and tropical jungle gave way to ramshackle wooden dwellings with brightly painted shutters flung open under corrugated tin roofs.

Kate slowed the Jeep on the narrow, partially paved streets. Women in colorful dresses sat on their small porches, holding infants. Those without babies to tend enjoyed a mid-day rest, fanning themselves while they chatted with their neighbors. A toddler with no diaper, wearing only a t-shirt, stood by his mother's chair, bouncing to the beat of the music from her radio. At the side of the road, a barefoot little girl held a dirty rope, the other end of it tied around the neck of a goat.

Kate eased the Jeep into the town's business district. She smiled to herself. She felt certain this would be a day she would always remember.

Rick checked his watch as Kate drove along the wharf. A quarter past one. Nine-fifteen in Orange County. Lila would check in with him soon, as she always did whenever he was away on company time. He didn't feel like talking to anyone from Executive Air today. He fished his cell phone from his pocket and turned it off, making a mental note to call Lila later.

He glanced at Kate. He had never slept with another

man's wife, not even the wife of a man guilty of betrayal. He hated himself for doing it. Even though he ached for Kate, he knew he couldn't let it happen again. Not now, anyway. She needed time to sort out her life.

Kate made a u-turn, sending Rick sliding across his seat, then pulled into a parking space in front of the outdoor marketplace across from the wharf. Peddlers crowded the sidewalk, sitting beneath colorful umbrellas, hawking household items and clothing piled atop tottering card tables.

"Arletta's is around the corner," Kate said, killing the motor. She slid out of the car, heading toward the throng.

"Come on," she said. "We can cut through here."

Stretching for nearly a block, the market was covered by a vaulted canopy of dark green trees. Rick and Grady followed Kate as she threaded her way through the narrow aisles packed with vibrant displays of ripe fruits and fragrant vegetables.

Rick loved the exotic sights and smells. He smiled at the women who tended barbeques and makeshift stoves, where peppery jerk chicken and curried goat lured hungry shoppers. Stopping beside a woman ladling something into plastic bowls, he asked, "What's that?"

"*Sancocho*," the woman replied.

"Spicy vegetable stew," Kate said. "If we ever run out of jet fuel, we can use it in the Lear."

He liked her sense of humor.

They continued toward the back of the market, passing a white-tiled stall where a side of beef hung from a steel hook. Next to the carcass, ducks, chickens, and one large bird that might have been a turkey hung by their limp necks, their feathers still attached. Flies buzzed about the butcher, who chatted with a customer.

They cut through the alley behind the market, emerging onto High Street where old Tipuana trees, like yellow-flowered umbrellas, shaded Lilliputian houses and businesses. At the corner house, a weathered clapboard, a large woman sat on the porch. She seemed to be watching them.

"That's Blossom," Kate said. "According to Marta she's the best fortuneteller on Santomar." Kate chuckled. "If you believe in that sort of thing."

They continued halfway down the street until they reached a whitewashed picket fence. Propped against the aging wood, a sign painted in bold red letters proclaimed, "Arletta's."

Arletta's, like so many small restaurants in the Caribbean, possessed no front wall and opened onto the street. Three inside tables and two others positioned under a blue canopy on the sidewalk were covered with shiny oilcloth printed with floral designs in carnival colors.

"Let's sit outside," Kate said, feeling a rivulet of sweat running between her breasts. "It's cooler out here."

Stopping beside a round table on the sidewalk, she dropped her handbag next to the large red cooler with

Coca Cola scripted in white. She slid onto one of the mismatched chairs, and Rick and Grady followed her. She sat close enough to Rick to inhale the subtle scent of his cologne, which triggered memories of their night together. A flush rose from her chest to her cheeks. She smiled at both men, fanning herself with her hand.

A small television set with rabbit-ear antennas sat atop a rickety table. Tuned to CNN, the sound was turned so low no one could hear the commentator. Inside the restaurant, Arletta stood before a primitive-looking stove, stirring the contents of a large cast iron skillet with one hand while she balanced a baby on her hip with the other.

"Welcome, welcome," she called out in her thick island accent, continuing to stir the food. The enticing fragrance of onions, garlic, and exotic spices wafted from the kitchen.

Grady leaned toward Kate. "It smells real good, but are you sure it's safe to eat here?"

"Are you kidding? Arletta's a great cook. Besides—" Kate cocked her head "—if you do get sick, the locals have a cure for anything from a splinter to a headache."

"What is it?" Grady asked.

"A cup of rum mixed with some ginger root and stirred with the foot of a freshly killed chicken."

Rick shrugged. "And if that doesn't work," he added, "we can always take you to the hospital. The only problem is you have to pay the doctor with either a goat or a rooster, and we're clean out of both." He winked at Kate.

"Okay, okay." Grady squirmed in his chair.

Arletta approached their table, the baby still perched on her hip. Leaning against the red cooler, she pulled a purple bandana out of her pocket with her free hand and wiped her dark forehead.

"Hello, Miss Kate," the heavyset woman said. She tucked the bandana back into her pocket and patted the baby's cheek.

"Hi, Arletta." Kate set her sunglasses on top of her head. She stroked the baby's chubby foot and smiled. "William's getting so big." The baby's large brown eyes struck a melancholy note in Kate, reminding her what she had given up to marry Sam.

Arletta hugged William and beamed. "He nearly be one year old." She bounced the baby on her hip, and he giggled and swung his legs wildly. "Soon dis child, he be big enough to cook for me." When Arletta laughed, sunlight glinted off one of her two gold teeth. "Your friends?" she asked, eying the two men.

"This is Rick Sanders," Kate said, pointing to Rick. "And this is Grady Burke."

Arletta's eyes narrowed. "I ain't seein' Mister Sam."

"He's working. He'll be here tomorrow," Kate said. "Now, what's for lunch today?"

Arletta's expression relaxed as she launched into her menu. "You like fresh curry chicken, fish stew, fried plantains? I make what you like."

"Surprise us," Kate said. "We're starving, and I've been telling my friends what a good cook you are."

"Yes, dat be very true." Arletta walked back to the

stove. She placed William in a playpen that showed signs of several generations of use, then busied herself with the task of preparing lunch for her three customers.

"How 'bout something cold to drink?" Kate said.

Rick stood and walked to the cooler, pulling out three bottles of Corona, dripping with ice and water. He held up a bottle and called to the kitchen, "Arletta, three beers." The woman nodded, apparently making a mental note to add the drinks to the bill.

Rick opened the bottles on the rusted metal opener attached to the side of the cooler, then handed one to Kate and one to Grady. He lifted his own while looking at Kate. "Here's to lots of happy landings."

"Those are my favorite kind." Kate grinned, longing for him to lean over and kiss her.

"I'll drink to that," Grady said.

The three of them clicked the long-necked bottles together and took a drink of cold beer.

Grady wiped his mouth with the back of his hand. "How 'bout it, Rick? I bet you never had a charter like this one before."

The corners of Rick's eyes crinkled when he grinned. "That's for sure." Under the table, Rick rubbed his knee against Kate's, and she stifled a smile.

Arletta appeared, bringing with her the scent of cardamon, curry, and cinnamon. She set a large platter, piled high with a variety of steaming dishes, in the center of the table, then went back to the kitchen. She returned with napkins, forks, and three crockery plates.

"You eat up," she ordered. Arletta paused on her trip

back to the kitchen and pointed to the mute television. "Look. Mr. Sam."

A photo of Sam appeared on the screen above the shoulder of the anchorman who read from a script.

A twinge of worry shot through Kate. "Can you turn up the sound?"

Grady, closest to the TV, searched for a volume button on the old set. "Arletta, how does this work?"

"No sound, it be broken. Only pictures." She shrugged her shoulders.

The photo on the small screen changed. The anchorman moved on to another news story.

"I wonder what that was about," Rick said.

"Sam's buying a radio station in Florida," Kate said, spooning a mound of pungent curry onto her plate. "I'm sure it has something to do with that." She didn't want to think about Sam now, or anything he might be doing in Florida.

Their lunch was a feast—curried chicken prepared with raisins, coconut, and mangos, a thick fish stew with carrots and onions, crisp plantains, and slices of succulent barbequed lamb.

When they finished, Grady sat back and patted his stomach. "I couldn't eat another bite."

Arletta cleared the table, then reappeared with three slices of creamy custard.

"Don't know what t'say 'bout people so skinny." She clicked her tongue as she placed a plate of the rich dessert in front of each of them. She walked away, shaking her head.

"Well, maybe just one more bite." Grady raised a spoonful of thick custard to his mouth. "Mm-mm." He rolled his eyes. A moment later, Grady pointed to the television set.

Kate and Rick looked at the small TV screen. Once more a picture of Sam appeared. A photo of Ellen Gordon followed. Kate's heart pounded. She felt embarrassed by Sam's behavior. *Some reporter probably saw them together*, Kate thought. *Great. Now the whole world knows Sam is cheating on me.*

Kate turned to look at Rick. A hint of a smile crossed his lips. Kate recognized the silent message his gaze conveyed. *You'll be okay, I'll be there for you.* In that instant, nothing else mattered to her.

Kate turned her back on the television. She didn't care where Sam and Ellen had dined the night before. She took one more bite of the sweet custard before pushing her plate away, then wiped her mouth on her paper napkin. She pulled her lip gloss from her purse and applied a coat of pink shine to her lips. Dropping the black Chanel tube into her purse, she pulled several bills from her wallet and dropped them on the table for Arletta.

She winked at her guests. "Lunch is on Sam." She stood up and tossed her purse strap over her shoulder. On the spur of the moment she added, "Let's go to Blossom's. I've never had my fortune read."

Chapter 16

E ven though it had been her idea, Kate approached Blossom's house with apprehension. She pushed open the gate to the fortuneteller's courtyard, unleashing a protest from the rusty hinges. Rick and Grady followed her.

Blossom held court daily on the porch of the white clapboard house she had inherited from her mother. The locals claimed she had also inherited her mother's gift of prophesy. Blossom, who resembled Louis Armstrong, sat beneath a Chinese umbrella in an old rocking chair that creaked under her weight. Dressed in a shocking pink caftan, she smiled broadly, her oversized white teeth flashing. Sitting forward, she beckoned them closer with her sequined fan, then used it to swat at a fly buzzing overhead.

"Welcome. Come, come," she said in a deep gravelly

voice. The woman not only looked like the jazzman, she sounded like him, too.

"Are you in the mood to know what the future holds?" she asked. In her other hand, she balanced a thin cigar.

"How much do you charge?" Kate inquired.

Blossom stopped rocking and rose from the chair, which continued to rock on its own.

"There are five other fortunetellers in Albert Town," the woman said with a flamboyant wave of her hands. The inch of ash on her cigar miraculously stayed put. "Everyone knows I'm the best. The others are thieves." Fluffing the scrawny ostrich feather boa that dangled from her neck to her knees, with an air of authority she said, "Ten dollars each, and I keep all bad news to myself."

Kate turned to Rick and Grady, who both nodded their agreement. "I'll be the guinea pig and go first," she said, grateful for the distraction. At least for a little while she wouldn't need to worry about Sam or Rick.

With one hand, Blossom drew back a heavy red drape, revealing the inside of her parlor. She gestured for Kate to follow her.

Kate glanced back at the pilots before stepping through the doorway, where the strong smell of incense greeted her. The curtain fell shut behind her. The dark cool space offered a welcome relief from the hot, dusty street. A worn red velvet sofa sat against a wall and four wooden chairs surrounded a small round table covered by a paisley tablecloth.

Blossom lit a match, then touched it to the candle in

the center of the table. The flickering light sprang to life in dozens of mirrors of all shapes and sizes that hung on every wall. Overhead an ancient crystal chandelier with six arms but only two dim light bulbs threw a curious glow over the room.

Blossom motioned Kate to the table, then sat down next to her. "I've seen you in town before. What's your name, dear?"

"My name is Kate."

"Put your hands on the table, Kate."

Kate put her hands on the table, her palms facing up.

Blossom shook her head and laughed, then she cleared her hoarse throat. "I don't read palms. Turn your hands over."

When Kate turned her palms down on the table, Blossom did the same. After several minutes of silence, the fortuneteller spoke.

"There's a struggle coming. And a secret waits to be revealed."

"What kind of secret?"

Blossom ignored her. "When it is uncovered, you will not be alone. And when you begin your journey, do not be afraid."

"What journey?" Kate asked.

"Set the course and follow your heart. He is always with you."

Kate listened with curiosity as Blossom went on about the need for Kate to remain strong and focused. Then, the heavyset woman shifted in her chair and blew out the candle. The room darkened.

"Wait," Kate said. "I have questions for you."

"No more today." Blossom pushed up to her feet.

Not knowing what to make of the experience, Kate opened her purse and pulled out a ten dollar bill.

Blossom tucked it into her bra. "Send in one of your friends," she said in her raspy voice.

Pulling back the red curtain and squinting at the bright sunlight, Kate found Rick and Grady sitting on the front step with their backs to her. She tapped Rick on the shoulder. "Next victim."

Rick emerged from Blossom's parlor irritated. He pointed to the bar across the street. "We'll meet you over there," he said to Grady. "Let's get a drink, Kate."

The bar was crowded and noisy. A television set bolted to the wall above the bartender quietly broadcast CNN. No one paid attention to it. While Kate made her way to an empty table by the wall, Rick placed their order with the bartender, then returned and slumped into his chair, a sense of unease settling over him. A waitress appeared with two bottles of Dos Equis.

"What's the matter?" Kate said.

Rick shrugged his shoulders. "Nothing." He put the bottle to his mouth and took a drink.

Kate shook his knee. "Come on. Don't be like that."

Rick took a deep breath. "I don't think it's a good idea to visit fortunetellers. There's no way they can know what's going to happen, and if they tell you something you don't like, you're stuck."

Kate's turquoise eyes crinkled at the corners. She failed to conceal her grin. "What did she say that was so horrible?"

"Fire in the sky will set me free. Right. A fire's the last thing I need when I'm flying."

Kate smiled. "She probably says that to everyone."

He relaxed into his chair and blew out a breath. "I guess I'm overreacting." Reaching under the table to find her hand, he stroked her soft skin, enjoying the feel of her long fingers and her smooth nail polish.

"This is the first time we've been alone since last night," she said.

"I know." He chose his words carefully, hoping she wouldn't misinterpret them. "I don't think it's a good idea for that to happen again."

She looked crushed, and she averted her gaze to the table.

"No," he said. "It's not like that."

He tilted her chin up to look into her eyes. "I mean right now." He squeezed her hand. "We just need to be careful. I'd probably get fired if anyone from Executive Air found out about it, and even if you are leaving your husband, for the moment, you're still married."

She nodded. "You're right."

"And while we're on the subject of your husband, I've gotta talk to him tonight. The runway will be open in the morning, and I need to know what time he wants to be picked up."

Kate sipped the beer, then twirled the brown bottle in her hands. "I'll call him when we get back to the house.

She sighed. "I hope he'll let me use the Lear to get my type-rating. I'm so close, and I'd hate to have to rent a plane."

"Don't worry about that now."

Rick lifted the bottle to his mouth but paused when, once again, a photo of Sam Randolph appeared on the screen. "There he is...again," Rick said, nodding toward the TV. The same picture of Ellen Gordon followed Sam's. But this time, a third picture stopped him dead in his tracks.

A photo of Sam and Kate filled the screen.

"Oh, my God," Kate gasped. "That's our wedding picture." Standing abruptly and knocking her chair into the one behind her, she called to the bartender. "Can you turn up the sound on the TV?"

The bartender cupped his hand to his ear. The picture on the screen disappeared, replaced by an ad for laundry detergent.

Kate turned to Rick. "I need to know what they're saying."

Rick sensed there was more to the story than a fling with an ex-lover. Spotting Grady at the entrance to the bar, Rick stood, pulled a few dollars from his pocket, and tossed them onto the table for the waitress.

"Let's go." He took Kate's arm, guiding her through the crowd and out onto the sidewalk. They joined Grady for the short walk back to the Jeep.

Kate took a short cut home that hugged the side of Lookout Mountain. She kept her eyes on the twisting road, trying her best to point out places of interest to her passengers, but her mind kept straying to Sam and Ellen Gordon. Once they reached the house, she intended to check her voice mail and monitor the news to discover just what was going on with Sam. She also needed to pack for the trip home in the morning.

She ached to reach out and touch Rick, but stayed focused on the road. After winding her way around Lookout Mountain, Kate rejoined the main route that led back to the villa. She turned into the driveway, stopping the Jeep in the courtyard.

Rick swung one leg out of the Jeep, then paused and turned to Kate. As though reading her mind, he said, "Let's check out CNN."

"That's the last thing I want to do," said Grady, who had jumped from the back seat and now stood behind Rick. Stretching, he yawned expansively. "I think I'll watch a movie and relax."

"Dinner's at eight," Kate reminded Grady as he ambled toward the guesthouse.

Grady waved. "See you guys later."

As he slid from the Jeep, Rick's hand grazed Kate's so casually no one would have even noticed. But Kate sensed his touch was meant to draw her attention, and it did.

"There's a TV on the *Fancy That,*" she said.

"Perfect. We can watch the news and the sunset." His broad smile helped to ease her tension and her troubled thoughts.

They walked through the garden, brushing against one another as they maneuvered down the narrow path. Hurrying along the dock to where the sailboat bobbed in the crystal clear water, Kate looked around, savoring their privacy.

They boarded the *Fancy That* and headed immediately down the ladder into the cabin. Before Kate reached the bottom step, Rick grabbed her hand. By the time he stood in the galley, he held her in his arms. Locked in an embrace, hungry for each other, they bumped against the stove, then the sink.

"Forget everything I said in the bar," Rick whispered into her ear. "I can't stay away from you."

"I'd like to feel that this is wrong," she sighed. "But I don't."

Rick's hard body pressed Kate's against the refrigerator before his mouth settled over hers. He reached under her Gucci scarf to cup her warm breast. His other hand grasped her hair, gently tilting her head back until she met his gaze. "I hated not touching you this afternoon," he admitted before he kissed her again.

She clasped him to her, trying to hold him so close he could never leave. Her knees nearly buckled from the sheer joy of being in his arms. "It was torture having to pretend we were just friends," she said.

"I know." He kissed her cheek, then tucked a strand

of hair behind her ear. "How about a glass of wine to go with the news?"

"The corkscrew's in the top drawer." Kate turned and opened the refrigerator. She withdrew a bottle of DuMol Chardonnay and handed it to Rick. He uncorked it while she pulled two glasses from a cupboard.

At the far end of the cabin, a queen-size bed occupied the bow of the sailboat. Across the room, a television sat atop a small built-in dresser.

After Kate turned on CNN, she climbed onto the bed, creating a backrest from the dozen or so blue and white pillows that covered the matching bedspread. Rick handed her a glass of wine, then climbed up beside her and sank back against the pillows. He gathered Kate into his arms, and she nestled close. They sipped the cold Chardonnay and waited.

They had emptied their glasses by the time the now familiar photo of Sam flashed onto the screen. The anchorman's eyes moved back and forth as he read from the teleprompter.

"We have unconfirmed reports that early this morning paramedics were summoned to the Palm Beach residence of Senator Ellen Gordon, where oilman and multi-media giant Sam Randolph was found dead...."

Shocked, Kate stiffened, hearing the story as though it were being told in a foreign language. Only a few key words registered in her stunned mind. "Dead...bedroom... heart attack...wife unavailable."

Heart pounding, Kate trembled. She sagged against Rick and buried her face in his chest and wept. He stroked her hair, and she cried until she couldn't catch her breath. She sat up, swiping at her tears as Rick handed her several tissues.

"I can't believe it," she said. "He can't be dead." She stood up, and then sat down again, feeling too disoriented to understand her own behavior."Why didn't someone call me?"

"Is your cell phone on?" Rick asked.

She shook her head. "I turned it off this morning. I just wanted to have a nice day with no interruptions."

Rick pulled his phone from his pocket and turned on the power. "Lila will be frantic."

"I just wanted to leave him," Kate said. "I didn't wish him harm. I wanted a divorce, not a funeral."

Falling onto the bed, she buried her face in her hands and sobbed. A few moments later, she stopped, sat up, and wiped her tear-stained cheeks.

Her jaw tightened. "I can't believe he died in his mistress's bed. God. That son-of-a-bitch."

Rick put his arms around her, whispering, "It's okay, Kate. It's okay."

"He wasn't a bad person," she moaned. "He was just...." She couldn't find the right words.

Sorrow. Mortification. Anger. One minute, Kate raged at her humiliation, the next she felt overwhelmed by grief. After a while, she finally calmed down, at least some of her emotions now spent. She stood, grabbed the box of tissues, and crossed the room to the dresser. With her back to Rick, she wiped her eyes and blew her nose.

He came up behind her. "Is there anything I can do?" He rubbed her shoulders.

She shook her head. "No." When she turned around and leaned against him, he pulled her close. "It's such a shock," she said.

Rick led her back to the bed and then poured her a fresh glass of wine. "Here, hon, this might help."

"Thank you," she said, taking a big gulp. She sank back against the pillows and looked at the ceiling as tears filled her eyes again. "I can't believe Sam's dead. Now I'm really on my own." Her eyes flooded, and she wept softly.

Rick stretched out beside her, pulled her close, and rocked her in his arms while he stroked her hair. He wiped her cheeks then kissed her. "You're not alone," he whispered. "I'm here."

She slid her arms around Rick and returned his kiss, never closing her eyes. And somewhere in the midst of sorrow, unbearable tenderness became unbearable desire. They formed a single entity, a tangle of arms and legs. Kate and Rick clung to each other as though struggling against an outside force that seemed intent on tearing them apart.

The *Fancy That* rocked in the crystal clear water, mimicking the motion of the lovers inside. While the sun set on Santomar, passions prevailed and fates were sealed.

Chapter 17

K ate refolded the *New York Times* neatly along its creases, then placed it beside her on the sofa. The air conditioning in the private air terminal at Miami International must have been set to sixty degrees. Zipping her apricot cashmere jacket, she surveyed the other people in the lounge. No one seemed to notice the chill.

During the week following Sam's death, Kate had remained on Santomar. The coroner took his time releasing the body. An autopsy revealed Sam had succumbed to a massive coronary. At least he hadn't suffered, she thought.

She had received a phone call from Derek, informing her of his plans for his father's memorial service on Saturday. True to form, he'd made all the arrangements without consulting her. But Kate had expected that. Since their first meeting, Derek made no secret of his hostility toward her. There was nothing she could have done that might have convinced him she'd married Sam because she'd loved him.

She stood and pulled her jacket tight around her shoulders. Given that she'd planned to leave Sam, the depth of her grief surprised her. Then again, she *had* loved him.

When the automatic doors to the tarmac opened, a gust of warm wind burst across the room. Rick, dressed in his captain's uniform, strode in, crossing the lounge until he stood before Kate.

"We can leave whenever you're ready," he said, his blue eyes soft with compassion.

Kate checked her watch. "They should be here any minute." She patted *The New York Times*. "Sam would have been pleased. His obituary filled half a page."

"I read it," Rick said. "I liked how they described you. 'Good-natured and gracious.'"

She smiled at him, saying a quick prayer of thanks that out of the billions of people on the planet, this strong yet gentle man had found her.

Rick's hand brushed hers. "I'm gonna check the weather. Sit tight. I'll be right back." He walked down the hall toward the flight planning room.

Kate settled into a corner of the overstuffed couch. Before long, a stocky man in a dark suit appeared in front of her, his grey jacket bearing the insignia, "Miami Funeral Services." He carried a package wrapped in brown paper and tied with black twine. His expression somber, he asked, "Mrs. Randolph?"

Kate got to her feet. "Yes."

"I have your parcel," he said. "It's rather heavy."

"Thank you," she whispered, emotion welling yet again.

He placed the box on the floor, then removed a handkerchief from his outside breast pocket and mopped his forehead. Reaching inside his jacket, he withdrew a sheaf of documents and a pen. "I need your signature," he said, unfolding two of the pages and handing them to her.

She signed both copies.

The man tucked the papers into his pocket. "Have a good flight." He nodded politely, turned, and left.

Kate bent to pick up the package. Finding it disproportionately heavy for its size, she left it on the floor.

Rick returned, crumpling the computerized weather briefing in his hands. "A few thundershowers over Houston, but other than that, it's clear skies all the way to California." He tossed the paper into an ashtray, then leaned over to pick up the box. "I'll get this for you."

They headed toward the exit. The sight of Rick in his captain's uniform prompted the security guard to unlock the glass doors that led out to the tarmac. Kate and Rick walked outside, threading their way between two rows of jets until they reached the Lear.

Grady stood at the foot of the stairs. "Preflight's done," he said. "We're ready to roll."

"Thanks," Rick said. "You can relax and watch a movie. Kate's gonna sit left seat."

"No problem," Grady said.

Rick handed him the box. "Take care of this."

Kate climbed the stairs, setting her purse behind the bulkhead while Rick locked the cabin door. She settled into the captain's seat and took out her checklist. Rick strapped into the seat beside her. Soon, the sound of the engines roared through the plane. Disengaging the emergency brake, Kate guided the Lear to the runway.

Shoulder to shoulder with Rick, she glanced at him. His presence beside her brought a sense of security. She reminded herself that the warm breezes and tropical magic of Santomar were gone. Could she count on him in the real world, as she faced a major change in her life? Just then, he smiled at her, and she felt a comforting warmth spread through her.

Poised at the end of the runway, Kate waited until she heard the familiar, "Cleared for take-off." Pausing a moment, she turned to look at the box positioned beside Grady on the sofa. Inside rested a bronze urn containing the remains of Sam Randolph. She was taking him home. Kate pushed the throttles all the way forward. Daunted by the tasks she knew lay ahead, she felt grateful for the temporary distraction of flying the Lear.

Lila sat across from Bob in his office. On the desk, the company checkbook lay open between them. A stack of unpaid bills loomed nearby. It wasn't easy keeping her mind on business. After Bob had asked her to dinner, she'd been on cloud nine. He had seemed so happy, but now he appeared more stressed than ever. She wanted to say something.

"If we don't get a handle on this cash flow," Bob said, "my whole operation could go under." He shifted in his chair, drumming his fingers in a steady motion. "Executive Air is hemorrhaging money," he said. "It's that damn yacht. With the economy so uncertain, I can't even sell that tub for what I owe."

The afternoon sun shone through the windows, creating a greenhouse effect. Lila removed her suit jacket and laid it on the chair beside her. She couldn't keep quiet a moment longer.

"It's not just the yacht," Lila said. "It's the pink elephant in the room."

"What?"

Lila rose from her chair and paced the carpet. "Two weeks ago Rick flies off to the Caribbean. You're happy as a clam. So happy, that after twenty years you invite me to dinner." She lowered her voice. "Then we go back to your house afterwards—which we also haven't done in twenty years. Next thing I know Sam Randolph dies, you go into mourning, and our relationship is back to square one. What the hell is going on?" Out of breath, she flopped back into her chair, her heart pounding.

Bob stood and came around the desk and sat beside her. "I'm sorry." He sighed. "Look, I'm tired of keeping this to myself anyway. Two days before he left, I made a deal with Sam Randolph. His attorney was drawing up partnership papers. Sam was going to transfer funds to our account to pay all the bills and arrears. As part of the arrangement, I was going to give Sam a great deal on the cost of maintaining and flying the Lear. When Sam got to Santomar, he was going to surprise his wife with the news he was buying into her passion, flying. Sam died before the papers were signed."

"Oh, my God." In dismay, Lila put her hand on Bob's shoulder. "What a disaster."

"Now you know why I'm so distracted," Bob said.

"I'm so sorry." Lila rubbed his back. Seeing him suffer tore at her heart. "I think Rick's been talking to some investors. Something will turn up."

"Do me a favor, keep this quiet," Bob said. "I don't want people to know this deal fell through."

The radio receiver Bob used to monitor the control tower hissed. Rick's voice called the "outer marker."

"They're on final approach," Bob said.

"It'll be good to have Rick back. Shall we go outside to meet them?"

"You go," Bob said.

Lila stood, smoothed her pleated skirt, and then put on her jacket. She squeezed Bob's hand and headed to the waiting room to watch the Lear land. Her boy was home, and a newly widowed Kate Randolph was with him.

The security guard unlocked the glass doors so Lila could walk out onto the apron. Squinting in the bright sunlight, she shaded her eyes as the Lear approached and then pivoted into its parking space. She grabbed her skirt and held it down when jet blast from the engines rushed by her. Through the cockpit window she saw

Kate in the captain's seat. *Poor woman*, she thought. *Too young to be a widow. But better than being married to that two-timing bastard.*

Lila waited until the chocks were in place on either side of the nosewheel and the engines had been shut down before she approached the door. It swung open, and a very suntanned Grady emerged first. As he clattered down the steps, a broad smile covered his face.

"Hey, Lila."

"Hi." She handed him a set of keys. "Can you bring Kate's car out here? It's the silver Porsche."

"Be right back." He headed for the parking lot.

Rick appeared in the doorway. "Hi, Mom."

Lila waved, watching him offer his hand to assist Kate down the stairway. She couldn't help thinking what a striking couple they made.

When Kate stepped onto the tarmac, Lila put her arms around the young woman and hugged her close. Kate held on tight, resting her head for a moment on Lila's shoulder in a gesture of intimacy that was so comfortable and common between women.

"I'm sorry about your husband," Lila said, stepping back.

Kate gave a weak smile, but her eyes telegraphed sadness. "Thank you."

Lila opened her arms to Rick. She pulled him toward her and hugged him hard. "I can't believe you've only been gone ten days," she said. "Seems like a month."

He squeezed her back. "It's good to see you."

Grady nosed the Porsche up to the side of the plane,

turned off the engine, and climbed out. He loaded Kate's luggage into the trunk while Rick set the package tied with black twine on the front passenger seat. He strapped it down with a seatbelt.

Kate sighed. "I've got to get home." She slid behind the wheel.

Rick leaned down to window level. "Things'll ease up after a few days," he whispered.

She nodded.

"Give me a few minutes," he said. "I'll be right behind you."

The engine turned over, and he stepped away from the car. Kate drove through the security gate, pausing in the parking lot to wait for him.

Rick slung his arm around Lila's shoulder, and they walked toward the office. "I'm gonna follow her home. Just to make sure she's alright."

Glancing sideways at him, Lila smiled. Her maternal instincts assumed that something was going on between Kate and Rick. It was just what she had hoped for, and she said a silent prayer of thanks.

The Randolph estate was legendary in Orange County, and Rick had to admit he was eager to see it. In the parking lot, he pulled his shiny black BMW behind Kate's Porsche, and flashed his headlights. She waved to him and pulled away from the curb. Following her out of the airport, he made a left turn onto Campus Drive, then a right on MacArthur Boulevard. They headed to Pacific Coast Highway, where they turned south toward Laguna.

Rick relaxed into the soft seat. He loved this stretch of highway. He took this route whenever he drove home from the airport—only this time, he wasn't going home, he was going to Kate's.

Coming to a stop at a red light, he flipped a lever on the dashboard. There was just enough time for the convertible top to fold back into the trunk before the signal turned green. Sucking in a breath of cool sea air, he adjusted the volume on the car's CD player. Led Zeppelin blared and the wind tousled his hair while the two cars played follow the leader past Pelican Point.

When he reached the curve in the road that paralleled the sandy dunes at Crystal Cove, Rick glanced at the ocean. He never tired of this view. *Not bad for a military brat,* he thought. In less than five years, the mortgage on his condo would be paid off. His backyard, one of the most beautiful beaches in California, made him smile. No doubt about it. He had done well.

Just past the clapboard cottage where beach-goers lined up for date shakes, the road arched high above the sand. Rick looked down, catching a glimpse of sparkling water and white foam crashing over the rocks at Morro Beach. A half-mile beyond, a green highway sign announced, "Laguna Beach, Home of the Pageant of the Masters."

Kate slowed, turning left onto a tree-lined lane. She

came to a stop beside the guardhouse that protected the entrance to the exclusive enclave of Emerald Bay.

Waiting behind her, Rick watched Kate speak to the officer on duty. After a moment, the tall iron gate, sequestering the privileged residents, swung open. Kate drove through. When Rick approached the guard, the uniformed officer waved him on.

Palladian palaces, New England farmhouses, and Mediterranean villas sat side by side in an eclectic mix common in Southern California. Ancient oaks and sycamores softened the mansions, and shady parks with tennis courts and children's playgrounds dotted the landscape. Rick followed Kate as she skimmed over the winding roads, finally entering a narrow tunnel carved through granite that took them beneath Coast Highway. They emerged to the sight of the private cove that made this community so exclusive—a crescent of white sand hugging a secluded bay where the glassy water barely rippled in the shimmering twilight. The deserted beach was sheltered from intruders by towering rock cliffs that stood like sentinels at both ends. The few houses built on this side of the highway ranked as the most expensive and most sought after. The largest residence on this elite stretch of land had been built by Sam Randolph.

Kate turned right, driving along the beachfront road for a short distance, then right again into a driveway flanked by massive pillars topped by ornate wrought iron lanterns. Once the colossal bronze gates swung open, Rick followed Kate up the driveway to the limestone villa with the bougainvillea-draped arches. He had never imagined that homes like this sat behind the simple guardhouse he had passed for years on his way to and from the airport. The house on Santomar, luxurious as it was, seemed like a beach shack in comparison.

He came to a stop behind Kate in the motor court. A man dressed in a butler's suit, along with a woman wearing a pink maid's uniform with a white lace collar and a white apron, waited at attention near the back entrance to the house. Rick turned off the engine, set the brake, then stepped out onto the slate courtyard. The house towered over him, making him feel small and insignificant. Like a twitching nerve he couldn't control, an unwelcome feeling shot through him. What was he doing here?

The butler rushed to open Kate's car door, the uniformed woman following close behind him. He helped Kate from her car while Rick strode across the driveway to join them.

Kate put her hand on Rick's arm. "This is Sam's pilot and my flight instructor, Rick Sanders," she said. "He was kind enough to escort me home."

Rick cringed inside. Hearing her refer to him as her flight instructor made him feel like an asset. Logic told him she was not going to introduce him as her lover, but nevertheless, the reality of the situation stung his pride.

"This is Patrick," Kate said, indicating her butler. "And this is Cora." The two domestics nodded in unison.

Rick felt uncomfortable standing in a lineup with the two servants. Was there something he was supposed to do or say? He had thought of nothing else on the flight home but his desire to be alone with Kate. Now, while Patrick and Cora filled her in on the events of the previous ten days, he stood awkwardly beside her with just one thought, *This house is too goddamn big.*

All Kate wanted was a hot bath and a cup of tea. But despite her exhaustion, she stood in the driveway and listened while Cora wrung her hands and delivered the details.

"Mr. Randolph's son was here, taking pictures of everything in the house the day after the story of Mr. Randolph's passing was on the news. He said nothing should be removed from the home without his permission."

"Don't worry, Cora," Kate said. "No one is taking anything out of the house." She turned to Patrick. "There's a box in the front seat of my car. Please put it upstairs in Mr. Randolph's study. You can set it on the floor by the fireplace." She looked at Cora. "I have a bag in the trunk. Would you mind putting it in my room? I'll unpack later."

When the servants left, Kate turned to Rick. "Sam's son has a one track mind. How much money did his father leave him, and how fast can he get his hands on it?"

Rick said nothing.

"I don't know what provisions Sam made for me in his will, but I'll find out soon enough."

"Stop worrying," Rick said. "It's not like you'll be homeless."

His words made her flinch. "Is something wrong? You seem upset."

He gestured around the courtyard. "It's just that my life is very simple next to yours."

His icy expression unnerved her. "Look," she said. "I'm the same person I was before you knew where I lived." She didn't know the cause of his peculiar mood, but she hoped it would pass.

He stood there, silent.

"I'd invite you to come in," she said, "but it's too dangerous. The servants would know, and with all the harassment I'm anticipating from Derek, appearances count right now."

His expression remained indifferent. "Don't worry about it."

Kate frowned as she looked up at him. "I don't...."

He cleared his throat. "I need to get home."

She couldn't let him leave like this. "Perhaps I could come to your place tomorrow. We could have dinner."

Rick frowned. "My place is a breadbox compared to this."

"It's not your breadbox that interests me. It's you."

He fell silent again.

Aching to touch him, Kate changed the subject. "Thank you for following me home."

"No problem." Rick shrugged.

Rattled by the distance he seemed determined to put between them, Kate fought the tears stinging her eyes.

They were both quiet, and then he made an effort with a weak smile. "I'm sorry. I'm just tired."

Kate nodded, desperate to make things right between them. "I know. It's been a long day."

"I'll call you tomorrow. Get some rest."

"I will," she said.

She waved as he disappeared down the driveway. Her heart sank a bit more when Rick didn't wave back.

Kate exhaled a deep breath of exasperation. "I haven't even unpacked, Derek," she said into the telephone. "Let's wait until the hurdle of the memorial service is over. It's only two more days." She shook her head. "You've lost your father. But whatever you may have thought of Sam's and my marriage, I've had a loss too, not to mention the humiliation of having my husband die in another woman's bed."

"I'm sure you'll get over it," Derek said.

Talking with Derek Randolph exhausted her. She'd never known anyone who lived in a more egocentric universe. Picking up her vodka and tonic, she placed the icy glass against her temple, hoping to ease her headache.

"You'll get the house, Derek, but I'm not going to let you bully me," Kate said.

"And I said you should start packing."

She set her drink down on the coffee table and stood, crossing the room to pace in front of the fireplace while he raged at her.

Her lips tightened. "Fine. Have Sam's attorney call me."

She should have slammed down the phone. Instead, she placed it in its cradle on the table behind the couch, flopped onto the sofa, and answered it when it rang again two seconds later.

"Hello."

"Kate, it's Roberta, from Safe Haven. I just wanted to let you know how sorry I was to hear about your loss."

Kate answered five more calls, accepting condolences from two more volunteers at Safe Haven, her hairdresser, a neighbor, and Sam's secretary. She finally took the phone off the hook.

There was a knock on the door. Patrick entered the room, carrying a silver tray with a smoked chicken sandwich and a tomato salad. He unrolled a linen placemat onto the coffee table, and placed Kate's dinner on it, along with a napkin and silverware.

"Can I get you anything else?" he asked.

Kate sat forward on the couch, unfolded her napkin and draped it across her lap. "Everything's fine, Patrick. Thank you."

The butler poured her a glass of Pelligrino and left the room, closing the door behind him.

Kate took a bite of the sandwich, the savory chicken satisfying her hunger. She pondered Rick's behavior. He'd surprised her, and a troubling thought plagued her. Santomar's magic had ignited their passion, but would the emotions born on the tropical island be allowed to grow, or would they wither like an untended garden now that they were home?

Chapter 18

With Brandy beside her, Kate climbed the curved staircase, fatigue and Sam's absence weighing heavily on her. Although he'd traveled constantly during their marriage, he'd always found his way home. This time, however, he wouldn't be coming home.

At the top of the stairs, the golden retriever turned toward the bedroom, but Kate noticed the light on in Sam's study. She walked to the doorway and peered into the room. Everything was just as he had left it. She entered the walnut paneled room and walked to the center, making a slow pirouette as she surveyed the distinctly masculine space. The study, comfortably furnished with two dark green leather sofas and matching leather chairs, contained a floor-to-ceiling wall of bookshelves that held reference books, history tomes, and novels. A rolling ladder attached to a shiny brass rail at the ceiling insured easy access to the volumes lining the highest shelf. Opposite the bookshelves, a wall of French doors opened onto a balcony overlooking Emerald Bay.

She felt strange, like a little girl in the principal's office. She had never entered this room without Sam being present. Strolling to the box Patrick had placed on the floor near the fireplace, she knelt and untied the black twine, letting it fall onto the Persian carpet. Then she unwrapped the plain paper, exposing a corrugated cardboard container. Lifting the lid, she reached inside. Grasping the heavy bronze urn by its handles, she pried it out of the box, set it on Sam's desk, and gave it a tender pat.

"For the time being, I think you'll be most comfortable here." Then, she crossed the room, turned out the light, and shut the door.

Trailing her fingertips along the balustrade that lined the upper gallery, she walked to the end of the hallway and through the double doors. She bypassed the bedroom, moving into her dressing room where her suitcase lay on the floor next to the shopping bag with the red biplane cookie jar. Kate bent to look at it. It was the last gift Sam had given her. She sighed, imagining it sitting atop a kitchen counter, somewhere away from this mansion that had been her home for the last six years. She placed the ceramic jar on her dressing table, then turned her attention to unpacking.

Neatly folded inside her suitcase was the mystery dress. She removed it and hugged it close, remembering how Sam liked to joke about it. Tears filled her eyes when she thought about the good times they had shared. She had no idea how long he'd been cheating on her. At this point, she doubted it mattered. All she knew was he'd died too young, and she would miss him. She took a deep breath, wiped her eyes, and draped the dress over the back of the chaise lounge so that the housekeeper would know it needed cleaning and pressing.

When she pulled a pair of sandals from the suitcase, they brushed against the interior storage pocket. Kate heard a crinkling sound. Stretching open the elastic pouch, she peered inside. She retrieved a piece of paper torn from a yellow legal pad and folded into thirds. She immediately recognized it.

One afternoon during their last visit to Santomar together, she and Sam had been lounging by the pool. While Kate worked a crossword puzzle, Sam made notes on a yellow legal pad for an upcoming meeting with his Texas oil industry cronies. She had finally noticed that Sam had stopped his scribbling to look at her.

She smiled at him. "What?"

"Derek hasn't been down here since the year I built this place," Sam said.

"He's young. He likes the beaches on the French Riviera. St. Tropez is where the action is."

"You're young, and you like it here."

"I don't like it here...I love it here. It's heaven on earth. I wish we never had to go back to California."

Kate watched Sam turn his attention to the ocean. For a while he appeared to be deep in thought, then he flipped open a fresh page and began to write again.

When he finished, he tore the piece of paper from the pad.

"Marta," he called out to the cook who'd just brought them a pitcher of iced tea.

"Yes, Mr. Sam?"

"Please get John and come back here with him."

"What's going on?" Kate asked.

"I've never gotten around to making out my will." Sam shook his head. "Bill Casey keeps hounding me, and I'm going to take care of it as soon as I get home, but this is one thing I absolutely must do...and right now."

Kate put her hand on Sam's arm. "Let's handle this when we get home," she said.

"No." Sam sat straight up. "Derek has no feelings for Santomar. I want to make sure he never gets his hands on it. He'd sell it off in two seconds flat to a developer. When I die," Sam said, "I want this place to go to someone who loves it as much as I do."

Kate refocused on her crossword puzzle. Talk of death bothered her. "Sam, we're on vacation. Let's not discuss this now."

Marta and John hurried to Sam's chair.

Sam held out the yellow piece of paper and his pen to the couple. "I want you both to witness my signature," he said. "Please sign your names, provide your legal address, and date the bottom."

After they'd signed the paper, the couple retreated into the house. Sam folded the paper into thirds, then held it out to Kate.

"I want to be cremated," he said. "And then I want

you to bring my ashes back here and scatter them on top of Lookout Mountain. It's the highest point on the island. I'll have a three hundred and sixty degree view."

Kate ignored the paper. "Do you have to keep going on about dying?"

He looked at her, his expression earnest. "I'm giving you Santomar, but you won't be free to move on after I'm gone unless you do this for me." He thrust the impromptu bequest into her hands. "Promise me you'll scatter my ashes on Lookout Mountain, Kate."

Kate gripped the paper, Sam's gaze holding her captive. She finally understood the importance of his request. "I promise," she had said. And she had meant it.

Kate reread Sam's handwritten letter, which gave Santomar to her. She pressed it to her heart. Tears slipped down her cheeks. "Bless you, Sam."

She refolded the paper and slid it into a drawer with her scarves, finished unpacking, and then got ready for bed. Walking into the bedroom, she noticed the turned-down bed and the kindling and logs in the fireplace. Just like always.

Fighting the urge for sleep, she crossed the room and reached for the antique match striker that sat atop the carved mantle. She pulled a match from the center of the oversized crystal globe, drew the head down the serrations, and watched it erupt into an orange flame. She knelt on the cold marble hearth, and lowered the burning match to the kindling. The fireplace crackled as it sprang to life, sending a column of smoke up the chimney. The aroma of piñon pine filled the room. With her gaze fixed on the dancing flames, Kate said a prayer for Sam, and renewed her promise to fulfill his wish.

Two days later, Sam's memorial service took place at noon at the Laguna Presbyterian Church. Relatives, friends and business associates filled the pews, with the overflow crowd listening to the service from speakers set up on the sidewalk. Kate held Janet's hand throughout the eulogies. Rick, Lila, and Bob Hansen sat several rows behind her, the house staff near the back of the chapel. Derek Randolph sat across the aisle. The rest of the crowd blurred into nameless familiar faces and strangers.

When the service ended, the mourners moved to the house in Emerald Bay. The guests, many of whom Kate didn't know, jammed the dining room, where the caterers had set up a lavish buffet.

Kate slipped into the kitchen to catch her breath.

Janet cornered her there. "Here," she said, holding out a goblet.

Kate shook her head. "No thanks."

"It's ginger ale."

Kate accepted the soft drink and took a sip.

"I've got to tell you something." Janet led Kate to a quiet corner of the butler's panty. "I think you need to get a lawyer."

Kate leaned against the wall. "I'm so overwhelmed, I just can't think of that now."

"I've been talking to Derek," Janet said. "I'm certain he's going to try to screw you out of any money Sam left you."

"Thanks for looking out for me." Kate squeezed her friend's hand. "I will consult with an attorney, but right now I've got a house full of people to feed."

The guests ate and drank well into the night, many remarking on Kate's graciousness. Kate felt on the verge of a meltdown, but she continued to attend to her guests. She meandered the house and gardens, visiting with as many people as possible, thanking them for coming. At a quarter to eleven, the last person left and Kate tumbled into bed.

The doorbell jarred her from her slumber. Glancing at the clock, she saw it was after nine. Brandy's low-pitched bark suggested the golden retriever didn't care for the unexpected visitor. Kate swung her legs over the side of the bed and reached for her bathrobe. Knotting the belt at her waist, she walked through the double doors leading to the upper gallery. She recognized the voice echoing from the foyer below, and she steadied herself on the railing as she hurried down the curved staircase.

Patrick and Cora came into view along with Derek

Randolph. Cora bent toward the dog, trying to calm her. "Shush."

"It's alright," Kate said. "I'm up."

The servants gave her a "we're in the other room" look and left Kate alone with her stepson.

Derek's aloofness throughout her marriage to Sam didn't prevent her from offering sympathy over the loss of his father. She crossed the foyer and put her arms around him, giving him a hug. "Hello, Derek, how are you today?"

Derek stiffened. He reminded Kate of a prissy British banker in his dark pinstripe suit. She had never seen him dressed any other way. *He never lets his guard down.*

Taking a step back from her, Derek smoothed the front of his suit jacket. "I came to pick up my father's ashes."

"Your father wanted his ashes spread on Santomar," Kate said.

Derek's reply dripped contempt. "My father wanted to be buried in the family crypt with my mother."

"That's not true." *Stay calm*, Kate told herself.

Derek snarled, "I want those ashes now."

Kate exhaled slowly. "The last time we were there, your father made me promise to bring his ashes back to the island."

"I don't believe you. You're just trying to keep yourself involved, because you think there's some money in it for you."

Kate moved her hands to her hips. Although she

had done her best to forge a relationship with Derek, he never masked his disdain for her. She steeled herself for a showdown. "Derek, don't let your greed impair your reasoning."

Taking a menacing step toward her, Derek poked his finger into Kate's shoulder. "Get those ashes for me now, or I'll have a court order in one hour for you to do it."

Kate's pulse quickened. "I can't betray an oath I made to your father."

Derek's eyes blazed with hatred. "Take your pick. Now, or an hour from now."

Kate stood fast, her heart pounding.

He lifted an eyebrow and growled, "I said, now."

How could she let this spoiled brat force her to break her promise to Sam? She didn't budge.

Derek stormed toward the library."I'll find them myself." He barged through the double doors.

A moment later, he marched back into the foyer, Brandy close behind him and barking. Derek booted the dog in her side. Brandy yelped.

"Stop this. Are you crazy?" Kate rushed to comfort Brandy.

Derek headed toward the staircase. Kate cut him off. Worried that he might strike her or the dog, she put her free hand out to stop him.

"Wait here," she said, her voice softening. She knew it was useless to argue. "I'll get them for you."

When she returned with the bronze urn, she held it out to him. Her hands trembled. "Your father loved you. I can't believe you can disregard his wishes."

Ignoring her remark, Derek snatched the urn from her. "My attorney will get in touch with you," he sneered. "I want you out of here as soon as possible."

She watched a triumphant smile spread across his thin-lipped face before he spun around and marched out the door with the urn clutched under his arm.

Chapter 19

Lila was bent over one of the rose bushes outside the Executive Air office. She snipped a thick stem, heavy with a colossal *Mr. Lincoln* bloom, then held the red blossom to her nose, inhaling its perfume. She looked up when she heard the whine of a high performance car engine. Kate pulled into a nearby parking space. Lila strolled over to greet her, wondering if there might be some potential for happiness for Rick with Kate. *That would be perfect*, she thought.

"Hi, honey," Lila said. "Ready to get back in the saddle?"

Kate swivelled out of her car. "I know it's only been two weeks since Sam died, but I'm afraid if I don't go for the type-rating now, I may never get it. I'm sure the moment Derek Randolph remembers the Lear, he'll put my name at the top of the 'no fly' list."

She locked her car, then leaned down to smell the rose. "Um-mm, delicious," she said, squinting in the bright sunlight, tiny lines framing her aquamarine eyes.

Lila put her arm around Kate. "How are you doing in that big house all by yourself?"

"I'm okay. At least I still have a place to live. But Derek is circling like a buzzard."

As the two women walked toward the building, Kate sighed. "I may have to ask Bob for a job once I get my type-rating."

Lila smiled, opening the door for Kate. "You'll have to ask Rick," she said. "He does all the hiring around here." Lila noticed a change in Kate's expression at the mention of Rick's name.

Crossing the room to her desk, Lila plucked several thorns from the roses before she dropped the long-stemmed beauties into a waiting crystal vase filled with water. "There," she said. "I love roses on my desk." She sat down and scrutinized Kate, who leaned against the counter in front of her. Lila decided to play detective. "So, what did the three of you do, stuck on that island for so long?" she asked.

"Well," Kate said. "Up until we heard about Sam, we were having a pretty good time. We explored the island, had our fortunes read, and tried some of the local cuisine." She shrugged. "And we spent a lot of time on the beach."

Lila nodded.

"Oh, yes." The soft expression on Kate's face spoke volumes to Lila. "One day, I took Rick for a sail to a secret lagoon."

Lila rested her chin on her hands, and, locking eyes with Kate, donned her most innocent smile. "Rick is like a son to me," she said. "Great guy, isn't he?"

Kate lowered her gaze and sighed. "Yes, he's wonderful."

Lila felt like slapping her own thigh in triumph. The look in Kate's eyes and the sound in her voice told Lila what she wanted to know. No doubt about it. There was more to the story of what had happened on the island than Rick had told her.

The sound of footsteps caused both women to turn. Dressed in his captain's uniform and radiating sex appeal, Rick came striding down the hallway.

"Hello, ladies," he said. And when he winked, Lila beamed inside; her Rick was crazy about the beautiful widow.

Three hours later, after precision instrument landings at Mojave, Chino, and Palm Springs, Kate touched down at John Wayne Airport. She knew she'd aced every approach. Slowing the Lear, she pulled off the runway at the first exit.

"Great job," Rick said while they waited for their taxi clearance. "I don't think there's anything else I can teach you. Now, it's all about racking up the hours in that seat."

Kate grinned. "So you think I'm ready for my check-ride?"

"I do," he said warmly. "After some preparation for the oral exam, you'll do fine."

Exhilarated, Kate taxied the plane to the hangar, then swung it into position so the maintenance crew could pull it inside. She shut down the engines, keeping her feet on the brakes until the wheels were chocked.

Unbuckling his seat belt, Rick crawled out of the second seat and swung open the door. Kate followed him out of the plane.

She hadn't seen Rick or spoken to him since the memorial service on Saturday. When she made arrangements for her flight lesson, she'd taken it for granted that afterward they'd be spending the evening together. Now, she stood watching him fold the stairs and lock the door, feeling awkward that he had yet to mention anything about getting together with her.

When he turned around, she touched his arm. "Are we having dinner tonight?"

He averted his gaze. "I was gone for ten days. I've got a lot of catch-up work here at the office."

Shock and disappointment made the blood pound in her temples. *What's wrong?* she wanted to ask, but pride kept her silent. She didn't say a word, just kept pace with his long strides across the tarmac. During the previous two weeks, her husband had died in his mistress's bed and her stepson was threatening to evict her. Now, the only man who had ever made her feel like a real woman seemed determined to give her the brush-off.

Rick stuffed his hands into his pockets. He hated himself for acting this way. He glanced at Kate out of the corner of his eye as she silently walked beside him. Her skin and her hair reflected the golden radiance of the setting sun. God, she was beautiful. He craved her as much now as he had in Santomar. Why had he lied and said he was busy tonight?

The scent of her perfume snagged his attention and tantalized his senses. He needed to stop playing games, because, more than anything, he longed for this woman in ways he'd never experienced before.

Turning to face her, he offered an apologetic smile. "I can come in early tomorrow to catch up. I want you to come to my place for dinner tonight."

Her gaze rose to meet his, and a smile spread across her face. "Are you sure?" She brushed a strand of hair away from her eyes.

Removing a business card from his wallet, Rick pulled a pen out of his shirt pocket. He wrote something on the back of the card, then handed it to her. "This is my address," he said. "Come over around seven."

Kate looked at the card. Next to his address, he had written, "Can't wait for dessert."

Rick's ocean-front condo looked out from the top floor of a three-story Mediterranean building in the heart of Laguna. Strolling about his home, Kate felt a sense of excitement. It was a stylish space, distinctively masculine. In the living room, two black leather Barcelona chairs faced a beige tweed sofa. A wooden bowl on the coffee table overflowed with lemons from a tree on the patio. Four modern chairs, upholstered in the same fabric as the sofa, surrounded a dining table near the windows.

Kate recognized a Scott Moore print hanging above the fireplace. She smiled at the surreal juxtaposition of a couple enjoying a candlelit dinner inside a Ronzoni lasagna box, with a three-story bottle of wine nearby.

She took a sip of cold Chardonnay and wandered into Rick's bedroom.

"After I bought the place," he called from the kitchen, "I knocked down the wall between the two bedrooms and made it into one big one."

A king-sized bed faced a wall of glass that opened to a broad balcony originating outside the living room. A home office was tucked into one corner.

Kate walked back to the kitchen. "Your place is so neat."

He laughed. "What did you expect, a frat house?"

"That's not what I meant. I was giving you a compliment."

She peeked into the laundry room just off the kitchen. A neatly pressed camouflage shirt hung from a coat hanger. Kate picked up the shirt and held it out to Rick.

"You going on safari?" she asked.

"Every so often I help a friend of mine who flies into war zones." Rick said.

"What?" It wasn't that she hadn't heard him. She was trying to wrap her mind around what he'd said.

Rick stood at the counter arranging a platter of sushi. "We fly a big cargo plane, a C-130. Sometimes it's too dangerous to land, so when we're over the target, a kicker, a guy in the back who's hooked up to a harness, opens the side door and kicks out boxes of hospital supplies, food and sometimes guns."

"Doesn't everything smash when it hits the ground?"

"We fly slow and low, about two hundred feet. Sometimes we find shrubbery in the landing gear." He explained all this with nonchalance, as if describing how a florist delivers an orchid.

She cringed. Her expression must have reflected the alarm she felt.

"There are lots of bad guys out there, Kate. The good guys need help. Some of the flights are financed by our own government."

"It just sounds so scary."

She replaced the shirt and returned to the kitchen. She came up behind Rick, circled her arms about his waist, and tried to erase the mental image of him on some God-forsaken runway.

He seemed to sense her thought. "Come on," he said.

He grasped the sushi platter with one hand and the bottle of Chardonnay with the other. "Can you get my wine?"

Kate picked up his glass and followed him to the patio, where a table had been set for two.

She watched him move aside a vase of blue cornflowers and two votive candles to make room for the platter. After lighting the candles, he joined her at the railing. She held out his glass.

Taking a swallow of the Chardonnay, he said, "I never get tired of this view."

Kate peered over the edge of the balcony. The sound of the surf three stories below conjured memories of Santomar. To her right, Main Beach appeared deserted except for a couple walking hand-in-hand along the boardwalk. To the south, the glittering lights of the shoreline resembled a necklace fit for a queen.

Turning to face Rick, Kate leaned back against the railing, a gentle sea breeze caressing her skin. "There used to be a restaurant called Victor Hugo's on the bluffs north of town."

"I've heard of it."

"When I was a little girl, my mother took me there for lunch. She said when she was young, it was the kind of place where women wore hats and white gloves." She sighed, the memory triggering long-forgotten insecurities. "We sat outside under a blue canvas awning beside the rose garden. After my father died, I worried constantly that my mother would die too, and there'd be no one to take care of me. But that day, I remember worrying about something else. I kept wondering if she had enough money to pay the bill."

Rick gathered Kate into his arms. She pressed her head against his shoulder, grateful for the comfort he provided. His embrace wiped away all traces of her bittersweet memory. She also recalled seeking out Sam for comfort after her mother died. Was she doing the same thing again?

Rick's warm breath fluttered on her skin where he had pushed back her hair to reach the sensitive area at the side of her neck. "Victor Hugo's closed years ago," he said, "but the building is still there, and so is the rose garden." His lips brushed her cheek. "It's a Mexican restaurant now. I'll take you there."

His mouth found hers. She marveled at his kiss, sweet and lustful at the same time. He drew her close, his arms circling her waist. She melted into his hard, strong body.

He took her hand, guiding her to the glass door outside his bedroom. He slid open the door, leading her inside toward the bed. Her mind and body fused into a single entity, swirling in a whirlpool of heat and desire, capable of only one thought. *Rick*.

"You know what they say?" he whispered, his blue smoldering eyes and seductive smile sending a shudder of ecstasy through her. "Life is short." He unbuttoned his shirt. "Let's have dessert first."

The following morning, Kate passed the flight test for commercial pilots, the last hurdle in qualifying for her check ride in the Lear. That afternoon, her new commercial pilot's license tucked inside her wallet, she met Derek Randolph in the office of Bill Casey, the family's attorney.

Derek was already seated in Bill's office when Kate arrived. "Here for your lottery winnings?" Derek said.

Kate didn't bother to answer him.

Bill Casey, clad in an olive green suit, rose from his desk like a frog popping off a lily pad. Taking several long strides, he stood before Kate with an outstretched hand and a smarmy grin.

"So nice to see you, dear," he crooned, guiding Kate to a comfortable armchair. "These things are never pleasant, so we'll try to run through this as quickly as possible."

The attorney returned to his desk, opening a bulky manila file.

Kate settled into the chair, smoothing the skirt of her red Armani suit.

"As you know," Bill said, "I was Sam's attorney for years. I now represent Derek. We're trying to sort out Sam's estate as quickly as possible, but it's all rather complicated."

Bill drew a document from the file, placing it on the desk in front of him. "I'll get right to the point." The lawyer adjusted his glasses and looked directly at her. "The reason you never had a pre-nup is that Sam's estate was protected from any divorce settlement by a series of trusts that have been in place for years, long before the two of you were married. Based upon the length of your marriage, and the amount of Sam's assets, five million dollars is the figure Derek has come up with to settle your interests in the estate. Derek would pay it out to you over a ten year period," Bill Casey said.

Five hundred thousand dollars a year for ten years. That was more money than Kate could have imagined. She was stunned, and comforted.

Bill Casey squirmed in his seat and peered at Kate. "As an alternative—" he cleared his throat "—Derek thought it might make more sense to clear this all up now and rather than wait for your money, you could take it up front, all at once. Sort of the way the lottery works." The attorney chuckled. "If you would like a lump sum, he would give you two and a half million now."

What a conniver, Kate thought about Derek. She had read the article in *Forbes Magazine*. She knew that Sam's estate was worth close to a billion dollars, and Derek was scrounging for a pittance. Derek's gaze darted between the attorney's file and Kate's eyes.

"Thank you," Kate said, her heart pounding with relief. "I'm sure Sam would want me to be patient and do things in a conservative way. The ten year pay-out will be fine."

When Derek shrugged his shoulders, it seemed to be a cue for the attorney to continue.

Bill Casey cleared his throat. "The house in Emerald Bay is being put up for sale. You can stay there for the next thirty days."

Even though Kate was prepared for bad news, this came as a jolt.

"I never expected to stay in the house," she said. "But why can't I live there until it's sold? It's not like Derek is going to move in."

Derek glared. "I want you gone from my life."

Kate turned to Bill. "I can watch over things while it's on the market. It's better than leaving it empty."

The attorney took a deep breath. "She has a point, Derek."

"Alright," Derek said, his tone impatient. "Let's get on with this."

At least they haven't mentioned anything about my use of the Lear, Kate thought.

Bill Casey closed the manila folder. "When you leave the house, Kate, the only items you can take with you are your clothes. Everything else must remain in the residence."

Kate pursed her lips. "What about personal gifts that my husband gave to me?" she asked. "Clearly, Sam wanted me to have them."

"Well, obviously if you have some proof that certain things belong to you, a bill of sale perhaps...." The attorney didn't get a chance to finish his sentence.

Derek jumped up to face Kate. "My father didn't make any provisions for you to take anything out of the house, so don't get any ideas. And that Porsche you drive is in my father's name." Derek sneered. "So leave the keys on the kitchen counter."

No stranger to Derek's disagreeable nature, Kate still felt shocked by his cruelty. She swallowed hard and opened her purse, pulling out the folded yellow sheet. Kate spoke in a controlled voice, looking directly at Derek. "The last time your father and I were in Santomar, he told me he wanted me to have the place." She held up the document. "He signed this paper, which leaves the property to me."

"My father would never give you that house," Derek hissed.

"Well, he did, and this proves it."

Derek grabbed for the paper. He missed when Kate turned away from him, protecting the bequest contained in the hand-written document.

Bill Casey chimed in, "This is very irregular. Sam didn't say a word about it to me. Surely I would have known if he wanted you to have that property."

"Not only did he want me to have it, he made me promise to bring his ashes back there." Glaring at Derek, Kate raised her voice for the first time since the meeting had begun. "He never wanted to be in the family crypt. You deliberately defied his wishes."

Derek's eyes narrowed into murky slits, completing the rattlesnake image. "Who are you, Little Miss Psychic?"

"Calm down," Casey said. "Let's keep this civil."

Derek ignored him. "You don't know what my father wanted, and you'll never get your hands on Santomar."

The possibility of this injustice shocked Kate into action. She stuffed the paper back into her purse.

"Derek, I'm sick of your bullying." She stood, and smoothed her skirt. "You bulldoze your way through life, hurting and intimidating whoever you please. Well, you're not doing it to me."

Kate marched across the room, opened the door, and turned to Derek and Bill. "My lawyer will call you," she said before she walked out.

She left the building and headed toward her car. It had felt good, and a little scary, to say those things to Derek. But now she had a slight problem. Every lawyer she knew worked for Sam. She didn't have one of her own, but she knew where to go in order to find one.

Chapter 20

Lila pulled a client's itinerary off the laser printer, then swivelled her chair to face Kate, who was seated across the desk from her.

"My boss knows everyone in this town," Lila said, feeling a maternal concern for Kate. "Don't you worry."

"You're sure?" Kate nervously twisted the strap of her handbag.

"Come on," Lila said. "Everything's gonna be okay. Bob'll make sure you get a good lawyer." Lila stretched out her hand, cradling a bowl of rainbow-colored candies. "Jelly bean?"

Kate shook her head. "No, thanks."

Setting the bowl back on her desk, Lila fixed her gaze on Kate. She liked the young woman's combination of warmth and spunk. She was so perfect for Rick.

Kate rubbed her temple. "I appreciate your help. I

didn't know where to turn. I could never have gone to any of Sam's friends."

"You came to the right place." Lila patted Kate's hand. "By the way," she said, using her most nonchalant voice, "I know about you and Rick."

Kate's eyebrows lifted. "You do?"

Lila slapped her thigh and grinned. "Well, I do now."

Kate flushed. Her hand flew to her forehead. "Oh, God. No one's supposed to know about this. He could lose his job."

Walking around to the front of her desk, Lila put her hand on Kate's shoulder and whispered. "Don't worry. Your secret's safe with me."

When Kate looked up at the older woman, the expression on her face and the fire in her eyes told Lila all she needed to know. "It's okay, Kate," Lila said. "I love him, too. Just in a different way."

Bob watched Kate shift in her chair on the opposite side of his desk.

"Yeah," he said into the phone. "She's got it in writing." His gaze returned to the yellow sheet of paper Kate had placed in front of him. "It's in his own hand. He even had two witnesses sign it."

Bob sat back in his chair, listening and nodding his head. "Just a second," he said, covering the mouthpiece. He looked at Kate. "Are you free at ten tomorrow morning?"

Kate nodded.

"That'll be fine. I'll bring her over," Bob said. "Thanks, Max." He hung up the phone. "I've known Max Abbot since he was a kid. He's a piranha in the courtroom. If anyone can get you that house in the islands, it's Max."

She'd have a bundle then, Bob thought—maybe enough to honor Sam's deal and bail him out of his mess.

Max Abbot's waiting room was stylish and comfortable. Kate was glad Bob had insisted on meeting her here in Century City to personally introduce her to the attorney.

"Before this area became a high-rise Mecca for rich and famous lawyers," Bob explained, "it functioned as the back lot of Twentieth Century Fox Studios." He clearly enjoyed playing tour guide. "Max Abbot's office stands on the exact spot where Cary Grant appeared in drag in a WAC's uniform for *I Was A Male War Bride*. And where Marilyn Monroe, as the gold-digging Loralie Lee, crooned "Diamonds are a Girl's Best Friend" in *Gentlemen Prefer Blondes*."

Kate could barely register his comments. Her stomach was twisted into knots. She watched Bob stroll over to chat with the receptionist. At precisely ten o'clock, Max Abbot's secretary appeared and ushered the two visitors into his office, twenty-four flights above Century Park East.

Max, who appeared to be in his early forties, looked up from the stack of papers in front of him. He flashed a winning smile, then rose from his desk, a subtle limp slowing his progress across the maroon Persian carpet. Dressed in grey slacks, a white shirt and a red bow tie that matched the suspenders holding up his pants, the dapper attorney looked like an actor left behind when Twentieth Century Fox abdicated the property to the real estate developers.

"Good to see you, Bob," Max Abbot said. The two men clasped hands in a hearty greeting.

"You, too, Max. How's your old man?"

"Ornery as ever." The lawyer chuckled.

"Max's dad and I go way back," Bob said to Kate. He put his hand on her shoulder. "Max, this is Kate Randolph. Kate, let me introduce you to Max Abbot, the best man for this job."

"Hello." Kate extended her hand to the attorney, who looked about as formidable as a child's stuffed bear.

Max clasped her hand in both of his. Although a simple handshake, Kate felt comforted by the strength and sensitivity it conveyed.

"Please, sit down." Max motioned Kate and Bob to the camel-colored leather chairs opposite his desk.

"Would you prefer to talk to Max alone?" Bob asked Kate. "I have an appointment in Santa Monica at noon. I can head out there early."

"No, please stay," Kate said.

Kate and Bob watched Max limp to his black swivel chair. The handsome attorney held onto the desk and lowered himself into the seat. Kate wondered what had caused his infirmity.

Max faced her, his back to the floor-to-ceiling windows that framed Santa Monica Bay from the Palos Verdes peninsula to Malibu.

"That's quite a view," Kate said, looking past the lawyer to the panorama behind him. "But I think your desk is facing the wrong direction."

"It's intentional," Max said. "I don't like to be distracted from the matters at hand." His face relaxed into a friendly smile. "Now, young lady, let's talk about you. When Bob called yesterday, he gave me an overview of your problem. Why don't you tell me, in your own words, what you think I can do for you."

"My husband died several weeks ago," Kate said. Embarrassed by the circumstances of Sam's death, she studied the contents of her purse. "You've probably read about it in the papers." She fished the yellow paper out of her bag, finally lifting her gaze to the lawyer's face. "He owned a home on a large tract of land in the Caribbean, and he wanted me to have it."

She handed the paper to Max. "His son, along with an attorney, told me this document is invalid. I'd like your opinion."

Max read the bequest, then pressed a button on his phone. Almost immediately, the office door opened and a young assistant appeared at his side. He held out the yellow paper. "I need a copy of this," he said. The assistant disappeared with the paper.

Max folded his hands on his desk. "What I think,

young lady, is that these men are trying to cheat you out of what was meant to be yours."

"You do?" She heaved a sigh and relaxed into her chair. Perhaps it was the relief of having someone on her side, but Kate suddenly felt faint. She leaned forward, lowering her forehead to her knees as spots danced before her eyes. "I'm sorry." She took a steadying breath and slowly straightened. "Too much stress."

Max Abbot's brow furrowed. "I don't doubt it. I know what Derek Randolph is capable of."

"What do you mean?" Kate asked.

"I had a run-in with him a long time ago."

Kate turned to Bob, whose smug expression added to her confusion. "Did you know about this?"

Bob nodded, darting a glance at Max. "I did," he said. "It's one of the reasons I thought he'd be perfect for the job. I knew he'd go after Derek Randolph with both barrels."

"What's between me and Derek Randolph is history," Max said. He addressed Kate. "Let's get on with your problem." He leaned back in his chair. "Where is your husband's will?"

Kate's gaze moved between the two men before she exhaled a long breath. "I don't think he had one," she said. "His attorney was always after him to make one but...." Her voice trailed off.

"Right," said Max. "Everyone thinks they have lots of time, until they don't."

"Derek doesn't want the place," Kate said. "He just doesn't want me to have it. He never went down there. And he ignored his father's request to have his ashes scattered there. He's behaving despicably, and I...." She paused when the assistant reappeared with the copy Max had requested.

The lawyer handed Kate the original. "If you don't have a safe deposit box, get one. And put this in it." Max tapped his copy with his index finger. "Derek Randolph doesn't know what he's up against. We're gonna demand a whole lot more than that house."

"I don't want anything I'm not entitled to," Kate said. "I just want what my husband left me."

Max Abbot's eyes darkened. "Don't worry," he said. "You'll get your house." He looked at the ceiling for a moment, lost in a thought or a memory he did not share with his client. Then, he sat forward and smiled at Kate. "You came to the right place." He sounded eager for the coming battle.

After a stop at a lobby kiosk for a cup of Starbuck's and a blueberry muffin, Kate reclaimed her car from the valet in the parking garage. As she drove down Santa Monica Boulevard, she mulled over Max Abbot's comment about a past run-in with Derek. She swung the car onto a side street, and fished out her iPhone. No juice. Too curious to wait until she got home to see what Google turned up, she headed north toward UCLA, her alma mater.

Kate knew every inch of the campus and soon found a parking space just off Hilgard Avenue. She slid her credit card into the meter, gave herself enough time to stave off the ubiquitous parking police, then wound her way through narrow pathways and across broad plazas until she came to the University Research Library. When she pulled open the heavy door, the musty aroma of aging paper and ink engulfed her. Inside were millions of volumes, arranged neatly and tightly like sardines in a can—five floors of information, indexed and cross-referenced. Heading toward the bank of computers to her left, she spotted an empty chair and sat down.

She typed "Derek Randolph + Max Abbot" into the search box. After a few flutters, the results appeared on the screen—two articles from *The Orange County Register* and one from *The Los Angeles Times*, both twenty years old.

She read the stories directly from the monitor, then studied the accompanying photos of Max. His winning smile hadn't changed, but his young, fresh face spoke to his youth. She sank back in her chair, pondering the news that Derek Randolph was the reason behind Max Abbot's limp.

Chapter 21

Shielding her eyes from the late afternoon sun, Kate sprinted across the Executive Air parking lot, copies of the newspaper articles tucked into her purse. She pushed open the glass door to the passenger lounge, and rushed inside. The room contained half a dozen passengers, all waiting for their planes. Some lounged in club chairs and read magazines, others stood at the window, watching the activity on the tarmac, sipping cold drinks or cups of hot coffee. A well-dressed businessman with the requisite leather briefcase nodded to her as she glided by him.

Kate paused at Lila's desk, then pumped the chrome bell several times with her palm, sending a barrage of high-pitched rings echoing throughout the room. Too impatient to wait, Kate flew down the corridor to the pilot's lounge. Finding it empty, she hurried back to the reception area and pounded the bell again.

The aroma reached her nostrils before she heard the footsteps. Kate turned and saw Lila coming toward her from the long hallway that led to Bob's office and the kitchen. Carrying an enormous bowl of popcorn, Lila waved.

Kate rushed toward her. "Is Bob back from L.A. yet?"

"Calm down," Lila said. "You're gonna drive off all our customers, making such a racket with that bell."

"Is he back?" Kate repeated. She followed Lila to the refreshment table, watching the woman set out the bowl of popcorn and a stack of napkins for the waiting passengers.

Lila took Kate's arm, and led her to a corner of the room. "What's going on?"

Kate sagged, suddenly exhausted. "I need to talk to Bob. Is he here?"

"He's in his office, briefing Steve and Pete. They're leaving on a charter to the Seychelles."

Walking to a nearby chair, Kate flopped down and opened her purse. She unfolded the newspaper articles and showed them to Lila. "This is the lawyer Bob sent me to."

Bob appeared in the hallway with Steve and Pete. Both pilots looked sharp in their starched white shirts and blue ties, the gold braid on their jacket sleeves shining under the bright overhead lights.

Kate stood, straightening the shoulder strap of her purse. She nodded to Bob, who returned her nod.

"Hey, Kate," Steve said. "When are you gonna ditch Rick and go flying with me instead?"

"Don't listen to him," Pete teased. "Let me take you for an E-Ticket ride."

Kate smiled. "By the time you two get back from the Seychelles, I'll have my type-rating and I'll be taking you for a ride."

"Look forward to that." Steve grinned.

Pete agreed. "Me, too."

Kate hugged both men. "Have a great trip."

Bob clasped each man's shoulder and shook their hands. "See you soon, guys."

Steve and Pete waved to Lila before they walked outside to the Falcon 900 that was fueled and ready to go.

Bob's gaze fell on the newspaper articles in Kate's hand. "I suppose you want to talk to me."

She raised her eyebrows. "I certainly do."

Kate sat in Bob's office and studied the framed photo of two shirtless soldiers. They were lifting bottles of beer to each other in a toast, looking as if they stood in a sports bar instead of a Middle-Eastern desert.

"Leon Abbot and I were discharged after we got back to the States," Bob said, pacing between his desk and the bookcase. "He was a lot older than me...had a wife waiting at home for him, and a five-year-old son... Max. The kid became a runner. Made the Olympic team his second year of college. The whole family was set to go to France. Leon could hardly wait to watch his son take the gold in the marathon. Max was a sure thing. Everyone knew it."

Kate handed the picture frame back to Bob. He traced his fingers across the glass, and then put the memory back on the bookshelf.

"Max bicycled ten miles a day," Bob said. "Part of his training routine. When the police measured the skid marks, they estimated the car that hit him was going twice the speed limit." Bob stared out the window, as though watching an instant replay of the event. "His dad broke down when the doctor said he wasn't sure if Max would ever walk again, let alone run. The kid spent two months in the hospital. His hip and both legs were shattered. He had four broken ribs and a punctured lung."

Kate shuddered.

Bob turned away from the window and looked directly at Kate.

"An old man out for a walk was the only eyewitness to the hit and run," he said. "Derek stopped and backed up before he sped away. That's how the guy got his license number." Bob paused and shook his head. "Sam paid off the old guy, who then conveniently forgot what he had seen. Derek's car disappeared. When the district attorney didn't file any charges, everyone suspected he'd been paid off, too."

Bob sat down behind his desk, and drummed his fingertips on the arms of his black swivel chair. "So, that's the story. Max got two years in rehab, and Derek got off."

"Why did you pretend you didn't know Sam when you sold him the Lear?" Kate asked.

"I wasn't pretending. I didn't know him." Bob shrugged. "I only knew what his son had done to my buddy's kid."

Bob stood and walked around his desk, sitting down in the chair next to Kate. "Max deserves this chance to rake Derek over the coals. God knows that son-of-a-bitch deserves it."

"I don't know." Kate shook her head. "I'm grateful to have your help, Bob. But I wish you'd told me ahead of time."

"My apologies, Kate. I should have." Bob leaned closer to her. "But Derek Randolph has plenty of money. Losing some of it is the only way to punish him."

Kate massaged her throbbing temples as she considered Bob's words. "I don't want anything I'm not entitled to. It wouldn't feel right."

Bob's eyes pleaded. "If it makes you that uncomfortable," he said, "you could give some of the money away. Do nice things for other people...people in real need."

Kate relaxed into the chair, mulling over that possibility.

"Please, don't bail on Max now," Bob said. "Let him have his justice."

Kate left Bob's office, feeling torn. Being greedy was not in her nature. But she couldn't help but wonder if there was a reason why, of all the lawyers in town, she'd found herself in Max Abbot's office.

Chapter 22

Kate peered across the stacks of papers at Rick and groaned. "I can't do this anymore." Crossing her arms on the table, she rested her head. "I'm exhausted." She glanced up at the clock on the wall in the conference room. "It's nearly eight. We've been at this since three o'clock. Everyone's gone home, even Lila."

"Come on, Kate," Rick said. "I don't want you to have to do this twice."

She glanced at the table strewn with operational manuals, charts, and flight data, all pertaining to the Lear Kate would fly the next day. The difference between tomorrow's flight and all the others would be that, this time, instead of Rick, the right seat would be occupied by an examiner from the FAA—a nerve-jangling situation for even the most experienced pilot.

Kate closed her eyes. "You know that I know this backwards and forwards."

For a moment, Rick didn't reply. Then, he sighed and got up from his chair. Standing behind her, he leaned down and clasped her shoulders, his warm breath washing across her neck.

"You're right," he said. "If you don't know it by now, you never will. You're gonna do great."

She spun around to look up at him.

"After all, you had a great teacher." He winked at her. "Come on," he said, guiding her out of the chair. "I'm taking you out. We both need a break."

After steaks and salads at Flemings, they strolled through the parking lot toward their cars. Despite the cool night air, Kate felt warmed by Rick's nearness.

"I want you to get a good night's sleep," he said.

"How am I supposed to do that?" Kate replied. "I'm so nervous."

Rick checked his watch, and then slung his arm around her shoulder. "It's only nine-thirty. Why don't I come by your place for a little while?" He grinned. "We'll have to be quiet so the house staff doesn't hear us, but I know something we can do that will help you relax."

At nine o'clock the next morning, Kate breezed through the Executive Air waiting room, energized and excited. Today, she intended to collect her reward for months of arduous work. She had mastered the Lear. She knew every inch of the colossal aircraft, every nuance of its instruments, every subtlety of its control surfaces. By noontime, if everything went right, she would be "Captain Kate."

Unable to contain the grin on her face, she headed toward Lila's desk. Kate looked forward to their visits. Each day when she was finished with her flying lesson, Kate lingered. The two women shared life stories, lunches, and an affection for each other rooted in their mutual love for Rick.

When she saw Lila's expression, Kate sensed something was wrong.

"Bob's in his office with Rick," Lila said. "I'm glad you got here early. They want to talk to you."

Kate's heartbeat quickened. What was going on? She sped down the hall to Bob's office, hesitating at the open doorway. Both men turned at the sound of her knock.

"May I come in?" she asked.

Bob stood behind his desk. "Of course."

Rick strode toward her. He put his hand on the small of her back, guiding her to one of the chairs that faced Bob's desk. They all sat down.

"What's wrong?" she asked.

Rick leaned forward. "We received a call from Derek Randolph this morning. You can't use the Lear anymore."

Kate felt all the wind knocked out of her. "My checkride is off?" She looked at Bob. "No. Not after months of preparation."

The cost of using Sam's plane for her training, which

ran nearly a thousand dollars an hour, had been absorbed by Sam's business. Now that Derek Randolph had denied her that privilege, if she wanted to go flying she would need to rent a plane. Even though she knew she would be well provided for, she didn't have that kind of money. All that work for nothing.

"There's one way you can still do it," Bob said. "You can use Eight Six Juliet Bravo. We have a deal with the owner. We can use it if we pay for the fuel."

Kate knew the plane, the only other Lear like Sam's on the field.

"That's impossible." She shook her head. "How can I fly that plane for an FAA check-ride? I've never even been inside it." She turned to Rick.

"It's just like the plane you've been flying every day for months," he said.

Tears of anger and disappointment welled behind her eyes. She looked down, determined not to cry in front of Bob and Rick. "It's not the same. You know every plane responds differently. And there's no room for mistakes on a check-ride."

Rick put his hand on her arm. "You know that Lear backwards and forwards. You'll never be better prepared than you are right now."

"What good is all my preparation?" She swallowed against the lump in her throat. "I'm sure the cockpit layout is different. I'd be searching all over for instruments and levers."

"It's a little different," Bob conceded, "but nothing you can't handle."

Kate looked up at Rick.

"You can do it," he said. "Either you know it, or you don't. And you know it. A change of machinery won't make any difference." His hint of a smile was irresistible, and got her heart going.

"I've never failed a check ride before," she said.

Rick's voice was soft and soothing. "You're not going to fail." He rose from the chair, pulling her to her feet. "Come on. We've got forty-five minutes before the check airman arrives." He nudged her toward the door. "I'm going to get you a glass of orange juice, then we're going out to the plane so you can memorize the layout."

"That's him," Rick said, pointing to the tall, balding man seated at the far side of the waiting room.

Kate willed the butterflies in her stomach to be still, and stared at the FAA check airman. Dressed in a business suit, his jacket tossed over the chair beside him, he had his briefcase perched on his knees and appeared to be filling out forms.

"He looks pretty nice," Kate said. It came out more like a question than a statement.

She had passed her private, instrument, and commercial check-rides on the first try, but each go-around had been more difficult than the last, and she expected this one to be no different. The orals always proved grueling. If the examiner asked a question you couldn't answer, you felt like a child standing in front of your teacher without your homework. Or worse, like you were in that dream where you arrive at school to take a test you haven't studied for, you have no idea what room to go to, and you've left your clothes at home.

Kate shuddered. "I hate flight tests. They're like being examined by your doctor, scolded by your mother, and interrogated by Torquemada all at once."

"It'll be a piece of cake," Rick said. "All you have to do is convince that guy you can fly the Lear in a snowstorm on one engine by yourself if something happens to your co-pilot."

"That sounds like way too much work for one person," Kate said.

"What do you think I've been teaching you to do for the last four months?" Rick grinned.

"I wish you could be in there with me."

He put his arm around her shoulder. "Even if you don't see me there, every time you get in that plane I'll be with you."

She looked up at him. Drawing encouragement from his gaze, she squared her shoulders and straightened her spine.

Rick gave her a gentle push. "Baby, it's time to do your stuff." His expression told her he knew exactly how she felt.

She hoped the forty-five minutes she had spent in the new cockpit would be enough.

"Go on," he said.

Stealing a last glance at Rick, she crossed the room.

I'm relaxed, and I can do it. I'm relaxed, and I can do it. She silently repeated the phrase until she stood before the stranger who, if she passed the oral exam, would be her copilot for the check-ride.

"Hello," she said. "I believe you're here to see me." She extended her hand and smiled. "I'm Kate Randolph."

Rick pulled up a chair beside Lila's desk and watched her flip through the pages of the latest issue of *Bon Appetit.*

"Doesn't this look good?" Lila showed him a picture of a Thai noodle salad.

He glanced at the picture and absently nodded. "They've been in there almost an hour."

Lila glanced at the door to the conference room. "You, of all people, should know how long this takes." She grabbed a pair of scissors and cut out the recipe for the noodle salad.

Rick stretched his arms over his head. After training twelve of the fifteen pilots who worked at Executive Air and sweating out each of their check-rides, he always felt a surge of pride when the flight test ended and the candidate returned with a wide grin. That telltale grin indicated a passed test, moving the pilot up a notch in the ranks of the flying elite. A young guy with a new type-rating in his pocket never walked anywhere. He swaggered with the kind of self-assurance that shouted, "I'm hot shit. Bring on the babes." Kate was the first woman Rick had ever trained.

When the conference room door opened, he tapped Lila's shoulder.

Kate emerged first, eyes downcast. The examiner walked behind her. She approached Rick and Lila wearing a glum expression. She looked at Rick, then shrugged her shoulders as if to say, *I gave it my best shot.*

Impossible, Rick thought. How could she have failed the oral? She knew that plane inside out. Besides, all of his students passed their exams on the first try.

Kate hesitated, fastening her gaze on him. Rick felt the impulse to reach out to comfort her, but he decided to wait for a private moment with her. He stuffed his hands into his pockets.

Then without warning, Kate burst into a smile. *Gotcha!* She winked as she whisked past Rick and Lila. "We're going flying."

Rick couldn't help grinning back at her, and then he thought, *I hope she remembers where the landing gear is on that plane.*

"She's the best thing that's ever happened to you," Lila said.

Rick put his arm around Lila's shoulder. He agreed.

"Come on. Let's go to Starbucks," he said. "I'll buy you one of those chocolate-mocha-caramel-latte things you like."

"You're on." Lila grabbed her purse.

They exited the building and strolled toward the

Starbucks at the corner. Tall eucalyptus trees shaded a broad sidewalk edged with marigolds and geraniums.

"I want to tell you something," Lila said.

Rick stopped short. "You're not sick, are you?"

"No." She swatted his arm with a gentle hand. "Don't be ridiculous. I'm fine." They resumed their walk. "It's about Bob. And don't worry, he's not sick either. The company's sick. Money is flowing out the door like water."

"Is it that bad?" Rick asked.

"Business is booming," Lila said. "It's never been better, but the expenses are out of control. He owes more on that stupid yacht than it's worth, plus he's behind on his taxes. If a new partner with cash to invest doesn't show up soon, Bob will end up in chapter eleven, or, heaven forbid, bankruptcy." Lila sighed. "It's a sound business if someone can get in here and clean out the chaff."

"You know I've been putting away money," Rick said. "And talking to other pilots who are looking to invest. But it's going to take more than we have."

They had arrived at Starbucks. The place was packed. Rick held the door open so two girls carrying coffee cups, handbags and computers could exit, then he followed Lila inside and they got in line.

All I need is one solid investor to make this work, Rick thought. In an instant, Wally Runnels came to mind. Rick had been flying Wally for years—make that Wally and all of his wives, since Wally traded in his spouses the way other men traded in their cars. Wally had his hand in dozens of pies. Rick would talk to him as soon as possible.

Kate felt energized. Her oral test had been flawless. Rick had taught her well. Now, she would prove that she could fly the big bird. Buzz Hall, the FAA examiner, followed her while she performed the Lear's preflight. She explained everything she checked as they slowly circled the plane.

"I'm looking to make sure the outside skin isn't damaged and no rivets are loose," she said, running her hand across the top surface of one of the wings. She had meant to toss her shoulder bag into the plane, and now it bounced on her hip while she inspected the aircraft, an irritant. "Static ports are clear, antennas are in good shape, connecting hinges okay."

She pushed on the left aileron and watched the one on the right wing rise, then she checked the elevator. "Control surfaces are fine." Bending over, she examined the landing gear. "I'm checking to be sure the tires are inflated properly, and that there are no foreign objects in the wheel well." Buzz followed behind her, making notes and occasionally nodding his head. FAA inspectors were notorious for their lack of conversation during check-rides.

Kate felt certain she'd examined every inch of the fuselage, but she went through the list in her mind a second time, as Buzz had the power to fail her for the slightest oversight.

She took a deep breath and turned to him. "She's good to go. Let's hop in."

Buzz followed her up the stairs. Inside the aircraft, he watched her every move. She retracted the stairway and locked the door. Kneeling to straighten the mat, she spoke to herself. *Just pretend he's Rick. Do everything just like he's Rick.*

Checking the handle to be sure the door was locked, Kate stood and turned quickly. The long strap of her shoulder bag catapulted it into the air. She watched in horror as it smacked Buzz on his ear.

Kate's mouth dropped open. "Oh, my God. I'm so sorry."

Buzz looked dazed.

"Are you okay?" Kate asked.

Buzz gave her a bemused look. "I'm fine. Guess I was standing too close to you."

Not knowing what else to do, Kate walked to the cockpit and slid into the captain's seat. What a way to start a check-ride, she thought, chagrined by the mishap.

After Buzz lowered himself into the co-pilot's seat and they were both strapped in, she gave him a safety briefing— emergency exits, oxygen, fire extinguisher.

Kate pulled her checklist from the pocket beside her. She pointed to the gauges while she spoke. "I'm looking at the fuel levels, the batteries and lights."

Show time. Kate said a quick prayer, then pressed the start button. Running her fingers down the checklist, she began to explain her every action to Buzz. "Engine pressure looks good, oil pressure's coming up." Kate pointed to the appropriate indicators.

"What's the maximum starting temperature?" Buzz asked.

"One hundred eighty-five degrees," she answered with confidence.

Kate called ground control for clearance for an instrument takeoff and permission to taxi. Pushing the throttle ever so slightly, she maneuvered the plane along the centerline of the taxiway, remembering with a faint smile her first attempt and the way she had zigzagged across the yellow line.

"I'm going to do a noise abatement departure," she said. "It's required here."

Buzz nodded.

Even though Kate knew he was familiar with the procedure, she briefed him on the details.

Braking at the runway's edge, Kate contacted the tower. She felt not a single doubt. She was prepared. Confidence rose in her chest, spreading up her shoulders and neck until it reached her mouth and culminated in a smile. This was her moment. It didn't matter that she'd never been in this particular aircraft before. She'd fly the hell out of it, anyway.

Kate moistened her lips before she keyed the microphone. "John Wayne tower, this is Eight Six Juliet Bravo. We're ready for takeoff."

A disembodied voice filled the cockpit. "Eight Six Juliet Bravo, you're cleared for takeoff."

Kate eased the throttles forward. Pinned to the back of her seat, she kept the nosewheel fastened to the centerline of the runway. The Lear thundered forward.

Like a well-trained co-pilot, Buzz called out their speed. "Seventy knots, eighty knots, ninety knots."

The Lear wanted to soar. If Kate hadn't been holding onto the control wheel, it would have leapt into the air by itself.

"V One," said Buzz.

Kate moved her hand from the throttle to the wheel. "Rotate."

Kate pulled back the controls and the Lear was airborne in a steep climb over the back bay. In seconds they reached five hundred feet. As the pilot-in-command, Kate knew her role.

"Gear up," she called to her co-pilot.

Buzz complied, and the wheels retracted with a thump into the belly of the plane.

Kate fired off another order. "Flaps up."

At fifteen hundred feet, Kate notified Buzz of her intention to comply with the noise abatement requirement. She pulled back the throttles, and the cockpit became quiet. As if it had just cleared the crest of a giant roller coaster on its way to a free fall, the Lear slowed. This was the part of a flight in which inexperienced passengers gripped the armrests, mild panic prompting them to seek protection against the sensation of sinking into a cloud.

When the plane cleared the coastline, Kate adjusted the throttles to cruise position. Practice was over. This was the real thing—the moment she had trained for. Setting her jaw in determination and unwilling to entertain even the slightest possibility of failure, she aimed the speeding aircraft toward the open ocean.

Bob Hansen stood at the window in his office, watching Kate's plane rise over the field. He was glad he had let her use 86JB for her check ride. Besides, he could write it off.

He tapped the pocket of his sport coat. Reassured that his wallet was there, he headed toward the sandwich shop in the main terminal for a meatball sandwich. He stepped out onto the tarmac, waving to Rick and Lila.

Bob strolled along the apron, feeling very satisfied with his introduction of Kate to Max Abbot. Definitely a good move. His old army buddy's kid could wreak his well-deserved revenge against Derek Randolph, and in the process, Kate would end up one of the wealthiest women in Orange County. Wealthy enough to help him out of his mess at Executive Air. Bob smiled. He knew he shouldn't count his chickens before they'd hatched, but if Kate went along with his idea, he could pay off his debts and enjoy the yacht that had caused him all this trouble in the first place.

Five miles out over the Pacific, the adrenaline coursing through Kate's veins helped her focus. She followed Buzz's commands, turning the Lear to specific headings or intercepting a particular radial of a navigational aid. Then the easy part of her check ride ended.

"Let's head to Long Beach Airport and shoot an instrument landing to a missed approach," Buzz said.

Kate called SoCal Approach to communicate her intentions. In the middle of her conversation with the controller, Buzz pulled back the right engine. The Lear heaved to one side. Like a preprogrammed robot, Kate pressed the opposite rudder and lowered the left wing. In seconds, the plane stabilized and returned to a straight and level flight path. Buzz nodded and restored the right engine. They sped toward Long Beach.

After shooting a textbook I-L-S to a missed approach to Long Beach, Kate stayed on track, flying a perfect non-precision VOR approach into Chino. *This is too easy*, she thought. Buzz suddenly yanked the left engine. The airplane shuddered, sending prickles up the back of Kate's neck. Her heart pounded. Engine failures at slow landing speeds could be tricky, but Kate had practiced with Rick until the recovery procedure had become second nature. In less than ten seconds, the Lear again flew straight and level.

"Nice job," Buzz said. "Head back over the ocean and climb to seventeen thousand."

Five minutes later, as she passed through sixteen thousand feet, Kate checked the clock on the instrument panel. She'd been flying, handling one emergency scenario after another, for nearly an hour. She felt fatigue start to set in. Buzz was giving her a heading to turn to when the pain struck. She pressed her hand to her right ear. Buzz had depressurized the cabin.

Kate jammed the throttles all the way back and pushed the nose down for an emergency descent. The airspeed indicator pinned at red line, and the altimeter needle spun furiously. In less than a minute, they lost eight thousand feet. Once Kate leveled out at a safe altitude, Buzz said, "Call SoCal Approach for an instrument landing at John Wayne."

Confident she could handle whatever Buzz threw at her, she picked up the microphone. Her heart still raced.

"It wouldn't be a problem if she didn't have so damn much money," Rick said. Seated in a chair behind Lila's desk, he braced his tan loafers against the bottom drawer.

Lila looked up from opening the mail. "How can you have too much money? It's not like having fleas."

Tilting back in his chair until it balanced on two legs, Rick stuffed his hands into his pockets. "I could never do anything for her she couldn't do for herself."

Lila glared. "What are you talking about?"

Rick nearly lost his balance when she shook his arm.

"You're more exasperating than all my ex-husbands

put together." Lila placed her hands on her hips. "What can you give her? Only the things every woman wants. Love, attention, affection. Things money can't buy. Didn't you ever hear that song, *The Best Things in Life are Free*?"

Rick gave her a skeptical look and said nothing more.

Kate swiped her hand across her brow before she keyed the microphone. "John Wayne tower, Eight Six Juliet Bravo is at the outer marker."

"Eight Six Juliet Bravo, you're cleared to land."

Kate checked the cross hairs on the instrument landing system. She was right on the money, even with one engine cut to idle. After jumping through hoops for FAA Buzz for an hour, she was glad it was over. Although one never knew about these things, she felt pretty confident she had passed.

The Lear landed with a thump. Kate braked and turned off at the first taxiway. She brought the plane to a stop, exhaled, then looked at Buzz. She waited while he wrote something on the notepad in his lap. Eager to get the plane back to the hangar, she asked, "Taxi to park?"

"No," he said. "Call the tower and ask for a straight out departure. We're going up again."

A brisk breeze swirled through the reception area. Lila dove to cover the papers lying on her desk, and Rick ran to catch several bills already sailing down the hallway. A well-dressed businessman, an overcoat slung over one arm, had entered from the parking lot, joining a colleague to wait for their plane.

Rick returned the errant papers to Lila, then strolled to the large window and peered through the sparkling glass. He smiled when he spotted the Lear as it exited the runway. "Here she comes."

Lila joined him at the window.

"You've taught so many guys to fly so many different kinds of planes," she said. "How does it feel?"

Rick looked up at the sky, reflecting on the coterie of men at Executive Air who considered him their mentor.

"It always feels great," he said. "But this time feels especially good. I was pretty tough on her. I worked her harder than anyone I've ever trained. But I knew she could take it."

"She's tough," Lila said.

"She's got perseverance," Rick replied. "I've never met a woman who loves to fly as much as Kate. It's like she was born with wings." He paused to squint at the runway. "What the...she's going out again."

Inching her way to the runway behind an American Airlines 767, Kate felt drained. What had she done wrong? Why was the examiner ordering her up again? Her shoulders ached from holding the control wheel too tight and a bead of sweat dripped from between her breasts to her waist. She replayed the last hour in her mind, going over all the maneuvers she had performed. She couldn't recall a single misstep or mistake.

Just ahead of the Lear, the American Airlines jet took off, leaving columns of black exhaust in its wake.

Kate picked up the microphone, trying to ignore her tension and threatening headache. "Eight Six Juliet Bravo's ready," she said.

"Eight Six Juliet Bravo, cleared for take off."

A wave of nausea hit Kate. Swiveling the air vent nozzle toward her face, she took a steadying breath, then thrust the throttles forward. Her feet danced on the rudder pedals as the Lear sped down the centerline of the runway.

Buzz called out the numbers. "Seventy knots, eighty knots."

At ninety knots he pulled a V One engine cut. The Lear lurched to the right.

"You lost an engine!"

Never forgetting the lesson she'd learned after nearly careening off the runway with Rick at Palomar Airport, she responded without hesitation. Kate slammed the second throttle back and stomped on the brakes. The Lear shrieked to a stop, half of the runway still ahead of them.

Kate turned to Buzz. *What now?* she wondered.

Chapter 23

B uzz offered Kate a generous smile. "We have some paperwork to fill out."

Kate beamed. FAA Buzz had spoken the magic words. All pilots understood them. She had passed. She grinned so hard her cheeks hurt. She'd done it. How many female Learjet pilots were there? A hundred? Two hundred? Even if there were a thousand, she could now claim membership in this elite group of aviators.

Taxiing the plane to Executive Air, she shut down the left engine. Following the lineman's arm signals, she used the thrust from the right engine to pivot the plane ninety degrees to the left. When she reached the mark, the lineman crossed his arms over his chest, a signal to shut down the remaining engine. She left the emergency brake off so the plane could be towed to the hangar.

She climbed out of her seat. Buzz followed. Unlocking the door, Kate swung it open, then extended the stairs. Rick stood on the tarmac, smiling up at her. She hesitated an instant in the doorway to savor the moment.

When he opened his arms, she bolted down the steps and hurled herself into his embrace.

"I passed," she whispered into his ear.

"Of course you did," he said, hugging her back.

Kate gazed up into his clear blue eyes, aching for him to kiss her. She wished they didn't have to keep their relationship a secret.

As if reading her mind, his white teeth flashed behind his seductive grin. "Because you were a perfect student and made your instructor look good with the FAA," he said, "I've got a big reward for you at my place."

Kate raised her eyebrows. "And just how big is this reward?"

He winked at her. "Come by around seven and find out."

In the conference room where she had attended safety training so many months ago, Kate's gaze rested on FAA Buzz. Her foot tapped the carpet. *Can't he write any faster?* She was bursting with energy, feeling as though she might self-destruct like those secret messages in *Mission Impossible*.

Buzz signed his name to her temporary license.

Tearing the three-inch square of pink paper from his pad, he held it out to her. "You earned this, young lady."

Kate grasped it with both hands. Grinning, she read it, even though she already knew what it said. Added to her commercial pilot's license were the words *Aircraft Certified to Fly, Lear 60*. She'd done it!

After Buzz snapped his briefcase closed, Kate followed him to the corridor.

"You did a fine job," he said, extending his hand.

Kate grasped it. "Thank you."

She said goodbye, and waited until she saw him exit the building. Then she headed toward the reception area. She used all of her willpower to walk down the hallway in a dignified manner, even though she felt like running and jumping and yelling like a crazed soccer fan whose team had just taken the championship.

Rick always felt triumphant when a student passed a check-ride. Today, his feelings for Kate heightened those emotions tenfold. He took personal pride in her accomplishment. He waited near Lila's desk until Kate said goodbye to Buzz, then watched her turn and make her way to him. Her eyes sparkled. He grabbed the red rose wrapped in cellophane he had purchased from the flower stand in the terminal, and met her halfway.

"I did it," she said.

Rick hugged her. "Congratulations, honey." He held out the rose.

She clasped the flower to her chest as if it were an Academy Award. Her gaze softened as she looked up at him. "Thank you...for the rose and for everything else you've taught me." She held out her license, displaying the biggest grin he'd ever seen. "Can you believe it? I'm really a Learjet pilot."

"And, you're the prettiest Learjet pilot I've ever seen," Lila said. She nudged Rick out of the way to plant a kiss on Kate's cheek. "Congratulations."

A voice boomed behind them. "Is there a Captain Kate here?" Bob Hansen sported a jolly smile. "Good job," he said, clasping Kate's shoulder.

The muffled jingle of a cell phone caused Bob to freeze in the middle of his one-armed hug. Rick patted his pockets, and Lila looked at her desk.

"It's mine," Kate said, tapping her purse. "I'll be right back." She walked to a corner of the room to answer the call.

Kate flipped open her cell phone. "Hello," she said, still staring at her license.

"Mrs. Randolph?" a female voice asked.

"Yes."

"Please hold for Mr. Abbot."

Max Abbot sounded cheery. "Kate, can you be at my office at nine tomorrow morning?"

"Sure, Max. What's going on?"

"Derek Randolph's attorney just called. Your stepson's going ballistic."

"That's no surprise." Kate buried her nose in the soft petals of the rose, and inhaled its sweetness.

"Derek wants his inheritance yesterday," Max said. "He's impatient. That's good. He wants to meet with you. Let's see what the kid's got up his sleeve."

Pleased with her decision to use Max to represent her claim to Santomar, Kate said, "I'll be there." She ended the call. Feeling invincible, she smiled at her reflection in the window, at her new license, and at the red rose in her hand.

Kate had never seen Derek Randolph so out of control. His temper flared and flashed like fireworks gone mad. Glaring at Kate, he leapt from his chair in Max Abbot's conference room and slammed a bundle of papers on the table.

"This is my father's will," Derek shouted, "and there's no mention of you in it. It's been in the safe in his office for years, and it leaves the house in Santomar to me."

Max Abbot and Bill Casey watched him with wide eyes.

Kate knew Derek was lying. She'd remained quiet

since the mayhem began, but now said, "Lying again, Derek? Bad idea."

Max Abbot spoke softly. "Derek, I don't know where you found this will, but my client assures me that her husband didn't have a will, and I have no reason to doubt her."

"Liar!" Derek shrieked, lunging across the table toward Kate.

Bill Casey grabbed Derek. "Sit down," he commanded, tugging on his client's arm. "Let me see that." He snatched the will off the table, reached into his pocket, and pulled out a pair of reading glasses. "Where did you get this?"

Derek dropped into his chair. "I told you, it was in my father's safe."

"That's odd," Kate said. "Sam told me he'd never gotten around to making a will."

"Well, he did," Derek snarled. "And this is it."

Kate sighed and stared out the window, past the granite skyscrapers to an oil tanker crossing Santa Monica Bay. She'd let Max battle it out with Derek and Bill Casey. Mesmerized by the sparkling wake trailing behind the tanker, Kate let her mind wander to the memory of the celebration in Rick's condo the night before.

Rick's front door was open when she arrived at seven. Wandering into the kitchen, she found him barefoot in a pair of faded jeans, uncorking a chilled bottle of Dom Perignon. His long sleeves were rolled up, and his tan chest and flat stomach peeked from behind his unbuttoned blue cotton shirt.

"*People* magazine got it wrong," she said. "You're the sexiest man alive."

He laughed.

She walked over, circled her arms about his waist, and he bent to kiss her. He smelled like sandalwood soap.

He placed the champagne cork on the granite counter, and poured two glasses of golden liquid.

"Do you know," he said, "that Dom Perignon was a blind Benedictine monk who made the first champagne by accident?"

"I do," she said.

He handed her a glass. "And do you know that, when the old guy took his first sip of this stuff, he said, 'I have tasted the stars.'"

Clicking her glass against Rick's, Kate said, "Here's to soaring among the stars."

He flashed her a sexy grin. "To the most glamorous pilot I've soared with."

They sipped their drinks. Rick slipped his arm around Kate's waist, and they walked into the living room. Rod Stewart's raspy voice crooned "It Had to be You."

Kate curled up on the sofa beside Rick.

He took a swallow of champagne, then set his glass on the coffee table. "I made a reservation at *Roy's* for eight-thirty," he said.

Kate sipped the Dom Perignon. "I love their calamari."

Setting her glass next to Rick's, she looked up at him and grinned. "It's hot and spicy."

Rick drew her into his arms. Their lips hovered a breath apart.

"You're hot and spicy," he whispered. He brought his mouth down to hers. It was warm and sweet from the wine. His hands slipped beneath her shirt, and he undid the single hook on her bra. The sensation of his hands on her bare skin shot a rush of heat and dizzying desire through her.

They never made it to the restaurant. Within minutes, their clothes littered the living room floor, and they lay sprawled across Rick's bed, enfolded in each other's arms.

Hours later, as they caught their breath in the quiet aftermath of the storm amid a tangle of sheets and pillows, Rick gathered Kate close and pressed her cheek against his chest.

She listened to his heartbeat.

"I love being with you," he murmured.

I love being with you. Nice, she thought, but not *I love you.* She yearned to hear him say those words, just as she longed for the freedom to say them to him, too. Instead, she played it safe. "I love being with you, too, Rick."

Derek slammed his hand on the conference table, snapping Kate back to the chaos in Max's Century City conference room.

"This document is genuine," Derek seethed. "It's on my father's stationery. He typed it himself. That's his signature."

Bill Casey removed his glasses and rubbed his eyes. "I need a few minutes alone with my client," he said. Pushing his chair away from the table, he stood and motioned for Derek to follow him. Casey ushered Derek from the room, closing the door behind them. Kate watched through the glass wall as the attorney prodded Derek down the corridor until they both disappeared from view.

Max turned to Kate. "So, what do you think about that will?"

Kate shrugged. "I don't know what to make of the whole situation. First Sam says he doesn't have a will, then suddenly one appears."

"I'd bet my practice the kid forged it," Max said. "If I'm right, you know what that means?"

Kate grinned. "That Derek will be sent to a penal colony in South America for fraud?"

Max laughed. "It would probably do him some good, but no. If it's confirmed that Sam left no will, under community property laws, half of Sam's estate automatically goes to you."

Kate's jaw went slack. "Half of Sam's estate? I never thought of it being community property because of all the trusts and corporations."

"That's not all," Max said. "If there's no will, the estate passes under the laws of intestacy. Do you understand what that means?"

Kate shook her head. "Haven't got a clue."

"It means that after your half is taken out, you'll get one half of the remaining half of Sam's estate. So you'd actually come out with seventy-five percent of Sam's holdings."

Too stunned to speak, Kate stared at her attorney.

Max smiled broadly. "Do you think you can make do with eight hundred million dollars?"

ORANGE COUNTY REGISTER
SANTA ANA, CALIFORNIA, JUNE 12TH

Chaos reigned today in the courtroom of Judge Dennis Phinney, when the question of who would inherit the Sam Randolph estate was settled after two days of testimony. The dispute arose last spring when the oil and media baron died intestate while with his mistress, Florida Senator Ellen Gordon.

The judge handed Randolph's widow, Katherine Kendall Randolph, the bulk of the Randolph estate, including a Caribbean villa and a Learjet. A frenzy erupted when Mrs. Randolph's stepson, Derek Randolph, who will reportedly receive three hundred million dollars in the settlement, spat at the judge when he delivered his ruling. Mr. Randolph was immediately remanded into custody and sentenced to thirty days in Orange County jail for contempt. Katherine Randolph, instantly cast into the spotlight as Orange County's wealthiest woman, slipped from the courthouse once the proceedings adjourned. Mrs. Randolph could not be reached for comment.

The following week, the paper ran a short story about the sale of ten acres of prime Newport Beach real estate to Safe Haven. An anonymous donor had presented the non-profit organization with two hundred million dollars to purchase the land and build a state-of-the-art campus. The same benefactor generously provided an additional fifty million to endow the after-school program.

In a corner of the covered terrace outside Rick's kitchen, a whisper of a warm Santa Ana wind rustled the leaves of the weeping banyan. Three floors below, a high tide crashed against the sea wall. Rick folded the newspaper and tossed it onto the patio table beside his empty coffee mug.

His investor had said he would call this morning. Why hadn't he? Rick was keyed up, excited to put a deal together. When he was a partner in Executive Air, he would shower Kate with gifts. And he'd feel a little more equal, he admitted. He'd been a grouch lately with this deal in the wings. He couldn't wait to surprise her with the news and make it up to her big time.

The news story about Kate had rocked the foundation of Rick's besieged ego. Since their return from Santomar six months ago, he and Kate had spent most of their time together at his condo. On the few occasions he had ventured back to her Emerald Bay home, he felt stifled, almost claustrophobic. Each time he thought he'd gotten over the roadblock of her wealth, another facet of the problem reared its ugly head.

At first simply a matter of masculine pride, Rick now recognized that his pride was a symptom of a more pervasive problem. Since he had walked out of his marriage all those years ago, he'd sidelined his emotions and used women for his own pleasure whenever he needed them. Being in control of his relationships, a matter of self-preservation, made sense to him. Until Kate, he'd embraced the theory that women were expendable and easily replaced.

Without warning, Kate had penetrated a crack in his armor, shaking his resolve and sending him into an emotional tailspin that left him feeling vulnerable. His desire for her had made him edgy from the start, but now her unfathomable wealth and power heightened his discomfort.

Were his feelings for Kate strong enough to break down the wall of self-protection he had built around his heart? Rick didn't even know where or how to search out an answer to that question.

His cell phone rang, and his heart rate picked up. He answered it.

"Hi Rick. It's Wally Runnels."

"What's up, Wally?"

"Say. About that aviation investment...."

At the ominous pause, Rick's heart sank.

"I've got some financial issues," Wally said, "which I'm sure will resolve. But I can't commit to anything right now."

Rick felt certain the financial issues facing the distinguished Mr. Runnels had to do with the man's soon-to-be-ex fourth trophy wife.

"I'm still working on the deal, so let me know if anything changes," Rick said, keeping his tone upbeat.

"I sure will."

Crushed, Rick hung up. His gut churned. He was back to square one. He needed to find someone else. Fast. Bob was going under, Rick's dream with him. Rick's loyalty was also his Achilles heel, and he would walk through fire to preserve the camaraderie at Executive Air. He recalled every man he'd trained, and thought, *I've got your back, guys. So help me.* He had a full day of flying ahead of him, but he'd start the search for another investor today.

Carol Burke, Max Abbot's receptionist, nodded from behind her desk when Kate walked into the office.

"Good morning, Mrs. Randolph." Carol spoke a few words into the intercom, then stood. "I'll show you to the conference room."

Kate followed Carol through a set of double doors. They veered to the right, down a carpeted corridor past the offices of several of Max's associates.

"I saw your picture in *TIME* and *Newsweek* online," Carol whispered.

Nearly a month since the newspapers and magazines had publicized the details of her inheritance, Kate still felt bewildered that people were interested. She offered her standard reply.

"Hmm," she said, smiling at Carol. She hoped her laconic response would quash the woman's curiosity and any further discussion of what Kate considered private matters.

When they had reached the glass enclosed conference room, Carol pushed open the heavy glass door. It made a whooshing sound as it scraped against the carpet. "Coffee, Mrs. Randolph?"

Kate set her Gucci handbag on one of the chairs surrounding the conference table. "Sure. Black, please."

Carol disappeared down the hallway.

By the time Kate slipped off the jacket of her white Chanel suit and hung it over the back of a chair, Carol returned with a mug of piping hot coffee. "Can I get you anything else?"

Kate shook her head. "No. Thank you."

Carol smiled. "They'll be right in." The whoosh of the door signaled her departure.

Kate settled into a chair and sipped the steaming coffee.

Max and Bob came into view on the other side of the glass wall. The conference room door swung open and they greeted Kate.

Max sat down and slid the contract toward her.

She picked up the three-page document. Bob paced the floor as she read it.

"I thought it would be more complex than this," she said when she finished.

"It's just a temporary arrangement," Max explained. "Nothing complicated."

"I can't tell you how much I appreciate what you're doing," Bob said to her.

"I'm glad to help," Kate said. "When you told me Sam intended to do this, it was only right for me to follow through for him. And I'd hate to see you lose everything." She shifted her gaze between the two men. "But we're all in agreement. I know nothing about running an aircraft charter company, and this is just temporary."

"It's an interim arrangement so Bob doesn't have to declare bankruptcy," Max confirmed.

Bob cleared his throat. "And thanks for not telling anyone. If word got out I'm having financial problems, I'd never find a serious buyer. Rick's been working on putting together a consortium of pilots and investors to buy in, but he hasn't finalized anything yet."

Kate froze. "Why am I just learning this now?" She turned to Bob. "Don't you think he should have been consulted about this?"

"I feel terrible about this whole mess," Bob said. "But his investor fell through several days ago. Didn't he mention it?"

"No," said Kate. Rick had been preoccupied for a few weeks, and despite her urging, he wouldn't tell her what was bothering him. The only time he was himself was when he was with her in the Lear…or in bed. Then it was glorious. Was there something wrong with her that men always pulled away after the glow wore off?

"It's not right," said Kate.

"Bob's out of time," said Max.

Slumping into a chair, Bob said, "We're down to the wire."

Kate felt sick. She couldn't disappoint Bob. He was counting on her bailing him out of his mess. But would Rick feel betrayed? She'd have to explain to him. She wasn't edging him out, only making sure there was a company left for him to buy into. Picking up a pen from the round leather container on the table, she turned to the document's last page. Her pen hovered over the signature line. It's just temporary, she reminded herself in an effort to control the unease coursing through her. Taking a deep breath, Kate signed the bill of sale that sealed her fate. She now owned one half of Executive Air.

Chapter 24

R ick strode through the waiting room of Executive Air, and then headed down the corridor to his office. His flight case dangled in one hand, and a *New York Times* poked out from under his arm. Irritated that the deal with Wally Runnels fell through, Rick intended to scour his Rolodex. It was full of potential investors, and he wouldn't rest until he found one.

This morning, as on many others, Rick had arrived first at Executive Air. The smell of Pine-Sol rising from the freshly mopped floors tickled his nose, announcing another pre-dawn foray by the janitorial crew.

Nudging the half-open door to his office with his knee, he pushed it all the way, crossed the room, and set down his things. Then he stopped a moment to gaze through the large picture window above the couch. An American Airlines 757 was lifting off the runway, leaving two trails of exhaust drifting toward the taxi-way where a Southwest 737, two United jets, and a single-engine Cessna were already lined up and ready to go.

Pleasure welled up in him. He felt grateful to be one of those rare creatures lucky enough to spend his life doing what he loved. Early in his flying career, he had made a pilgrimage to the outer banks of North Carolina. He had walked the four miles from Kitty Hawk to Kill Devil Hill, the actual site of the Wright brothers' flight. Each step he took over the grass-covered dunes cemented his camaraderie with the bicycle-makers-turned-aviators who'd lived and breathed airplanes.

Atop a stack of mail on his desk, Rick saw that Lila had left him a note with the day's itinerary. It was going to be hectic.

First stop, Sun Valley to pick up a supermodel and her tennis-pro boyfriend. Drop them in San Francisco, then fly down to LAX to collect the chef-owner of the hottest new restaurant on the Las Vegas strip. Shoot over to McCarran field to drop off the chef and pick up five thirty-somethings who had been holed up at Caesar's Palace for two days in a news-making bachelor party. With late-afternoon thunderstorms predicted for southern Nevada, he hoped they wouldn't get sick all over the plane before he dropped them off in San Diego. If time permitted, he'd make a quick hop to Phoenix to pick up the new altimeter for the company's Gulfstream. Aircraft stuck in maintenance made no money.

Rick checked the time on his stainless steel Rolex, a

gift from a passenger he had flown years before. He folded the day's schedule and tucked it into his shirt pocket.

He reached for the phone to call Kate, but changed his mind when he remembered she had an early meeting in L.A. today. He'd see her tonight. Noticing the message light on his phone flashing, he pushed the button and listened.

"Hey, buddy." He recognized Decatur Crane's voice. "I gotta talk to you today. It's urgent. Call me as soon as you get this."

Kate rode the elevator from Max's office to the parking garage, clutching her knotted stomach. She should have discussed this with Rick. Sam's death and the legal battle with Derek had clouded her judgment. She knew Rick had a full day of flying scheduled, but she'd see him tonight for dinner and explain her predicament.

When Bob had confided his financial crisis to her, and revealed Sam's plan to become a partner in Executive Air, Kate had agreed to help. She would follow through with Sam's offer, but her partnership would be temporary.

"I just need some time," Bob had said. "The truth is, with some restructuring, Executive Air will recover and prosper. The only provision I ask is confidentiality."

"That's fine," Kate had said. "When I'm at the airport, I feel like one of the guys. If Lila and the pilots find out, it'll change the way they treat me and think about me."

The valet appeared with Kate's car. She handed him her claim check and a tip, took a deep breath, and slid behind the wheel. *Everything will work out fine,* she told herself.

Lightning sizzled across the dark sky seconds before a crack of thunder shook the massive Falcon 900. Rick didn't flinch. He had flown through worse, but it had been a long day. Corporate pilots didn't have the same restrictions as airline pilots who, by law, could be on duty no more than eight hours straight at a time. Rick had left the ground at seven-thirty that morning. It was nearly six o'clock and the runway wasn't even in sight yet.

Angry winds tossed the plane, rattling dishes and crystal in the galley. Rick wished he could call Kate, but this damn thunderstorm demanded his full attention.

The radio crackled. "Falcon Bravo Bravo, contact tower at one twenty-six point eight."

Pete, the copilot, dialed in the frequency. "John Wayne tower, Falcon Bravo Bravo is on approach."

"Winds are out of the west," the tower responded. "Gusting to twenty-five knots with half mile visibility. You're the only one out there right now, and you're cleared to land."

"Glideslope's coming in," Pete said to Rick.

Rick watched the cross hairs line up. The aircraft

lurched to the left. Correcting for the wind, Rick kept his gaze glued to the instrument panel, scanning every gauge. He wouldn't lift his head to look out the window until Pete notified him the runway was in sight. *Never trust your body cues when you're in the soup.* He remembered the first time he'd heard that warning during his initial lesson in instrument flying. He had just lifted off from Santa Monica Airport and was soaring toward the Malibu hills, when Jake, his instructor, had handed him a plastic baseball cap with the longest visor Rick had ever seen.

"Put this on," Jake had said.

With the visor in place, the only thing visible to Rick was the instrument panel. Every visual cue outside the plane was obscured by the duckbill visor.

Jake tapped the instruments with his pen. "Attitude indicator is home base. Always come back here. Scan the instruments, five seconds each. Attitude, airspeed, attitude, vertical speed, attitude, compass, attitude, engine instruments, always back to attitude."

Rick had been doing a good job of keeping the plane straight and level when Jake gave him an order.

"Put your head in your lap," Jake said.

As Rick lowered his head, Jake put the plane into a steep dive with a sharp turn to the left. Rick felt light-headed for a moment, then crushed into his seat as the instructor pulled the nose up so high the stall warning horn blared.

"Feels like the Matterhorn at Disneyland," Rick said.

"That's the idea."

Jake dove and then climbed while banking the plane from side to side.

"You can lift your head," Jake said.

Due to the visor, Rick still couldn't see outside the plane.

Jake covered the instrument panel with a magazine. "Using only the information you receive from your body, get us back to straight and level."

No problem, Rick thought. He banked left, then corrected right until he felt the wings were level. He pushed and pulled the control wheel, and when he felt certain he had stabilized their cruising altitude, he smiled. "Piece of cake," he said.

"You're sure now?" Jake asked. "You can still make a slight correction if you want to."

Rick hesitated, then, feeling sure of himself, said, "No. It feels okay to me."

"Great job." Jake sounded pleased. "Take off the hat and check out your instincts."

Lifting the visor, Rick squinted at the sunlight. A chill sped up his spine. The plane was in a thirty-degree bank to the left, the airspeed pegged past redline. They were heading straight for the ground at rocket speed.

"Oh, shit." Rick yanked the throttle back and raised the nose, narrowly clearing a stand of evergreen trees. He glanced at Jake.

The instructor furrowed his brow. "Never trust your body cues when you're in the soup. They'll play tricks on you that'll lead you straight into the ground.

Trust your instruments. They'll tell you everything you need to know to get this baby back to earth."

Pete Smalley called out from the right seat. "Gear down."

Rick pressed a lever. The landing gear whined, then locked into place.

"I've got the runway," Pete said, alerting Rick it was safe to transition from instruments to visual flight rules.

Rick looked up from the instrument panel for the first time since initiating their descent into Orange County. Before them, the runway glistened under a sheet of water.

"I'm gonna take five knots off our landing speed," Rick said. He glanced at the clock on the instrument panel. Nearly seven o'clock. He'd call Kate from his office. By the time he arrived at his condo, she would be waiting outside his door with supper. The first time she offered, he had protested. Kate insisted, however, and he quickly grew accustomed to the luxury of a home-cooked meal after a day in the cockpit.

He smiled to himself. After tonight, she wouldn't have to wait outside. He put his hand over his shirt pocket and felt the extra key to his condo. He never thought he'd allow a woman into his heart again, but Kate was different. He trusted her. He couldn't wait to see the expression on her face when he gave her the key.

Rick pulled the throttles back and lowered the flaps the final ten degrees. The Falcon touched down just above stall speed. Blue taxi lights guided them to Executive Air. Rick parked the aircraft as close as he could to the building, then shut down the engines.

Unbuckling his seat belt, he turned to Pete. "Make sure you put the engine covers on before they haul her to the hangar." They climbed out of their seats. Pete unlocked the door and extended the stairway.

Rick grabbed his flight case and the altimeter he had picked up in Phoenix for the maintenance department, and headed for his office. Dropping his case on the floor, he set the altimeter on his desk. He leaned over and pulled a blank flight report form from the second drawer on the left, then slid into his chair. He grabbed a pen, filled in the tail number of the Falcon, then set aside the pen. The report could wait. He picked up the phone and dialed Kate's number. Before it had a chance to ring, he heard a noise from the hallway.

Setting the receiver back in its cradle, he made his way to the corridor. He noticed the lights were on in the spare office Lila used for storing old business records. He marched toward the office and poked his head into the doorway.

Bob Hansen, who had been shuffling through a cardboard file box labeled "Accounts Payable," looked up.

"Hey, buddy," Bob said. "I heard you come in. Those guys get back to San Diego okay?"

Rick shoved his hands into his pockets and leaned against the doorframe. "That must have been some bachelor party. They smelled like a whiskey factory. We could've flown to San Diego on their fumes."

"Did you have time for the Phoenix run?" Bob asked.

"The part's in my office," Rick said. "I'll walk it over to maintenance in the morning."

"I need to talk to those guys," said Bob. "Put it on my desk, and I'll take it over myself."

"You're here late," Rick observed.

Bob put the cover back on the box. "I've been playing in the fast lane, now I'm getting my ducks in order."

"I've noticed you've been pretty stressed...."

"Everything's fine," Bob said. "In fact, I'm off to meet a friend for dinner at Flemings."

Bob flicked off the storeroom light, and headed out the side door to his car. Rick strolled back to his office, picked up the altimeter, and headed down the hall. He found the light still on when he entered Bob's office. He crossed the room to the desk, carefully placing the altimeter next to a stack of business papers. Rick didn't pry, but the top document, in full view, caught his eye. Purchase Agreement for Executive Air. Rick's stomach knotted. He skimmed down the page, his anger building as he searched for the identity of the buyer. When he saw the name, he froze. He blinked, hoping he'd misread the name. He looked again. Katherine Randolph. Bob had sold Rick's dream to Kate.

Furious, Rick strode back to his office. How in hell could he work for her? And what the hell did she know about running a charter fleet? In the aftermath of his discovery, he felt his career and his personal life implode. Kate Randolph—a one-woman wrecking ball. Damn her. And damn him for being such a fool. Kate and Bob had both duped him.

Kate drummed her fingers on the granite counter. *Where are you, Rick?* she wondered as she looked out the window above her kitchen sink. In the night sky, the moon peeked through the remnants of the thunderstorm. Its light ringed the clouds in a silvery glow. Rick usually called when he was on final approach, and he'd said he expected to be home at seven. Kate glanced at the clock. It was now eight.

She reached for the phone and dialed his number. When she heard his recorded message, she disconnected. As she paced the kitchen, Kate's gaze fell on the picnic basket that Cora had packed for her to take to Rick's. A voice in her head began to chant: *He knows. He knows. He knows....* Kate's stomach churned. Grabbing the picnic basket and her purse, she called out to Cora, "I'm leaving...don't forget to turn on the alarm."

She drove through Emerald Bay and down the Coast Highway, barely registering the stoplights and other vehicles. She parked, her heart racing as she ran to the stairs that led to his third-floor condo. Kate suddenly whirled around, retraced her steps, and looked at Rick's BMW sitting at an angle in his parking space.

"He knows." The two words emerged from her like a groan. She tightened her grip on the picnic basket and climbed the three flights of stairs, her purse banging against her hip every step of the way. She heard the television just before she knocked on his door.

Rick threw open the door, but he stood in the doorway like a barrier designed to prevent an enemy's incursion. His icy glare confirmed her worst fear.

"Hi. I...." she began.

He cut in, "My job description doesn't include sleeping with my boss."

"What...?"

"You knew I wanted to put together a deal to buy into Bob's company."

"It's not like that."

He stared at her. "And you beat me to it."

"No. I'm just helping him. You don't understand."

"Yes, I do. You went behind my back. You're about as trustworthy as a surface-to-air missile."

"You need to calm down," she said.

He stood there, not moving a muscle, then calmly said, "I don't want to see you."

Rick closed the door.

Kate's knees threatened to buckle.

"Let me explain," she called through the door.

Kate heard the volume on the television in the condo climb several notches. She braced herself against the wall. The picnic basket slid out of her hands. Something deep within her shattered, and she knew it was her heart. An old adage flitted through her mind—*no good deed goes unpunished*. She'd rescued Executive Air, she'd even saved Rick's job, but she'd lost him. Worse yet, his pride wouldn't allow her the opportunity to explain.

Chapter 25

Rick leaned back against the door. *She must take me for an idiot. Did she think she could just show up here as though nothing had happened?* He walked to the sofa and sank onto the soft tweed, grabbed the TV remote and turned up the volume even louder.

Spotting the key he'd made for Kate on the coffee table, he laid his head back against the cushion and tried not to think about her. He took a deep breath, wanting nothing more than to zone out. A fist banged three times against his front door. *Shit!* He rose and headed back to the foyer. *Okay, okay.* If she insisted on having it out right now, he was ready.

He threw open the door. The last person he expected to see was Decatur Crane—six and a half feet of muscle with curly blond hair and a shit-eating grin. Beside him stood a man Rick didn't recognize.

Decatur held a picnic basket. "This was just sittin' out here," he said. "Somebody likes you."

Kate.

Decatur set the basket down inside the condo. "Hey, buddy." He clasped Rick's shoulder, and the two men shared a bear hug. "Don't you answer your messages?" he drawled in his Oklahoma baritone. "I've been calling you all day."

"Been to hell and back today," Rick said.

Decatur side-stepped and motioned to his companion. "Rick, meet Hap Walton."

Hap extended his hand. "Glad to meet you."

"You, too." Rick shook Hap's hand. "Come on in."

"This guy's face was plastered in the rear-view mirror on that F-18 I flew around the Gulf," Decatur said to Hap.

The two men wandered to the leather chairs in the living room while Rick gathered three Heinekens from the fridge.

"Where you been?" Rick motioned to his guests' camouflage shirts and jeans. He handed each man a beer and returned to his place on the sofa.

Decatur took a slug from the bottle. "Hap and I just delivered fifteen cases of supplies to rebels fighting some bad-ass warlord in Naga Jolika. A little place west of Mongolia."

"Blew two tires taking off outta there, but we beat the devil and lived to tell about it," Hap said.

"And made enough in three days for a new Porsche and six weeks in Maui." Decatur grinned.

Rick nodded. He had flown a dozen of these perilous, high-paying jobs with Decatur during the last ten years. Non-military covert operations. "You'd think we'd have gotten enough of that rush in the Marines," he said.

Decatur nodded. "It's like a drug, man. Once you get used to it, you're addicted."

Rick took a swig from the bottle. "Sometimes I think it beats the hell out of wearing a necktie and hauling drunk rock stars around in flying buses."

Decatur slapped his thigh. "That's the reason I'm here. I normally wouldn't take a job so soon after another, but I got a call this morning for the mother of all jobs."

The three men faced each other. Rick studied Hap. The guy looked ready to jump out of his skin with excitement.

"It's your lucky day," Decatur announced. "Hap's wife is about to pop their first kid."

Hap shrugged. "She threatened to leave me if I'm not with her when the baby's born."

"You gotta help me out, Rick," Decatur said. "I need an ace pilot sittin' next to me to pull this one off." He lowered his voice. "This one is too good to turn down. A little civil war on a spit of land in the South Pacific. The Hercules won't work there. No kickers. We'll have to land in the jungle. How about it?"

Rick shook his head. "Civil wars are tricky."

"It's a clean deal," Decatur said. "A touch-and-go."

"The thrill of sleeping on a concrete floor in some third-world prison doesn't do it for me," Rick said.

"Come on," Decatur said. "If you don't go, I'll have to

strap Hap, kicking and screaming, into the co-pilot's seat."
He shook his head. "It won't be a pretty sight. Come over
to the Marriott. There's someone I want you to meet. We'll
have a drink, and I'll fill you in on the details."

Rick glanced at the picnic basket. "I wouldn't mind
getting out of town for a few days."

"Then it's settled." Decatur stood.

Rick shook his head. "I just remembered. I'm flying
George Clooney to Lake Como day after tomorrow."

"Cancel it. Let someone else take him."

"I can't."

Decatur's mouth spread into a wide smile. He
leaned forward. "Not even for half a million in cold
cash to stuff in your mattress?"

An hour later, Rick entered the Marriott elevator and
pushed the button marked "twelve." The wood-paneled
car whisked him up a dozen flights. Half-a-million
added to the stash he'd already saved could stake him
to a small charter business or training school. He hoped
the client was legit so he could say yes to the mission.

When the elevator doors parted, Rick made his way
down the hallway to Decatur's room. He knocked on
the door. It swung open a moment later.

Decatur filled the doorway. He pulled Rick into the
room. "I got someone here I want you to meet."

The door shut behind them. The room was like

hundreds, perhaps thousands, of others Rick had slept in during his years of flying at Executive Air—two queen-size beds separated by a table with a lamp, a walnut-colored dresser with a TV perched on top, and a round table with two chairs near the floor-to-ceiling windows.

A heavyset man with a broad forehead and a receding hairline sat at the table. The man's head tilted back, a ribbon of cigar smoke curling from his mouth toward the ceiling. Rick recognized the aroma of an authentic Montecristo from Havana. *Who is this guy?* he wondered.

After three long strides, Rick stood before the stranger. The man peered at Rick with close-set ebony eyes, guaranteed to chill the recipient of his gaze.

"This is Rick Sanders, the man I was telling you about," said Decatur. Then he motioned toward the stranger. "Rick, meet Mr. Zamarcos."

Without bothering to stand, Zamarcos extended his hand. Rick shook it, noting the flash of a jelly bean-sized diamond in the man's pinky ring

Decatur sat on the corner of the bed. He pointed to the vacant chair. "Have a seat, Rick."

Rick sat down opposite Zamarcos. The man withdrew a Montecristo from the breast pocket of his rumpled suit jacket, holding it out to Rick. "Smoke?"

Rick shook his head. Zamarcos returned the cigar to his pocket, and then cleared his throat. "Mr. Crane tells me you two flew together in the Marines."

Rick didn't say anything.

The large man smiled, revealing tobacco-stained

teeth. He inhaled a deep breath. "I represent a humani-tarian organization," he wheezed. "We want to fly a planeload of medical supplies to Tagoro. You may have heard of it, a tiny island southeast of Bali. They are in the midst of a civil war and, as usual in these situations, innocent people are caught in the cross-fire."

Rick looked at the man. "Why not put your sup-plies on a commercial flight?"

"There aren't any," Zamarcos said. "Shanghai Air was the last carrier to fly in there, but since the rebels from God's Path started shooting at everything in sight, even the Chinese won't go near the place."

Decatur broke in. "It'll be a nighttime operation. Quick stop 'n go. Drop off the stuff and blow outta there."

Rick studied Zamarcos. The guy seemed sleazy. "I'm not interested in flying drugs," Rick said. "Not my style."

Zamarcos laughed. "Mr. Sanders, if I wanted to sell drugs, I'd bring them here where people can afford them, not some impoverished island."

Rick drummed his fingers on the table. Even if it wasn't drugs, it sure as hell wasn't medical supplies. "A half-a-million bucks apiece is a pretty hefty fee for delivering band-aids. What's the deal?"

The fat man sucked on his cigar and blew two smoke rings toward the ceiling. He stared at Rick. When he spoke, his voice sounded glacial. "The deal is, either you want the job or you don't."

Rick rubbed his chin, pondering Zamarcos's offer. It

intrigued him, and although a half million—or whatever would be left after taxes—might not put him in Kate's league, at least he would earn the paycheck for this job on his own merits. Crap! He mentally pushed Kate into a far corner of his mind, but not before his gut assured him she would hate it if he took this assignment.

Rick recalled the rush of flying his F-16 over the Gulf, the G-forces crushing him into his seat while he sought his target and locked onto it—a grown man's version of the ultimate video game. This operation would be a taffy-pull compared to dodging missiles, and it sure beat the hell out of sitting at home thinking about Kate. He didn't like or trust Zamarcos, but he needed a time-out. This mission was the answer.

Rick said, "I want the money up front."

Zamarcos nodded. "Of course."

Decatur pulled out his cell phone. "I know a guy in Seattle. He's got a DC-3 we can use."

"Are you kidding?" Rick said. "It'll take us till Christmas to get there in a DC-3."

"But it's perfect for the job," said Decatur. "The Tagoro airstrip's in a jungle, and it's shorter than my last marriage."

The long day finally caught up with Rick. Exhausted, he relaxed into his chair. He said to Zamarcos, "When do you want your packages delivered?"

Chapter 26

Sunlight radiated through a gap in Kate's bedroom curtains. She rolled over and clutched the down pillow to her chest. The simple act of awakening triggered her memory of the previous night's quarrel with Rick. With an aching heart, she sat up and swung her legs over the side of the bed. She bent to pet Brandy, and then opened the bedroom door so the dog could make her way downstairs to Cora.

Trudging into the bathroom, Kate absently turned on the shower faucets and stepped into the swirling mist. She stood under the warm cascade, wishing the soap and water could wash away her pain.

Determined to act professionally despite her grief, she dressed in a white piqué suit. She had a meeting at ten-thirty with an architect for the Safe Haven project.

She headed downstairs, the scent of butter and

cinnamon doing little to stimulate her appetite. The aroma of freshly brewed coffee proved to be the lure that drew her into the kitchen. She found Cora removing a hot tray from the oven.

The cook smiled proudly at her work. "I've made you some cinnamon buns," she said, placing two round pans on a cooling rack.

Kate didn't want to hurt Cora's feelings. "They look delicious. If you pack a few up, I'll take them with me."

Grabbing a flowered mug, Kate filled it with coffee then walked outside. She meandered through the rose garden where the groundskeeper was removing wilted blossoms.

She nodded. "Good morning, Andrew."

Andrew tipped his hat. "Morning, ma'am." He returned to his task.

Kate wandered down the path to the table and chairs under the jacaranda. Morning sunlight filtered through the purple canopy. She sat down, facing the ocean.

She didn't know which would be worse, the lonely night she'd just spent tossing and turning, or the empty day ahead. *It can't be over*, she thought. She sipped her coffee and wondered what he was doing.

That morning, Rick packed a small bag with his passport and a few essentials. He called Lila and asked her to assign another pilot to the Lake Como job. He had to admit a part of him craved the risks and challenges like the operation Decatur had planned. With a mixture of excitement and wariness, Rick walked into the Newport Beach branch of City National Bank, and following the directions provided by Zamarcos, Rick asked for the manager.

Under a whirling ceiling fan, John Reynolds, dressed in a dark blue suit, greeted him. "Mr. Zamarcos told me to expect you." He led Rick into a private office.

Within ten minutes, the bank manager had set up an account for Rick. It took an additional fifteen to verify that the half million dollars Zamarcos had promised had been wired into that account.

With a couple of hours to kill, Rick headed to Mozza on Coast Highway. It was barely noon, but the parking lot was packed. He found a seat at the bar. After an order of eggplant tapenade on Texas-size toast, followed by a Margarita pizza, he drove to Balboa Island and strolled along the south bayfront. He took pleasure watching the sailboats maneuver the narrow channel in a steady breeze. He'd always been drawn to the ocean, relying on the endless ebb and flow of the tide to bring tranquility to his world of schedules and duties.

He walked for a long time, enjoying the sound of the water lapping at the docks of multi-million dollar beach cottages. When memories of Kate popped into his head, he forced her out of his mind by turning his thoughts to the serious task ahead. It was time for Rick to perform his part of the bargain for Zamarcos.

He checked his watch. Two-thirty. He hoped he

could get a couple of hours of sleep on the plane. God knows he'd need it.

Rick caught a commercial flight to Seattle, where Decatur had secured the DC3 and readied it for over-water travel. Fitted with auxiliary fuel tanks, the twin-engine goliath had a range of 3,400 miles. With all the seats removed, the cabin would provide ample space for Mr. Zamarcos's cargo.

Rick pushed open the terminal's glass door and walked outside. The Seattle drizzle fell on the cars, taxis, and limousines dropping off their passengers on Sea-Tac Airport's upper level. The narrow strap on his duffle bag cut into his shoulder. He adjusted it before he pulled up the zipper of his leather flight jacket. He scanned the area.

A beat-up white Honda Civic pulled to the curb. When the passenger window slid down, Decatur Crane leaned over from the driver's side. "Welcome to sunny Seattle. Hop in."

Rick tossed his bag onto the back seat and climbed inside. The door creaked and moaned when he pulled it closed behind him.

"Where did you find this hunk of junk?" Rick asked.

"Belongs to the FBO. Anyone who buys fuel there can use it." Decatur pulled out into the traffic lanes. "I'll drop you at a coffee shop. Get some dinner and order half a dozen sandwiches to go. I'll finish the preflight and come back to get you." Navigating the terminal maze, Decatur turned onto a side road. "Did you sleep on the plane?"

"There's nothin' else to do if you're not the pilot," Rick said.

"Good, 'cause we're leaving tonight instead of tomorrow."

"Suits me fine." Rick leaned back in his seat. "The sooner we get over there, the sooner we get back."

While Decatur tied up some loose ends at the hangar, Rick sat in a corner booth in a coffee shop not far from the airport. He wiped his mouth on a paper napkin. The enchiladas weren't as good as Javier's, but they would do. He turned the page of the *USA Today*, not really focusing on any story in particular. He felt antsy. Where the hell was Decatur?

A leggy brunette in a miniskirt, with a butterfly tattoo on her shoulder, stopped by his table with a coffee pot. "Fill 'er up?"

"Sure." He pushed his cup toward her.

"You from around here?" She smiled.

Rick set down the paper. "Southern California. The O.C."

Hand on one hip she gave a wink. "How 'bout some peach pie? It's fresh today."

"Sounds good."

She nodded and, with obvious reluctance, moved on to pour coffee for two United flight attendants seated nearby. Turning her green-eyed gaze back to Rick, she winked before she sauntered behind the counter to pick up his order.

Her hips swayed when she walked, and she had the kind of legs he liked—long and lean. She returned with a slice of pie and slowly moistened her lips with the tip of her tongue as she set the plate down in front of him. Her vamping should have produced a stirring in him, but he felt nothing. Even her dazzling smile left him cold.

He pulled out his cell phone and pressed a number on his speed dial menu.

Lila answered on the second ring. "Executive Air."

"Hi. Don't you ever go home?"

"I was just thinking about you," she said. "The boys are fueling the Gulfstream. You should be flying it to Italy. Tomorrow morning you could be sitting in a café overlooking Lake Como, drinking an espresso, reading the paper. Instead, you're on some cockamamie plane...." She paused. Exhaled. "What are you doing?"

"I just had to get out of town for a few days," Rick said.

The door opened, and a blast of cold air rushed across the table, ruffling his newspaper. Decatur strode toward him.

"Gotta go," Rick said.

"Wait. Kate came in here with red eyes today, and you can't fool me. I hear the pain in your voice. What's going on?"

"Nothing." He ignored the stab of heartache he felt at the mention of Kate. "I'll call you tomorrow. Bye, Mom."

Decatur slid into the seat across from him, his cell phone glued to his ear.

"We're on our way," Decatur said. He shoved the phone into his pocket. "The cargo's ready. We pick it up in Port Moresby in New Guinea."

"The charts?" Rick asked.

"Got 'em," Decatur said.

"Lifeboat?"

"On board and loaded with supplies. You ready to rock and roll?"

Rick stood. "Let's do it." He pulled a few bills from his wallet and dropped them on the table, leaving the waitress a generous tip.

The two men walked toward the parking lot.

Decatur checked his watch. "Looks like we'll be in Hawaii by daybreak."

The DC3, a legendary aircraft, took her maiden flight on December 17th, 1935, thirty-two years to the day after Orville and Wilbur's *Wright Flyer* lifted into the sky at Kitty Hawk. Every pilot Rick knew coveted the chance to fly it. The first time he'd been at the controls of one, he'd meticulously entered the flight in his logbook, knowing it would be an event he would always remember.

That flight, nearly twenty years ago, was a far cry

from this one. It had lasted forty-five minutes, concluding with a round of drinks amidst the World War I aviation memorabilia at the 94th Aero Squadron, the restaurant perched at the edge of the runway at old Stapleton International in Denver.

Rick thought about that flight now as the silver-winged workhorse transported him across the Pacific. Its Pratt & Whitney radial engines possessed a reputation for reliability, and he was glad Decatur had chosen this particular model. Hitting a patch of unstable air, the plane bounced and lurched. The two 14-cylinder behemoths droned on. Rick looked down, beyond the wide propellers biting into the thin high-altitude air, to the reflection of the moon on the ocean below. His gaze followed the streak of light to the horizon, where it blurred at the dividing line between sea and sky. In an hour the sun would be up, and he and Decatur would breakfast in Honolulu.

They descended over the lush landscape of southeast Oahu. Rick called out their altitude as Decatur guided the DC3 through puffs of cotton candy clouds.

Rick gazed down at Waikiki Beach, where the famous curve of white sand surrendered to aqua water. "I wouldn't mind spending the day down there."

"Don't worry," said Decatur. "In three days we'll be back here, sipping Mai Tai's at the Royal Hawaiian."

They intercepted the glideslope over Nimitz Highway, and with Pearl Harbor in the distance, touched down at Honolulu International. Taxiing to Hawaii Air Service, Decatur spun the plane close to the waiting fuel truck Rick had ordered.

Unbuckling his seat belt, Rick braced one hand against the tan-colored curtain that separated the cockpit from the cabin, and slid out of his seat. After extending the stairway, he jogged down to the tarmac. He nodded to the lineman as the man finished chocking the wheels.

"She's got four tanks," Rick shouted over the still-running right engine. "After you top off the wings, get these." Rick pointed toward the fuselage and to the latch for the left auxiliary fuel tank. "There's another one on the other side."

Hawaii Air Service had been the fixed base operator for as long as Rick had been flying. As he walked in the door, Big Betty, the two-hundred-pound receptionist, recognized him.

"Hey, big boy. Couldn't stay away from me, could you?" She threw back her head. Her lusty laughter filled the small room.

Rick leaned over the counter and winked at her. "I haven't even looked at another woman."

Glancing outside, Big Betty gave a nod to the DC3. "You didn't fly all the way from the mainland in that thing, did you?"

"Sure did."

"When did you leave? Last Tuesday?" She laughed again, then held out her hand. "Credit card?" she said.

"We'll pay cash for the fuel," Rick said.

She arched an eyebrow and grinned. "I see you took your sexy pills this morning."

After a breakfast of scrambled eggs with bacon and hash browns, Rick and Decatur were back in the air, a cooler full of roast beef, turkey, and ham and cheese sandwiches stashed behind the bulkhead. Hawaii disappeared behind them. Nothing but thousands of miles of water lay ahead.

"Let's skip the stop at Beru," Decatur said. "We can push it to the Solomon's."

"We're not *pushing* anything," Rick replied. "We're going to get home in the same number of pieces we left in." Leveling off at their cruising altitude, he loosened his seat belt and turned to Decatur. "Why don't you get some sleep? I'll take the first shift."

Decatur nodded, crossed his arms over his chest, and closed his eyes. "Wake me in two hours," he said, slouching down into his seat.

Rick reached for the thermos he had tucked into a side pocket, poured a cup of coffee, and took a sip, savoring the Kona bean flavor. He unfolded a chart of the South Pacific, spread it across his lap, and allowed his gaze to travel south from Hawaii to the Society Islands. He'd once spent three weeks there, flying Steven Spielberg and his family from Papeete to Bora

Bora, and then on to Rarotonga. "All we want is a little privacy," Spielberg had said.

Looking northwest on the chart, Rick found their next stop, the Marshall Islands. In ten hours they would refuel at Beru. From there it would be a half-day's flight to Port Moresby, where they would rendezvous with Zamarcos and his cargo.

Rick refolded the map and slipped it under his seat. Staring at the ocean below, he thought about his home on the beach in Laguna. He found it difficult to believe his life had changed so dramatically in the last two days. He hated to admit it, but he missed Kate.

Hell, Rick thought, he didn't simply miss Kate—he ached for her, a soul-deep kind of ache that both terrified and fascinated him. He grudgingly admitted to himself that she embodied nearly every fantasy he'd ever entertained about his ideal woman. Not just his sexual fantasies, which she more than met and exceeded, but others as well. Her compassion, her intellect, the daredevil in her that embraced the challenges inherent in aviation, her commitment to Safe Haven, and, of course, her effervescent smile—the latter enhancing her physical beauty and grace. All these attributes and many more translated into Kate Randolph.

But despite everything he knew about her, Rick still felt the sting of Kate's ownership of Executive Air. *Was it his pride, or was it something more?* Since his divorce, he'd made it his policy to hold all women at bay, and to always keep the upper hand in his personal relationships. But Kate wasn't like other women. And because of her, Rick knew he'd lowered his defenses and allowed himself to become emotionally vulnerable. Then, she'd betrayed him. Just as he no longer trusted her, he no longer trusted the longing in his heart to see her, either.

The engines hummed. Rick's gaze skimmed the horizon. To distract his thoughts from Kate, he checked the autopilot and the fuel gauges, remembering the old saying, "Flying is long periods of boredom interrupted by moments of terror." He poured another cup of coffee. He needed to remain alert. Their lives depended on it. With nothing but water ahead of them for thousands of miles, it would be easy to disappear into the Pacific and be lost forever. Hadn't Amelia Earhart vanished along this very route?

Scanning the control panel again, he checked the oil pressure and engine temperature, then he glanced at Decatur, who slept soundly beside him. Again, he thought of Kate. *God, I wish you were here instead of Decatur*. A heartbeat later, he wished he could forget her. Some instinct deep inside assured him he never would.

Two hours later, Rick wakened Decatur. Satisfied that his friend was alert and in control of the aircraft, Rick relaxed in his seat, closed his eyes, and drifted into a light sleep. A half hour later, he jerked awake. He stared at the endless stretch of water ahead, then looked to his right. Decatur's head was slumped down, and he snored like a freight train. Rick elbowed him.

Decatur snapped to attention, obviously disoriented.

"Am I interrupting something?" Rick barked.

Decatur seemed to shrink into himself. "Sorry, buddy. It won't happen again, I swear."

Rick craved sleep. He rested his head against the seat, angry that for the remainder of the operation he'd have to sleep with one eye open.

The ground crew on Beru, the largest in the Marshall Island chain, was quick and efficient. The turn-around time at the little airport, a popular refueling stop for aircraft that lacked trans-continental capability, clocked in at just under thirty minutes. Six hours later, as morning dawned on the second day of their journey, the DC3 bucked like a rodeo bronco as they descended through a maze of thunderclouds toward Port Moresby, New Guinea. The cloud layer hugged the rugged mountaintops where wild jungle foliage stretched for an occasional glimpse of the sun.

Rick tightened his seat belt. "You're sure Zamarcos is gonna be here?"

"This is the third time I've done business with him," Decatur said. "He looks slippery, but he's reliable. Always keeps his end of the bargain, and, as you know, he pays up front."

A cloudburst hammered the plane, echoing through the cabin like rain on a tin roof. Vibrations from the propellers coursed through the fuselage into the control wheel. Touching down in the final fury of a tropical storm, they used up every inch of the slick runway. Decatur spun the plane around, then headed for the small terminal.

When they came to a stop, Rick jumped out of his seat. He rotated the heavy door latch. A gust of wind swung it open, splashing water into the plane. Decatur had shut down the engines and feathered the props so they wouldn't catch the wind, but they wound down slowly, and sprays of water shot out from each blade.

Hurrying down the stairs, Rick unzipped his flight jacket. Despite the storm the air felt sultry. He turned to see Decatur step out of the plane. It had stopped raining, but beads of water sheeted on the stairs and dripped off the handrail. Decatur took two steps before he slipped, tumbling down the steel stairs and landing hard on the tarmac.

Rick walked over to him. "You'll have plenty of time for sitting on your ass when the job's done."

He pulled Decatur to his feet. The man flinched, his hand flying to his knee.

"You okay, buddy?" Rick asked.

Decatur brushed himself off. "I'm fine." He hobbled beside Rick toward the Customs and Immigration office.

You'd better be, thought Rick.

New Guinea, South Pacific
A two-dollar cab ride from Port Moresby Airport, the

Tamarind Club occupied the bottom floor of a shabby hotel on High Street and reeked of whiskey, fried fish, and sweat. A teenage hooker seated at the bar watched Rick and Decatur enter the dive. She took a drag on her cigarette, smiled, and patted the barstool beside her. "I give you good time," she promised, her childlike voice competing with Tony Bennett crooning, "I Left My Heart in San Francisco" from a set of tinny speakers.

Rick pulled a few dollars from his wallet and stuffed them into the girl's pocket.

"Get yourself a good breakfast. It's the most important meal of the day." His gaze swept past her to a table positioned against the back wall. Zamarcos sat in the shadows, eating his breakfast.

"There he is." Decatur winced as he limped ahead of Rick.

The hooker smiled, counted her money, then swivelled back to the bar.

Stuffing a forkful of eggs, rice, and some sort of seafood into his mouth, Zamarcos glanced at his watch.

"Right on schedule," he said. "Impressive." He motioned them into chairs and snapped his fingers, calling to the waiter. "Two plates for my friends."

Rick looked on in amazement. He'd never seen a man eat so ravenously or so recklessly.

Zamarcos washed down a mouthful of food with a gulp of Chinese beer. He got right to the point. "After a hot meal and a nap, we'll load the plane." A piece of fish flew out of his mouth as he spoke and landed on his sleeve.

The waiter returned with two steaming plates, setting them in front of Rick and Decatur.

"Refresh yourselves," Zamarcos said, lighting a cigarette and easing back in his chair. "You need to take off by three this afternoon if you're going to be on time. My contact on Tagoro will meet you at ten tonight."

"No problem." Rick picked up his fork.

Decatur groaned. "Not quite true." He pulled up the leg of his cargo pants. His knee, as purple as a ripe eggplant, looked swollen to the size of a volleyball. "I can't fly. I think I've broken my kneecap."

After breakfast, four hour's sleep, and a hot shower in one of the five shabby hotel rooms above the Tamarind Club, Rick was eager to get going. He hadn't planned on making the trip to Tagoro alone, but hell, no big deal. Besides, with Decatur out cold from three Vicodin tablets provided by the bartender, what help would he be? Rick just wanted to get the job done and go home. The half-million bucks Zamarcos had already paid him, plus the quarter-million Decatur insisted he was going to transfer from his share to Rick's account when they got home, offered him new options. His life's dream of self-employment was now within reach. But he could also take some time off, go fishing down in Cabo for a few weeks. There were plenty of women there who might even be able to help him forget Kate. *But did he*

really want to forget her? He swore in frustration as he slammed the door of his hotel room.

Rick caught a cab to the airport, where he taxied the DC3 to a far corner of the field. Overgrown tropical foliage spilling over the edge of the concrete nearly obscured the long-bed pickup truck parked in the tall grass.

Zamarcos stood nearby while the driver loaded the truck's contents, sixty sealed cartons marked with a large red cross, onto the DC3. When the driver approached the stairway with the last carton, Rick turned to Zamarcos. "I want to see the contents."

Zamarcos raised an eyebrow, but then nodded to the man, who dropped the carton on the ground. Walking to the box, Zamarcos withdrew from his pocket a five-inch blade that glinted in the sunlight. Grinning, he sliced through the packing tape and then stepped back as he folded the switch-blade and stowed it in his pocket. "Be my guest."

Rick tore open the carton. Surprised to find bottles of antibiotics, he closed it, then nodded to the worker, who hoisted it onto his shoulder and carried it into the plane. Rick frowned. Why would Zamarcos pay two men a million bucks to deliver medical supplies to a third-world country?

The driver scrambled down the stairs and slid behind the wheel of the pickup to wait for Zamarcos.

The afternoon sun beat down on Rick's shoulders, gluing his damp shirt to his skin. "I'll be back here at seven tomorrow morning to pick up Decatur," he said. "Make sure he's ready to go."

"Don't worry," Zamarcos said, his voice sharply edged. "He'll be here, and I'll be here with him." Zamarcos's eyes narrowed. "When you make your delivery on Tagoro," he said, "the man who meets you will give you a package. It's for me."

Bingo, Rick thought. He felt stupid, wondering why he hadn't seen this coming. Nobody pays millions for the delivery of bandages and antibiotics. A flash of apprehension shot through him. This wasn't about what he would *deliver* to Tagoro. This was about what he would transport *out* for delivery to Zamarcos. *Son-of-a-bitch.*

As he climbed the stairs and made his way into the cockpit, Rick couldn't help wondering if he would ever see Kate again.

Chapter 27

At a quarter to ten that night, fifteen miles off the coast of Tagoro, Rick radioed his contact. The quarter moon had yet to rise, and the dark night made it impossible to find the runway without help from those on the ground. Five minutes later, in a clearing in the jungle, steel barrels filled with kerosene burst into flames, illuminating an old pockmarked landing strip. From above, the blazing barrels reminded Rick of luminarias at a Mexican fiesta. Excitement prickled his skin.

Whistling "It's Five O'Clock Somewhere," he brought the DC3 in slowly. Once on the ground, he came to a stop beside a grove of palm trees. He spun the plane around, and taxied back to the other end of the field. If he had to make a quick getaway, at least he'd already be facing into the wind. He didn't bother to shut down the engines.

Instead, he set them to idle, feathered the props, and secured the emergency brake.

Two men, illuminated by the burning barrels, ran out of the jungle toward the plane, ducking their heads to avoid the whirling propellers. Dressed in shorts and tank tops, they appeared unarmed. Rick jumped out of his seat, unlatched the door, and pushed it open. A blast of steamy hot air slapped him in the face. He didn't unfurl the stairs. Instead, he flung the boxes he had carried from Port Moresby, one by one, out of the plane. The two men caught them, hiding them in the tall grass behind the palm trees.

When he had cast down the last box, Rick brushed his hands, then held them up. "*No more,*" he yelled over the thundering engines.

The older of the two men gave him a "thumbs up," then reached down to unbutton a pocket on his cargo shorts. He withdrew a leather pouch and tossed it up to Rick, who caught it with one hand.

Suddenly, the distant sound of shouting shattered the tropical night. The two men turned and ran into the tall grass.

Rick stuffed the pouch into his shirt pocket. He'd check out the contents later. Two rifle shots rang out, and then another. Birds screamed in protest. Rick spotted the muzzle flashes at the edge of the jungle. His gut clenched, and his mouth went dry. A bullet hit the plane, the blast reverberating through the cabin. He slammed shut the door.

With his heart pounding, he hurled himself into the

left seat. Without stopping to buckle his safety belt, he adjusted the angle of the props and rammed the throttles all the way forward. Hours spent alone in his F-18 over The Gulf had taught him the art of focusing. Worrying about potential or impending danger wasted time.

Men with rifles emerged from the jungle at the far end of the field. They continued to shoot at him.

The massive radial engines roared as they spooled up to takeoff speed. The runway was short. Rick gritted his teeth. The DC3 rumbled and vibrated while he counted to ten. He released the brakes. Gripping the wheel with both hands, he pulled it all the way to his chest.

No rocket ship, the reliable old tail-dragger lifted into the dark night. Rick banked to the left, one silver wing pivoting around the flaming barrels. The gunmen disappeared as he soared skyward.

Rick allowed himself a deep breath only after he cleared the coastline. He set the autopilot for eighty-six degrees, trimmed the plane for thirteen thousand feet, and glanced at the fuel gauges. Two hours of flying time. Since refueling on Tagoro had never been a possibility, his plan called for a short stop in Darwin, Australia. He checked his watch—ten forty-five. That would put him in Port Moresby at daybreak. He would hand over the pouch to Zamarcos, and after catching a few hours of sleep, he'd load a sedated Decatur onto the plane and head home.

Rick pulled a can of Coke from the cooler. Then he reached into his shirt pocket to withdraw the brown leather pouch. He untied the drawstring, curious to see the real reason for his flight to Tagoro. He turned the pouch upside down. Like plump summer berries tumbling from a basket, eight rubies landed in the palm of his hand. Three overflowed his hand and dropped into his lap. He picked them up, their brilliance flashing even in the dim light of the old DC3 cockpit.

Rick let out a long whistle. He knew Burmese rubies fetched a higher price than diamonds. He didn't know the value of these gems, but he guessed it must be enormous if Zamarcos willingly parted with a million bucks to get them. He remembered Kate telling him she liked rubies. God, he wished he could give them to her. He'd always felt there was nothing he could ever give her that she couldn't buy for herself. These beauties would sure fit that bill. *What was he thinking? He was never going to see her again.*

Exhaling, he slid the glimmering stones back into the pouch and tightened the drawstring. Grabbing his leather flight jacket from the seat beside him, he tucked the pouch securely into the pocket.

He gazed below, where tiny islands glowed like stepping stones. The sight reminded him of Santomar. He'd never be able to erase the memory of his first night on the beach with Kate—the warm water of the Caribbean, moonlight caressing naked bodies. An image of Kate formed in his mind. He had memorized every detail of her face...especially her eyes. A dull ache lodged in his chest and tightened his throat. He closed his eyes, remembering the scent of her perfume. He could almost feel the silk of her blond hair brushing his cheek.

No matter how hard he tried not to, he missed her. Here he was in the middle of nowhere, suddenly realizing how badly he had treated her. He had accused her of lying to him, and hadn't let her explain. He had caused his own misery. In the beginning, Kate's wealth had intimidated him, but he had made an effort to adjust to it. The bigger problem, he now realized, was his inability to accept the intense feelings she aroused in him. He'd abandoned her to protect himself. He had walked out on her because he needed her, and that need unnerved him. He hadn't had the courage to admit it then, but here, alone over the ocean and with eight thousand miles separating them, he knew the truth. He loved her. And suddenly, all he wanted to do was tell her.

For the first time since his departure from Orange County, Rick felt a sense of inner lightness and peace. He knew now what he wanted to do. He clasped his hands behind his neck and sat back in his seat. Things would be different once he returned home. He would see to it.

Startled by a sudden jolt, Rick snapped his attention to the instrument panel. He stared in horror at the red warning light on the left fuel gauge. The tank couldn't be empty. He tapped the glass, hoping the indicator was just stuck. It didn't budge. The engine sputtered. Shit! One of the rifle shots must have nicked the fuel line. His pulse raced as he feathered the prop. He'd never make it to Darwin on one tank. He grabbed his chart. He needed a place to land. Now.

Lila watched Kate approach her desk.

"Need any help?" Kate asked.

Since Rick's departure, Kate had been inconsolable. She'd taken to spending long blocks of time at Executive Air, waiting for his return. She sat in the passenger lounge either working on Safe Haven projects or reading a novel. She was determined to set things straight with Rick, and nothing short of his reappearing would ever soothe her.

"It's not that I don't like your company," Lila said, "but shouldn't you be at the Safe Haven office?"

"I hired a full-time assistant. I don't have to take care of the day-to-day minutiae."

Lila set down her pen. "How are things going there?"

Kate's eyes lit up. "The architect is a genius. The site's going to be excavated so the whole campus sits lower than street level. Once it's surrounded by full-grown stone pines, you'll hardly notice it. And it's going to be a model program. People from Atlanta and St. Louis are coming out to see what we're doing." When there was no more to tell, her cheerful expression faded.

Lila patted Kate's hand. "Look. I don't think he's coming back today. Go out with a friend. Have lunch. Go shopping."

Kate's weak smile told Lila there wasn't enough chocolate, margaritas, or Jimmy Choo shoes to fill the huge space Rick had left in her heart.

The phone rang. Lila reached for the receiver. "Executive Air. This is Lila."

The minute the caller identified himself, Lila's stomach filled with butterflies. Grabbing her pen, she scribbled "Decatur Crane" on a pink *While You Were Out* message pad.

"I'm calling from New Guinea," Decatur said.

"Is something wrong?"

"Rick told me to call you in case of an emergency."

A feeling of dread washed over Lila. "Rick's okay, isn't he?" She spoke the words deliberately, as though saying them would make the statement true. Her gaze met Kate's, and fear jumped from one woman to the other like static electricity.

"Okay, now don't get excited," Decatur said in a calm voice. "Rick's down in the South Pacific, and he's in jail."

"No, no, no," Lila stuttered. Her heart pounded. "He can't be."

Wide-eyed, Kate hurried around the desk and crouched beside her. "What's the matter?" she whispered.

Knitting her brow, Lila shook her head. She held an index finger in the air to shush Kate, then pressed the phone closer to her ear. She continued to listen while Decatur explained the situation. When he finished, Lila asked, "Where can I reach you?" On the pink pad she wrote *Golden Lotus Hotel* and an international phone number. "I've got to make some calls," she said. "I'll get right back to you."

The room felt like it was spinning. Lila set the phone down. "This can't be happening." She sat frozen in her chair, staring into Kate's questioning eyes. She opened her mouth to say something, but nothing emerged.

Kate shook her arm. "What's going on? Is Rick all right?"

Lila lowered her head, cradling her forehead in her hands. She felt like she was in a dream. When she spoke, her voice echoed like a stranger's in her ears.

"Rick's plane." She shook her head. "It went down north of Australia—a little island called Rantora." Her voice rose when she said "Rantora," as though she were asking a question. "He's in custody, and...and...they've charged him with violating their airspace."

Kate stood, her turquoise eyes blazing. "What?" She grabbed Lila's shoulders. "Are you sure?"

Lila nodded. "That's what the man said." She picked up the note with Decatur's name and phone number. "That was a friend of Rick's. He said things went wrong on a job they were doing together, some-place near Bali." She handed the notepad to Kate. "He told me the State Department handles this sort of thing. Said I should call my senator to get the ball rolling."

For a moment, the two women stared at each other. Then, Kate sprang to life. "Find Bob," she ordered, slid-ing into the chair behind Lila's desk.

Lila hesitated.

"Hurry," Kate commanded her. "And tell the boys to top off the Lear."

Kate picked up the phone and dialed information.

"City and state, please."

"Washington, D.C.," Kate answered, her heart pounding.

Kate dialed the number and waited. The phone rang a half dozen times before the switchboard operator answered.

"United States Senate."

Kate cleared her throat, identified herself as Mrs. Sam Randolph, and asked for the senator's office. She had never used Sam's name to obtain special treatment, but his name still carried clout, and that's what she needed now.

Drumming her fingers on the desk, Kate stared at the clock on the waiting room wall. Nearly three o'clock. Rush hour. She needed to go back to Emerald Bay and pack a bag. If Coast Highway wasn't too jammed, she could be back at the airport by six and in the air by seven. She would fly through the night. Already pumped full of adrenalin, it would probably take that long for her to calm down anyway, so she might as well be in the cockpit.

Kate endured being shuffled from one surly assistant to another, until a soft voice came on the line.

"This is Senator Gordon. How may I help you?"

Kate took a deep breath. "This is Kate Randolph," she said to her late husband's long-time mistress. "I need to see you. It's urgent."

Chapter 28

Every fiber in Kate's body ached for Rick. Like a movie in her mind, she replayed their first night together in Santomar, over and over, until she nearly made herself crazy. She would stop by the sheer force of her will, only to start again a short while later.

She thought about him now as she stood over the open suitcase on the chaise lounge in her dressing room. She didn't care what hoops she had to jump through, she vowed to get him back. She would make him understand she hadn't the slightest interest in owning Executive Air. She'd only wanted to help Bob before he lost everything.

She folded her black Armani jacket and placed it atop the neatly packed matching skirt, then zipped shut the case.

Since her phone conversation with Ellen Gordon,

Kate had been going full force. Now, she suddenly sank down onto the chaise lounge.

What if the government on Rantora wouldn't release Rick? What if he never came back to her? What if they freed him, but he still wanted nothing to do with her? What if...what if...? Her mind wandered through a host of unpleasant outcomes. She finally grabbed the tattered pillow with the bouquet of balloons, and squeezed it to her chest. Her finger accidentally poked through a frayed seam and penetrated the pillow. Janet was right. It was threadbare. If there was anything she needed right now, it was courage, not this lumpy pillow from her childhood.

As she dragged her finger out of the hole, it scraped on something sharp. A drop of blood oozed from a tiny prick in her skin. She put her finger in her mouth to stop the bleeding as she fetched her manicure scissors. Moving toward the light to get a better look, she cautiously cut the threads that held the seam. What in the world had her mother used to stuff her pillow?

With great care, Kate withdrew a brown leather flight jacket. She unfolded it, gazing in shock at the brass name badge that had pricked her. She ran a trembling finger over it. Joe Kendall. Her father. A lump formed in her throat.

Kate's knees felt weak, and she leaned against the wall for support. With tears blurring her vision, she pressed the worn leather to her cheek. Her mother had given her the pillow for her eighth birthday, a month after her father's death. It had taken a quarter of a century for Kate to discover the true gift hidden within. Kate marveled at her mother's fortitude, that in the midst of her grief, she had thought to prepare this secret gift for her. Kate nuzzled the jacket, inhaling the scent of her mother's sorrow, imagining the woman who'd lovingly folded the jacket and tucked it inside. Kate realized that her mother must have hoped she would find it when she was better able to grasp the enormity of love and loss.

Kate unbuttoned the jacket and slipped it on. She hugged it close, embracing the memory of the man who'd vowed to always protect her. She patted the side pockets. Empty. She tucked her finger into the breast pocket and found a folded slip of paper. She spread it out on her dressing table. On the sheet of paper, her father had written:

COME TO THE EDGE.

WE MIGHT FALL.

COME TO THE EDGE.

IT'S TOO HIGH!

COME TO THE EDGE!

SO THEY CAME

AND HE PUSHED

AND THEY FLEW.

CHRISTOPHER LOGUE

The poem had obviously meant something to her father, and it had rested in his jacket all these years, as if waiting for the right moment when Kate would understand its meaning. And she did understand. She had relied too much on men—to take care of her, to heal her, to make her feel safe. Had Rick felt her neediness? Was that why he'd left her?

She stood and gazed at her reflection in the mirror. She didn't need anyone to take care of her anymore. She could and would take care of herself. She had just needed this push. Now, she could fly.

Blossom's prophesy flashed through her mind. "A secret waits to be revealed. When it comes out, you will not be alone. He'll always be with you." Kate had wondered at the fortuneteller's meaning. Now, she knew.

Kate grabbed her suitcase. Still clad in her father's jacket, she left for the airport.

"Eight Six Sierra Romeo, descend and maintain five thousand. Contact tower, one-two-six-point-three."

Kate keyed the microphone. "Roger, one-two-six-point-three," she replied.

Grady Burke, her co-pilot, reset the altimeter, and Kate initiated the Lear's descent. She pulled back the throttles and at the same time pushed down the nose, creating a momentary sensation of weightlessness that sent a chill up her spine.

She peered down from the night sky onto the inspired vision of Pierre Charles L'Enfant, the architect hired by George Washington to design his fledgling country's new capitol. Straight ahead of her, the Lincoln Memorial perched at the edge of the Potomac and the Jefferson Memorial overlooking the Tidal Basin gleamed like moral beacons through the crystal clear night. Luminescent monuments to integrity and intellect, the concrete, steel, and marble proclaimed, "These men are worth remembering."

Grady nodded toward the granite structures. "Those guys had faith in what they were doing," he said. "They knew their destiny."

"You have to really believe you can do something before you can succeed at it," Kate replied.

Unexpectedly, the words she spoke inspired her. She straightened in her seat. She did believe in her quest, and she wouldn't allow anything or anyone to thwart her. If she had to stand on her head in Ellen Gordon's office and spit wooden nickels, she'd get Rick out of that jail. She felt suddenly invincible...whatever she had to do, however long it took. And once she freed Rick, she intended to get him back. It didn't matter if it took the rest of her life, she vowed to get him back.

Kate's gaze swept across the Reflecting Pool to the Washington Monument, and up the National Mall to the gleaming dome of the Capitol. Wide, tree-lined avenues, radiating from the building, reminded Kate of the Étoile in Paris. That's where they would go when she got him out. The city of lovers. A city made for Kate and Rick.

Kate glanced at her watch. Four in the morning. Her appointment with Ellen Gordon would occur in less than seven hours. She disengaged the auto-pilot, even though it was programmed to guide the Lear all the way to the ground.

"Always fly it in yourself," Rick had taught her. The memory of his voice made her heart ache.

This time, the anguish she felt seemed somewhat tempered by hope and optimism. She stole a glance at Grady, sitting in the copilot's seat. He was such a sweet guy, and very competent, but he wasn't Rick.

Rick's presence in the cockpit had always electrified Kate. Whether he was talking to Center, folding flight charts, or studying an approach plate, alpha maleness radiated from him, enveloping her until she couldn't tell if the excitement she felt came from piloting the Lear or the brush of Rick's shoulder against hers. Flying with him resembled a most subtle form of foreplay, for it brought them together in body, spirit, and mind. Her grief was not only for the man, but for the loss of the thrill she experienced when he sat beside her in the Lear. But soon he'd be back, sitting next to her again. She just knew it. She refused to have it any other way.

"Sierra Romeo," a voice from the tower called. "You're the only one out there. How 'bout a straight-in for two-four?"

Kate nodded to Grady.

"Straight in. Runway two-four," he replied.

"Spoilers," Kate said.

Grady deployed the small flaps on the upper surface

of the wings. The plane dove at a slower, steeper angle, intercepting the glideslope several miles from the runway. When they intercepted the red and white vasi lights, the visual approach system that hugged the threshold of all runways, Kate smiled.

"Red over white, everything's right." All beginning pilots learned the little rhyme, and Kate always spoke it aloud on final approach, the way her first flight instructor had taught her.

The usually backed-up runways at Reagan National were deserted. After a smooth touchdown, Kate taxied the plane to Signature Flight Support. A lone lineman guided the Lear to a spot close to the dark building, then crossed his arms over his chest. When Kate shut down the engines, the man tossed chocks on either side of the wheels, kicking them into place. A limousine parked nearby approached the Lear.

Kate yawned, stretching her arms over her head. "Thanks, Grady. Great flight."

"No problem." Grady slid out of his seat. "Glad to help." He unlatched the door and opened it. "You know we'd all do anything to help Rick."

He handed Kate's overnight bag to the limo's chauffeur, who placed it in the trunk. Kate scooted across the limo's back seat.

"Can I give you a lift to your hotel?" she asked Grady.

"Naw. Thanks, anyway. I wanna lock down the plane and cover the engines. Give me a call tomorrow when you're ready to leave. I'll meet you here." He closed the door.

The driver slipped behind the wheel and turned his attention to his passenger.

"The Four Seasons, Georgetown," Kate said. She laid her head against the headrest. In no time, a construction detour sent them skimming past the Smithsonian. Kate leaned forward, addressing the driver.

"Can you pick me up at nine-forty-five tomorrow morning? I'll be going to the Capitol."

"You here to save the rain forests or something?" the driver asked.

Sinking back into the soft leather, Kate said, "No." She closed her eyes. "I'm here to save something much dearer to my heart."

At ten-fifteen the next morning, Kate followed an aide down a midnight blue carpeted corridor on the third floor of the Senate Dirksen Office Building. The young man momentarily turned his head to look at her, never slowing his pace. "It's just a bit further." Kate opened her purse to feel for the slip of paper Lila had given her with the details of Rick's detainment. She ran her fingers over it as though it were Rick's cheek, then closed her purse. At the end of the hallway, the aide halted before an old-fashioned wood framed door. Two-inch gold lettering extending the width of a glass panel read: Senator Ellen Gordon, Room 314.

The aide opened the door, holding it for Kate to enter

first. Closing it behind them, he pointed to an oxblood leather sofa. "I'll let the senator know you're here." The young man knocked softly on the carved oak door to an inner office, opened it, and disappeared inside.

Kate surveyed the small waiting room. Across from the sofa, two beige and black tweed armchairs hugged a polished walnut table holding a Tiffany-style lamp, a small terra-cotta bust of a young woman, and a bud vase sprouting one red rose. Kate sat on the sofa, tucking her purse on the floor beside her. The leather sofa felt cold against her legs. Folding her hands in her lap, she scanned the room. A wide marble sill supported a tall window that framed a view of the White House. Everywhere else, photographs of the senator and her constituents covered the walls.

Kate stood and browsed through the display. Photographs of the current and a former president, personally autographed to the senator, hung side by side, as well as dozens of photos of Ellen Gordon with well-known politicians and Hollywood celebrities. Kate paused before a formal shot of the senator curtsying to the Queen of England. She heard the door open.

Kate turned, expecting to see the aide. Instead, a petite, dark-haired woman in her late fifties hesitated in the doorway. Sam's mistress.

Dressed in black and white hounds-tooth slacks and a red blazer, Ellen Gordon seemed smaller than Kate expected her to be. The softness of her features also surprised Kate.

The senator spoke in a gentle tone. "Come in." She

stepped aside so Kate could enter, then nodded to her aide, who stood beside two wooden flag poles. One bore the Florida state flag. From the other hung the flag of the United States, both trimmed in heavy gold braid.

"Thank you, Scott," the Senator said. "I'll call you when Mrs. Randolph needs an escort downstairs."

The young man walked to the door, shutting it softly behind him, leaving Kate face to face with the woman who had been her rival for her husband's affection.

"Thank you for seeing me, Senator Gordon," Kate said.

"Please, call me Ellen."

Instead of using the chair behind her oversized desk, which was stacked with piles of documents, the senator sat down in one of the two visitors' chairs. She motioned toward the other. "Please."

That simple gesture said, *We are not senator and voter, we are just two women.* Kate settled into the chair, struck by Ellen Gordon's gentility. *But, of course,* she thought, smiling to herself. *Sam wouldn't have settled for anything less.*

Kate was relieved by the ease she felt as she and Ellen Gordon talked. Any animosity she had harbored disappeared as the seasoned politician listened, asked questions, and took notes. If her cordiality emanated from her guilt about Sam, Kate didn't care. She cared only that the senator possessed the power to cut through the red tape that ensnared the man she loved.

If the senator felt awkward, she never revealed those feelings. Kate soon discovered that the woman was not only polite, she was effective. Reaching for her phone several times during their conversation, Ellen Gordon called the secretary of State, the Transportation Department, and the White House with as much ease as if she were ordering out for a pizza.

After forty-five minutes, Kate heard a knock on the door.

"Come in," said the senator, rising from her chair.

The door opened to reveal a white-gloved waiter, who carried a silver tray.

Ellen Gordon smiled at Kate. "I thought we could have lunch together."

Opening the portable stand he had brought along, the waiter placed it between the two women, balancing the tray on top of it.

"Thank you, Carl," said the senator.

The waiter draped a white cloth napkin across each woman's lap. "Just call if you need anything else, Ma'am," he said, then quietly closed the door behind him.

Ellen Gordon handed Kate a bone china plate, decorated with the blue and gold Senate insignia. The plate held four small finger sandwiches arranged around a salad of field greens.

Unwrapping her straw, Kate dropped it into her glass and took a sip of passion fruit tea. Smiling at the senator, she thought it odd that they had once loved the same man. Ellen Gordon must have read her mind.

"You know, it wasn't just a reckless fling with Sam. I loved him. I always will."

Kate took a bite of a chicken salad sandwich. She didn't know how to reply.

The senator set her plate on her desk. She looked straight at Kate.

"I met Sam when I was twenty-nine," Ellen said. "A little younger than you are now. I was an aide to the secretary of the Interior, and Sam had come to Washington to lobby for an easement across some government land near his oil wells."

Ellen reclined into her chair, laughing softly. "He told me the only reason he invited me to dinner that first night was so he could use me to get to the secretary. Instead, we became inseparable. For six months, we were hardly ever apart. I stayed at his Texas ranch, or he flew to Washington to be with me. But Sam wanted a woman who'd be waiting at home for him at the end of the day."

Ellen shifted her gaze to the window. Rays of sunlight pouring through the glass gave her skin the appearance of alabaster. She stared out toward the White House.

"Sam knew I loved him," she said, "but the power here in Washington was seductive. I couldn't leave. So, we made a plan. I'd stay here and make a life for myself in politics. Sam would be free to take a wife and have a family. But our first allegiance would always be to each other."

The senator briefly looked up at the ceiling, clearly lost in a past memory, then she sighed. "After Cindy died, I encouraged him to marry again. I didn't want him to be alone. He was getting older."

The muscles in Kate's shoulders tightened. "I always thought something was wrong. I always thought it was me."

"It wasn't," the Senator said. "Sam's lifestyle demanded a wife for show. There was never a chance it would've worked out for the two of you. Sam hoped you'd find a lover and be discrete about it. He was sorry he'd dragged you into a marriage that was so lonely for you."

Kate shook her head. She could hardly believe her ears. "All of the guilt I felt...."

The senator patted her hand. And for the first time, Kate noticed the bracelet she wore. It was gold carved into the shape of Pegasus, the mythological flying horse, its wings tipped with diamonds.

"I think he'd have been happy and relieved to know you fell in love with your pilot."

Ellen Gordon slipped her arm through Kate's as the two women strode through the Capitol rotunda where Lincoln, Kennedy, and unknown soldiers from two world wars had lain in state.

"How are you coping?" Kate asked, keeping step

with the senator and speaking in a hushed tone in deference to the hallowed space.

"I try not to have any free time," Ellen replied. "Around here, that's not hard. And every night when I get into bed, I cry. What else is there to do? Half of me is missing."

The senator stopped under one of eight historical paintings that adorned the curved sandstone walls. "Isn't it magnificent?" she asked, changing the subject as they both admired the artwork. "The Surrender of Lord Cornwallis by John Trumbull." She shook her head. "No matter how many times I walk through here, I never tire of looking at it."

She stopped and faced Kate. "Cases like yours are unpredictable," she cautioned, her kind eyes crinkling at the corners. "You never know what sort of power trip the local authorities are on. It could take two days or two months." She hugged Kate. "Go home to California," she said, holding Kate's shoulders. "I already came between you and one man. I promise, I'll help you get this one back. You deserve to be happy, Kate."

Chapter 29

The following day, Kate sat with Lila in the Emerald Bay dining room. Neither had eaten much of the poached salmon and cucumber salad Cora had prepared for lunch. The phone rang.

A moment later Cora appeared in the dining room. "I'm sorry to interrupt, but Senator Gordon says she needs to speak to you."

A spark of hope shot through Kate. She exchanged a fleeting glance with Lila, then pushed her chair away from the table and hurried to the phone that sat at the edge of the marble-topped sideboard. Lila huddled close, and Kate pressed the speaker button.

"It's Kate. I've got you on speaker with Lila Stern."

"Time to go get him, honey," Ellen Gordon said.

Kate's legs felt as wobbly as Jello. "What?"

"They're releasing Rick Sanders."

"Oh, God." Kate reached for Lila's hand. Hot tears of relief spilled onto her cheeks. "Thank you, Ellen. Thank you so much." Kate smiled at Lila, who also had tears in her eyes.

Kate pulled a pen and paper from a drawer in the sideboard and scribbled while Ellen spoke.

"You've got permission to land on Rantora," the senator said. "You can stay just long enough to pick him up."

"That's all the time I need," said Kate, her heart racing with anticipation.

"I need the names of everyone who'll be traveling with you, their passport and Social Security numbers. Everyone needs a visa," the senator said. "There's a courier leaving for Los Angeles at seven this evening. If I receive the information in the next hour, you'll have your visas by tonight."

Kate thought it wise to include a relief pilot on the trip to Rantora. With two people in the cockpit, the third person would be able to catch a few hours sleep. Every man at Executive Air volunteered to accompany her on the rescue mission. At three o'clock the next afternoon, with Grady occupying the copilot's seat and Steve relaxing with a magazine in the back, Kate steered the Lear down the centerline of the runway. When they had accelerated to one hundred and eighteen knots, she heard Grady call out, "V-One."

Kate moved her hand from the throttles to the control wheel. The plane quivered. It wanted to fly. She held the wheel steady. The plane fought back, struggling against her, its aerodynamic wings clambering for freedom from the bonds of earth. The Lear leapt forward down the runway as though it shared Kate's mission to reach Rick as quickly as possible.

"Rotate," Grady called at one hundred and thirty-six knots.

Kate pulled the wheel back until the attitude indicator read *thirty degrees*.

The Lear sprang from the earth and into the afternoon sun, steeply banked over Catalina, and then raced west across the Pacific.

A shaft of sunlight pierced the gray confines of Rick's concrete cell, falling on a cockroach as it crawled up a leg of the rusted army cot in the corner. Seven days since he'd crossed the Pacific with Decatur. Or was it eight? To Rick, it felt like a year.

When he had landed his fuel-starved DC3, the men who immediately surrounded the plane eagerly demonstrated their dominance over him. And thanks to the sharp pain he felt whenever he took a deep breath, Rick suspected they'd also fractured a rib.

Despite his discomfort, Rick gritted his teeth and powered through his morning routine of push-ups, crunches, and knee squats. The military had toughened him, taught him discipline and that being cooped up in a ten by ten cell didn't justify a lapse in physical fitness. When he finished, he dropped onto the cot, sending up a squeal of protest from its corroded coils. He flicked away the cockroach now in residence atop the flimsy mattress. He appreciated that as long as his captors continued to bring him a daily ration of rice and onions with a piece of fish thrown in now and then, he wouldn't need to resort to cannibalizing his six-legged roommates. He hadn't enjoyed the crunchy insects during survival school, and he doubted he would now.

He raised his right hand to his cheek, running a finger along the inch-long cut below his eye. It felt like it was healing. Rolling his flight jacket into a pillow, he stretched out and waited, allowing his thoughts to return to Kate. He drew a deep breath that filled him with infinite regret and pain. If he ever made it home, he intended to make up for the hurt he knew he'd caused her. His thoughts drifted to that night on the beach...the feel of her body next to his...the moonlight on the water... the unexpected depths of her passion....

He soon sprang up from the cot, his body so aroused he groaned his frustration. This was getting him nowhere. He began to pace the cell, summoning mental images other than Kate's naked body. When he'd first landed, he remembered seeing two old Piper Cubs at the east end of the runway. He knew he could start them without a key. He just needed to get to them, but how?

Hearing the sound of footsteps, Rick whirled around.

A guard in a drab khaki uniform, armed with a semi-automatic rifle, unlocked his cell and tossed him a half-used bar of Irish Spring and a frayed towel.

The man pointed down the hall. "You go there... wash," he ordered in a thick accent. "Your country... come for you."

For the first time in two weeks, Rick smiled. A second later, his delight turned to suspicion. What if this was a trick?

After Rick showered and dressed again in his filthy clothes, the guard prodded him outside to a rickety Jeep. A uniformed soldier sat behind the wheel. The driver motioned to the passenger seat.

Rick climbed in. "Where are we going?"

"What you care?"

Even with a fractured rib, Rick knew he could take the guy down, although the short-barreled automatic weapon holstered at the man's side might give him a slight advantage.

They headed across a rutted dirt path that led away from the jail compound. When they turned onto a black-top road, the driver asked Rick, "How many children you have?"

"None," Rick replied.

"Huh. You not a man. You boy." The guard pointed to himself. "Eleven children," he said.

Rick smiled, pitying the man's offspring their cretin of a father. "Congratulations."

"You know Julia Roberts?" the man asked.

"Yeah. She does my laundry every Tuesday."

The guard glared, and then fell silent.

Ten minutes later, they arrived at the Rantora airport, a clear-cut strip of land of indeterminate length, wreathed by jungle foliage. The driver pulled up beside a concrete hut at the edge of the runway. Rick spotted the two Piper Cubs as the soldier shoved him out of the Jeep. A sharp pain pierced Rick's side as he stumbled, barely staying on his feet. He fought the urge to break the guy's neck.

The guard pointed to the hut. "You wait there." Glaring at Rick, he reached inside his wrinkled khaki shirt and pulled out a pack of Camels.

Rick's mind raced. How could he get to one of the Pipers? He doubted anyone was coming for him. And if the locals moved him to another prison, it might be so remote, no one would ever find him. He stepped out of the hut, addressing the soldier, "Very hot inside." Rick pointed to the grassy area behind the hut. "I sit there?"

The guard puffed on his Camel and nodded.

Sitting on the ground, Rick surveyed the area. In order to make it to one of the Piper Cubs, he needed to get past the jackass in the Jeep, as well as a half dozen other soldiers scattered between him and the planes. He trailed his hands through the long grass, his senses heightened as he scanned the area. A threatening wall of thunderstorms was forming in the west. He leaned his head back against the concrete hut that provided the only shade in sight. *Shit*, he thought, frustrated by the lack of cover.

A breeze whipped the weeds at the edge of the

runway. Rick rubbed his week-old beard, regretting that he hadn't been able to shave.

Suddenly Rick heard a plane overhead. He jumped up, his pulse racing. Shading his eyes with his hands, he searched the sky. He could tell from the sound, it wasn't a piston plane. A military jet? The aircraft eluded him at first, then he zeroed in on it. He grinned, waving his arms when he spotted the Lear, its contrails streaming like ribbons on a kite. Only one plane in the world had those dark blue, maroon, and orange stripes, and he'd taught Kate to fly it. *My God*, he thought, *she's coming for me.*

The guard appeared beside Rick. Both men watched as the Lear made a low pass over the landing strip. The two trails of black smoke streaming from the engines sparked Rick's memory of Blossom's prediction on Santomar. *Fire in the sky will set you free.* His mouth curved into a broad smile. The fortuneteller really was psychic.

The Lear touched down flawlessly, a faint spray of dust trailing from its wheels. Four rusted Jeeps drove onto the runway, corralling the aircraft when it came to a stop. The hairs on the back of Rick's neck lifted, tension suffusing his rugged frame. He hoped this wasn't a trap.

"Go." The guard pushed Rick in the direction of the plane. They set off by foot across the runway.

The Lear was situated so that the door faced away from Rick. It wasn't until he advanced around the fuselage that he saw Kate standing at the foot of the stairs, Grady and Steve beside her. Her back to him, she waited while a government official dressed in a colonel's uniform examined the handful of documents she held out for his inspection. Five armed guards surrounded them. At first sight of her, Rick released a ragged sigh of relief. He took a step toward her.

The guard grabbed his shirt. "Wait."

Kate turned, raising her free hand to brush away a lock of hair the wind had blown into her eyes. Dressed in white overalls and a bright yellow t-shirt, she was the most beautiful thing Rick had ever seen. She spotted him, smiled, then returned her attention to the colonel.

Kate gestured emphatically as she spoke to the man. Rick couldn't hear her words, but he read her body language. At one point, she poked the official's chest and shook her head. Then, she pointed to the cockpit. She appeared exasperated. *She's amazing*, Rick thought, laughing to himself. *She's absolutely fearless. If I'm ever in another jam, I know who to call.*

Kate motioned the colonel away from his armed cronies. When Grady stepped toward them, the man brandished his sidearm. Kate stepped between Grady and the gun.

"No." Her voice carried on the wind. "We have a gift for you."

She slowly reached into the side pocket of her overalls and withdrew two one-inch stacks of currency. Grady pulled three more from his pockets. Rick estimated the bribe came to fifty thousand dollars.

The man fanned the bills, eyed Rick, then shook his head.

Kate refused to give ground. She inched into the man's face. "My president will send his troops." A crack of thunder punctuated her remark.

The official and Kate stood toe-to-toe, wind ripping at their clothing. Rick sucked in a sharp breath at Kate's fierce determination and her courage.

Apparently after contemplating the stubborn American female's words, the colonel pointed to Rick and snapped his fingers.

The guard shoved Rick forward. Kate turned. She didn't move a muscle, but her eyes locked on Rick's and conveyed a clear message. She would not leave the island without him.

The colonel impatiently motioned for Kate, Grady, and Steve to board the plane. The two pilots obeyed the command, but Kate defiantly ignored the man and stayed put, extending her hand to Rick. Rushing forward, he gripped her hand and pulled her toward the Lear. Together, they scrambled up the stairs.

Once they ducked into the cabin, Steve locked the door. Rick pulled Kate into him, not speaking as he enfolded her in his arms and buried his face in her soft blond hair.

She hugged him back, tears of relief stinging her eyes. He winced, hunched forward, and grabbed his side.

Alarmed, Kate stepped back. "What's wrong? Are you hurt?"

Rick straightened. "My hosts had a helluva welcoming committee. It's nothing, a fractured rib." He moved forward toward the cockpit. "Come on, Kate. Let's get the hell outta here before they change their minds."

Kate nudged Rick back into the passenger cabin. "You stretch out on the sofa and try to get some sleep. Steve can copilot for me."

Rick ignored her, moving into the cockpit. "You must be kidding," he said. "A fractured rib or two never stopped me from doing anything." He winked at her. "And I mean anything."

"I remembered the most important thing." Kate grinned.

He looked puzzled.

"The coffee dispenser's filled to the top."

He laughed, slipped into the right seat, and patted the one beside him.

"There's a killer storm brewing," Kate said, climbing into her seat and fastening her safety harness. "I've never seen anything like it. Thunderheads at forty thousand feet and climbing." She nodded toward the west. "There are a few gaps in it that haven't filled in yet. Let's hope we can thread our way through."

Rick glanced back toward the passenger cabin. Grady and Steve gave him a thumb's up.

"Buckle up tight," he called to them.

Three of the Jeeps had left the runway, but one remained positioned directly in front of the Lear, as though to block their departure.

"Can we get around him?" Kate asked as she cast a worried look at the glowing black sky. "This weather scares me."

Rick reached for her, clasped her chin, and turned her face toward him. "As long as I'm with you, you don't have anything to worry about."

Kate's lips parted in a weak smile. "Okay, but I still think we're going to get hammered." As if in agreement, the wind picked up, sending small shrubs and other lose debris flying every which way, shaking the Lear with every punishing gust.

Rick squeezed her hand. "Be patient. It's all about power. They're showing us who has it." A flash of lightning punctuated his sentence.

Rick grabbed the checklist. "Let's get ready to blast out of here." He ran his finger down the page. After he called out the last item, he tucked the list into a side pocket.

A jagged streak of lightning illuminated the sky, followed by a rumble of thunder that shook the Lear.

Rick looked at Kate. There was so much he wanted to tell her. "I'm sorry I..." he said quietly.

"Me too," she said. "I was just trying to save Bob from bankruptcy. Sam had made a deal with him, and I couldn't let him down. I didn't do it to betray you."

Before he could reply, the angry sky exploded. A tropical downpour pounded the plane like a jackhammer.

Although the torrents of water sheeting the cockpit window blurred his view, Rick saw the Jeep race for cover. "He's gone. Battery on."

Kate flipped the lever. The lights on the control panel sprang to life.

"Start button," Rick called out above the noise.

They waited. Soon, the roar of the engines spooling up engulfed the cabin. Rain continued to bash the plane. *This is gonna be one hell of a ride*, Rick thought. He knew he'd trained Kate well, and he felt confident about her skill in the cockpit. But he also knew that thunderstorms could be treacherous.

"There's no centerline," Rick said. "And even if there was, you wouldn't be able to see it in this downpour. Look out the side window, and estimate your position by watching the edge of the runway."

Rick's eyes darted across the control panel, scanning the gauges. He tightened his seat belt, then squeezed her hand once more. "It's time, Kate. The wind's shifted," he said. "We're gonna take off to the west, right into it."

He inched the right throttle forward and stomped on the left rudder. The Lear made a tight pivot until the runway lay before it.

"It's just like Palomar," Rick said. "Don't let go of the brakes till you've got full power. The minute we're airborne, I'll call Darwin Approach Control."

Kate planted her feet on the brakes and pushed the throttles forward. When the engines reached peak power, she released the brakes.

Violent gusts of wind battered the Lear as it shot down the runway, thrashing it like a leaf blower blasting a solitary blade of grass down a driveway. Seconds later the cockpit darkened. They were in the clouds.

Jammed against his seatback by the G-force, Rick kept his eyes glued to the radar screen. He'd never seen it lit up like this. Green meant turbulence, yellow meant more of it. Red meant pray the plane doesn't come apart. He'd keep his concern to himself. No need to tell Kate and frighten her. A crash of thunder punctuated his thought. A flash of lightning followed. The Lear bucked like an outraged bronc, sending china from the galley crashing to the floor.

Kate gasped. "What's that?"

"Just keep the wings level."

"I will if they don't fall off," she said.

The engines, howling at max power, tore through the wild weather. Like a life-and-death video game, they evaded the red blips, and wound through lines of embedded thunderheads.

"We're at thirty-nine thousand," Rick said. "This can't last forever."

The Lear shook and creaked.

"Don't take your eyes off the instruments," he said.

They broke out of the clouds at forty-three thousand feet. Sunlight streamed into the cockpit. Kate leaned back in her seat, running her hands through her hair.

"You okay?" Rick asked.

She nodded. "Yeah."

Rick set the autopilot for ninety-eight degrees. He squeezed Kate's hand. "Good job."

Grady appeared behind them with two cold Cokes. He handed one to each of them. "You two rock," he said.

As Kate and Rick settled in for the rest of the flight, Rick turned to her. "I've got to know one thing."

"Sure," she said.

"What in the world were you saying to that guy down there?"

Kate smiled. "I was just giving him a piece of my mind."

"About what?" Rick asked.

"The idiot had the gall to ask me why two pilots needed a stewardess."

Two hours later, they landed in Port Moresby. A black sedan drove out onto the tarmac. Rick watched Decatur Crane, followed by a young man in khaki pants and a blue blazer, emerge from the back seat.

Hobbling toward the plane, his leg in a cast, Decatur threw his arm around Rick's shoulder. "Good to see you, buddy. I knew they couldn't keep you for long."

The other man approached and extended his hand to Rick. "I'm Leonard Roberts. I work for the State Department." They shook hands.

"We just want to make sure you're alright," Roberts said.

"I'm fine, thanks to her." Rick motioned toward Kate, who stood talking to the fuel truck driver who had just arrived to service the Lear.

"Where's Zamarcos?" Rick asked.

Decatur shook his head. "It's a good thing he paid us up front. I thought he was gonna have a stroke when he heard your plane went down. Instead, he bought the farm the next day. Choked on his breakfast. Literally. The guy fell head first into his scrambled eggs."

"I had a bad feeling about him from the beginning." Rick pulled the pouch of rubies from his pocket and handed it to Leonard Roberts. "You should be able to figure out who these really belong to."

Decatur patted Rick's back. "What happened to the DC3?"

Rick laughed. "Can you spell *insurance*?"

Chapter 30

K ate came to a halt along the narrow trail. She leaned
sideways, allowing the blue Gor-Tex backpack to
slide off her shoulders. It plopped gently to the ground,
startling a lizard that darted for cover in a stand of wild
onions growing beside the path. Kate knelt, lifted one
of the nylon flaps, and pulled a bottle of water from a
side pocket. She stood, taking a few sips.

Gazing down on the switchback, Kate waved to her
hiking companion. "You're doing great," she shouted.
"We're almost there."

She tucked the water bottle back into its pouch,
then turned toward the afternoon sun and closed her
eyes. She loved the feel of the sun's warmth on her
skin. The salty scent of the Caribbean reached her, and
she took a deep breath. The sound of sea birds in the
distance mingled with the songs of the sparrows in the

nearby bushes. Kate stood very still. *No doubt about it,* she thought, *Santomar is heaven.*

When she heard Ellen Gordon's footsteps, she opened her eyes. The senator, dressed in shorts and a t-shirt and sporting her first pair of hiking boots, stopped beside a boulder that had insinuated itself onto the path. The dark-haired woman sat down, waving her hand like a fan in front of her face.

"I'd like to send a few of my colleagues from Congress down here." She laughed and caught her breath. "This would do wonders for clearing cobwebs from their minds."

Kate wiped her forehead with the back of her hand. "How 'bout some water?"

Ellen shook her head. "No thanks." She pushed herself back up to her feet and took a deep breath. "Come on. Let's go."

Kate hoisted the backpack and led the way over a small rise where the trail flattened out and widened. The two women walked side by side in a companionable silence.

A carnival of colors greeted them as they approached the summit of Lookout Mountain. Tropical grasses and shrubs covered the ground, and the breeze carried the scent of frangipani and wild roses. Fragrant clusters of white flowers hung from thorny locust trees. Branches, heavy with tamarinds and guavas, drooped to the ground. Bees buzzed beside flowering manjack. Soon, the sweet white blossoms would ripen into fruit, and the locals would scrape out the pulp and use it to maintain their dreadlocks.

Kate hesitated near the edge of a plateau, which overlooked a small valley below and the glistening Caribbean beyond.

"It's beautiful," Ellen whispered, coming to a stop beside her.

"This is the spot." Kate set down her backpack near a clump of sword ferns. She knelt to unzip it. Reaching inside, she withdrew a flowered tablecloth.

"Let me help you," said Ellen. The two women spread the cloth on the ground beside the knapsack.

Ellen sat down while Kate fished inside the pack, locating a bottle of Dom Perignon and three crystal glasses.

"It's only fitting we have a drink to Sam here," said Kate. "He really loved this place."

She uncorked the champagne and filled the three glasses. She left one of them on the tablecloth, picked up the other two, and gave one to Ellen.

"To Sam," Kate said, lifting her glass in a toast.

"To Sam," Ellen echoed as she raised her champagne.

Both women looked at the third glass before taking sips of the sparkling wine.

Kate leaned back, resting on one elbow. "You can't imagine the chaos on the morning Derek stormed into the house and demanded Sam's ashes." She shook her head. "I told him his father had made me promise to scatter them here, but that maniac wouldn't take no for an answer."

"There was never any reasoning with Derek," said Ellen. "No matter what Sam did for him, it was never enough. Excuse my French, but I'm sure he'll piss his entire inheritance away on hookers and race cars."

"What about you?" Kate asked. "Did Sam make any provisions for you over the years?"

"Sam was very generous," Ellen admitted, taking a sip of champagne. She smiled at Kate. "If you've ever shopped on Worth Avenue, you've been in one of my buildings."

Kate set aside her glass, pushed herself up, and then reached into the backpack. "Luckily this was still in my dressing room. Sam gave it to me the night before we left for Santomar." She pulled out the red biplane cookie jar, its lid taped closed.

"I was frantic," Kate said. "I could hear Derek ranting downstairs, and then the idea came to me. I emptied Sam's ashes into the cookie jar, and filled the memorial urn with ashes from my fireplace."

Kate cocked her head, looking at Ellen. "Apparently Derek never knew the difference." She grinned. "He buried the fireplace ashes in the Randolph family crypt."

Both women laughed. "You did the right thing, Kate," Ellen said. "Sam would have applauded your quick thinking."

Kate took a deep breath. "Sam once told me that after he was gone, I wouldn't be free to move on until I scattered his ashes here." She raised her glass, downing the last of the champagne, and then gazed out over the ocean.

"I think it's time to set you both free," said Ellen. Her eyes sparkled with warmth.

Kate nodded. Both women carefully untaped the

cookie jar. Ellen stood, and Kate handed her the red biplane before getting to her feet. Together, they carried Sam's remains to the cliff.

Kate nodded to Ellen. Both women lifted the lid together. With their backs to the wind, they tilted the cookie jar. The breeze caught the ashes as they spilled free, swirling them over the flowers and trees. Some of the ashes, carried aloft with the breeze, floated toward the shore.

Kate and Ellen looked at one another. Tears rolled down both women's cheeks.

Ellen turned her face to the sea. As she spoke, her voice quivered. "Goodbye, my darling Sam. Safe journey."

Kate put her arm around Ellen as Santomar embraced Sam Randolph's ashes. "Goodbye," said Kate softly. "And thank you, Sam."

While Kate and Ellen said their farewells to Sam, Rick swam laps in the villa's pool. He emerged from the water thirty minutes later, feeling invigorated. Easing onto a chaise lounge, he inhaled the fragrance of gardenias and salty sea air that scented the breezy Caribbean afternoon. The sun penetrated his tired muscles and warmed his skin.

Lila and Bob sat nearby under an umbrella, enjoying slices of Marta's coconut cake.

"I could get used to this," Bob said.

Lila cocked her head. "Maybe it's time to sell the other half of Executive Air."

Bob touched Lila's hand. "Maybe it is."

Rick smiled and thought to himself. *Maybe it is.*

Scattering Sam's ashes to fulfill her promise to him left Kate at peace. After showering and changing into white slacks and a black halter top, she relaxed on a double-wide chaise lounge by the pool. When she heard the bedroom door open, she looked up. Barefoot and tan, Rick looked almost too handsome in an island-print shirt and white jeans. Five weeks since their return from the South Pacific, and the only remaining trace of his captors' bad manners was a small scar beneath his right eye.

Rick crossed the flagstone patio until he stood beside her. He bent down to kiss her.

"Mmm-mm. You smell good," she said.

He stretched out beside her, weaving his fingers through hers and bringing them to his lips. Then, he moved her hand until it rested on his chest. "How did it go?" he asked.

Kate smiled. "Fine. She's a nice woman. I like her, and I can understand why Sam loved her."

The sound of jet engines broke the stillness. Kate pointed to the Lear silhouetted against the sun just now dipping into the ocean.

"There she goes," Kate said. "I was afraid they might not make it out before the curfew."

"Grady and Steve will take good care of her," Rick said.

The kitchen door opened. Lila stepped out of the house, carrying a tray of piña coladas. "You two look comfortable."

Bob Hansen appeared on the path that led from the guesthouse. "Here, let me get that." Bob hurried to take the tray from Lila. He placed it on a nearby table.

Lila served the frothy pineapple and coconut drinks, then lifted her own from the tray. "Here's to a wonderful hostess," Lila said.

"And here's to another wonderful woman." Bob raised his glass to Lila. "I don't know what I'd have done without you at Executive Air."

"I love going to work every day," she said.

Bob took a swig of his drink. "Lila, it may be time for both of us to wind down our work schedule. Retirement doesn't sound so bad."

Lila laughed. "Let me get that in writing."

"What about you, Rick?" Bob said.

"I've got a few ideas." He raised his glass to Bob and Lila. "In the meantime, I'll be forever grateful for the home you both gave me when I left the service."

Marta emerged from the house with a tray of baby crab cakes. She set them on the table, then smoothed the front of her uniform. "Dinner will be served in half an hour," she announced before she returned to the house.

Rick stood and stretched. "Who wants to walk on the beach before dinner?"

Bob took a seat near Lila. "I've had enough exercise for one day," he said. "I've already been up and down that cove three times. Think I'll stay here."

"Me, too." Lila winked at Rick.

Rick stared at her. Lila always insisted her thirty-year-old romance with Bob was history. *Had Santomar rekindled it?* he wondered. He got his answer when she glared at him, making a shooing motion with her hands.

Rick reached out to Kate. "Come on," he said, taking her hand and drawing her up from the chaise. "I have something I want to show you."

He laced his fingers through hers, leading the way onto the brick path that meandered down to the beach. By the time they reached the stone wall that separated the lawn from the sand, a pale blue twilight had begun to settle over the island and the first stars twinkled in the velvet sky.

Rick stepped over the wall, then turned to help Kate. They held hands as they strolled on the sand. Not far from shore, a sailboat, tiny white lights strung from its three masts, glided through the water. The sound of music drifting from the boat blended with the song of the surf.

Rick's heartbeat quickened. He was accustomed to Kate having that effect on him. But this time, the response felt heightened by his need to set things right between them.

He stopped at the water's edge and turned to face

her. "I'm sorry." He swallowed hard against the emotion lodged in his throat. "My ego grabbed the captain's seat."

Kate sighed. "I should've told...."

He interrupted her. "No, let me finish. I was angry at Bob for selling half the company, and I took it out on you. I got exactly what I deserved. I figured if I took that job in the South Pacific, I'd get far enough away to forget you. It never happened. The whole time I sat in that jail, I thought about you. All I wanted was to see your face one more time."

Kate stepped forward, sliding her arms around him. She rested her cheek against his chest, the steady beating of his heart a source of comfort and reassurance.

"It's okay," she whispered. "We're together now."

With his fingertips, Rick tilted her chin up until he saw her eyes. He put one arm around her waist, drawing her near, then he brushed his fingers through her hair. He leaned down to kiss her, his tongue seeking the sweetness of her mouth. Her breath came fast, and she held him close, her soft feminine scent warming his heart.

He kissed her nose and her eyes, running his lips across her cheek. Burrowing his face into the curve of her neck, he held her close with the knowledge that she was the woman he loved and had always wanted. His heart raced. He needed to speak now. For God's sake, he had flown combat missions, surely he could do this.

He put his lips to her ear. "I love you, Kate," he whispered.

Kate sighed. "I love you, too," she whispered back, melting into him.

He hugged her closer, realizing he could never be without her.

Stepping back, Kate gazed up at him, her eyes sparkling in the moonlight. "Do you remember the night we went swimming here?" she asked.

"How could I ever forget it?"

"Let's do it again."

"How 'bout tonight?" Rick said, reaching into his back pocket. "Only this time, you've got to wear something."

Kate frowned. "Really?"

Rick reached inside the velvet pouch he had withdrawn from his pocket.

"Yes, really." He smiled. "I want you to wear this."

He pulled out a necklace with a ruby as large as a ripe raspberry.

Kate gasped. "This looks like one of the rubies you showed me before we landed in Port Moresby."

"It is. It slipped through a hole in the lining of my jacket pocket. I found it a few days after I got home."

"We have to give this back."

"I tried," Rick said. "I called the guy from the State Department, the man I gave them to. He sent the rubies, plus a ton of paperwork, by courier to our embassy in Sydney, and they sent them on to Washington. He said returning this one would be a bureaucratic nightmare since he doesn't even know who has the others or where they are now."

Eyes wide, Kate stared at the gleaming necklace.

"He told me to keep it, to save him a world-class headache. Said it's mine." Rick smiled. "And now it's yours."

He placed it in her hand, and she held it against her heart as she gazed up at Rick.

"You can wear it when we go to Paris," he said.

"We're going to Paris?"

"Of course. And anywhere else you want to go."

Her eyes lit up. "I've always wanted to kiss the Blarney Stone."

"Start making a list."

"How about Venice?" she said. "Venice is the most romantic spot on earth."

"Wherever you say."

He drew her into his arms and claimed her mouth in a devastating display of his love and desire for her—now and forever.

"Fly with me, Kate...for the rest of our lives."

At the table in the great room, Bob pushed his plate away. "Marta is one great cook. Let's take her home with us."

"Her husband won't let her go without a fight," Kate said.

Lila took a sip of Cabernet, then dabbed her lips with a linen napkin. "That's some hunk of jewelry," she said, casting a glance at the ruby necklace gracing Kate's neck.

Kate raised her hand to her throat, caressing the stone.

"I finally got Kate something she couldn't buy herself," Rick said. He raised his glass to Lila. "And we can thank you for that. If you'd have gotten 'round to fixing that hole in my jacket pocket, it couldn't have fallen through."

Bob reached for Lila's hand. "You've been a lifesaver to all of us."

"Glad I could help." Lila said. She took another sip of wine. "So Rick, you still working on that consortium of pilots and investors?"

"I've got a better idea," Rick said. He regarded Bob and Lila, their hands entwined on the tabletop. "How about selling me the other half of Executive Air, Bob? Kate and I want to be partners."

"It's not like I haven't thought about it," said Bob.

"You and Lila could spend more time here in Santomar," Kate said.

Lila raised her glass. "I vote for that."

"I'm a good negotiator," Bob said. "It'll probably take all your profit from that South Pacific job."

Rick grinned. "You gotta leave me a little bit. There's something else I want to do."

"Is it a secret?" A wry smile crossed Lila's lips.

"No." Rick gazed at Kate. Her eyes shone with love. "After I fuel up the Lear," he said, "I'm taking the woman I love on one hell of a honeymoon."

Kate's Santomar Orange Blossom Liqueur

(For people over 21!)

Pick 2 -3 cups of fresh orange blossoms. Put them in a glass bowl and cover them with 1 bottle of unflavored vodka. Cover the bowl and put it in a dark place for 7-12 days. The longer the blossoms stay in the vodka, the more intense the flavor will be.

Put 2 cups of water into a pot. Add 2 cups of sugar and heat until the sugar is completely dissolved. Let sugar solution cool to room temperature.

Pour orange blossoms and vodka solution through a strainer into the cool sugar water. Stir. Pour liqueur into bottles. Store in the freezer.

Acknowledgments

I wish to acknowledge and thank the following people.

Lou Nelson and all the past and present members of my writing group, especially Dennis Phinney, Dennis Copelan, Susan Angard, Wally Runnels, Will Hager, Marcia Sargent, Janet Simcic, and Mary Guleserian. Thank you for nurturing and encouraging me through the journey of writing this novel.

Laura Taylor, Lou Nelson, Lisa Leonard-Cook, and Beth Leiberman for their editing skills at various stages of this novel's development.

My many flight instructors. Thank you for sharing your knowledge and love of aviation with me. Your patience and skills took me from white-knuckle flyer to Learjet pilot. Special thanks to Dean Waters, my first flight instructor, who guided me through my first take-off in a single-engine plane, and Mike Thornton, my last flight instructor, who taught me to fly a jet.

Kristin Lindstrom at Flying Pig Media for handling all the publishing details.

My husband Wes, who never asked me, "What's for dinner?"

Enormous thanks to all of you.

Made in the USA
Columbia, SC
01 October 2021